MINDY, MORGU

Revenge is a Bitch

Cass Milla

Copyright © 2018 Cass Milla

ISBN: 978-0-244-67669-8

All rights reserved, including the right to reproduce this book, or portions thereof in any form. No part of this text may be reproduced, transmitted, downloaded, decompiled, reverse engineered, or stored, in any form or introduced into any information storage and retrieval system, in any form or by any means, whether electronic or mechanical without the express written permission of the author.

This is a work of fiction. Names and characters are the product of the author's imagination and any resemblance to actual persons, living or dead, is entirely coincidental.

'I haven't got any fucking odds.'
And Edie

Revenge for the Cunning
Part One

Soap star Chad Rise was hungover, hungry and horny as fuck. This lethal 'H' trio made regular appearances in his rich life along with drunk and disorderly fines, love struck stalkers with an endless supply of stationery and unexplained bruises on his forearms - an unnecessary pain for his peculiar agent Greg Locust to cover up, but Chad was worth the twenty five percent.

Chad loved to party. He loved being the centre of attention a daytime soap star brought, on par as addictive as a tanorexic and UV lights. The endless amount of money to earn from deals sponsored his morning wank. The chasing level of fame raced with his addiction to achieve the next high, where the celebrity parties were bigger, and the bling even bigger, and media attention a mere aphrodisiac for him. Chad loved to experience life outside of the box; sadly, one day death would each grab a limb and put him in a box - just not yet.

Today the hangover peaked at mammoth proportions, and the only way out down the helter skelter of depression and destruction. Previous hangovers that had put a notch on his sexy body were at this point a hazy memory of a Chinese whisper. This one was for the history books. This one would start the unstoppable ball rolling directly towards the demolition of his lavish life, pushed by revenge. The unsteady avalanche was ready to drop a ton of destruction on his Adonis body in coming weeks from the least person he would ever expect.

Stale aftershave marked him unwashed, and the thirty thousand dollar bought teeth felt unfamiliarly gritty as he ran his parched tongue over them. His carb-free body ached as a result of the massive bender, and not the gay type.

Was it still night or day?
How many days might have passed?
Had he won the TV award?
Questions tripped over themselves, waiting impatiently for Chad to answer - he didn't.

A more important question barged to the front, knocking the competition out of the way - who the fuck was he with? Some horizontal action lifted the thin sheet, coming and going like a gentle tide. Hearing a slight groan working below his athletic waist, under the poor quality sheets like a cheap Halloween ghost costume, gave away that he was not alone. His aching erection was wet, gripped between the fast working lips pleasurably. His expensive rhinoplasty nose ached for an economy priced line, while his head banged for a glass of water to drown his thirsty headache. This sad situation started to become more frequent when he drank, becoming more out of control. Was he was losing will power, or wanting to abuse his celebrity power? Which was more dangerous to a troubled soul?

Naked in the double bed, he had no idea of what time of day it was as the question roamed around inside his heavy head, clueless. He felt the sensation as if his head was in a rusty clamp slowly being crushed by his harassing neighbours, to rid this debauchery clear from his memory. The dense darkness of the hotel room gave him the false impression that everything seemed ok, everything was fine. Something – despite having no legs - was making its deadly way towards him. Engulfing anything in its way, its anger hot, it was here for one victim, and only one - TV star Chad Rise.

Dark designer stubble shadowed his famous square face, acting all shady like villains of Disney films - warning young and naïve but sexually frustrated and disobedient princesses, who were happy to joy ride on a rug from the market - to stay away. Pairing up with his cut, chiselled body, his minor successful calendar adorned teenager girls' walls across America and gained him a small profit. Mainly due to it being in the discount bin of Walmart, it was early material to finger blast themselves into self-discovery and masturbation, innocently in the shade of their idol, the real Chad Rise. This man was dynamite to women on a devastating level - especially the weak, vulnerable, or the willing to be paid. His stubble length was two days old, and so was the hooker sucking on his fat, erect cock. He had the gift of stamina every Kenyan marathon runner wished for; this made Chad Rise the irresistible hunk that he was.

Drink and the variety of drugs, a combination that baked the toxic comedown to take at least a day's visit to rehab to cure, he feared burnt his senses. Smelling it so realistically, the smell of burning itched at his nose - but not enough to register. His concentration was dazed and confused by drugs serenading his sharpness to relax a little, but a little too dangerously this morning.

What was the cause for this ballistic bender? Not that Chad Rise ever needed a reason. This was a man who drank vodka straight for fun before noon, put cocaine up his nose like a vapour stick, and played with hookers the way that toddlers do with a Barbie doll. Missing out on 'Best Actor' in a soap award again - fourth year running - dented his plywood pride, losing out to his archenemy, pig-nosed fat twat Jermaine Mont, a Latino, over-fifty silver fox, whose role on daytime television as a widowed doctor had propelled him back into the living rooms of bored housewives. The knife in his already public open wound stabbed deeper, and he faintly remembered that his best pal Jack - who lived in an iconic bottle - consoled his overblown ego by drowning it.

His star power thought nothing of abusing his cock with hordes of hookers picked up from the strip bars, wearing a uniform of inflated tits and bloated lips - both bigger than their neon thongs. All of them wanting the dollar more than the dick, it was a kind of MOT to his dick, he humoured, once a month. A carnal sin of a meeting between two addictions, each abusing the other, yet only one came out richer for the experience. While the hooker worked for an hour or two, once finished he threw her out like a stray dog, with a flimsy fifty dollars and an aching below was all she would have to show for it.

All his life he used women like a razor - one use to rid the irritation and then gone. He used them to get to where he was today - they climbed onto his cock, and he climbed over them to gain power. Women, in his eyes, were weak; they were a small luxury like fine champagne to indulge in every now and then. The memory of his lovely mother rushed towards him, but was knocked out by a satisfying groan from his dry throat. Unaware of the dismissive derailing heading his way and closing in, he hoovered up a white line. What the hell was that smell?

Faint shouting stirred him to semi-consciousness enough to light up a half-used spliff from the wooden bedside table. Sucking a long drag due to his low energy, he noticed compact smoke blanketing the hotel room. His wrist was light and bare of his Rolex - only a watch-thick strap of pale skin free from the sun's tanning showed the parking space of such Rolex. Most hookers in Los Angeles wore one of his Rolex watches, like most criminals wore electronic tags.

The heavy curtains were closed, keeping the afternoon sunlight from entering the room and raising awareness of the danger in the room for both him and his hooker. Peril was the morning bird song. No noise penetrated the room - only his penis into her mouth, and a slight gasping of her mouth opening and closing faintly fractured the silence. Sweat stuck to his overheated, toned body like morning dew; he could feel his pubes soaked.

The glamorous hotel room, like thousands across the world (especially across the Strip) grew numb to the abuse of stars and celebrities. They thought nothing of enduring its glamour and good hospitality with a seedy night of drugs, drunken debauchery and sordid sex - mostly uncomfortable, mostly paid, and sadly forced. The hotel rooms became an extension of their workforce; celebrities were fickle, destructive creatures who only thought that maids were an urban myth, and not a real person who whose jobs were to return the room back to its former beauty - like surgeons do with botched tit jobs. Still, it was a paid service to do, and that's what it was doing. If only walls could talk.

His short, selfish attention span drew him back to the pleasurable action going on under the sheets. Removing the thin sheets, he revealed the blonde head bobbing up and down like a buoy. For a man who lost his virginity quite late for a London lad, Chad had made up for this. She was the last surviving whore from the three he remembered bringing back. If the room had kidnapped his attention for three seconds longer, he would have realised that his glamorous life was in dear danger of coming to a fiery end. His cut abs, a waterfall of muscles descending from his pumped chest to his groin, were a delicious sight stained with lipstick. Turned on by the sight of himself, it sent back up his already erect knob and he expected it to explode.

*

Sally the hooker worked solidly on his fleshy cock, feeling it harden more in her dried-up mouth, coarse friction hit the inside of her cheeks. She was amazed at the hardness of it, as if his cock was made from concrete and not pink flesh. It was one of the finest cocks she had worked on, to be fair. She had put worse in her mouth, that was for sure; she remembered one time her cousin Jake had put a slimy slug in it in a childhood game. It had good girth - enough to tease your lips of a tear, and his marble smooth, deep plum head led a generous length to water your eyes - Chad's cock, not the slug. Sucking on the meaty piece deep and fast, she worked well for the fifty dollars, certainly getting his monies worth. She was the last to survive from the three he had invited back, reigning supreme like Diana Ross – the only one to go on to a stellar solo career, and have the only name from the three, the world remembered.

"Is that good baby?" She tenderly questioned in husky Californian tones, looking up with pleading eyes. Her mascara was days old, lipstick smeared lost three shades, and white foam growing at the corners of her mouth watered by dehydration gave impression she swallowed a washing tablet not spunk. Every guy getting his hungry cock sucked was always 'baby'; it made them feel comforted, vulnerable and naughty all in one. It gave them a break from being the bored, sexually frustrated husband, and left them a few dollars poorer, beat buying the wife shoes.

Chad ignored her, and pushed her head back on to him harshly. Her blonde hair was extremely soft and reminded him of Roxy, which led him to think of Maria. *Fuck Maria!* Even when she was not in the room she still managed to ruin his day. That woman was nothing but a problem, pain in his arse, she didn't even like anal, and he scolded. His swollen cock hitting the soft flesh of the back of her throat proved his manly worth, and rid Maria from his toxic mind like brush sweep on pile of dust.

"Suck it deeper, you slut."

All women loved to be called a slut - it made them feel naughty, he chuckled. Nobody ever disagreed with him. The gagging noise from his shaft suffocating her airway turned him on. She was defenceless, and he smirked as he took another pull of his shortening spliff in celebration. Defenceless women were always a turn on to him; the faint memory of his recent engagement night gave him a slight kick of guilt.

Sally held her breath with the span of a blue whale and the gag reflexes of an anaconda, as her soft lips hit the hard base of his penis each time in a woodpecker rhythmic beat. Smelling stale sweat in his trimmed pubic hair, she knew she had been here a while, thank fuck she didn't leave her car in the carpark, clamped and pounded for sure. She was tempted to rim his waxed arsehole and drink the small puddle of sweat forming to wet her dry mouth; she could murder a drink right now. She fingered his hard pink nipples as if she was looking for a tap to make him spunk, and pulled gently on his big balls to release his reluctant load. Her overworked jaw was starting to stiffen after fifteen minutes of working on his generous cock, praying for a release. When he would finally shoot a creamy load she imagined the relief would be on par with Nelson Mandela's. *'Hurry the fuck up'*, she said in her head. Her poor cat Pepe had been left unfed for two days and was probably eating himself. She was dying for a green smoothie and a catch up of *The Kardashians*. She wanted out, she wanted spunk in her mouth, and she wanted home. The room was so hot she feared she was sucking off Satan.

"Mmmmmmmm, this cock is so good." No lie. "Such a big boy, show me what you're hiding in there." She pleaded.

Dirty talk always aroused the man towards a quicker finish like loved ones cheering on from the sides of a marathon, make you faster. Sally came up for a response, and more importantly, air. Her eyes met with his. His eyes were bright blue - so blue that she felt inspired by the blueness to turn Pornstar. This man was something else; he was extremely beautiful. She felt intimidated just looking at him, and lucky that she was the chosen one, using her hand to roam across his chest of muscles.

In her years of servicing men - and a few women - Sally had fucked the good, the bad, and the damn right kinky with a baseball bat. But, this man was up there in the best looking by far. Sally had been clever enough to learn a lot about men over the years from their behaviour, to their kinks, to why they used sex. Her evening classes in psychology told her that this guy was trouble - more trouble than a squirrel with a nut allergy.

Chad was either deaf or read her mind of her opinion of him and simply rammed her head down; the deep throat such a completely new level that he half expected it to pop out of her arse. The queue of Viagra patiently waited their turn like eager fans wanting to glimpse their favourite boy band. Loyal they were, and not in any rush to work their purple power of a lasting erection on the popular cock disappearing into her willing mouth just yet. Sally worked proudly on her blowjob, like a kind of penis Picasso. She was glad that all of the hard work only benefitted her; childless, she would have begrudged working this hard just to give the money to her child to buy baseball stickers. Famous for her vigorous stamina to suck cock, she was a legend on the seedy strip. He on the other hand, expected to blow dust. He spunked so much in any hole that Sally required filling that he was amused she had not suffocated. He remembered that there had been another two females, but they must have left - one with fifty dollars, and one with a Rolex, the lucky bitch.

The dryness from her dehydrated mouth and the odd clash of botched veneers on his tender prick made it less enjoyable. His pale foreskin was slightly torn with each touch of her energetic, dry tongue on his overworked, swollen shaft, sending pain and not pleasure. He needed to piss; he wondered if Sally would take a golden shower, feeling his bladder heavy. His balls ached to empty, and she must be dying for a drink. He certainly was, and his whiskey tumbler was empty.

The fact that the hard liquor booze was wearing off and his conscience was coming up for air made him feel guilty for Maria, his loyal, faithful - if not slightly boring – model fiancée back in Atlanta. The arousal of the lengthy blowjob and the building strength of someone calling his famous name paired up with the pressure on his bladder, the crack-like craving for greasy food and the angry man hitting a sledgehammer against his head, along with one hundred denier-thick smoke wanting out all joined forces like *The Avengers*. They took a limb each and shook him awake enough to realise that the seedy hotel room was on fucking fire.

The mattress threw Chad Rise from the bed with a speed as if it was made from hot nails, not springs. The utter fear of potential death shot a measly load into her hungry mouth. Chad feared death more than anything else in the world. Sally screamed with the huge relief of a lottery winner, and her jaw had been relieved of duty. Chad's jumping-jack out of the bed knocked Sally off the bed, and naked, she hit the hard floor that was solid enough to knock her out cold. A dozen fire-fighters crashed down the hotel door moments later. The hungry fire reached the seedy bed, grabbed hold of Sally's flammable hair extensions and refused to let go. The '*Do Not Disturb*' sign was shocked that it had been disturbed, and fell off.

Pity…if revenge had got to him first before the fire-fighters, the bargain hotel room would have witnessed a celebrity murder - another to add to its tally. But, good things come to those who wait, and she could wait. After all, revenge was a bitch.

New York City,
Central Park

Central Park in early spring was her favourite time of year. Pocket of oasis among the tall concrete jungle, dropped by the grace of God, brought greenery to a grey city. A maturing sun gained confidence with each minute of light, joining the protest to banish the dark days and lift the dense depression that the city had suffered of late; it brought instant cheer in the way that horny females lifting up a tartan kilt on a Scottish hunk would, praying he kept true to tradition. Sadly, it was also a beautiful day to end a life.

Cheekily the warm sun dared to give a gluttonous taste of summer in the way that a secret alcoholic might sample a taster for all of the wine on the menu, hoping that their date does not click on to their addiction. The rise in the weather infected promising cheer among the fast-paced New Yorkers in their morning rush of the day, like a celebrated illness that people wanted to catch.

Joggers blurred past in outfits of warmth, hoping to shed these for as little as possible in the summer, ridding their summer, sun-starved bodies of the few extra pounds that Thanksgiving peer pressure indulgence had left. One woman in her mid-forties, Edna guessed who looked extremely determined to lose the evil pounds, passed by wearing a pink bin bag two-piece drinking a weight-loss milkshake with a small tyre dragging behind her, the tyre as reluctant as her to move. The miserable fact was that her husband of twenty years had left her for a twenty-one-year-old who thought that cellulite was the name of a girl band. The raw image of finding her nearly-there knickers with less material than a napkin stuffed down the side of the chaise pushed her around the park one more time. Her revenge would not be the petrol bombing of his car that she had first thought of high on wine courage, but in achieving the weight loss all on her own, bagging her own sun-kissed toy boy on a trip to Bali.

The evidence that Mother Nature looked forward to the cold pissing off too, fed up, was that she had been dressed in blankets of snow and then stripped off in spontaneous heatwaves, reserving menopause every year with fleeting hot flushes, her change starting from the ground up. Determined buds of spring flowers punctured triumphantly with clasped fists of green out of the lifeless brown ground, like zombies from the films of the eighties - only they were screaming with joy, not fright. Unless you were a person that suffered from hay fever, then you were fucked; wet eyes, sniffles and a sprint of sneezes enough to give you a quarter of an orgasm waited for you in every open space to attack like a serial killer on the loose. The small buds gave the winter-battered park premature freckles dotted sparely in shades of green all over, like a kind of mould to the ground as if it was a slice of stale bread.

The buds brought hope, bold colour and changing promise to the famous park previously hidden under a cling film of frost and ice, with no one witnessing their long struggle to achieve their breaking of the ground, reflecting the struggles of life for those who walked the park. The famous park for the past four months had played submissive to the dominant big freeze. Whipped harshly by Arctic winds and spanked by snowstorms, tied down solidly under a forceful frost, the city was exhausted and was in need of a solar power recharging from the prodigal hot sun.

A few frozen dead homeless people hit the local paper vouched for winter's serial killer kink. It was time for a change, and that change was spring. *Change was good, wasn't it?* Edna asked nobody in particular. She was old, practically invisible in the youthful city; she might as well be dead.

City living squirrels wore their grey fur coats, which had been an inspiration for one deranged Italian designer at New York Fashion Week who had collected live squirrels to skin; the flower bombs and protests from angry animal protesters brought more exposure than the whole of the famous FRow. The skittish squirrels rushed a furry circuit around the park at the speed of electricity; the heat of the city subway and twenty-four-hour lighting made hibernation an urban myth. Sleep was for the weak; their nutty single mothers told them. They were more sleep deprived than a new mother in fear of not hearing their child at night. The agitated squirrels looked forward to death, if just to sleep. Edna felt a joy to watch them hurrying along the thawing park ground with a cocaine anxiety and crack paranoia about losing their protein-fat nuts. It brought a flashback of herself as a young mother with three toddlers, racing after them, and then racing around dropping them off at various school clubs, and then ferrying them all over the city to parties as they left their teenager years, few times she forgot where she left them. Memories gave a smile to her face, but hell panic at the time. These family memories distracted Edna's attention briefly from the real reason why she was in Central Park on a chilly Tuesday morning, and not down at the knitting club. The fresh air beat the matured BO smell of Patrick, the old guy who stalked any seat next to her. The language that the hectic city spoke of pure noise respectfully filtered around the park, and left the park in peace. The silence was heavenly.

Edna's pale blue cashmere cardigan, a perfect survivor from a trip to Venice, became ideal to keep the determined chill of lingering winter at bay. A classic, it gave her small shoulders film star chic, whilst being warm enough for her prolonged stay on the green park bench as her plan took effect and she was found and carried away. The bench was scarred with *Selma loves Tuck*, carved in the arm like some young love ritual of cutting your skin. She gently stroked the bench's graffiti scar and smiled - she hoped Selma and Tuck were happy.

The Tuesday mid-morning park consisted of Chanel-dressed nannies and dog walkers; she did not want to do it on the weekend when the park was at bursting point with children - no child should see a dead body, Edna thought, again putting others before her own needs. In awe of its glamour and peace, the park was the perfect place to kill yourself. The sky was clear of clouds, so there would be no collisions as her spirit left to go to heaven. She hoped heaven and not hell; Edna never had been a fan of the heat or of going down for that matter.

Life had always been precious to Edna, but today she was against her blessed life and its betrayal. She had given life to her own three children, who were all busy adults juggling their hectic careers with their own children named after popstars, and country retreats at the weekends. On first hearing of Edna's illness, they had been glad when she assured them that it was not worth cancelling little Trixie's pony lesson to come and visit, and that Mum would be fine – again, she lied. Edna wanted to protect her children. That's what parents did, wasn't it? Protection from an imaginary monster under their bed at age seven, to an untreatable illness cutting her mobility and life quality when they were at the age of mortgages taking over. Her children had failed to visit that weekend to make sure their mum was ok.

The pain in her body would end today, controlled by her in stable mind and matter. Winter was ending, part of the deal between the seasons. Supermodels wished themselves to be as thin as the beautifully bare trees. Her ruby-long happy marriage had ended when her beloved Barney had passed away. Give him his due, he had held on for four days after the bus hit him. Slowly her own life was to end before the vicious illness crippled her creative flare and her betraying bones broke down, immobilised her like a statue. Hospital bound, she would be a burden, a problem, and another elderly life left to rot. A tube-fed dependant, she doubted the tube would feed her beloved homemade stews or delicious soups. She would need someone to wipe her arse; her arse was whiter and more wrinkled than chicken skin and had always lacked volume. She pictured it tucked away in a human nappy, and the thought made her shiver.

The over-worked, under-paid, living on four hours sleep night nurse annoyed Edna, taking up a ward bed for her Sleeping Beauty audition, wiping her deflated arse as a chore not worthy of her nursing degree. Edna opened her small wrinkled hand on the thought of her saggy arse being wiped, by God forbid, her family.

Four tiny tablets let out a celebrated gasp for air. She had clasped her hand so tight from the moment she met the shaggily dressed man on the corner. Reggie dressed in clothes too big for him, his baggy jeans exposing his designer underwear, and a gold tooth that made all his other teeth look a poor, poverty stained yellow. Edna thought his good looks were wasted as a drug dealer. Unknown to him, Reggie had happily offered to help with her plan of revenge. Smirking while taking her money, he thought to himself that druggies came in all sizes, races, backgrounds and ages, and he did not give a fuck about the old bird. Business was business. He thought she was probably a doting Grandma helping her drug addicted Grandson - if only.

Her hand ached - was it the illness or the fear? She clamped her fist hard hoping nobody would stop her. Racing, with her limited energy she created a hurried speed, weaving her tiny wren frame among the human congestion of the New York City sidewalk. She had never stopped until she found the secluded bench, shaded by a huge tree. Only now could she relax, collecting her rational mind and popping a Mint Imperial into her mouth to ease the dehydration. The cancer had started off so slightly, and then Parkinson's had joined in the march to minimise the use of her body, causing simple shaking in her hands. Grace, her friend, had joked at the coffee morning that she wasted those shakes not giving out wanks, seeing Edna spilling coffee on to the saucer drowning her ginger nut biscuit. Grace was an ex-madam, always had been a filthy broad. Edna smiled, remembering how her illness had brought light humour.

Spontaneous sickness ruled her day, and both elements gained strength over the months fighting to be the gladiator in the arena of her failing health until an everyday chore that most people took for granted like something as trivial as opening the bread became a frustration that would cripple her into a completely helpless invalid, crouched on the kitchen floor. Tears drowned her into a depression each day more dangerously than her postnatal depression with Alan, her second born. Simply drinking water, one of life's essentials, brought on a sickness spree to outdo projectile vomiting from the menopausal, bulimic Emily Rose of Exorcist fame; the weight loss failed to lift her shattered spirit.

Paying for her healthcare, she demanded that Dr Smith, a lovely Asian doctor who had treated her for two decades and had seen her more vulnerable than any of her children – and possibly her vagina more than her husband had - be brutal with the negative outcome. His brutal, yet extremely honest reply for one of his favourite patients, who knowing very well he was on a diet, would bring in a freshly baked banana and cherry cake for him, was: *"You will be encased in a living coma until it's ready to kill you."* He held back his unprofessional upset, but his blunt confession was enough for her to vote for the Brexit of her life. Edna had two phobias in life; one was being unable to care for herself in old age, and the second was flying - so a visit to Dignitas was out of the question. Plus, she worried that her children would be horrified if she was dipping into their inheritance to fund her death vacation. She decided that suicide was the only dignified way to end her life on the noisy subway ride back three days previously. Selfish, maybe, but Edna had always been selfless throughout her seventy-six years. Sometimes you had to put yourself first, and for once, she was going to abide by this motto on this chilly yet bright morning. Overdosing was the in-control option worthy to end her blessed life, and loads of celebrities did it too, giving it an edge of glamour. You controlled your finances, your bills. You controlled your car, you controlled what you ate, and nowadays you could control your bloody periods - so why not control your life ending?

She was too weak to hang herself, and her vertigo was a nightmare. She forbade herself from ruining anyone's day by jumping in front of the Subway - cutting their pay that day from work could snowball negative events for them. Throwing herself off Brooklyn Bridge seemed like too much hard work, and knowing her luck she would probably hit the deck of a passing boat and survive to become a sensation on YouTube. God knows where you would buy a gun; Edna was the only American who protected her home with a chain link lock.

The park's pigeons were a bit partial to human flesh and could possibly peck her to death, and lastly, if not found for a few days - as New Yorkers might presume her homeless and asleep, too busy to be concerned to check for a pulse - she hoped she would remain human looking. Liza, the beauty consultant at Bloomingdales beauty counter hoping to hit her holiday deposit commission had told her in a southern sweet drawl, *'not even a tsunami could wash this mascara off, doll'* that morning.

The tiny tablet looked like nothing more than a sweetener bulked up on steroids, as she opened her crinkled hand. It was smooth and innocent looking against the wrinkled folds of her paper-thin palms. The contrast of life in the form of the wrinkled palm of her hands created by human invention, and the small, pimped-up, also human invented tablet, was the reason these hands would no longer age, nor play trumpet, or touch her beautiful, spoilt grandchildren's faces. Strangely it was a beautiful, compromising image, but not enough to stop her.

She knew that in the tiny compact tablets the power to end your life was an outcome; it amazed her at how Atom Bomb deadly these tablets were to the body. It was the most nerve-wracking, crazy thing she had ever done, beating the time she had visited a nudist beach, yet the most peaceful she had ever felt about a decision in her life. She wanted the deadly deal done with her diseased body, and she wanted to conquer it. She wondered how something so small could be so deadly, but the saying *'size doesn't always matter'* took a well-earned break from being compared to penis size. The tablets revelled in the deadly fact.

She wanted revenge on her own body for turning against her, revenge for leaving her to rot away inside and end up vegetated in a ward - or god forbid, a moth-dogging meeting place of an armchair. She wanted revenge on her own body that had given birth, made love, helped raise money, donated a kidney to her sister Janice, and made memories about everything good the body did. She wanted revenge for its betrayal on all of the healthy food she had cooked and daily exercise she had done, drinking omega oil like the youths of Spring Break drank tequila. She would be damned if she was going to let her body kill her. Revenge was the least she owed herself. The choice to end her life with a dignified, stable mind was all hers.

These four simple tablets held the deadly power to end her seven decades on earth within an hour. The first tablet was a struggle to swallow. The rest made revenge create history.

London

His youthful, naked, athletic body proudly displayed inch deep raised abs to all in the windowless room, like skin instead of feathers on a horny peacock - male vanity at its worst. Mindy wanted to touch them with either her fingers or her tongue, knowing that his sponsored silence meant there could be no sexual harassment charge. Mindy prayed for abs this flat when she and Stacey hit the gym. Mindy had stuck to the same routine for the past five years. Mindy was so committed like a crusty clam to the bottom of a sea ruined boat, while Stacey ran feeble affairs with most machines and a few members even, resulting in her need to swallow the morning after pill with her fat burners.

Feeling the tight muscles underneath the tips of her fingers, running them along the way Elton John does to the keys on a grand piano while making sweet music, a teasing, and flirty temptation gnawed at her fingertips; luckily her will power was iron-strong when it came to clients and professionalism. It had been a while since she had felt the body of a man. The last time had been on a horrific Tinder date where Alf, her banker date, descended into an explanation of everything wrong with women today with each whiskey. He was fixated on why they would never succeed or become the superior sex. The only skin to touch was her hand to slap his cheek.

This guy would probably have no time to commit to you; men seemed to think that commitment was paying for a Sky Sports subscription each month. A guy this good looking must devote all of his spare time to having a huge affair with the gym, not a woman. The only breasts going into his mouth were chicken. An aftershave of protein shakes scented his breath; she guessed that kale would be his most featured post on Instagram. Cute, boyish looks told you he was a looker, and he would not be out of place at a surfer beach or an Abercrombie shoot with his sun-kissed body and loose blonde hair tickling his neck. She imagined herself as the crazy, jealous, still a stone away from her ideal weight girlfriend, having to fight off many admirers when in public, taking up kickboxing as a hobby, and wearing a knuckle-duster instead of an Argos engagement ring. Good looks and a good body - two ticks off her potential boyfriend list…another hundred or so to go.

"So, I thought that's it, can't watch it no more. Nothing worse than when the character you like dies. Know what I mean?" Mindy offered insight into her dislike of TV shows killing off their main characters, ignoring the fact it was a hook to keep you glued, create a global buzz. Free to talk away to herself, he wouldn't answer. She sounded word-perfect, despite having two make-up brushes made from swan-down perched in her mouth. Mindy liked routine and consistency, so with the sudden death of a character, it took a few days for her to settle. Mindy was not a massive fan of social media, so she never had a heads-up on potential cast killings, and to her, a troll had neon pink hair and was a nudist.

Carrying on, "I used to be a vegetarian back in art school. All top artists used to starve themselves, you see, to create a masterpiece. One even cut his ear off, could you imagine?" She applied a bit of blusher. Mindy had no chance of cutting her ear off to improve her art; it had taken her till the age of twenty-seven to get her ears pierced. Her horror filled screaming sent all of the three years old in the queue running out of the high street shop in tears. Alex had to sit on her for the beautician to finish the other ear.

"But coming off meat shocked my body like a hairdryer in the bath! Plus, the mother was dating Barry the butcher at the time, so all the free sausages she could handle would go to waste. World War three broke out when told her I was going vegetarian," laughing loudly thinking she was Peter Kay. She recalled the memory of Poppy on a sausage marathon. Every dish had come with a sausage like a free toy in a Happy Meal, and she had brought a priest friend around to conduct an exorcism on Mindy for her protests to become a vegetarian. A phobia of holy water developed, and a wooden crucifix and old men in ill-fitting dresses terrified Mindy's dreams for weeks after.

Why couldn't all men be as patient as him and just listen she wondered? "That should be it, darling," placing her make-up brush down; the magic was finished. Releasing her breath, the smell of mint escaped and echoed around the room like a morning mist of spring freshness. She always harboured a mint when working so close to her clients. This was also part of her mild OCD, and coffee breath was her nemesis. Everything had to be clean and fresh, including her breath. Stepping back to view the final touches, she had been scrutinising her work for the past hour and looking for the imaginary mistake, which like the lost city of Atlanta, was never found, nor had he complained about. She felt a little betrayed by her professional skills, as there was not a reason to go back and touch his beautiful face again. Perfectionism was an illness, she would declare.

She was her own worst critic was Mindy, and if she had been on Twitter she'd probably troll herself and win troll of the year. All through her straight-A school years, college years and University, she had gained the highest mark in Fine Art and a national award for her outstanding work, but her self-doubt still cheered louder and shook pom-poms with bells on, forever taunting Mindy. The internal bully never lost strength or weakened. Her homework was top notch and a joy for the teacher to mark, yet she always said '*sorry*' when handing it in, like it was unfinished. She never gave herself praise even when due, like now.

"Not bad" Eric told her, putting his thick glasses on, his short sight returning to normal, taking off his thin white gloves and disposing of them into the bin.

"Ya think so?" She was unsure if the foundation was a tad too deep for his beachy looks.

"Yeah, you can barely even see the mark on his neck, well done Mindy. I can see why you won make-up artist of the year more than once," patting her slim back with an aged, manly hand sporting a few age spots. The firm pat echoed confidently with praise for his favourite employee. She felt it was more like '*try better next time*', like when you throw a ball for your dog but it doesn't catch it, but you still pat it, hiding your disappointment that your dog is the shit ball catcher at the park, its pedigree bloodline failing to add canine credit, seeing your neighbours adopted mongrel, down to three legs, catching a Frisbee with smug ease.

Truly, she was a perfectionist - if not a little obsessive. In Zumba she had started as a backing dancer, two-stepping her salsa behind a woman who looked like she ate salsa, and the Mexican who served it at the back of the dance studio, whose chubby arse was forever making famous faces in her too small gym pants, like the way Jesus pops up on toast. One week she was convinced she saw Michael Jackson's face, his nose missing, lost in her hungry crack. By the fourth week Mindy was shaking her shimmy at the front as if she was Beyoncé in a ginger wig, twerking to the point where the instructor barred her from the class.

Eric lifted his '*I'm the boss*' mug up. A chip in the rim made each sip a hazard to his thin lips; it was the only time Eric lived dangerously. A present from the staff, he never let on that it was the prize possession in his lonely life. The tea left a crop-circle ring on the stainless steel table as the only indication that a cup had been there. Turning and leaving the cool, heavily sterilized room behind him, he told himself she was a clean freak as he noticed cleaning products in their masses of all sizes, strengths and smells, bigger than an army that Russia could muster together and powerful in their numbers. Germs told stories about their power when they were microscopic and invisible to the eye, before they matured into superbugs. He smiled, closing the light door quietly so as not to disturb Stevie Wonder's smooth tones as he sang *Superstition* on the fifties-inspired radio.

Mindy stepped back, then forward under the bright lights, and added a bit more foundation to his neck. Again, she stepped back, then again, nearly twisting her ankle in her doctor's shoes. She cocked her head to the left, then right like a bird of prey watching its helpless victim. She returned a stray strand of her red auburn hair behind her cute ear, which always reminded her mother of the sun setting in India that time she was hijacked by camel sellers. Job satisfaction was a daily fix for her, giving the same benefit that smokers got from a pull on a cigarette. She never received praise from her clients every day - rude maybe, but she did not mind. They could not help it; they didn't even pay the fee or leave a tip, and got family members to send cards of thanks like a PA would to a diva. She never thought she would end up being a make-up artist to the dead
.

Los Angeles

The hotel room was completely gutted. Burned back to its wooden skeleton and covered in charred ashes, its foundations were exposed, showing the hunger of the fatal fire with its destroying greed. The gluttonous fire had waited for Chad to spunk before it devoured the room and the hooker, watching the star in a free sex show. Luckily, the fire-fighter got into the room just in time for the fire to not leave a dead body. Chad was rescued first - he was after all the talent - while the hooker suffered slight burns to her pretty face due to her collapsing. She was not breathing as well as she should; she had been taking Chad's cock on a tour to the back of her throat, and adding to that the competing fire sucking the oxygen from the room, she lacked breath to move and her fake hair had acted as fuse lint.

Chad was grateful that he had not burned alive in a cheap hotel room with an even cheaper hooker. *Thank God for the lucky escape,* he thought - not the brave fire-fighters - taking tequila shot in the hotel bar. It was free, of course, from the manager who apologised for the fire. *Had he lit it?* Paranoia ransacked his mind. Celebrity status held the power to make the most humble and innocent of people take the blame.

The shame plastered in the media could ruin his small acting credits; it would certainly cull his attention-grabbing relationship with Maria Dieppe. Maria certainly would not be impressed if it was leaked that he had been caught with a hoe, but would wear a fabulous frock just in case she was papped. Running his hands through his sun kissed locks, his hair smooth, he was annoyed more at the fact that the hotel was not the Chateau Marmont. His locks fell gently back into place, afraid not to.

Chad sat at his open kitchen table alone in his rented villa, the pristine white walls giving them an endless appearance, and wide-open windows inviting fresh ocean air in while reading a collection of magazines. The near-death experience cremated any news of his failed win at the soap awards, crisping any attention on the winner like a left chicken wing on a BBQ; slight bonus for Chad. The fable story told the reader that soap star Chad Rise had saved the life of a female guest, carrying her through the flames to safety in only his underwear - pure Hollywood action hero, and utter bullshit. But, so was showbiz. A little exaggeration did wonders for the ego and harmed no one - or did it?

"Fucking good lie that one, isn't it?" his crisp American accent filtered around, but his question remained unanswered. Chad was pleased that he had been thrusted onto the front page without having to pay the paps or display bad behaviour, and for once he would gain sympathy. His unpredictable ego had been stroked giving him satisfaction, tearing the article out to glue later into his scrapbook, on his fifth volume of himself.

Being talk of the town fed his desire to gain strength and had the added bonus of Maria calling him in tears, thinking he was dead as it had taken two days for him to answer. It was all a game to him. He was sucking out her insecurity to fuel his desire to women - yet anyone eavesdropping in on that call would have known that her tears were tears of sadness that he had not died in the rogue blaze.

He lit up a Marlboro, his third in the past half hour, resting it between his thick lips; the same lips to be involved with a few sexy females while Maria was away, seeing a limp condom hanging over the bin rim like it was trying to escape and show evidence of his infidelity to Maria. It gave him a chuckle. He turned the thin pages of the Celebrity Weekly and yes, he dominated the pages with his bravery and lucky escape - just not his talent. Annoyed, he wondered if dying in the blaze would not have done his career any harm - it did James Dean no harm. His face was untouched, his bad boy looks were intact and his smile was perfect. 'Thank fuck,' said Greg Locust, his money-greedy agent's response when his first question was 'Is the face ok?' It was ideal that he shared the same name as a gluttonous insect.

This was perfect to kick out gossip over his quick exit from the Soap due to his unprofessional behaviour of fucking the producer's sixteen-year-old daughter, but the age-old showbiz reason of 'wanting to try other things' was plastered over the near-paedophile incident. This was just what he needed to show the studio bosses that they had been fucked over. He was number one trending on Twitter and had ten thousand more fans following him…it was the best free publicity so far this year. *'I'm a genius,'* he thought to himself, turning to another magazine to read their write-up on the incident.

Chad was extremely popular. His popularity was dangerous with his shady behaviour, especially when drunk; he was untouchable, he thought, and it was only a matter of time before he became an icon of the big screen. Demanding, bullying, and full of sickly self-confidence, he displayed the age old lethal trio of traits that a man harbouring secrets and loathing would have. His treatment of women was bad - mostly weak and vulnerable such as prostitutes - abusing their need for the paid pounding fuck for their survival. It was shallow, and for some ladies to cross his path, also life changing. But not all of the women Chad left in his trail of destruction were afraid or weak; some were on their way to come back into his life.

"*I hope Faith steps in before he makes the big time, or something more sinister like revenge*", one victim of his bad behaviour told her cell mate.

He was talented. Not on a Johnny Depp level, but who is? He had enough talent to hold his own on a prime-time American soap, was beautiful enough to enter the 'Top Ten Hunks' each year, and his rowdy behaviour was enough for the hyena journalists to print his name weekly. His looks were rugged but with a clean shine, and a strong jaw line used on many a Disney Prince framed his face amazingly. Botox kept him looking fresh, but froze his emotions as well as his wrinkles. His eyes were the innocent hue of a baby in the blue ocean water of the Maldives, as if every time he opened his eyes they were virgins to the world. His stare was a killer; he looked at you like he could read your dirty thoughts of what you wanted him to do to you and smirked knowing. His lips were forever wet as if they had just left a vagina soaked in satisfaction. His worked-out body was ripped, stripped of any processed fat, and with a sun kissed tan from the original tanner, the sun - or a bottle. His body was captured in a calendar every year, and was a best seller too. His blonde hair had been loosely brushed by the wind or his strong hands, and his crooked little finger even added cuteness. His penis was generous in length and girth, and was forever entertained by the many willing females he met - yet it was never enough for him. His Porsche was never fast enough, his home in Atlanta never bigger enough, and his career not winning awards enough. There was always something Chad was chasing - may that be a role or a skirt.

This free exposure exploded his hotness all over the media reminding all that he was free to hire, and sure to get the mega bucks offers in. Greg, his long-time percent greedy agent, was already on the case doing the rounds for possible projects, film being the number one priority, and maybe a cheeky visit to rehab too.

Chad rose from his table with the regal action of a King, and walked over to the large fridge fishing out two cold cans of Australian lager. They were the only lodgers in the fridge, feeling the fridge blow cold air on his insulting abs. This exposure deserved a toast. He went out onto the small decking, feeling the fresh air in his lungs and the sun bright on his tanned skin, closing his eyes to soak it in. He'd come far from his old life where Chad Rise was merely a mood board in his Action Man diary. He had been a dream to act out in his head every day, and it was the only thing to keep him going in dead end jobs and a stale life of just living. The dream was now reality.

The transformation was remarkable; it was praised actually. His determination to achieve everything he set out for over the past five years was to be admired, but the way he achieved it was criminal. Selling his soul to the devil twice over paid off, leaving loyal people hurt and destroyed by his deceiving. He took all of the money he could find and killed off his old life to create the star today, Chad Rise. Life was looking damn fucking good. He had built himself from the ground up. The gym worked his muscles to rip and shed and cover over his old body, and new, bigger muscles grew over his old body like ivy more poisonous. Shaping out and toning all over was the easy part, if not the longest. It took time to change your body, but not your face.

Arriving at the surgery, he had been in disbelief at how a person could pick out features as they reconstructed them onto a 3D picture of you. When the doctor had turned the TV around to show him the outcome, his new face, Chad Rise had shed a tear and fifty thousand dollars.

He shouted Roxy over from the lake, who as loyal as ever bounded over all golden locks and glossy eyes shining in the sun, ready to fall into his bicep happy arms. "Have a toast with me, beautiful lady." Roxy approached gasping for a drink, and she was mute from asking what the reason was for the early morning toast. She would do anything Chad said in a heartbeat. Chad ran his fingers through her soft mane. "Onwards and upwards. Dead is Chad Rise, the small TV star. Now it's time for the rise of Chad Rise, the movie star." Bending down to fill Roxy's water bowl up with cold lager, the golden Labrador was only too happy to please her owner; her pink tongue tasted the bitter drink on its first contact.

London

Becoming a make-up artist to the dead was one of those drunken promises you know that you just happen to make on a wet Wednesday, writing your bucket list on the back of a water bill envelope with an eyeliner pencil - along with losing weight, and stop stalking ex-boyfriends on social media. This was a familiar thing for her since she'd hit thirty, along with hangovers lasting longer than her drying out periods, and getting annoyed when ticking the third box on forms that asked your age. The killer sign she was getting close to old age - finding a grey hair in her pubes that morning of her great aunt's funeral. Ignoring the fact that it was a sign she was closer to getting a free travel pass didn't lift her depressed mood, with the bullying and nagging thought that she should be more spontaneous, not stale.

Through slurs accompanied by a few refills of White Grenache and a few soggy ham and cheese sandwiches, she had told the kind looking man quite loudly, "I could do better! (Hic) People deserve to (Hic) look amazing when they say their finally goodbyes! (Hic) Can I have a refill? Goodbye to the world (Hic)," then falling over into the buffet table ended her spontaneous rant. The gent turned out to be a successful funeral director, Eric May, and a few celebrities had left his parlour in oak wood and not McQueen. Needing a new mortuary make-up artist since Bonnie had followed the trend of her clients and passed away, he offered her a job on the spot.

Mindy had started in the make-up business the good old-fashioned way, from the bottom, back at the mere age of twenty-one. This was long before all the pretenders popped up on social media, having completed a make-up course in the back of a white transit van on a council estate, charging Mac prices for a McDonalds look, and using make-up bought on tick from the catalogue. Years it had taken to master her skills and secrets, with hard graft and hours in training, where different looks actually meant different looks, not just the same look using different colours. She had learned make-up to enhance natural features - not to shade your perfectly normal nose into rumours of a nose job, three shades too much, your nose giving

Janet Jackson the shivers. This was unlike today's trends of contouring and a dark eye, gathering more likes on Facebook than a successful charity fundraiser.

She had entered the world of make-up starting as a low paid assistant to an eccentric theatre make-up artist called Caddie Dillon, a good friend of Poppy her mother, back in their Greenpeace protesting days. Yet Poppy mainly forgot the peace bit, with cautions beached up in her police files better than the whales she tried saving did. Caddie looked like she applied Cleopatra's make-up she was that old, with a crew cut dyed ice white and neon orange lips. Dust coated her hair giving it a grey cap, cropped into a boyish crew with the stunted regrowth from chemo. Veneers nearly as long as her, skin pale and near transparent, and a face pierced by beady, tiny eyes that hid behind huge leopard framed glasses. She was a tiny woman so frail-figured that she stood on a beer crate sometimes to do her celebrity clients' make-up. Silent in her work, never muttering a word, all Mindy did was watch, timid and shy; Mindy stayed put in standing and with tongue.

To her surprise, Caddie Dillon was full of life. She had not a creaking bone in sight, and was full of surprises teaching her tricks and secret tips of the trade. She had invaluable skills and secrets to take you from applying make-up at children's parties for minimum wage, to applying make-up to the film stars and earning a living of luxury. Introducing her to her tightly knitted power clients, networking amongst the industry helped Mindy become a name within make-up. Mindy went from being a shy girl into a hardworking, workaholic, in-demand woman. She had no time for relationships as she threw herself into her celebrated work. Caddie Dillon became to Mindy what Noah was to animals - a saviour, and what Bill Clinton was to Monica Lewinsky - a pay cheque. Mindy became her successful successor when Caddie Dillon sadly passed away due to a hormonal ewe when trekking one summer in the Lake District.

Mindy threw herself into her ideal job, winning top awards including an Oscar for a period historical drama. She created a sell-out range of make-up, the first to be organic, anti-ageing make-up sold exclusively in Selfridges, *Miracle of Mindy*. Flying all over the world to apply make-up to celebrities for awards and ceremonies, she was in high demand. One day she would be in Cannes for the prestigious film festival, the next over to L.A for music awards and Oscars or back to England for Royalty. Anywhere that a star might need the best make-up to beat the other bitches of the industry, Mindy was flown to. Dashing between two rooms with plausible excuses as she was doing the rival's make-up in the other room, Mindy was too polite and work-proud to turn down work. One time she even applied make-up to a vagina to cover bruising on a famous TV star. The actress had decided to give in to the pressure of a threesome from the producer to land the lead role of his new film. The banging from the two well-endowed men lasted four hours and the bruising lasted a week, but the Oscar nomination was worth it.

Mindy reigned over the industry for years giving lectures, running workshops and building up an impressive clientele base, and even collecting a proposal from Boy George. But, over the years as trends started to last no more than a day, make-up was becoming competitive to the point where it started to be stressful more than fun. Competition cluttered up social media and the make-up industry sold its soul to reality TV socialites.

Make-up products were being churned out cheaply and as fast as Madonna throws out toy boys. Stars more famous for getting their enhanced tits out than their actual talent or starring as the female role in a sex tape, the fewer clothes they wore the less their talent was shown. People in the industry started to backstab each other, shag each other husbands and wives, and social media killed privacy. Mindy decided enough was enough and retired before she hit thirty - one tick off her bucket list.

The pleas from her collection of high earning clients fell on Mindy's unpierced ears and did not make her change her mind, and nor did Grace Jones turning up at her home begging her to reconsider and change her mind, waving an axe. Once Mindy dedicated herself to an idea she stuck by it, even the time she decided to learn pole dancing. The instructor had politely mentioned after ten weeks that maybe Mindy was not a pole dancer, watching Mindy mopping the floor with her arse as she attempted the swan. Being stubborn was a trait that benefitted Mindy. She eventually and happily became a total recluse in the industry. Vogue ran an article on her calling it the end of an era for make-up; it took pride on her fridge, and five years later it still made her smile stuck next to a portrait of her and her Mother dressed in African tribal wear on their safari trip for Poppy's sixtieth. Poppy loved Africa so much that she had broken tradition and went on the hunt for a toy boy and his green card. Another factor in her decision to leave - and if anything, sometimes bitterly and regrettably annoyed her - was her mother becoming seriously ill.

The handsome young guy laid pleasantly at peace from his tragic and distressing departure from the earth's living room knowing as life. The thin cloth covered his modesty; Maud had disgustingly asked if she could look at his penis. Only the deep, death-delivering gash on his neck told you that he was dead. The thin steel cable wire literally needed cutting out; it was embedded deep in his throat, and blood dried over the wire acting in protest for the wire not to be cut. Not found for three days, by his wife never to be, she was traumatised seeing him hanging from the brand-new loft conversion on her return to their new home. He looked like he had not a care in the world, which when you are dead, she supposed you didn't. He looked like he was dreaming of a better life – maybe where he was now, wherever that was.

Why was suicide so painful for others?

Does one not have the right to end life if it becomes unbearable for them?

Was suicide selfish, or was the selfish act in those left behind mourning their pain and ignoring the pain of the deceased.

Had Mindy's heart committed suicide, as dead as her poor client?

This was her work and she kept it as work, as cold as it sounds – she was paid a job to do. Her vacant heart had been chilled with the lack of loving someone, and vice versa.

She applied the same pride of sophisticated skill and tremendous talent as she did for the living, despite being paid a hell of a lot less. She painstakingly finished each corpse like they were about to be in a shoot for the cover of a style bible, instead of being encased in a coffin. Sometimes Eric stepped in to speed her up, yelling "the dead don't wait!" Ringing of a telephone in the background backed up his morbid claim. The satisfaction of the relatives when they saw their departed love ones, the tears of joy amongst the tears of torn hearts always made her heart glow that she had done the job properly. Mindy's skills were used a lot when the victim was brutally beaten, or burnt, and her touch brought peace to their faces.

The worst part of this job was dealing with babies. To see a life cut so short punched her heart, and it hurt constantly, so to imagine what the parents must have felt beckoned. Nobody who had not lost a child could even try to imagine, so Mindy never did. Each time a child came in she prayed that it was a natural death and not interference from battery, neglect or the sadness of fire. Placing a teddy bear in their arms as she worked her make-up, she liked to think that the softness of the bear comforted them. She drank a bottle of wine on those nights to help her sleep.

"There you go, you look brand new," she said spraying the wasted life with a gentle layer of hairspray to keep the make-up in place, like a kind of Botox for the dead. She regularly spoke to the deceased, comforting them while they lay in a strange place. She also had the added bonus of no-one interrupting one of her Mindy moan-alogues as they waited for the great heaven taxi to pick them up, which in this case was a thousand pound plus taxi fare for the funeral costs.

Funerals were probably the only business to gain a profit from a loss and never make a loss, profit always. Eric always joked that he was going to sponsor a serial killer to bring some business in. Maud gave him the number of her cousin who would be freed in two years from a manslaughter charge and would need a job.

Death had always fascinated Mindy from a young age; the death of Malibu Barbie to a hungry whippet had started it all. She understood the trauma of losing of a loved one from witnessing her own mum upset over a dear friend or relatives, but Mindy had prepared for it by telling herself that everyone must die - no matter how powerful, rich, famous or good that person was. We all had to die, and it was the only common link between all living things. It was a conversation that no matter how uneducated or foreign someone was, everyone around the globe could join in and discuss death. 'Mindy the Morbid' Alex called her when she started talking about her philosophy on death, and how strange it was to have an egg with a piece of chicken; the egg had been the start of the chicken and the breast was the end, two life stages on the same plate. Alex always ordered another bottle of wine with the rolling of her perfect eyes.

As long as the death was not too horrific and too hideous to leave unanswered questions being talked about by the buffet table, she appreciated the hunger that death brought to a life and always remained ready. If it was a loved one with weeks or months to live then at least activities of joy could be shared, bucket lists ticked off, and pictures and memories stacked high. If their death was due to old age, then she was forever congratulating the achievement to people who mentioned the age of the deceased.

There was another reason that Mindy became uncharacteristically friendly with death, and only addressed it whenever she came across the topic in conversation, print or news, or when drenched in wine - but she was neither at the minute. It always humoured Mindy that to come into the world it cost literally nothing but a quick leg over, yet to leave, some people had to remortgage their homes to cover funeral costs, what for? The poor dead person would probably enjoy the expense more alive than dead, and it was the only party where you were guaranteed to be the subject of – it was almost as if the deceased were acting like a diva by not turning up. You come into the world naked and you leave naked too. Though, Mindy remembered a woman buried in her thirty thousand pound Vera Wang wedding dress; it had taken all of her will power and the fact that she had just had her nails done by Sabrina that day not to grave-dig the dress up herself.

*

She wasn't completely un-dateable or hideous looking-wise for her to have to wear a burka, or for men to need to claim to be gay if she spoke to them. Having relationships in the past, they had never lasted longer than a Ramadan - but she never loved them as much as she loved her work or had loved 'Him', and no one had stabbed her once loving heart with a venom filled knife as much as his bonking betrayal.

Mindy looked twenty-seven to her thirty-six years with a complexion plain and blessed with a youthful glow, and light green eyes that broke up her plain, hydrated face, along with wild freckles that seemed to change places, playing hide and seek under the sun and popping up randomly like cute moles on a lawn. Her slim nose was her only venture into plastic surgery, due to a seagull flying dead into her face on Brighton beach and breaking her nose on a hen do. However, she had a flirtation with Botox once a year. Flowing locks of red waved down her back like lava from an eruption – it was the reason that men glanced at her in the first place, and it gave the impression that she could be Scottish. Forever picking up compliments, she looked similar to Henry Dooley – an Oscar winning British indie actor up there with Michael Caine. Mindy could never see it herself, but Mindy never ever knew her Dad.

She was attractive in a simple way; she had no fear of jealous attacks from acid-throwing women or ex-boyfriends. She was a bit taller than the average woman, slim with good sized breasts, and a warm and welcoming smile that made people want to talk to her. A few times she had missed her stop due to her chatting away to strangers on the tube. She was confident, but not in-your-face confident - just the kind of confidence that maturing brings. Her life was canal calm and slow flowing, bringing peace and beauty and enriching her friends' lives. She had no horrific hiccups in her younger life to sway her behaviour towards anything reckless, or a rebellion like promiscuous loving with local boys, or becoming size four from heroin addiction. Only the incident with 'Him' had brought shade on her adult life and tainted her trust in men. Mindy was a fan of positive thinking; it was a barrier to stop negativity since the incident was still strong in her mind.

She was single and living alone, apart from E.T, her ginger, three-legged cat reincarnated with the soul of a Cerberus, like Hades pet dog. She had once had to foot a vet bill for next door's Jack Russell missing an ear. Mindy preferred it if E.T brought in dead mice rather than dog ears as gifts. E.T was short for Elizabeth Taylor - his feminine name hid well behind people's mistaken assumption that he was christened after the alien needing to reverse the phone call home. Her other passion - apart from make-up, recycling, Stevie Wonder and Oreo cookie milkshakes - was watching the stunning legend in her old films. Mindy owned lilac contacts too, wearing them for the special film gatherings at the small fan club she had found in London. She hadn't really had a relationship since 'Him'. 'Him' was enough to make Mother Theresa become a serial killer, with men as her only victims. 'Him' was simply a cunt, her friends declared. Alex still couldn't believe that Mindy had let 'Him' get off so lightly; every time a skinful of wine was poured down her neck she badgered on about it, where she had got a caution for beating him up instead. Mindy failed to address the past with 'Him' but she would one day, and like Elizabeth Taylor, she never stopped hoping for that one true love - unlike Lizzy, luckily Mindy would only marry once.

Turning his greatest collection up with one hand, Stevie Wonder belted on about a *higher ground* as Mindy danced like a drunk uncle, packing away her make-up trolley with her other hand. She cleaned the studio up, emptied the recycling bin, and then she finally changed to head home.

Someone was on their way to Mindy in the cargo pit of a private jet currently crossing the Atlantic. Mindy was the only person in the world with the heart to help with the more than a decade-long revenge and her terrible make-up. Unfortunately, though, they were bringing Mindy real danger from an evil man. "Mindy best bloody be in," she muttered in her black body bag.

New York

Prostitution or turning to God to better her life were the only two options left at the crossroad five years ago as she faced another eviction, declared herself bankrupt and had been left by another abusive boyfriend as she laid spread eagle for a smear test. Only one could win, come out on top, and get her life back on track. They both worked similarities so she felt no guilt - both were mentioned in the bible, both made you drink wine and both made you get on your knees. The winning factor for 'team prostitution' was that it paid you.

This was exactly what Claudia was waiting for now as she picked at a dry cum stain on her shapeless skirt, as she sat on the edge of the hotel bed in cheap heels and her heavy tits on bare show. Her client this afternoon was a stud, a proper sexy guy. His beach body was ripped and he was all Hollywood smiles. Normally she preferred an older man in the hope that they had a heart attack, so she could loot the wallet before she fucked off. The stud came out from the bathroom, dissolving his hard body under a thin plain white shirt and his hair glistening wet from the shower. She couldn't quite picture where she knew his handsome face from, but she had seen it somewhere - she would scream in shock later that evening opening up the National Enquirer. The stud reached into the pocket of his vintage denim and pulled out a Chanel wallet fat with notes, fingered it like he had with her, took a few dollars and tossed them at her. They floated to the floor as if too worthy for Claudia to hold.

"Maybe we could have round two or something, soon?" she said, flicking her eyelashes caked in mascara as if she was sweet seventeen years old and had just lost her virginity, and not a thirty-seven-year-old with minor acne. To him it looked pathetic and made a puddle of bile flood his throat. Adult acne was never cute, and her harsh black hair, coarse and cut unevenly did fuck all for her round face; she looked like a female Jack Black. Her saving grace was her impressive tits that poured out from each handful he grabbed like kneading bread dough. Still on show, they nearly possessed the power to turn him around and drop to his knees to take them in his mouth. This hooker was a little plump for him; he preferred slim, near child-like skinny. Yet what she lacked in rib count she made up for in curves and sexual energy, watching her nearly topple over with their weight as she picked up the ashamed dollars. Feeling him slamming against her chubby arse cheeks had worked as a slight aphrodisiac, and her sweaty moans of '*more*' fed his thrust. It was a change to feel the comfort of her skin instead of bones with his normal heroin-diet hookers. Fat was disgusting, an emergency epidemic, and now that the haze from his horniness lifted, the reality was gut wrenching.

She had worked her chubbiness in the heated shag. Luckily, doggy-style hid her rolls and cellulite well; once he came, the Cinderella effect came off faster than the two condoms he wore. She turned back into a fat whore selling her fat fanny for cheap sex. It disgusted him, yet the next time he was alone in a hotel room high and horny, the only medication to curb his hunger for sordid, no-strings sex would be her willing pussy at the happy hour strip joint he had first found her in.

"Nah thanks, hookers are like teabags to me. One dip in then out in the bin." His cruel laugh met her ears mute to Claudia; most men's insults were like water off a duck's back. You couldn't be a prostitute if you were a little sensitive, she would tell the newbies on the strip. She noticed how beautifully his face lit up when he laughed. It was a shame he was a prick, but with a wonderful dick. She wondered how she would be able to go back to 'Mr Joe Average' after that dick. It would be like going back to a kitten heel after wearing Louboutin skyscrapers. "Have a nice day, anyway," his back told her, leaving the hotel room and closing the door behind him and on her. Claudia sat back on the bed and let out a fed-up sigh into the empty room. It echoed loudly and was about to remind her of the past, but she slapped it away. She counted the hundred dollars absent-mindedly, thinking it wasn't much for a two-hour session. "Oh, my day is looking mighty fine thank you," her delayed reply told the empty room. Reaching under her arse she pulled out the Rolex and held it up. The sunlight bounced off the sheer metal due to the expensiveness of it. She knew it was at least worth four thousand dollars; Wayne the pawnbroker would cum in his pants instead of her mouth for a change when she took it to him. *Not bad for a day's work*, she smirked, putting her impressive tits back into her off-white bra. Running one over on Chad Rise, "Revenge is a bitch sweetheart," she said tucking the Rolex into her bra with a smile.

*

Today was a good day. The sun was bright, and the clouds were clear like her conscience. Yes, it was definitely a good day for letter writing to reveal the overdue truth, to reveal her identity to him after these years. It was only fair all before it was too late. Her resemblance to him was gaining strength and attracting comments daily; it unnerved her at times. The more she kept it to herself, the more it showed on the face. Each morning she saw the lie before she saw her aged reflection. Could a three-decade secret find another way of exposing itself through someone's face rather than mouth? Was the saying 'it's written all over your face' true?

The letter that was over thirty years overdue was currently a blank piece of paper. She feared that once she started writing it would become a trilogy. She admired the innocence and enduring nature of the blank sheet. It seemed a shame to ruin it with words of discretion and ruin; she paused, it was a weak excuse to get out of it. The cute floral print in the corner of the page added a touch of expensiveness. Well, if you were about to ruin someone's day with words, a little luxury was worth it she thought. How was she meant to explain it, to ask for forgiveness, and give her reasons for not contacting sooner? He was easy to find. A public figure of his calibre would definitely demand a DNA test before admitting that the child was his. Her main priority for breaking the routine to her day - to write the letter and not watch Judge Judy kicking ass – was that she hoped they were able to build some sort of relationship before it was too late, before she left, and before she forgot.

A letter was old fashioned; it was an original, it had no way of being tampered with, or photobombed or something she could not remember - social media terrified her like a cyber Jack the Ripper. A letter was extremely personal. With this matter on so many levels of human deception and betrayal, she wondered where to start. The beginning, maybe? Yet the beginning was a little blurry for her as if dust had settled on that night so long ago in that field of protest. Only the ending and the last thirty six years were in full colour. She smiled at each memory and thanked the ecstasy tablet that she had taken that night to lose her inhibitions. She missed the days of free loving and living.

She was an old-fashioned type of lady with a youthful mind and a mischievous streak. Technology was for the lazy and the young, she blasted. The fountain pen paused before it touched the paper, dropping a tiny drop of navy ink as a tear. Was the pause due to her being afraid of what it was about to write, or did she have writers block? Sat at the small desk facing out from the window, the beautiful morning light warm on her old face reassured her that this was the right thing to do; it was time, time to end a chapter of her life and hopefully begin a new one for her daughter.

She did not have long to get this letter written; today was a good day to write the letter of confession, but tomorrow could be a whole new ball game. The address on the envelope was already written, there was no turning back. Plus, Maggie from Room Two had fumed handing over her last first-class stamp with the reluctance of handing a rationed egg in the war, so she best not waste it.

"Here goes," she said, letting out a thick sigh. The sharp tip touched the thick paper, and simple words with the power to change Poppy's daughter's life, bleed out in blue blood written within a paragraph.

Manhattan

Delia Von-Grouse never did two things in New York, ever. One was being seen out in Manhattan without her legendary beige mink coat that she never apologised for, and second, her trademark YSL ruby red vampire lips. The famous lipstick had left its iconic mark on many a war-famine inspired skinny fashionista's cheek at the many glamorous parties she attended, and many of Manhattan's horny bachelors cocks like a red notch on a bedpost. Here she was the wealthy socialite whose fortune had come begrudgingly from divorcing a bald, cheating Senator, out on the New York pavement without both. She was famous for her over-exaggerated love for animal skin glamour, and her resistance to flour bombs and PETA pressure. Her Parisian-thin posture on the high society scene of the skyscraper-loving city had worked many a paparazzi lens like illegal lovers kidnapped in a frame. Infamous for her bed-hopping, any conquest tagged as 'Dicked by Delia', she liked to use a diamond strap-on. Tits like boulders all made Delia a great column filler to shake up the boring drone of fashion write-ups. Tonight, why the fuck was she out on the cold pavement in only her lacy underwear, giving the homeless a break from the strange stares of passers-by gasping in sheer shock? One Chinese tourist had taken a selfie with the infamous Delia, great inspiration to stick to their fridge help with their temperamental dieting.

Delia was a high lady of excessive times, excessive dresses and excessive spending, and more importantly, excessive sex; a pioneer to pave the way for the term *cougar*. Delia loved nothing more than a young stud, or two inside her. She leased out her body more than her Manhattan penthouse suite, and had more deposits on her body than the monthly rent. Tonight, she again hit the front pages in a beautiful underwear set that was yet to grace the stores, a sell-out nicknamed 'Death by Delia'.

This evening, Delia Von-Grouse wore her skimpy underwear on the cold wet pavement floor, gave no reaction to the shocked crowd gathering. Light rain descended, making her wetter than any man of New York ever had, and all fifty-seven of her years were dead. Delia

Von-Grouse had liked a bang, but not the type to the head that killed you. Blood poured over her surgery-stretched face the way that strawberry syrup tickles down a Knickerbocker glory sundae. No single expression broke through the Botox barrier, and not a bone was intact; Delia was dead on impact.

Cartier, her Persian cat, looked out from the stony high ledge of her twenty-second floor posh apartment, licking his plump paw in sorrow. Chilly night air blew on his flat feline face due to the sheer height of the apartment block. Yet a professional cat whisperer would have known it was more to do with him being hungry than grief. He had witnessed the murder, and hearing the apartment door close after the designer-dressed killer beat his routine grooming. Being a cat, Cartier sensed the storm brewing, witnessing Storm 'Revenge is a Bitch' claim her first victim, Delia.

Notting Hill, London

The cheery doorbell rang impatiently throughout the land of the beautifully cream decorated home. It rang longer this time, pissed that it had not been answered, pressed again with the endurance of a Jehovah's Witness dying to rid the weight of leaflets from their cute briefcases. Mindy's two bedroom apartment sat proudly in plush, posh Notting Hill set back from the main road among cute trees and peaceful beige painted houses. She had bagged the little piece of property heaven when she had first set out on her flourishing career, receiving her fee for occupying a Latino superstar on her sell out world tour and paying the deposit; she sent a Christmas card to Mindy every year in Spanish.

It was a sensible investment paired with long term security, and her mother called it a rich husband trap. In the words of Meatloaf, *two out of three ain't bad.* Single men of London, notorious for the shallow dating of single women in the grip of fear, preying on their fear of being lonely with seven cats and an addiction to knitting and Midsomer Murders, like porn infecting them with false promise, lived in the prime property of the crippling prices of the city. It made getting on the property ladder a hell of a lot easier than being chained to a desk and saving for a mortgage, and was more ruthless than *Saving Private Ryan*. If you got these women pregnant then bingo, you were in - no successful woman wanted to raise their child in Zone Three.

Pinpricks in condoms, forgetting to pull out, or doggy style in the wrong hole were all of the tricks that came out of their loose pants to secure that property. The women needed a lodger in their hearts, while the men needed beds in enviable locations to score above other males - like birds of paradise competing in building a magnificent nest to attract a mate - just that the female did all the hard work. It was a new thing in the never-ending dating game that potential boyfriends looked for. This kink was slowly overtaking big tits for some men in their potential CV for girlfriends. Ten blissfully happy years later, it still made Mindy pinch herself every time she woke up in her Laura Ashley covered queen size bed.

"Fuck, about time! This wine was in fear of going from chilled to cooked. If I had to wait any longer I was going to drink it on the doorstep. Plus, Pervy Pete was twitching the curtains," the bold, brass northern lass declared with a crack in her voice like a firecracker caught in her throat, trying to dislodge it every sixth word, frantically waving three bottles of wine in Mindy's face to celebrate that it was Friday. Her brash words blew Mindy's midget fringe as she opened the front door. "Had one of those weeks haven't I?"

"Again" Mindy mocked, patting down her wayward fringe. "Yes, again," rolling her beautiful eyes, landing a kiss on her cheek and dropping a slap on her curvy backside. An expensive fragrance flicked her senses into a frenzy of internal electricity as the glamorous guest poured past Mindy with grace and demureness. Her destination was the cute kitchen, and the fridge was her target. The sleek brown, cocoa shiny hair, so shiny that you could see your own reflection in was glossed better than any Dulux paint, reminding Mindy that this girl was a hair model part-time.

With dick-hardening beauty, most red-blooded males wanted to fuck her. Leopard print heels with an iconic long lasting marriage to a red sole waved back. The thin heel clinked on the wooden floor as the leopard dressed sex bomb filtered through to the cute kitchen, and echoed into the silence.

"It can't be Pervy Pete, he died three months ago." Mindy wondered who her new neighbour was, closing her front door on the quaint street.

Alex - never Alexandra, or Al, Ally or, God forbid, Sandra, was a typical city hard-nose, throat-slicing solicitor, nicknamed 'The Pitbull' in the confrontational business of law. She had a good jaw gifted with tearing the hardest criminals to pieces using fierce vocabulary. Her brutal gob was her nuclear weapon, explosively blowing cases to bits. One prisoner serving a life sentence had her photo on his cell wall, signed too; it was his nightly wank bank material.

She took no prisoners when she meant business and she never cut corners or beat around the bush; she ran right through it, waving the muddy ripped up roots in the air. She was ruthless in court, attacking with the speed of a Great White shark and leaving the accuser breathless, confused and weak - and once, bleeding. This was teamed with her looks of exotic beauty mistaken for the Far East, when actually she was from Scotty Road forever lying, saying Cilla Black was her Aunty.

Six foot tall travelling up to the moon, she was a tidy size eight with a slim and slender frame blessing her high designer wardrobe, and made clothes look all the more beautiful on the walking human mannequin. Her fat free figure fed the male body with randy desires fed by regular sessions with a hunky personal trainer. Her skin was Botox smooth, her pout perfect lips when closed shaped full and plump all naturally, and it was becoming tiresome hearing cheap claims from people she would fight all her life that she hadn't had them done. Her face was an area of outstanding beauty. Most women, if naturally beautiful like Alex with features working together to create beauty, forever dodged rumours that they had a little help from Mother Artificial from jealous bitter women. Her lips produced many images - if you were a heterosexual male - of them rolling slowly down to the base of your penis, giving hard gratification instantly to most males. She was a British Amal Clooney but with her own dress sense, but she neither had a stylist nor a film star husband - yet Troy was forever being mistaken for Jason Statham by pissed tourists. Elle Magazine had named her 'woman of the year' once, when she had helped feminist Lady Emma Harold to be freed from a Thailand prison for protesting about ill treatment to animals. Alex had freed her, made the government tighten their laws on animal welfare, bagged a first class flight home, and got Lady Emma Harold's roots done all in less than an hour.

She had started as a model, spotted waiting for a friend at an STI clinic. Her beauty resembled a mixture of Linda Wagner in her heyday, with the sassiness of Miranda from Sex and the City, but with a body to make Pamela Anderson in her Baywatch days weep and dive into the ocean - not run along the beach.

"Work's as crazy as normal!" she called from the kitchen. "Who would think trying to bring justice to the world would take so much fucking effort?" She wanted to make a difference in people's lives, not just to their wardrobe. She studied solidly and found herself in a top city branch. She worked her way up like an elevator, passing her colleagues who crumbled under heated court confrontations in hired suits. Alex had grown up with confrontation living with three sisters, and world wars broke out every day over the weak excuse of someone using the hair mousse and not replacing it. Their loving parents had even discussed faking their deaths for a break, with the slamming of doors and echoes of 'bitch, I hate you!' every morning over a Hobnob and cup of stolen tea.

Mindy's best friend for over twenty years, they had first met at Blackpool Pier one summer while on a family holiday for half term. Mindy was mesmerized by her outgoing attitude, hypnotised by the massive hoop earrings dangling dangerously. Her loud toucan mouth fenced in by red lipstick, she had the ability to cause mischief with her 'living for the moment' motto. Mindy heard Alex before she saw her. The biggest draw was her thin, bright yellow shell suit. Never had Mindy seen something so vibrant in colour, yet so life-ending if close to a naked flame. She thought that Alex was dangerous and fearless just from wearing that yellow shell suit - and smoking in it - all at the age of twelve.

Alex adored Mindy's creative flare for fun, the positive outlook that she had on life and her love of looking for true love – she was her memory-making muse. The girls had bonded over wiry candyfloss, soggy sandcastles and a litre of cheap cut-away-at-your-stomach-lining cider. Both had been grounded by their parents who found them surrounded by youths under the pier as they flashed their budding breasts for a cigarette. Since that delightful summer they had kept in touch through letters until they were old enough for Mindy to travel to Liverpool and Alex to Cornwall. Alex had shit herself the first time she had come across a deer in the woods; the only thing that Alex came across in Liverpool's woods was burnt out cars or flashers. In their mid-twenties they had gone over to Newcastle for a brief weekend, getting mortal on happy hour gin cocktails; they had jointly decided to de-camp their family nests for an adventure. They set up in the concrete jungle that is London in a shared bedsit in Hendon, where they were still living to this present day, just not in a bedsit - Mindy in a house in Notting Hill, and Alex in a penthouse apartment overlooking the Thames.

"You change the kitchen again, Moo?" Alex peered from the open plan kitchen looking out to Mindy. The look she gave reflected how she repeated this home improvement sentence many times throughout the friendship. Last week teal tension fused with pacific breeze, and now it was apple white with a misted hills silk running through - light, fresh and cool feeling, unlike the wine if she didn't get it into the fridge. Alex chucked the ice cubes into the goldfish bowl sized wine glasses and headed out on to the terrace, placing the rosé filled glasses onto the simple chic café table that she'd nicked one night when drunk. Feeling the outdoor heater, they pretended to themselves that they were somewhere hot and not spending a miserable March in London.

"Yes, it's slowly coming into spring. You know I redecorate with each season!" Mindy was relieved that there were only four seasons. Being obsessed with colour was her OCD, and her Nan had called her Josie (a female version of Joseph and the Technicolour Dream Coat). She was forever decorating to celebrate promotions, hitting life goals, or if a sale in a local paint shop was going out onto the terrace. Alex sometimes thought that the redecorating fetish was probably to fill the void in her life that a man normally would, joining her friend in the fresh air. She could never understand why Mindy (who she nicknamed 'Moo') was still single. She was pretty, had a good job - if a little unusual - and bore a scary resemblance to Henry Dooley that grew stronger each year. But Alex knew that 'Him', the cunt, played a huge role in Mindy's mistrust of men, while her soul forbade her kind heart to move on and ached with each waking breath. The shiver of the scene they had witnessed that day made Alex gulp her wine.

*

"Another Rolex gone, another fucking hooker fucked more than my dick," Chad stormed out of the yellow taxi, slamming the door hard at his stupidity and cursing at a pigeon. He wanted to kill the big titted thieving bitch. *Not a bad idea*, his evil streak screamed; it had been a while. History repeating itself ate away at his funds, while his cock ached from overuse. He contemplated hailing another taxi to find the bitch. But, he had bigger fish to fry this afternoon, so she could wait.

He needed to bag a role, quick. Since his departure, other networks stayed quiet to offer him work and his reputation as a party boy and a diva on set kept them away. Being popular and in the media was an addictive thing for Chad, a dangerous addiction and one that he would eventually overdose on. It was the heroin that he needed to function, and like many addicts, they needed a hit bigger and stronger than the last - so some poxy Soap where a bare chest got complaints from prudish viewers was not going to engulf the world of his presence or curb his cravings. Therefore, a juicy role that was challenging his acting art was the ideal dealer that Chad craved. Awarding him with worldwide applause and a statue from the academy board to live rent fee on his Beverley Hills mansion fireplace (when he bought one), was the biggest fix his hunter focus was on. He wanted a media magnet to grace all the covers in the land and TV chat shows. He wanted roles to place him in the big league with the big boys; Pitt, Stallone, Depp, and Reynolds and so on fed his obsession. *'Strike while the iron is hot,'* his dear mother used to say. The memory of his sweet mother hurt and his heart, broken at the church, did not bother to register.

Greg, his agent seemed too bone-idle of late to get him auditions. Maybe Chad needed a fresh start with his sacking and a near-death experience as the perfect excuse to recharge his life. Within five years he had changed his whole life, *fuck*, including his fantastic face, so a new agent and representation would be piss easy. He took out his cell phone; fourteen missed calls from Maria. She could wait - he wanted to speak to Greg and threaten him with jumping ship to another agency unless he pulled his finger out of his shitty arse. His good looks, talent and fans would have Chad snapped up before the ink could even dry on the contract. He walked on, his fringe hiding his great eyes, and with his attention being paid to the cell phone, it made him invisible to passing fans.

The afternoon showed danger of breaking into a downpour as fat clouds, dark and moody, huddled in a football scrum discussing tactics overhead. Chad sped up his walk towards Greg Locust's office on hearing his call go to voicemail. One thing Chad wanted to avoid was getting soaked. The only time he wanted to feel the wet was inside a fanny, or for his typical 'just-stepped-out-of-the-shower' look for his calendar. In his hurried walk he avoided finding out that the death of Delia Von-Grouse was being counted as suspicious on a magazine stall. Turning the corner of his collar up and dissolving into the thick crowd, he was gone. His wish to grace every magazine cover in the world would come true soon, but why?

Meanwhile back at Mindy's

"Just what the body needs!" Alex emptied half her wine glass in one. Luckily, being Northern lass allowed such vulgar drinking in a woman. Her wide mouth glistened with whiteness, and the wetness of the wine made her lip gloss shimmer to the max. Her body relaxed from its short-lived drought, and crossing her leather-dressed legs over she was finally ready for Friday evening with her best friend.

Spring must have been coming around the cold corner of late winter, promising a hot one if the warm spell on this Friday evening was a taster. Birds boycotted their evening curfew to stay out longer and city foxes braved light evening bin raids; the city was ready for spring. The girls always met somewhere on Friday for a glass of wine, and today the colourful comfort of Mindy's home played host.

'Friendship Fridays', they christened them. Looking around, Alex noted the vast collection of plant pots running through the colour spectrum from bold and bright, to mosaic, to brick on the terrace. Their heights ranged like the London roof chimneys in the *Mary Poppins* scene – this was Mindy's preparation for the sunny months. The terrace looked small due to the pots overcrowding like at a glow rave gig. Bald due to the global warming, winter had cut their petals like a haircut on a war camp; it had been a harsh winter to the point where Alex had worn two pairs of tights to work, with Jean her PA asking if she had been overworking her calves.

In summer, the transformation of the garden burst better than a sequin disco ball at a gay pride party, with colours to rival the famous Notting Hill carnival samba passing each year. Where no life lived at the moment, paradise grew beneath the soft compost, invisible in its struggle, but once it came out of the darkness its beauty would be applauded. Exploding into the purest of nature's natural colours that man tried hard to match, but lacked the glow and honesty of the colour. Sunny sunflowers, taupe tulips, ruby red roses, dozy daffodils…if a rainbow was a garden, it would look like this. Playing host to many summer parties, drowning into the backdrop of the mish mash of colours, this girl knew her colour - just not how to get her fringe cut - Alex thought, noticing Mindy's new addition to her forehead.

"What the fuck's up with your fringe?" Being a lawyer, she was obviously straight to the point. Alex spent no time in waiting for the answer while there was wine to drink. "Is this a kind of self-harming? Most self-harmers hide their scars, not advertise them on their forehead."

"Sabrina's training to be a hairdresser." Mindy was comfortable with her follicle disability - just as comfortable as Alex was with her second toe freakishly bigger than her first. Happy to assist in her goddaughter's training, she ignored her.

"Is this Sabrina's latest career move?" Sabrina, Mindy's goddaughter, had changed career more times than OJ Simpson changed his story, and Mindy played the guinea pig godmother. Mindy just prayed that Sabrina did not want to become a brain surgeon.

"How was work, Ape?" Mindy asked, avoiding the attention from the fringe cut shorter than Bob Bobbitt's penis. 'Ape' was Alex's nickname. It was still unknown where it came from, but she remembered that a drunken night was the starting point. Mindy loved hearing about the dramas of Ape's job, with the bust-ups, fights, scandals and scams, who was shagging who…and this was all just in the office. Mindy worked with the dead all day where the only audio that she got was the sound of purging - when a dead body passed wind.

"Oh, well one guy got sent down for trying to steal a drag queen's identity, but unfortunately he didn't pay attention to detail and brought Max Factor touché foundation, instead of Max Factor touché matt - so that's how he got caught out!" she yawned. Lately, her cases seemed to be a walk in the park. Stuff that she could deal with when asleep and dreaming of Leon, Simone Delvin's other half and her celebrity crush. She wanted a juicy case for something to vent her anger on, to rage over facts, to reduce her opponents into residual lumps of fear, and give her mouth a good workout - not in the sexual sense; her fit fiancé took that role. She wanted a juicy steak of a case, but lately she was getting wafer-thin ham ones.

"It's a bit boring at the minute, the cases all passed over to me. You see, because I get results quickly they're giving me short cases to get them out of the way, to stop clogging the office up, and a fast way to make money." Her empty wine glass reflected her job load at the minute. Another thing Mindy loved in Alex was the confident fact that Alex knew she was the best in her game. She was not afraid to admit it and take the credit - some would say big-headed - but Alex's awards proved otherwise. She was a scouse Spice Girl dressed in Stella McCartney and dancing in killer heels.

Alex stood to fetch a refill and to look for some nibbles, feeling peckish again; being a northern lass had benefits that she found southern girls lacked, like not being afraid of eating carbs in front of a man who was not their father, drinking a pint in a pub without Wi-Fi, or going out on a Saturday night without a coat in winter. Mindy was dressed in denim jeans, and a salmon pink cashmere halter jumper gave her comfort. Her red hair was loosely up in a bun, her face make-up free and carefree casual. It had been a stressful week; the carnivorous winter had taken many victims, not just killed off her flowers. She looked forward to Friday's allowance to indulge in plenty of wine, chocolates and Elizabeth Taylor. Mindy lived for the weekends for another reason too - an affair of the heart. It darkened her life, and all she could do was walk through the dark and pray for light at the end.

Alex entered the petite kitchen, pulling open the blue fifty style fridge with a blast of fresh lemon, just as if the fridge suffered OCD brushing of its teeth, and chilling her skin. Unbeknown to her, her killer watched. He arrived.

She had been stalked by a killer from the moment that she turned into Mindy's cute street - a killer who would leave no trace from the practise of killing many times, an expert killer never caught in the city of CCTV. His brown eyes burned deadly and hungrily into her tender back. This male was rare; he was immune to the beauty of Alex, and straight too. He was one male to overpower her terrifying mouth, and his ripper-style silent attacks left victims dead in an instant. Despite being a ginger, there were never any eyewitnesses to testify to the ending of the life. He was buying his time after creeping in through the stupidly left open window, and sharpening his killer blades. Patience was his for the taking.

*

Eric and loneliness had become best friends ten years ago when his wife, Ruth, had died of ovarian cancer within three months of diagnosis. It was a massive blow to his ideal life, but he coped by telling anyone with sympathy on their tongue *'that's life,'* quite coldly. Keeping each other company over the long years in the big house, Eric engaged in conversation with loneliness by discussing the news on telly or asking questions out loud, chatting away to Sir Bobby his ten year old goldfish. Loneliness he actually felt through his evenings when he returned from work, hugging his arrival by jumping on him once through the door. The day she had died a light went out in his life, and a little bit of his soul disappeared with every descending inch of her white coffin devoured by the muddy, wet ground. Friday nights were hit by the absence of her the hardest.

Every Friday they used to go dancing down at the local country club. Jazz, jive, country - they conquered them all to applause and good times with friends. When certain songs aired on the radio, instead of cupping her hand to dance now he turned the radio off, muted the memories. The sad thing about grief is it took as much time as it wanted to stay around with no apology or regard for your cancerous pain, accompanying your day like some sicko stalker in the shadows, throwing obstacles in your way that reminded you of your loss. Perfumes sprayed innocently by a beauty consultant, each note knocking a reminder, made you feel like she was in on prolonging your pain - not commission. The favourite film that they had loved appearing on a Sunday evening was a kind of returning stain, his emotions racing for him to turn over, and praying for the day that he could watch it again. This happened with the dancing; the pain sadly became his partner with no love of dancing. Slowly he stopped going and slowly his small group of friends stopped badgering him to go. Ten years later the pain was there, but now he buried it beneath his workload of running the parlour, his trips out bird watching, and the odd game of golf with Howard, his younger brother.

Since Ruth had died, Eric had never dated again. He was a comfortable looking man with an enduring personality as big as his cake-fed chubby waist. He made intelligent conversation to engage all ages, but it was just that Ruth had been his soul mate; they were swans bonded together for life and he didn't want to settle for second best. Once you'd had ribeye steak it was hard to go back to gammon. So why did he feel like he was betraying her at this moment in time, breaking his marriage vows, even though his wife was dead, betraying her, still feeling like a coward and knowing she could not interfere?

His heart raced as if she was about to barge into the study and catch him in his act of infidelity, screaming like a banshee and launching his belongings into binbags to toss him out of the family home. Tiny beads of anticipating sweat congregated on his forehead to witness what he was about to do; was he really about to do this?

His plump fingers shook; misguided stares might think that alcoholism was to blame. Many souls, both sensible and suicidal drank alongside heartbreak, but not Eric - something else was the reason. Hovering over the keyboard he was sure he felt a force pushing his fingers away - was it Ruth? Yet Ruth was famous for her selflessness; she would never have stopped Eric's happiness. Instead of him speaking out his cheating, his fingers tapped them out. Being around dead people for ten hours a day brought home how much he missed human contact and conversation. Howard, his younger, three times divorced brother, told him to start getting a life and stop missing what could be. Optimistic was Howard, and he had presented Eric with a gift at a second cousin's child's christening two weekends previous.

Earmarking an article on online dating, he gave it to Eric as a piss take but Eric took it further and decided after a double scotch too many that maybe it was a sign from Ruth to move on. She forever loved hearing about people's lives; she would be so upset that Eric had stalled his life due to her quick death. So tonight, he found himself brave off a scotch and the positive article, and decided to become a modern single man in the modern world of singletons, jumping into the world of the unknown...this dark abyss called online dating. Preach what Abba sang and *Take a Chance*; it took him twenty attempts to find a suitable username that was security worthy. The information this site wanted beat any form he had filled out for his mortgage. Guilty, he hated feeling a little excited doing something so daring and new in his stale life. He would dread telling Maud - she would heckle him for the rest of his living days - yet he might gently mention it to Mindy and maybe encourage her to join herself. It was time that Mindy got back into the dating game, feeling that he was a proactive promoter for online dating, and maybe even a success story, he thought chuckling.

Clicking upload on all his information, a few potential dates appeared within a minute. It was strange how this informative paragraph available to the world for anyone to see had the power to find love; it grew his curiosity. If anything, logging on to the site added a little light entertainment to his dull evening, and who knows, maybe Cupid used a click instead of an arrow (knowing health and safety would have a field day). Cupid was closer than Eric knew.

*

Alex's head was in the fridge looking for something to eat that was not low fat, organic or good for you. "Fuck, she has some shit in this fridge," she said, looking at a glorious green cucumber that looked like it had been in a fight. That's if it was a cucumber. Mindy was forever buying alien looking food and treating her fridge like Calais, but among the carrots that ate your cellulite, or the onions that made your hair glow or something, she knew that Mindy held a stash like every dieter who was also a secret food junkie; chocolate - full fat calorie chocolate, that seriously did give you cellulite as a warning not to eat anymore.

"There you are!" The purple foil of the wanted item hidden beneath a packet of smoked salmon waved with joy from amongst the root vegetable rubble. Alex lent a hand to save her sweet survivor. Bringing her head out from the chilly air of the fridge, the murderer was standing deadly behind her with not even a single ginger hair left to trace him. Silently, inch-by-inch, he held his meat-laced breath while she fumbled with ice cubes. She was easy prey, busy thinking about herself - like most of his victims, consumed in food. She was completely unaware that an enemy of hers was ready to attack her; being a brilliant lawyer meant that she had many enemies, and now this one had caught her.

"Mindy! Your drawers are a disgrace!" closing away the disorganised mess. She turned to face behind her and before she could scream for help he pounced, his eyes hungry and dark wanting death. Mindy was daydreaming about a deep royal blue she had seen on a woman on the tube, and broke from it following a piercing scream, the smashing of glass and a swear word so blue that Mindy decided against painting the bathroom that colour. Frozen to the spot she thought, *what the hell?!* Mindy was fearful, hearing it all quite inside the house.

"That fucking cat is pushing its fucking luck with me!" Alex appeared back into the quaint garden, her hair looking like a matted mess of brunette weeds, gripping the wine bottle, knuckles white with fright. Her beautiful face burned with anger, then through her legs emerged a bundle of ginger with a satisfied smile, purring and leaping on top of the bird table - which had not yet ever had a bird visit. Stretching out his ginger limbs - all three of them - his ginger, stripy tail softly wagged with satisfaction. Alex was an easy target he thought, lengthening out his ginger body to sunbathe in the late evening warmth. He was impressed that he still had it; he never failed to scare Alex.

"Telling you, Moo, it's the reincarnation of a fucking furry psychopath! Crazy fucking cat." Throwing an ice cube at him, he lay unaffected by the icy attack.

"Alex! You'll hurt him!" Mindy protested, ignoring the time that he had dragged in a dead fox. E.T could be a little wild. He had the habit of attacking friends, trying to kill local wildlife and chasing children who crossed in front of the house. Alex seemed to be his favourite target - the louder the person screamed, the more he enjoyed it.

"I'll fucking hurt him!" Ape was annoyed that Mindy defended the psycho pussy, debating whether to bring over Troy's brother's staffy, but knowing very well that Rocky would lose against the cat.

It was a tiger reincarnated with a kink for terrorism. "Have you seen my hair?" Returning to her garden chair, sitting down and letting out a frustrated sigh, she looked in her Burberry bag for her blusher brush.

"My heart's just fell out my arse, girl." If this had been true, Alex would be classified as weightless. Alex declined to be a lady, swigging wine straight from the bottle to calm her murderous thoughts towards the mad moggy running amok inside. She brushed down her moneymaking hair with her perfectly polished manicured fingers like a comb, flicking it back and applying colour to her pale face from the shock.

"Oh, he likes you! That's why he does it," Mindy lied. Alex despised the cat, and she had told Mindy so when she brought him home as a kitten from the rescue centre. Alex told Mindy sternly within five minutes of meeting it that she should call it Damien. Alex was a dog person. Yet fate needed this angry cat for a dark night approaching like a storm towards Mindy.

"Here, have some chocolate," she said, handing a generous chunk over "compensation in chocolate." "Ta doll." The chocolate smoothed away the trauma. After a few minutes of gabbing about the latest Stella collection, Mindy remembered something.

"Ape, what was that smashing noise?" She had presumed it was the wine, but Alex emerged from the attack looking like a Bond girl from the kitchen, bottle intact.

"Oh, that? Bottle of perfume on the side in the little black bottle," not noticing the look on Mindy's face of '*why?!*'

"Alex that was a hundred quid for that little bottle" Mindy remembering the price and shuddering; she didn't give a fuck if it was the new Tom Ford, she wanted to tell the commission happy saleswoman. She was not poor, but still liked to watch her money.

"Either that or the wine chick, and seeing as the perfume would not be nice to drink, it was the only thing I could throw," looking at Moo with the look of '*what's the problem?*'. Mindy's look was of pure bewilderment at Alex's lack of awareness of the problem of smashing her perfume. Picking her newly filled glass up, the coldness of the chilled wine made her fingers jump a little. Mindy took a long sip to ease her mind of the tragic loss.

"Suppose ya right, it would have tasted vile," laughing and raising a toast for no apparent reason.

"Cheers," Alex joined in. The night carried on with more wine, takeaway pizza and a Whitney Houston sing off between the best mates.

*

On Sunday morning Mindy woke up in the pitch black; not voluntary blindness, just her pink velvet eyewear nestled on her petite nose. Saturday was a quiet one for her. She had a killer hangover, thanks to Ape, that immobilised any movement and only a long stay on the couch with a box of chocolate aided the discomfort of dying. E.T played the concerned relative, curled up on her lap waiting for her to die. Therefore, Saturday was Elizabeth Taylor day again. She never got bored of watching the screen legend in classics such as *Cleopatra* or *A Place in the Sun*. Alex enjoyed the films too, once, ten years ago - but every Saturday was a bit too much for Alex. She paired it with going to visit your Gran who insisted on serving uncooked food, but you had to eat it anyway knowing that your pocket-money followed...a compensatory catch-22 for a near death experience. If there was no wine or dancing involved, she was not game. Mindy rolled back her duvet weighing a comfortable ton, banishing bingo wings; it was a goose quilted workout from the comfort of your own bed. The weight of it was the bed's way of saying *stay in bed*, as it gently pressed down on her reassuring her that no matter how bad the day was, the bed was waiting at the end of the day to welcome her return.

Mindy adored this huge bed she had bought when she saw it in a funky club in New York named Bed while attending New York Fashion Week. The way it moulded to your body shape into the perfect position to sleep was a feeling that made her smile as she climbed in; she imagined this comfort was like being in the womb - an extremely dry womb. Huge in size and height, she felt like she slept up in the clouds. She remembered the first time she had fallen out of the bed. A black eye and a busted lip was not a look Eric said would work at work. Her bedroom was her favourite room in the whole house. Lightly painted in a blossom hill pale pink matt on the smooth walls, it created a subtle boudoir feeling. A huge promotional poster of her make-up range hung above the headboard in a gold frame like a halo. Dark, intense, truffle brown wooden floor leaked and covered the whole floor like a layer of chocolate on a cake. Huge, draping curtains in *redcurrant delight* red gave the room a scarlet attitude, flowing like a waterfall of beauty where a thousand salmon spilt blood along each side of the huge parlour window, and tiny diamantes twinkled, excited to see Mindy wake. Trinkets from her travels around the globe were littered in no order around the room like chess pieces. Each was a visual reminder from the amazing places she had visited, and how lucky she was to lead a life of luxury travel.

At the end of the bed on the far wall was the room's pot of gold at the end of this rainbow. Every girl had one focus 'take your breath away' piece in their bedroom - Alex's was a real life-size stuffed tiger confiscated from a raid; many was their wardrobes, but not Mindy. A huge antique wooden dressing table held status in size, enveloped in elegance, and varnished in history. She had received this treasure in her mentor's will. She remembered the first time she had seen it, covered in jewels, make-up, and a stunning leading lady sat there being prepared by Caddie. It was a breath-taking piece of craftsmanship, and Mindy had fallen in love with it there and then.

The bright bulbs made her face glow as if staring into the first rise of the sun. While sitting there, anything seemed possible and no problems of the world penetrated you, feeling nostalgic and happy. The table had been a throne to stage starlets all over stageland. If you got to sit at *this* table, you knew you had made it. Carved out of oak tree from the Queen's garden by an artist of the 1900s, it oozed glamour, had timeless style and was solid with whispers of gossip; she imagined the stories it could spill. This dressing table had once sat proudly in the main dressing room of the oldest theatre in the West End. Many a West End musical legend - Page, Streisand, Garland, Minnelli, Astaire and many more - had sat each night at this table applying their make-up ready for that performance, the greatest one of their life.

Mindy's pride and joy was her replacement for not having a firstborn. Mindy could not believe when it arrived, all wrapped up in battered newspaper. The poor delivery men had called in extra hands to carry it, one asking if it was a dead body, chuckling as sweat ran down his face and fearing drowning as it rolled into his mouth. The generous tip from Mindy added to her beauty. A simple note on personal headed paper said, *'Enjoy it and thank you. All my love, C. P.S. Don't tell anyone* x'.

Every time Mindy sat at this table in the run up to going out, she could never resist singing the musical showstopper *There's No Business like Show Business* in a Marilyn Monroe breathy tone. Alex caught her once and handed her a paper bag, thinking she was having an asthma attack.

She stretched her in need of a severe spray tan, sun-starved, pale, naked white body; a vampire was more tanned. She rolled out like a pastry roll, lumpy and white before it went into the oven to brown. Previously in the foetal position, Mindy had been dreaming of a couture-wedding gown in misty white embedded with innocent diamonds - never to have seen daylight before - across the lace bodice, yet she was in fact at a bus stop in Ireland. Each stretch made her body more awake, alive and ready for her day that would involve a gym visit, repainting a wall (again) and getting her uniforms ready for the week. But first, her religious visit to her Mother Poppy, which by looking at the gothic clock on the adjacent wall, meant she should have been there less than half an hour ago. Out of the bed rushing like a jack-in-a-box was not her favourite hobby.

Pulling into the huge drive, the mosaic gravel stones threatened to do damage to her plum purple Mini convertible - a symbol of her singleton status to men. The tiny stones were excited to scratch the paintwork. Luckily, Mindy had mastered the art of two-wheel driving; well, driving at a snail pace. Parking in front of two tall evergreen trees standing a little one-sided, a woodpigeon drunkenly balancing on the droopy branches, its grey stone plumage reflected the lack of afternoon sunshine.

Mindy peeled herself from her car turning off Stevie Wonder as she pulled the keys from the ignition, dressed casually in flared jeans with a tear in the knee. Fashion statement? No a fall over a broken curb. The deep denim in a solid colour had been too good to throw away, and a simple halter-shoulder cashmere in goose grey hugged her tiny waist. Her red, auburn, wild hair was up in a bun secured by a red patterned paisley scarf around her head acting like a hair band. Looking casually cool, this was just what Sunday's were for. She smiled as she saw a fiery red fox looking confident in the daylight, darting daringly across the facing field.

Her mother Poppy's home was in a vast old manor, a treasured jewel among the countryside and just outside of the crazy city. Green, lush fields swamped around it like stags around a lap-dancing table. A small green pond collected wild mallards while a few sheep belted around bored in a paddock. She was surrounded by the natural beauty that many women craved. It was peaceful, calm - just what her mother needed in her aging years, a stress-free place of pure, placid pleasure, and a nurturing nursing environment surrounded by perfection and professional carers with big hearts. It was the right place for her mother to live out her twilight years, battling her losing war with dementia.

Poppy in her younger days had looked like a young Bette Midler, goofy-looking but pretty. Five foot nothing, but what she lacked in height she made up for in personality and fight. She was a bit of a wild one, like an untamed dog; fierce and free living, and answering to no one. She was forever dyeing her hair on a weekly basis to the amusement of her neighbours, who nicknamed her Tie-Dye Diva. She was an environmental protester, a good friend of Vivienne Westwood, and a frequent diner with Sting. Protesting about the destruction of the rainforest, raising recycling schemes, and ruffling the feathers of bigwigs at wasting energy, she was free-loving to the point that she had a one-night stand while bored protesting in a field against deforestation. She decided that sitting on a stump belonging to a man would pass the time. Unfortunately, she fell pregnant with Mindy, though she was her biggest and proudest accomplishment. This slowed her down. Well, she at least got a proper home (not a tent in a tree), but built Mindy the best tree house on the street. A few police cautions under her belt kept her on her toes and young.

Her fighting spirit was in no danger of wilting, ensuring a successful neighbourhood watch that won a local award. She got speed bumps put outside the local school to reduce traffic accidents, helped families who were poor, and even took in battered women and raised money for a support group, not to mention a zoo of stray animals to rival a wildlife game park. The council even took note of her naked protest, her body painted like a fox as she laid pretending to be dead at the door of the town hall, promising to fund a rescue centre if she put her clothes back on. This home was where Poppy retired her twilight years until the illness had leaked over her brain, killing her memories like a gas leak.

Despite no father figure being around or mentioned, the only thing that Poppy remembered was that he wore red Doc Martens and had long hair. Poppy never made Mindy feel only half-loved from her single parent status; she was the only single parent on the estate, and it was Poppy's private achievement. She had done it all on her own, had struggled every day, yet watching Mindy blossom into a confident and beautiful woman was worth every debt letter, long hours in a dead-end job, and sacrifices of luxury - including never marrying or meeting a man.

Having Poppy for a mother had been embarrassing when Mindy was young, when children underestimated their mothers, when mums just shouted, made you eat peas and ragged the comb of torture through your hair called a nit comb. Yet all her school friends thought that Poppy was a legend, which gave Mindy a comfortable and enjoyable school experience. They all relished her dramatic stories of fighting for the less fortunate. Poppy was asked to turn on the town hall's Christmas lights, cementing her popularity for two years running back in the day. Her memories of borrowing her many fashionable outfits, and clubbing with Poppy when they turned legal were precious. Many a time the roles were swapped and Mindy became the mother, making sure that the house ran properly, bills were paid, and her mother was kept on the straight and narrow. As she got older, the role became more her own from picking her up from police stations, listening to her receive punishments in court, ignoring her hunger strikes to save the whales (even though the nearest sea was four hundred miles away), or living by candle light when the electricity company refused to supply it.

Poppy was a free soul searching for her next fight against injustice like a lone albatross, yet she soared on clouds of misjudgement raining down on those who wronged the community rather than searching for fish at sea. Forever fighting for justice for the helpless, she refused to calm down and be normal, whatever that meant. She used to shrug when coming home from a three week sit down in a field, handing Mindy her dirty clothes to be washed. Mindy adored her mother for all of this as she grew older, wiser and realizing slowly when losing her mother, who eventually became a frail shadow of herself, turning to dust until Mindy became a stranger to her and not her daughter.

When Mindy became a household name in make-up Poppy was the proudest mother in the world, on the same level as the Virgin Mary, smug about being picked to give birth to the Saviour. Poppy posted a thousand or so recycled leaflets to every address in Cornwall. Every time Mindy's name got mentioned she cried with overwhelming joy. She was Mindy's biggest fan, so proud of Mindy that she would tell anyone who listened (and those who wouldn't). Poor Wilma down at the community allotment turned off her hearing aid every time Poppy came through the gates.

Poppy bought anything that Mindy produced, recommended, bought, or was seen advertising, though Mindy offered her mum freebies - all animal cruelty-free of course - to the point where Poppy got the loft converted, and she was talking of turning it into a museum.

The disarming demise of her mother's creative, carefree mind started unnoticed like a gas leak silent and invisible, but deadly - and a loving memory was like lighting a match. It was creeping up on her mother slowly, crumbling away at her memories and dissolving them like a tablet in water. Events evaporated and were becoming frustrating to remember, creating tears of confusion at the inability to recognize people who all her life had supported her. One day, the illness became more than a faint comedy and a roll of the eyes scene - it turned deadly and dangerous the day she had left the chip pan on the cooker, burning down the whole kitchen. Even the smoke inhalation didn't make Poppy realise. Poppy was for first time in her life defeated - not by the Government or Pharmaceutical companies, nor by the law, but heartbroken and betrayed by her own mind.

Mindy remembered the day she had first realised that Poppy was a slice short of a full cake as if it was yesterday, not several years ago. Sitting at the dining table with its mix and match chairs of a variety of charity cast offs, Poppy had nursed a black crow's wing with matchsticks and a neon shoelace from her old skating boots. Brought to her by local kids who said they had found it, but Poppy had wondered if they had wounded it for fun and then felt guilty - yet really, they just wanted to perve on Poppy's big tits in her low-cut top. Mindy was reading an article on nothing that would change her life or mind, but the tackiness of it made her intrigued as she dipped a chunky bourbon into her tea absent-mindedly. Reading away about a man who had changed to a woman but then regretted it once the M&S women's sale had finished, he now wanted to be a man again. Her mother was humming an old song, something country, the battered crow in a state of pleasure at her sweet humming.

"Remember that day, Dolly, when we met those sailors and ended up on a stowaway to Ireland?" she said chuckling as she put the coal feathered crow into a box, stroking it and remembering being cautioned by the angry police.

"Sorry, Mum. What you say?" Mindy was confused at whether she had heard right, or was too wrapped up in the article to not be giving her full attention to the question. Her mother looked at her with her eyes big.

"You remember, that time we stowed away to Ireland!" clearing up the broken matchsticks and placing them in the recycling bin, not impressed by how her friend could forget such a landmark in their friendship. "Oh, Dolly, you must be losing ya mind. Dozy mare" patting Mindy on the shoulder as she passed her going into the living room, a hoarder's paradise, giggling to herself like a minx. Mindy sat looking forward, and her frown was in danger of doing permanent damage to her skin. Surely her mum must have mistaken her. She tried and failed to come up with an answer. Maybe concentrating on the injured crow had relaxed her enough to make her forget that she was in the present, not the past.

"Mindy throw the kettle on. Here's Mary coming up the path." This cut her diagnosis of the scene, snapping back into reality as the doorbell rang. *She called me Mindy, so she must be ok, mustn't she?* Mindy hoped this was the last time it would happen. The dreaded, dull feeling filling the pit of her stomach like water rushing into the Titanic and matching the doom of the great ship, told her it was not.

Wearing flats today was a lifesaver. The refilled gravel driveway made her feet sink deep under the layers, removing the possibility of any stable walking. She wobbled on her feet as a nurse passed her wondering to herself how she could be drunk at such a place, but her smile at Mindy was a perfect disguise. Mindy made it with only one near fall.

Poppy's suite was through the manor, across a little brick courtyard with reckless ivy growing up the walls with an ASBO beauty that it did not get the praise for. The entrance was like a luxury hotel, with big, majestic wooden furniture clattered through like guests in an art gallery. The staff forever plastered in smiles always freaked Alex out. She had commented they must be on magic mushrooms or there had been a Children of the Care Home style invasion. Their smiles were infectious too as Mindy smiled to numerous staff members. Her Blackberry called out that she had a text; it was from Alex who without fail texted her every Sunday to pass her love on to Poppy, who was like a second daughter to Poppy. Poppy adored Alex. Her demise with the illness and the thought of leaving Mindy was eased slightly knowing that Mindy had Alex in her life. Mindy just needed a husband, and to grow her fringe. Mindy replied to her best friend. The courtyard was not gravelled so she picked up speed, her head down as she was texting away, not seeing the obstacles laid out and waiting for her to make a spectacle of herself when she fell. "*Spk l8ter x*" Hitting send, she found herself inspired by hitting the hard, cold, grey crazy paving in sync.

Her head angrily ached as she pulled herself to her knees on all fours, her knee scraped against the floor resulting in a cut. A garden hoe lay tangled in her feet - the culprit of her embarrassing death trip – with her shoe upturned in the rose bush.

"You ok?" a voice appeared beside her. Irish, smooth and addictive like talking Irish liquor, the old gardener she assumed, slapping her eyes closed to ease the pain. *God, please do not let me cry*, she silently prayed - she never had been good with pain, our Mindy. Her first period gave her the idea that she was going to spontaneously combust, and the over-the-top screams made Poppy gag her with pair of socks.

A strong hand cupped her arm. "Ay there, ya ok?" the talking hot drink whispered close to her embarrassed face in a voice that a parent would use to comfort a child. It was working; Mindy was lusting over the voice even if it belonged to a friend of Jesus, forgetting the pain in her head and knee. She refused to open her eyes until the tears behind her closed eyes tide away. Being raised to her feet, another hand grabbed her shoulder. "Sorry, I'm bit of an unorganized guy," the guy with no face said as Mindy couldn't open her eyes just yet, the tears starting to recede back into her tear ducts. "Come on there, it'll be ok. I'll fetch ya a plaster." His tone was comically light; the old guy had a sense of humour. Mindy found the courage, and the whispers of the small crowd told her she was being looked at a bit too much. Slowly she started opening her eyes, ready to thank the old gardener for helping her up. She had seen him on many visits. He was a small, fragile man, with a slight hunch and a bony frame tending to the rainforest of foliage littered around the grounds. Yet she had never heard him speak until today, and with such youthfulness too; that was a surprise. Her vision came back to her after the brief hibernation with closed eyes.

The nurses smiled and carried on with their daily visits to patients, routine check-ups, and new arrivals. An elderly couple on a bench turned back to their conversation, still engrossed with each other after all these years. The gardener who had helped her up seemed to have disappeared, and she was sad at not being able to thank him. Remembering her shoe kidnapped by the rosebush, she turned to retrieve her shoe which appeared to be auditioning for the role of Cinderella's left-on-the-stair slipper. "Here ya go." The canvas pump appeared at her hand attached to the end of a hand, and holding out the shoe was not the old man who wore a flat cap one size too small, but instead, the pumpkin came in too quick with its cue and turned into a beautiful looking man. He had jet-black hair, black as the first night God created, with a long fringe that fell to one side revealing a shaved side. He had a strong, slim, pale face, but not sickly pale - the shade of 'interesting' pale face, and coal black and wild (yet with a hint of tameness from tweezers) eyebrows stood out against the white drop of his face. Cheeky dimples on either side of a cute mouth highlighted how sexy his smile was, like commas on a sexy word. Sparkling teeth lit his mouth up as three-day-old stubble around his thick lips advertised for you to try them. A narrow nose staircase up to two emerald green eyes, crystal clear, they looked at you, taking in your appearance and savouring the details. His body looked taut, toned and worked out under his red polo shirt, his biceps cut and tennis ball firm, with a blue vein flowing down to his wrist. If he was a junkie this vein would be his Amazon River. He reminded her of Tarzan.

The red cotton clashed sexily with his pale complexion making him look more esquire, innocent looking, with a hint of vampire. She found herself very intrigued by him, more than normal. A little taken aback by this man, maybe she had banged her head harder than she thought. And he was Irish. Remembering her dream, maybe this was a sign?

"Thank you," she whispered, her hand reached out. She was horrified to notice that she had missed one nail out when applying her naked nude matt varnish as she drove to the home running late.

"No problem, my fault for leaving out me tools. I'm messy, it's me downfall!" He was perished by this woman; she was curvy, with a womanly body formed to have babies - his babies - he rudely thought. A petite face smiled with life, like a timeless piece of perfection. She had the old school beauty of the scarlet era of golden, pure grace. His Granny C would tell stories about her time as a costume designer when he was just knee high.

Her hand was feminine, her fingers beautifully preserved, perfect for a wedding ring. She'd left just the one nail unpainted too, *daring*. The most striking thing about this woman was her head; racy red hair was woven up off her face as if curtains rising up on a musical. Her eyes changed colour when they caught the light, yet he could also see a slight sadness - like raindrops in the whitest of clouds. Had she witnessed a life changing sadness? Or maybe she was just hungover. Faint freckles were splashed around her nose and cheeks. She caught his breath and for once he was speechless - which for an Irish man, was unheard off. Joe-Ryan was never shy around the female sex. He was the only son born into a gypsy family so there were plenty of females to build confidence with - he really should have been gay with the amount of female influence around him. This red head was different. He did not need confidence around her; she made him feel at such ease that he could just be himself.

"Thanks," Mindy repeated as the strange gardener held her runaway shoe in his grip. He looked frozen to the spot. Feeling that it was being a bit too long to stand there with her bare foot hanging out, she said, "Excuse me, can I have my shoe back?" She smiled as the strange guy snapped out of his spontaneous silence.

"Sorry. Here," fumbling as he passed over the cute looking flower print shoe. Dropping it out of his hand it fell like a baby bird testing for its first flight, diving down like a peregrine falcon drops from the sky onto its helpless prey. Mindy feared that this time the shoe would decide to roll around in the compost of the flowerbed like a just-groomed dog does, and instinctively went to grab the shoe with the speed of a bungee jumper jumping from a crane.

It was one of those life changing moments, and if it had been an animation, love hearts would have fallen onto their heads like snow. Was this the modern-day equivalent to being hit by Cupid's arrow? Head butting each other with matching force seemed to work for mating mountain goats.

*

New York was in mourning for two of its greatest socialite women, dead within the same week. *Is a serial killer on the loose?* One wacky magazine questioned for sales. Delia Von-Grouse had met her death falling from her penthouse suite, hitting the cold pavement in a sensational skimpy underwear set, and Mad Mabel had been found dead in her apartment, vintage Dior clung to her body like a grieving lover.

Henry Dooley read the article about the sudden deaths; he knew both women well, starring with Mabel in iconic film Queens of Dallas and Delia a lot more personally. Henry was a rare man who favoured powerful women, and these two broads were generous, took no shit and were now dead. It saddened him how life simply ended at anytime, anywhere. Flying first class over the vast Atlantic, Henry prayed that the pilot was not due. Ordering another gin and tonic from the skin-tight dressed flight attendant, he leaned back in his reclining seat kicking off his Russell & Bromley beige loafers, noticing Tom Hanks coming out from the toilet who waved, his cheeky grin still fresh.

Henry Dooley settled back with only his gin and tonic and wandering thoughts for company on this flight to England. Henry Dooley was a man of routine in his life. His stellar film career meant he was successful enough to be meticulous over acting jobs, and he had never married nor had children - something he regretted at times like this when friends were dying. Six hours later, he woke from one of the most restless sleeps ever. In his broken dream, a faceless figure had provoked him to think hard and trace back through the memories of his life for something, but what?

London

"OH, HELLO! HERE SHE IS EVERYONE, OUR MINDY. YOU TOOK YOUR TIME!" Poppy's sweet, crackling voice called out loudly over the busy Green Room. Other residents turned their heads looking like dominoes as Mindy walked in, her forehead covered with a cold compress and her mini fringe looking wayward. One resident, Nina, clapped. The embarrassment of the incident made her feel like jumping into the nearest never-ending well (if they even existed), never having to see him or anyone else again. Mindy knew very well that by the time it took her to climb over the wall and into the well she would have been talked out of it anyway. So why could she not stop smiling a warm smile, as a glow hugged her out of practice heart and giving it CPR while her forehead ached. The last man to have such a strong impact on her was 'Him', yet his impact was life shattering in a bad way – it took more than a blue plaster to mend and cease the pain.

She reached her mother who was sitting in a huge armchair dressed in a flower explosion cat suit, looking divine. Pink, orange and yellow wrestled on the silk cat suit to stand out the most, a tie-dye disaster dating her slim frame while a battered baseball cap sat on her head. Mindy remembered this creation from parents' evening many moons ago. Poppy still fitted in it. Mindy smiled, loving the vibrant aura of her crazy mother working the colourful reject outfit.

"Sorry Mum," planting a loving kiss on her mother's skin, which as usual smelled of berries and left a taste on her lips. She felt a sadness that these kisses were limited and numbered, and she wished she could throw this rude fact away. Poppy was only sixty-nine but looked at least ten years younger, which Mindy hoped she would inherit and smiled brightly. Sitting in the armchair already vacant for Mindy to sit in, it faced out onto the adamantly beautiful garden groomed to perfection. The weather was clean, bright and the green view was calming. Mindy felt her body relaxing, yet could murder vodka.

"Hi Mindy" Alf, an elderly gent called out.

"Hi" Mindy politely passed back.

"Hi Mindy," a blue rinsed dear declared from her seat.

"Hi Deirdre" Mindy called back, smiling, turning to face her mother and about to speak.

"Hi Mindy," croaked an aged woman or man, so wrinkly that it was hard to tell. There was no clue what sex either; the name was both female and male.

"Hi Lesley," Mindy beamed.

This ritual followed every visit. She ended up saying hello to about fifty residents and drank a cup of tea in a flat moment to rehydrate. Her mother was forever banging on about Mindy to them until her throat became hoarse, and that was their reason for being so friendly.

"You're popular today" Poppy patted her daughter's back. Her daughter had been brought up polite and kind, and it showed through the way that she treated people - it always made Poppy smile. Even though her illness was at a stage where medication was prescribed, Poppy still had bouts of pure erasure memories, so these strangers saying hello to her daughter was sweet. She forgot that she was forever telling them stories of *Mindy the Marvellous*. Mindy tended to give makeovers to some of the residents to brighten up their groundhog days, and a few when they unfortunately left the Peaceful Palace.

"You look cute. I like this new head accessory. Not sure on the fringe" looking at the plaster on her daughter's head above her eyebrows, and the fringe squatting on her hairline. "Don't think it will catch on" Poppy wondered if it was Mindy losing her mind, not her. "A fringe that short gives the confusion that you could be undecided on what sex to be?"

"Oh Mum, just made a huge mess outside, butted the gardener, didn't I!" expecting a cup of tea from the nurse helper who made the most noise possible with her trolley rattling away. A funny feeling like Irish dancing was happening inside her as she remembered the handsome stranger and her dream again. Handing Poppy a black tea, who added a sweetener. "I remember, I butted a police officer" Poppy sat back with the delicious thought of the incident matching the delicious taste of the sweet tea. "Yes Mum, but mine was an accident - yours was on purpose. Plus, I got a bandage to show for it, you got a caution." Mindy collected a small plate of assorted biscuits from the training nurse who was shaking her head at her Mother's recollection. The nurse smiled. She adored Poppy; she was a favourite among the staff. The spectacular stories, her frantic in-your-face fashion brightened up the home, her humour was like a missile launcher - spot on - and she flirted with any man with a pulse. Poppy laughed, Mindy smiled. Today her Mum looked like the Mother she was: vibrant, dramatic, animated, and still no clue how to apply makeup, noticing the eyeshadow that was too heavy. To look at her you would think she was normal, not fighting a losing battle with her mind – with no medicine or tireless fundraising as an ally in fighting. Visits like these were a huge boost for Mindy, who would make the most of it by asking her Mother for motherly advice and words of wisdom, as one day she would no longer be able to remember. Asking her to retell a story she had heard a hundred times before, she would relish in the glory of her heyday and storytelling charms. All of this was so that she could have her Mother back and keeping her memories alive, her mind working like a database keeping data, doing what it does best, remembering. Sadly, unstoppable, the dreaded day would arrive when her Mother would look at her and think *'what is she on about?'*, not remembering her colourful past or even her daughter, this painful thought made Mindy shed a tear on many nights alone in bed.

Poppy finished telling Mindy about the time she had tied herself naked to the railings of a powerful oil tycoon in protest to stop them from causing harm to marine sea life. Poppy loved the naked body. Most protests always involved her birthday suit - and a caution as a birthday gift from the police. This day she protested until she realised Dolly had given her the wrong address; she thought that Poppy had asked for *Typhoo* the tea maker, she was two zones away and naked, being held prisoner by a Yale padlock due to the keys being chucked down a grid.

"Oh, I had visions of being pecked to death by the pigeons!" Poppy's shoulders shook as she laughed huskily. Mindy loved her Mother's crass, loud, short laugh, like a rook in a tree. She would miss that sound; the thought sadly squashed her heart. "Oh, I had this lovely new healthy bread for breakfast." Poppy waved over the tea nurse, changing the conversation. "Oh yeah, what was it called?" Mindy loved health foods, anything to make you younger, live longer, make organs work properly, make your hair glow, nails strong, cellulite vanish - anything like that, she ate. Alex was more in to products, creams, lunch hour temporary surgery to keep her model looks, but Mindy wanted the natural version. She felt that if you got it from the horse's mouth, it was at its best.

"Erm, oh, bisexual bread?" proud she'd remembered such a detail.

"Bisexual bread?" Mindy laughed, passing her mum a look of doubt from her beautiful eyes, drowning another biscuit in her hot tea.

"What's funny?" Poppy was confused; she swore she remembered it. She used little things like this to keep her mind healthy, like trying to remember dates or songs she liked on the radio. It was a mind exercise class, keeping it fit and healthy.

"Never heard of it" Mindy wracked her brains, had she come across it in a magazine knowing most magazines on the coffee table inside out, or had she heard any word of mouth?

"Nurse, please tell our Mindy, who thinks the mind has finally collapsed this morning and thinks I'm nuts!" rolling her eyes at Mindy who hated it when her Mother said stuff like that, it gave her a sick feeling in her stomach, similar to seeing abs in the gym on someone wiping their faces with the rim of their gym t-shirt.

"About that bread that I had for my breakfast, you know what it's called? Bisexual." Poppy waved a mish-mash blur of colour from her arm, a few dozen jade bangles knocking into each other like commuters on a packed tube creating noise.

"Oh, you mean the *Best of Both*," the Nurse innocently replied, wondering what the joke was. Mindy roared laughing out loud and long, her poor fringe shit itself, lifting up with the outburst of air.

"Best of both bloody bisexual bread." Her belly ached.

"Oh yeah, best of both." Poppy realized her mistake and mocked slapping her forehead, her baseball cap fell off. "Where the hell did I get bisexual from?" Joining in the belly pit of laugher produced by the two generations of women drew confused looks from the other residents at the home, but this memory maker was too strong to stop.

Lesley heard Poppy from his battered chair and was relieved that Poppy had forgotten his revelation to her about his secret sexuality, when she had asked how come the same woman visits on one day, and a man visits on another day…turns out both were his partners.

New York

The contrast between the two naked bodies entwined in the afternoon light, dripping with wetness, was quite beautiful in an artistic way that would make Francis Bacon bash out his paint set. Black and white skin, showing that age was just a number when it came to sex. His cut muscle-blessed body wore onyx, and the skin deep dark inkling of tattoos mapped all over his fit body added to his sexiness, shimmering in the afternoon light from the sex sweat seeping from his taut skin.

His hard buttocks thrust forward hard as if lobbing a kettle bell between his legs, not an eight-inch fat cock into her. His black, coarse pubes greeted her with soft friction, rubbing against the contrast of her white, slim, toned body; she felt it was like another pair of hands in the room. The body that was still able to work a bikini shuddered with each forceful slap of pleasure. His penis penetrating her sending ripples across her flesh felt so fucking good. Bent over her dressing table, her perfumes and luxury lotions knocked over by the human landslide spilled onto the floor. With a body that a woman in her late thirties/early forties would work hard to get, this body was in shape and fit enough for Reggie to have all her seventy years bent over a dressing table in only heels and pearls - pleasurable and sexy. Saffron liked her sex hard, despite being at an age where sexual libido tended to race to the finish line alongside the menopause. Reggie gave it hard, fast and regular. This afternoon, like many others, witnessed Saffron's sexual appetite - something never to leave her or waiver as the decades rolled past and birthday cake ran out of space for the candles. Reggie was ideal. Young, gym fit with a street edge and a dangerous glint in his eyes for the older rich woman and packaging a glorious dick like most black men did.

Feeling him inside her made her feel young, alive and exciting, as if his cock was a magic wand to grant eternal youth, working on your insides first. He fucked her like it was her first time to ever accommodate a dick. He was all of her past lovers in one, and more. Every romantic lead in the novels - he was them all, as if he had jumped straight from the page to service her, and worship her with hot, fast sex instead of flowers and diamonds. Sometimes when she came, vehement tears fell from her eyes; he took her to places neither other lovers nor a space shuttle could. She had tried sleeping with men over fifty, but they lasted the same amount of time as it took to swallow an Aspirin. Most of them were out of shape, botched lifting her up against the wall, putting their backs out, and all of them relied on that little purple pill like it was a threesome. It was becoming a common occurrence, Reggie's visits, and with each visit the scorching, sordid sex became more daring, kinkier and more experimental. Saffron did things with Reggie that she only thought took place in hard-core porn.

His hot breath burned the back of her neck, singe fledging grey hairs, but she was in a cosmic state of wanting to cum and wanting him to cum - it all added to the bubble building up inside. Benefit of being of an age where your periods were a distance memory, so far back that you forgot the bloody pain, was that you could fuck without the care of a pregnancy. Saffron was in no danger of visiting an abortion clinic; a woman of her seventy plus years and celebrity calibre, world news, had an on-call private doctor who could treat any STI - and for a slag, she had yet to suffer one.

"I'm about to cum, me Lady," he whispered intensely into her ear, each word escorted with a thrust deeper into her, knocking her up a gear. Taking her earlobe between his gold teeth, cold on her earlobe, it was a far contrast from the heat running around in her tiring body, thrilled with his broadcast of syrupy semen, and smelling the faint tobacco turned her on.

"Not yet, I'm nearly there!" she moaned back. Her peals banged at her chest like they were knocking her back deeper onto him like a nail into wood - the wood being his desirable cock. Taking his thrusting into the next gear, it was a sure sign that he was about to cum.

"Where do you want my hot load?" he said nipping at her neck, kicking up a flutter of vanilla and taking her pearl necklace into his mouth. His thrusting for the last half hour lost no stamina and showed no sign of losing it for next half hour either, so hard her reply came out stuttered.

"Where would you like?" She didn't give a fuck where his spunk covered her, she just wanted it in her, or on her, or both, knowing his load could over spill a test-tube at a fertility clinic. It was his honey load reward for accommodating his huge black cock for the past half hour, and he was glad that she was manoeuvring into doggy style. She feared for her body that it would not take the orgasm - her fourth that week.

Feeling him swollen, his black balls repeatedly banging on the entrance and her clit, asking for permission to release in her, it was impossible to think straight before he answered, pulling out and turning her around, showing her where he wanted to spunk all over her famous face. Washing the remaining sperm off his knob using her willing mouth, he looked down at her on her knees, her make-up watercolour faint due to the sweat and spunk - but she still displayed her beauty in a regal way. "Now your turn to cum," smiling, he produced a flesh coloured dildo from the desk. Its girth and weight made it fall lopsided. "Get on the table and spread those legs, you whore."

Helena was disgusted as she listened from behind the bedroom door, clutching her duster tighter with each octave of Saffron's cries for more. Saffron was a right slut; no woman of a certain age should engage in sexual activity of this kind. But her boss paid a generous wage, a kind of 'silence money'. Helena could not wait for the old bitch to pop her clogs; it would be amazing if she suffered a heart attack while having sex. Helena wondered if she should drop speed into her tea, and not sugar. She had nearly finished the sensational, explosive manuscript, a killer of a story about working for the rich bitch. It was ready to be sent off for a bidding war, she was sure of it - certainly now with the slight suspicion that Saffron was the reason why Delia Von-Grouse was laying naked in a morgue. Hooking up a meeting with New York's hottest agent Greg Locust, he literally cummed in his pants reading only the first chapter of *What the Scrubber Saw,* admitting "Jackie who?" with a cruel, moneymaking laugh.

She turned to go and finish her chores, wondering if today was the day that Saffron would die. Her fingers ached from a decade of being crossed in the hope that today was the day for Helena's revenge.

London

"I'll have a cuppa while you're there," a bland cockney voice shouted over from her small reception desk, her manners absent as usual, creating a disturbing noise in the tranquil reception. The huge bunch of flowers greeting customers bent with the force of her gob and the smell of her breath; Hurricane Maud was reading a magazine whose special this week was all about revenge and how to get it. Maud wrote down a few pointers on a post-it note beside her.

Maud Mower, the employed guard dog of the place, a mastiff-sized piece of human, was the receptionist on paper. She had tendencies to be lazy, loud, and Britain's biggest tea drinker; the woman consumed a bath full of the stuff a day, yet never seemed to go for a piss. The three packets of digestives accompanying her tea blocked her bladder like a dam or something. A haggard bob two inches too long to be a style with three colours in all different stages of growing out sat lifeless on her head like a bike helmet. An unconditioned spilt-end heaven screamed out for a hot oil treatment and for hunky fingers to be run through it. Bright red cheap lipstick stuck to her cracked lips, and her teeth, and the odd time to her chin - all three of them. She looked like an ugly Dawn French but less funny, older, and disliked *Terry's Chocolate Orange*.

She was watching the kettle like a hawk does with its prey from her swivel perch known as a chair. She had 360 degree vision of anyone who neared it to make him or herself a cup, approaching the tea urn like a frightened wildebeest approaching a crocodile-infested river. They would reach it successfully with a sigh of relief, then from nowhere they would hear her motto. "Been bloody gasping for a cuppa all bloody morning" The predator had successfully gotten its prey - Maud getting a cup of tea without moving. Mindy smiled, bending down for another cup from under the tea urn, the smallest one she could find just to piss the lazy bitch off. She was oblivious to Maud's little list of names under the title 'Revenge' doodled in her boredom - Mindy's was top.

The reception was tastefully painted in a calm *Just Walnut* silk with a *Raspberry Bellini* matt feature wall to ooze warmth, and there were huge, hand-painted acrylic tulips commissioned by her good friend Fred on a canvas the size of a small island to create a cheery focal point. Mindy was crazy about colours. She loved colour clashes, calming colours, feng shui fading, and silky shades. When she had first arrived, the blinding white covering every wall surface was very cold and clinical feeling, giving migraines to most staff - not something that she felt was very welcoming to grieving members of families. Now it was warm, calm and soothing, with a black leather sofa and floral print oversized cushions to give it a homely feel. Eric at first thought it was bit too much – a bit too interior-design fashion for the parlour. Seeing that he had worn the same style of shoes for the last fifty years and ordered his clothes from a catalogue, him being afraid of change was understandable. However, comments from the many customers told of how it made them smile, giving the compliment that it felt like they were at home was comforting. This, to a smiling Eric, was the best compliment and he never tired of hearing it, being a sucker for customer feedback.

"How's that poor guy? You know the one who hung himself and his girlfriend found him?" Sucking the ingredients out of a dry digestive biscuit with the sex appeal of a slug sliding across a limp lettuce leaf, Maud was not interested in Mindy's work or anyone as a matter of fact. If it did not involve herself or a celebrity, especially Simone Delvin, she was not arsed about knowing.

"Dead" Mindy stated the obvious. Maud loved gossip, hence her knowing details of the deadly demise of the dead clients passing through. The people from the morgue always told her how they had died for a digestive biscuit in return. Maud found the information to be like verbal foreplay.

Maud fixed a button on her piscine-crisp blouse which was forever popping open like a flasher's trench coat, putting her chubby fingers in danger of speeding her arthritis up. If the world's supply of biscuits she ate didn't go to her chubby stomach, it certainly went to her lumpy bust. Huge, heavy, wonky-looking and a hindrance to the vases, many a time she had toppled them over. Yet when the lads from the morgue came, her fat tits sitting under her chin with at least one wonky nipple hard pushing against her blouse got her some male attention. For the first port of call at the parlour, she was rude regularly and a bit too cold at times. If she just upped her body temperature by a degree or three, she would probably get more mentions on the feedback forms - and a boyfriend.

Peaceful Palace was successful, established family-run funeral directors, known with great respect within this crazy city and serving the community for nearly fifty years. It was respectable and very popular due to the detail of the funerals and the support that they offered to the families. No request was too small. If you wanted pink doves, you would have pink doves.

Set in a quiet area of the city, west among the trendy trees, planes of parks, and a clean canal peacefully passing behind bringing a bevy of waterfowl in the summer, most trailed by fatherless offspring. Most of the summer funeral planning took place in the rose garden, which was a personal touch and very picturesque. For some reason the barge owners - like pirates riding cursed seas - always did the sign of the cross when passing, like a good omen or something.

Eric the owner was the lovely gent who had endured the drunken promise made by a very tipsy Mindy. In the family business since he was sixteen, he was a school leaver starting out as a coffin maker, then moved into planning, and then finally took over when his Father got too old. Eric took Mindy's drunken rant with good humour, including her awful impression of Marilyn Monroe singing happy birthday a lot more out of tune; he was a lovely man. He reminded her of an owl, with an oval shaped head, and his eyes huge from the magnification of his thick glasses and thick white eyelashes. His fluffy, fraying hair moulted every time he moved his head, and he was Santa Claus cuddly. Kind, and a widower himself, he knew the devastation that death caused, hence his personal approach to dealing with the loss of loved ones. He was quiet but with a strong presence, wise from many years of dealing with all walks of life who had needed his help. Eric didn't see class, race or richness; each person who came in needed his help, and each person was treated the same. Eric's only downfall was that he was a big bird watcher, boring his employees to death about the local thugs of seagulls terrorizing the canal on a daily basis, and the posse of pigeons pick-pocketing school kid's lunches in the park. The magpie insisted on moaning, lording it on the roof each time an Elvis funeral left the building - Elvis themes were popular.

Mindy made the tea, and as the kettle boiled so did her reminiscing of the weekend. The weekend visit with Poppy was marvellous, and the head butting of the gardener had butted into her thoughts ever since. Every time she slept her dreams ran a theme of green, Ireland, and one kinky one involving having sex with a leprechaun. She'd certainly have to stop the shot of fish oil before bed. *What is it about that man,* she asked an organic ginger nut as she nibbled, waiting for the kettle.Why was he stirring up the dead leaves that had fallen from her once thriving heart, kicking them to clear the way for new leaves to grow, maybe? Mindy's run of lacklustre sex with a knob of late was running low, but the gardener was probably gay. Either way, she would happily let him rent the space in her mind and occupy her daydreams for free.

The click of the kettle boiled away her hypnotised state. She poured the hot water and turned to go and give Maud her tea. "Oh, bleeding hell Mindy! You on another recycling program of yours again?" Maud tutted loudly, mortified her chocolate biscuit would not drown in the lacking cup of tea. Half of the water was still waiting to be collected the next time it rained, by the looks of it.

"Sorry Maud" Mindy shouted as she entered back into her studio, a vengeful smile of tiny pleasure plastering her face as she lock the door just for good measure.

Poppy was sitting in the well-maintained garden with Mavis, an old bird who smoked two cigarettes at a time and was more jumpy than Skippy - she was enjoying the company. Mavis's stress levels were forever running high, her dirty grey hair in dire need of a colour, or a kind relative to visit to gently brush it. The morning promised to be bright and dry, as the very early days of spring should be.

Sitting, reading a book on the migration of Australian birds with a cool glass of water, her straw hat was probably a bit too early in the year to wear, with a huge daisy sewed onto the side of it giving it an edge like a beacon drawing attention to insomniac bees but Poppy beat to her own drum. Mavis was gabbing about a new mobility scooter that her eldest daughter was buying her, and Poppy was automatically nodding and humming in the right places. Engrossed in a chapter on the great fire of the Australian outback, she was thinking about the time that she helped build a well in Africa - a voice interrupted her memory of being chased by an ostrich. "Morning ladies, nice hat," a young Irish, lustful, full-of-life cheery voice sang. It was a perfect soundtrack to the morning, outdoing the birdsong for the most beautiful sound.

Looking up, the early morning sun's glare shined off this guy making him the vision of an Angel. Silky, soft hair covered one side of his face, his emerald eyes told you he was genuine, and a black eye told you he either enjoyed a good punch-up or was completely accident prone.

"Hello hot stuff" Poppy flirted, as you can with younger men when you reach her age and mental state. This man was handsome; she had not seen him around here and she had been here for four years. He was certainly a change from the other men who inhabited the place - even if their scooters could reverse or they could fill a colostomy bag in under an hour, they were not her type.

This man for some reason made her brain ache; she was sure the black eye was like a clue. She was losing her mind - not developing the gift of premonitions - so she must have been told about this guy, but who the hell was it? They just came on her out of nowhere the mental blocks, her mind wiped clean like chalk off a board, washed away by a monsoon of memories, all confused and out of order of time. She shut her book, furious at the lack of memory. Tossing it aside, it hit an anxious Mavis with a thump who lit up another two fags in fright.

The feeling that this guy was sent for a reason kicked her hard mind, craving attention to the detail of this man. She had a good feeling, like taking the vacant job in someone's heart, but she only remembered that he was connected to the red-headed make-up girl who visited now and then, who bore a frightening resemblance to the great Henry Dooley.

Joe-Ryan looked at the mature woman with her crazy hat on; she looked like she had been a fun person before her illness took over. She reminded him of someone, but then his black eye that was created by that mesmerizing woman fuzzed his vision. Saying his polite goodbyes to the two women and wishing them a good day, he went to tend to the bushes in the extensive grounds. Poppy frustrated, she resumed the reading of the book trying harder to remember, scolding herself.

*

It was exactly how she had left it on Friday, spotless and not a thing out of place. Her make-up tray was stacked tidily away looking like it was bought brand new; it had not been used for the past five years. The balancing booty of cleaning products greeted her like a puppy – well, if they were living objects, they would have pounced on her. Mindy was addicted to cleanliness in her studio, her cleaning skills matching her design skills. 'Clean Freak' was a name she had heard from a family of familiar faces, but she had always had a thing for cleaning and she couldn't understand where it came from. Poppy's way of cleaning was just throwing something out or into a cupboard. She wondered if her father was a clean freak, or a doctor, or maybe an artist? She always felt that she was not 100%, like she needed to find her father to complete her being. Still, Mindy took to cleaning like it was an art – at least she knew that no germs lingered - well, ones she could deal with.

"Here ya go," burst in Maud. A small car with exhaust problems backing out of a garage would have made less noise than her. With a mug the size of a paint bucket, it made her thick fingers look slim - like Mindy said, only germs she could deal with.

"Thanks," said Mindy, hiding her horrified look as tea spilt on the floor, masking her itch to go and fetch the mop. Maud placed down some burned toast on the side table, crumbs running riot on the stainless steel, fleeing with freedom and escaping her gob. Mindy was dying inside to slap Maud and wipe the mess up using her frank fringe.

"You had a clean-up?" Maud said this every time she ventured into the studio - which was not that common, thank god - as if Mindy was a mess all the time. Maud chewed the toast rudely, and each slapping of her lips seemed to increase in volume. This wound Mindy up. Maud lingered, unaware that she was not really welcome - like a fox around a rubbish bag leaving a trail of mess when she left, with her chubby, fat fingers touching everything.

Mindy pulled out her huge tower of make-up. Every colour ever made was laid out perfectly and patiently waiting to be used in her magic. She had enough foundations to fill a truck, and eye shadow to outdo a whole Mac shop. Lipsticks in every shade were aligned perfectly together like cars in a multi-storey car park. She had brushes as thin as eyelashes ranging up to as thick as yard brushes, every single item needed, treasured and part of the mixture of miracles she created - each was just as important as the other, all with a colourful role to play. "Oh, this is a nice colour!" Maud picked up a pastel palm pink lipstick, trying a bit on.

"Maud!" Mindy snatched the make-up from her chubby hands with horror. "You can't use make-up that has been used on dead people, it's unhygienic and disrespectful!" Mindy wished sometimes that she was ruder so she could tell Maud to fuck right off and get lost.

"Eurgh" Maud nearly ripped her podgy lips off - a dead woman's lips on her own? People would think she was a freaky fetish lesbian or something. The tension in the room shifted up a gear, Maud oblivious to Mindy ignoring her, picking things up and placing them back somewhere different. *Mindy is a clean freak*, Maud muttered under her breath. Everything had its place, its purpose. This kicked Maud in her sad heart - did Maud have a purpose and a place, beyond just being an employee? Maud was insanely jealous of Mindy, though she wouldn't dare to tell anyone - only her makeshift voodoo doll minus the pins and burns. She was beautiful and talented with a hotshot career - Mindy was the glossy billboard of a successful, single woman. Maud had been the only woman here for a decade before Mindy swarmed in. Suddenly, she was pushed onto the reception answering phones, dealing with upset customers who were all negative and depressing, stuck in front when all the action went on in the back. Many a time she was left out on the jokes, but still, she was in a job that paid her well, plus Mindy was a loner. Sometimes Maud thought she was a lesbian every time that Alex phoned and asked if her Wifey was there, whereas Maud had her website dating profile, which remained with her still waiting for a reply off Boredcockerall, exiting the room without so much as a bye.

Mindy was relieved that the big shadow of her unwelcoming presence was gone so she could get on with her appointments. The only man who was stable, who stayed in her life without fail and was there at every hurdle life threw at her, mini heartbreaks and drunken nights, crooned around the stainless-steel space about *Superstition*. Mindy's first client was an elderly woman who had passed away in her sleep aged seventy-two, when respiratory problems had failed to give her any more breath. One Sunday after a classic Heartbeat episode, with a mug of hot chocolate, she had gotten into bed, reading a book, never to wake up again and find out if the hopeless romantic lead had got her man. Her skin was soft and loose, free from life's stresses. Her old body was light and no longer heavily weighted down with life's worries - she seemed at peace. "Let's get you looking wonderful, dear," putting on her little mouth mask and gloves; Mindy was ready to work. You see, sometimes, if the deceased has been, say, murdered, the stress shows on their face - their bodies look taut, tense from the fight for life. They seem tormented in their faces. It's not visible to people who don't work with the dead, but like Mindy, if you do, you can see the traits of a terrified death's un-peaceful pass over etched all over their face like bad patchwork. She started dusting a light base of baby fawn foundation with simple strokes to smooth out her weathered, wrinkled face. Each fold of her flesh was a milestone to show her long life, and a little blusher livened up her sunken cheeks to instantly add warmth to the dead woman's face. Mindy's bruise on her head from the sexy gardener was covered by her mini short fringe, which despite Alex saying it would suit her, and it didn't, it now did have its uses.

She had dreamed of the Irish stranger all night. His smile was so wide that it hugged your eyes. His eyes looked beneath your clothes - not in a rapey way, but a complimentary way - deep into your soul, wanting more than just the outside. His voice was like verbal cream pouring over hot cake, and lyrically his tongue played his teeth like a harp. Opposites attract and all that. She wondered what he hid underneath that red uniform, what he would be like to kiss, and what his hobbies were. More rude thoughts digressed to the point that she aroused herself into a state of sexual tension. She awoke and pleasured herself with a mental note to do this more often, and satisfied, she slept with a smile.

The big concerning question she asked herself was - would she see him again? The memory of that fatal afternoon that changed her outlook on love, shattered, falling to pieces on the floor, was 'Him'. The relationship with 'Him' had started off promising, with dinners capping off the working day, her favourite flowers blooming weekly, love notes stalking her most of the day. Yet that all ended when she had walked in on him in *her* house on *her* corner sofa that *she* had saved a fortune to buy. She couldn't see his face due to a slim blonde sitting on his face, wearing her vagina like a fleshy balaclava. At the same time, an identical skinny blonde was bouncing up and down on his knob like a pogo stick, moaning with a deep lust of sexual desire fulfilled. Both girls must have been at least twenty-one and had clearly not heard of a carb. Their girly, confident groans of granting sexual satisfaction rang in her ears a long time after she left him.

Mindy froze dead in that moment of time; the image forever scarred her memory. She could not move or make a noise, and shock shut her down with its best defence. The naked scene before her was porn-inspired, the three bodies so closely entwined together that it looked like the Loch Ness monster - but with tits instead of humps. Where one body started and another one ended was anyone's guess.

Despite her not seeing Edward's face, due to it being squashed by a fanny, or his cock, for it being inside a clit, the tight curly hair on his chest gave him away. So did his tattoo of an eagle on his ankle, and his little finger crooked and bent from an accident. Not that Mindy had expected three people to break into her home and have sex, but she had hoped that's maybe what had happened, so naïve to the situation that her own hand wanted to slap her. It was only when Alex - who was helping to bring in the shopping - barged past an immobile Mindy that it brought her back to the reality of her fiancé fucking not one, but two girls on her suede couch. Mindy had already been thinking to herself how to get rid of the stains of sperm and fanny juice.

Alex and her Scorpio anger, greeted with the naked threesome of her best friend's fiancé and two slappers, blew the roof off the small detached house, and charged towards them with the clamped fists of her amateur boxing skills. She launched at the sofa as if she was a pit-bull released from her cage to fight; the two mongrels didn't stand a chance.

Alex gave out black eyes to anyone who dared to challenge her leaving the recipients swollen. Edward took the worst beating with a black eye, cut lip and cracked rib. She choked one of the girls with their own hair extensions, booting the other one so hard that she fled half-dressed out of the window with a shoe print tattooed on her bare arse. Mindy simply stood still. Edward's mercy pleas of his 'moment of weakness', that 'he couldn't remember', that maybe 'if she had paid more attention to him than her work', and the one that stung the most - 'I love you, Baby' - fell on deaf ears. She simply watched Alex do what she should have been doing, ripping his designer clothes up and throwing his naked body out of the house. What made the whole thing worse was that this happened on the first anniversary of her miscarriage…

Her fourth, and last, client of the day was a notorious criminal who had died in prison under suspicious circumstances. Really, he had choked on a sausage that he'd sneaked into his cell - but to keep the press interested and a lawsuit off their hands, they had said he was strangled. He was a mean-looking man with a face of stone, and no symmetry to his face - just round, with a round head, round nose, round thin mouth, yet he had reigned over a part of London for years. He was quite short too, like a tree stump, bulky, and cut wrong with adult acne too. The funeral parlour was quiet all day, with most of the staff paying home visits to grievers. Mindy was looking forward to a microwavable chicken dinner and a Bio channel documentary on Elizabeth Taylor, even though she had already seen it eight times. The legend let her escape into her world for at least an hour. Inviting Alex over to join her for the premiere of the film, Alex seemed to get the world's quickest food poisoning ever in the same breath between being asked. She replied that she couldn't make it due to food poisoning off, of all things, a flapjack.

Laying the cloth over the mini mountain of menace, Mindy finished and was ready to head home. Wiping around the stainless-steel fence of tables until she could see her pretty reflection, she had been wiping the imaginary mess for an hour. Why was it so hard to wipe the past away? 'Him' seemed to be a stain that was stubborn and hard to wipe away. Each day the image was slowly fading out, but God, it was taking its time. Forcing the cloth out of her hand, a struggle between her hands came to life and she finally out-tied the hand gripping the cloth.

Mindy entered the cosy reception and the sunflowers beamed at her. Throughout the day they grew bigger, blooming brighter as if they were alive with pride. Whether this was a sign of her life to come yet she did not know, but she knew that they made her smile a pure smile, flowers always did. Freshening up the water by adding a dash of sugar in the mix too, giving energy for the flowers to blossom overnight, she was ready to leave. Minding her own business, she was humming away unaware that she was not alone in the building - apart from the lifeless bodies lying around bored and waiting to be buried. Something she had never seen before, a frightening sight lurked.

"WHAT THE HELL?" Mindy screamed, knocking the vase over and watching the sunflowers wash up on the desk with the tide of sugary water pouring from the vase, they trying to escape the sight. This was all a result of being tapped on the shoulder by the shadow that had crept up on her. She jumped around on the spot to face a clown exclaiming 'Ta Da!' – Well, she looked like a clown. For some reason, Maud had decided that dipping her face in paint was a new Hollywood therapy - or was she actually wearing make-up?

"Sorry did I scare ya?" Maud stood looking at Mindy's frightened face, unaware that putting make-up on without a mirror could have had such a dramatic effect.

"Maud, are you ok?" Mindy asked cautionary, hoping that this was not a psychopath killing. Was Maud having a break down? Her make-up needed one.

Eye shadow of bubble-gum blue covered her eyelids, correct, but also a quarter of her forehead. Mascara was missing on one eye. Her lipstick was so red that she would probably stop traffic, looking like a stop sign. Her Lego-inspired stiff hair unfortunately had the pleasure of glitter spray threw at it that a seven-year-old would refuse to wear, even on Halloween.

Her outfit was a cross between a draping curtain and a balding leopard - something that a child might wear for dress-up play. "Got a date, haven't I?!" Maud triumphed; a date to end her boring day. Knowing that Mindy was going home alone, a smile of slyness stretched the baboon arse coloured lipstick, with at least three of her teeth covered in it.

"A date?" Mindy did not mean to shout it, but shock can do that to you. Was Mindy missing something that men looked for now?

"Yes, a date," debating whether Mindy was excited for her or surprised.

"Oh, well have a lovely time. Oh here, have a spray of this - he won't be able to resist ya." Mindy dug in her bag for a bottle of spray, handing her a clear bottled scent. Maud was flabbergasted at this random act of kindness, and it touched gently on her sour soul. Spraying her whole body with the clean smelling spray - probably a designer, Maud thought - using too much, she was hoping to waste it on poor Mindy. She faced Mindy before leaving the door.

"Wish me luck" flouncing out, the tail of her dress begging Mindy to stop her from going.

"You need more than luck lovely," she whispered to herself, watching the plump midget dressed in a curtain telling a car passer to go fuck himself with a finger gesture, as he narrowly avoided hitting her. Mindy thanked God that Maud fell for the 'perfume' - not everyone could carry off a hygienic hand spray as a scent.

New York

Chad Rise landed in New York in the early hours from Los Angeles. Greg Locust had triumphed with a casting for a cop role on the new, hyped-up Bruce Willis film with an award-winning top director, big bucks payroll, and big exposure - two things that Chad craved. Chad was delighted that Greg had finally come up good off his twenty percent, and snorted a gram to celebrate at 75,000 feet in the air.

He knew that this was his big break. What actor wouldn't wank at the thought of this chance? He looked the part with a fan base of young, hot girls and horny, bored housewives; he felt he was right for the part of a rogue rookie. Plus, he knew he would look sexy in a police uniform. If he landed the part, he was done with TV work forever. He wanted the big screen, more adoring fans, bigger money, and privacy-ending fame. Becoming a power player on the movie scene would be an addiction more hazardous to him than any drug he piled into his body. Chad adored popularity, and it made him feel alive. He needed it, and he was God in Chad World - a God graduating from Hades' school of horrors.

Maria was going to join him in two days. The reason for her absence now was that she was tending to a family engagement in Mexico. This suited Chad fine. If Maria was away, the dick could play. He tried calling Delia Von-Grouse, who for a fifty-seven-year-old, plastic surgery addicted divorcee, had a vagina that had kept the tightness of a twenty-year-old, with the hunger of a cougar. Delia was kinky for S&M, used chains for decoration, adored fast fucking, laying on her expensive collection of real furs, and wearing every eye watering diamond she had bought with her divorce money. A picture of her cheating, bald husband looked on from the bedside table like a peep show. She was yet to return the several missed calls. Chad did not mind; there was plenty of willing pussy to feed his undernourished male ego until Maria arrived, then he would have to behave. Women appeared on a conveyor belt to him, his choice of women was never-ending - like a lion, he was always looking for fresh prey.

Maria was beautiful and bold with it; her black, thick hair smelled divine every time she flicked it away from her erotic face as if she washed it in the ocean. Her olive skin, kissed by the sun since birth, was smooth and soft to the touch, and never tired or dull-looking. Mexican fiery foods kept her figure slender but shapely, and clothes revelled in her wearing them - she made clothes come alive. Her walk made men hungry; she was a sex bomb of rare beauty. Her tits were heavy with real flesh, none of that fake shit that so many L.A chicks worked. They felt great cupped in his hands, with pert, dark nipples that were forever firm, igniting his sexual lust with this simple image of her suckable nipples. Maria was a vision of seduction and sex to look at for many hot-blooded males, yet in the bedroom she was so stiff of late, so dull that Chad wondered whether to pimp her out to necrophilia shaggers.

He had met Maria three years ago on the set of *Sunset Dawn*, the hit soap opera that he had been recently fired from. Maria played a con woman and they had hit it off instantly, with her flirty banter and tomboy attitude to life, and the fact that she liked lager was a hit with him and his small circles of friends. They became small enough gossip to be printed in the *National Enquirer*, and common interest for social gossip sites to be name dropping them least once a week. She was feisty, funny and incredible with her mouth, so they eloped to Las Vegas and got engaged - egged on by tequila and sleep deprived nights of gambling and partying. Before the platinum engagement ring was even a day old, Maria had turned from Mexican man-eater to moaning fiancé. Since then, Maria changed. She had become a prude in the bedroom and erection-killingly dull. She would mutter, "A wife-to-be would not do that." It gnawed on Chad painfully to the core. Each time he nudged her with his thick cock indicating he wanted to try anal, she would shrivel up away from him as if looking for a shell to retreat into, appalled by his cock and by him. Repelled by his mere touch, she looked weary and unsure every time he hinted at lovemaking - her complaint of a constant headache made Chad book a brain scan for her in case she had a tumour – again, just to benefit himself, and not her. Her body made a man want to enjoy and caress it, and to be denied that was about as devastating to his ego as torrential rainfall devastates countries. Her cock-stimulating curves guided your hands to her places of sensation and joy, yet she was the biggest dick tease ever and Chad hated it. He was Chad Rise, irresistible to women! Each time Maria turned him down she chipped away at his ego, allowing fractures to fester, and needing the touch of another woman to fill them in.

Maria suddenly lacked imagination. She lacked ambition, yet moaned to anyone who would listen that she was about to get her big break. Being boring replaced being fun, and an overgrown bush replaced a Brazilian. Her only redeeming quality was that Maria dressed fucking sensationally, and the fashion world pawed over her as if she was the messiah. Each time she was mentioned in the fashion pages, his name was also. Designers dropped off dress after dress like orphans at a nunnery to grace her womanly body. She was Team Curvy, adored by women for her refusal to diet into an unattainable shape that she would not enjoy. She was good to have on his arm, especially if he wanted more exposure in the tabloids. Cheating was his secret hobby; it was less harmful than his drug habit and cheaper than his gambling, with his debts outdoing his winnings. However, her moaning was getting louder of late and his patience was thin, literally cracking like ice. As long as Maria kept shopping until she dropped and never found out, all would be blissful. Chad refused to allow the memory of what happened in their Las Vegas hotel that night of their engagement that changed Maria into the woman that she was today. After all, what happens in Vegas stays in Vegas - but not for Maria.

Chad arrived at his hotel, checked in, and after the bellboy left with a generous tip, he was alone. Chad being British - despite talking with an American accent - always made a brew. The only English thing that he kept from his previous life back in England was his love of tea. Since his makeover and brand new face, he had kept up his new life and identity. Would his teachers still think he was dumb now? Looking in the bathroom mirror, his new handsome face smiled back at him wide with a perfectly polished set of veneers. Buying the features he needed to become a star was expensive and time consuming. His lack of patience made him aggressive, and his girlfriend at the time - pretty Jane, a nurse - took the brunt of it, dished out by his fists. But having a nurse around was useful for minor slips and wounds refusing to heal. Chad hated having no patience. He had no time to sit and wait for scars to heal and bruises to fade when he could be out auditioning, networking, and fucking. Each cosmetic surgery plunged him into a lengthy tunnel of darkness while healing, but the glow from the star that he craved brought him one step forward to becoming a global star.

To achieve this grand makeover the funds in his account had run out fast and he needed a new flow of cash – here stepped in his loving, elderly parents. Conning his parents into selling their big home produced the massive funds to enable him to pick out his finishing features, as if flicking through a catalogue to furnish your home. He wanted to create Chad Rise, a superstar of the screen. Taking the rip out features of celebrity men, he glued them into his scrap book, moulding them into the flesh of himself – like a kind of Frankenstein minus the tell-tale scars, the green tinge replaced instead by a sun-kissed glow. He had millions in his bank and millions adoring his work and face. He was glad that he was an anonymous 'Mr Average' when he had come to L.A to start his plastic fantastic transformation, unnoticed as he healed. He still marvelled at the magic the surgeon was able to complete, with neither a visible scar nor the look that he had had work done, checking out the usual sites for giveaway scars. This was the face he was meant to have, and every time he saw his picture in the media or topping the hot list, it was worth every back stabbing, hurtful action he had delivered to anyone with the amenities to complete his change. He had a little bible-thick book of cuttings (which a parent or obsessive fan might keep) which was now into its trilogy - no fan was more obsessive or stalked Chad Rise more than he did himself.

Fleecing his ex-fiancée had funded his acting school in New York, a con job had bumped up his deposit on an L.A bedsit, and his appearance in a few blue movies had paid for extensive personal training. Lastly, brilliantly faking his own death had left the door open to be whoever he wanted to become, and his choice was the untouchable Chad Rise.

The English tea tasted heavenly. Lying down on the huge soft bed, he kicked off his patent Prada brogues, wriggled his bare toes into comfort, slipped off his washed-out Levi's, pulled off his white t-shirt, and only his white underwear survived his private strip. The tea - his only company - was just as hot as his body, and for some strange reason at that precise moment, it made him think of 'Her', his ex-fiancée. He wondered how she was getting on, his alien conscious asked. He hated when his mind asked unwanted questions of his abandoned past; it always set off a domino effect of questions of 'if only' and 'why'. He fidgeted with the TV remote; the power to change the hundred channels of pointlessness was distracting his mind from flooding with guilt, slamming closed the canal lock before the flood swept over him and drowned him in his hell, bound by betrayals of a bad nature. Where the fuck was Delia? He picked up his phone - no missed calls from her awaited his reply. Longing for distraction to help keep closed the lock as the heavy flood was robust and rolling towards him, questions like logs were floating down. What was his poor mother going through? Poor Jane, battered and bruised and never to ever trust another man again. And 'Her', his ex-fiancée left back in London, heartbroken - his adultery was the reason why. *Fuck the slut* he muttered, deciding to dial his drug dealer Reggie to kill his boredom until Delia called. Time was ticking down until he became the most famous man in the world - but not for his acting.

Mindy's Home, London

E.T purred, pawing and pining for his generous, kind owner and pounding Mindy's leg before she made it through the front door. "Ow, get off!" With Mindy not having a high pain threshold the claws felt like hot knives - getting her eyebrows threaded took three painkillers and a large glass of wine. The loving welcome of her return made her smile, his little button nose crinkled as she rubbed her face into E.T's. She could not understand why everyone thought the cat was pure evil. Maybe she suffered from 'child blindness', you know, where parents are completely and utterly blind to their little Damien's bad behaviour, blaming everything from the terrible twos to ADHD for their serial killer streak at the park with a scooter. The tube ride home was surprisingly tranquil and quiet, without anyone throwing him or herself in front to delay it, neither anyone playing irritating loud music to annoy others, nor a suspicious bag left to blow up. She also bagged an E! Magazine free from chewing gum, explicit swears and unidentifiable wet pages which had saved a seat for her - not a bad end to a dull day.

The answering machine nestled on the faux marble table along with a minuscule layer of vintage *Vogue* covers flashed like a beacon on the rough sea. Mindy enjoyed the old school feel of having an answering machine. It took her three days to record her greeting. In her first attempt she sounded like a newsreader mentioning the crazy heatwave, sulkily wishing to report the news from the park and not a hot, stuffy studio. The second attempt sounded like she was an asthmatic call girl begging for your money and services, and an inhaler. The third was done when she was a little merry - afternoon prosecco in the park was never a good idea – and was a rap so slow that she ran out of recording space...no need to lose sleep just yet, Jay-Z. It was Poppy who finally became the voice to let you know that Mindy could not take the call but to please leave a message; she was jolly, and straight to the point. It was beautiful, her voice. Mindy knew that one day she would be calling her own house to let it ring out, just to feel the comfort that Poppy's voice brought.

"You - have - one - new - message..."

"OHMYGODMAKESUREYOUREADTHESTANDARDPAGE FIVEYOU'RENEVERGOINGTOBELIEVEIT!" The speed of Scouse poured out without breathing between each dense word of information. Alex always spoke fast when she was excited, happy or drunk, or calling from the treadmill. Her thick Scouse accent was incoherent to the everyday person, and alien to any foreigner asking for directions, but luckily Mindy had an honorary degree in understanding it from the University of Ape. She enjoyed its singing, rhyming style.

Collapsing like a Jenga block onto her cream sofa, the cool couch caved in around her curvy frame and snuggled into her for the evening. She pulled out the folded evening paper from her black leather Mulberry bag - a gift from an aunt - ironing out the front page. There was a footballer draped with a blonde, with tits pushing her chin up to her forehead in a skimpy dress like a sausage wrapper, a seedy Politician draped in flour and not hookers for once, and a free offer on Lush products. Mindy loved Lush products - all that natural goodness drenching your skin with nourishing nutrients. The first page showed off a hotshot crack-skinny artist opening a show, an exhibition of illustrations of London using human fluids - nothing special but Kate Moss had showed up, hence the first page coverage. Her mind started to wander back to when she would be invited to such events, even if she didn't know the person. The dress code was air kisses. She loved the free bubbly, the people watching, and the excuse to get dolled-up to the heavens on a school night. Oh, how she missed those days. She sometimes felt bi-polar over the present and past...one made her happy, the other made her sad, shifting the blame onto each other too.

Being a gossip freak - alongside being a hopeless romantic, terrible cook and Zumba member - the *Evening Standard* kept her up-to-speed and inner city knowledgeable on what was happening in the ever-changing London, the biggest gossiper in the Capital. Picking the paper up for a second time and ready to read any future information with a large glass of chilled rosé, she turned to page five a little too late. The icy temperature of the White Grenache blissfully blessed her lips, and the pleasure of blending aromatic fruits restoring her body instantly. It clouded over her earlier memory of

Maud's manic, clown inspired make-up. Turning to page five expecting it to be a piece on Alex or something related to her, she gasped at the announcement. It caused her wine to perform an emergency stop midway down her throat, choking her for a second. She couldn't believe what she was reading. *'Mad Mabel Found Dead'* was written in big, bright gold letters - extremely fitting for the dead woman - screaming the sad news. A double page spread featured a picture of Mad Mabel smiling out, her eyes twinkling with mischief and drama. Her neck, the owner of the finest diamonds to ever grace the Manhattan elite society scene, was found dead. Mindy started to frantically read, missing words out of sentences. Only the words *murder, found, suspicious, dead, mob* pulsed out of the page like a beating heart. Tears dropped heavily as she realised her mother's friend had passed away, while the wine glass visited her mouth more than the dentist did.

Lady Marbella Mill-Miner was a glamorous, fur-loving good time gal. She was a celebrity in her own right, aka *Mad Mabel*. She was a diamond collector among the professionals and had been rumoured to sponsor a diamond mine in Africa. Dragged up before the high court with a famous supermodel on the possession of blood diamonds from a warlord, Mab Mabel had refused to give the diamond back and swallowed it whole, spending a year inside and passing the most expensive kidney stone ever. Her neck and fingers possessed some of the world's finest diamonds, gifted by some of the world's most influential men of film and politics - each was a love-bite of the time she had spent with them. A Texan born and bred, she honoured the cartoon image of big hair, big make-up and a big personality that millionaire Texan broads were famous for.

She was a red carpet regular at all the hottest invitations in New York, from Oscar-nominated premieres in Beverley Hills to pot-smoking rapper's album launches down in the Bronx. She possessed the ability to appeal to all, no matter if it was a shoeless homeless guy or a President. Her filthy sense of humour loved across all generations made her popular and much loved on television shows. And she had been a mega hit on a reality show following the rich housewives of New York.

Mabel's mouth was like a gutter - never dredged or cleaned, she cracked a joke every fourth second, and had fascinating stories of old Hollywood. Think Shirley Maclaine crossed with Joan Rivers - but with less plastic features. She was a strong inspiration for her good friend Jackie's femme fatale characters in her bonk-buster books. A power player of a popular lady, a huge beacon of hope in encouraging charitable aid, a heavyweight fundraiser for unfortunate causes, and a good friend of her mother's was dead.

A legendary journalist out of rich retirement had scripted the piece, telling the whole city of Mad Mabel found dead in her penthouse suite in New York. She was dressed to attend the Race for Racehorse rally in classic couture Dior. W*hat a way to go*, Mindy smiled sadly. Despite her being treated like a prized racehorse, she was *'merely a donkey keeping up'* she had famously said.

The champagne chugging, coiffed old widow, once photographed coming out of a brothel in Amsterdam at the opening of a whore's leg as long as the good time that was had, was thought to die of natural causes. Gossipmonger's started to emerge from their reality hibernation, spitting to spill conspiracy money-making stories. Stories included Mabel being addicted to a selection of sleeping pills, taking too many while playing sleeping beauty with a Brazilian escort - role play gone wrong. Another was that she was prone to taking ecstasy, wanting to recapture her fun-loving youth - like the years where she had met Poppy on a hitchhiker's trip in the early 80's. Bonnie and Clyde they had named themselves, high as a kite.

The weirdest one to hit the gossip vine was that she was into erotic asphyxiation, suffocating herself with a Cartier bag - the feeling of passing out giving her a sexual high. Others though retold a more believable account; she was murdered by the Italian Mob. Their raw anger had failed to calm since they were still out of pocket for the 1984 kidnapping of Ballet Foot, the greatest Italian racehorse ever to touch hoof in America. The purest breed of pure bred horses, the mould never to be created again – apart from Red Rum, nearly. He was an undefeated champion, a chesty chestnut stud with legs of steel, a speed beating the records each race, a multi-million-pound money-making machine who loved to run and eat hay. One night the majestic horse had mysteriously vanished, disappeared, wiped from existence, rubbed out - you get the idea - from a stay at Mabel's countryside stables. Not a trace was left at all. It was a mystery to baffled experts; every stone was turned in the land but not a strand of his thick mane was found. It kept any other news of the year off the front pages.

Then the sightings of a wild horse roaming the vast fields and galloping at the speed of a comet began a made-up story to stir up commotion. It was even blamed on an alien abduction. It had gripped the headlines with startling force that summer, and even the record breaking drought was blamed on the kidnapping of the horse. Someone had to take the blame, and playing the main role was Mabel in all her vintage expensive mink. It was the unsolved crime of the decade. Psychics from around the globe failed to see anything from the horse in their cards, crystal bowls and medium powers. The magnificent horse was sorely missed to the point where a minute's silence was held at Ascot. A cast iron statue was made in every racecourse in the world to mark their respect and loss.

Mabel was suddenly thrust into a global media game of Cluedo. Everyone said it was her, not the butler; she pleaded her innocence to every TV show and paper in the land. A diamond horseshoe shaped earring was found belonging to Mabel, yet apart from that, the evidence was low with no witnesses stepping forward, and ultimately no charges were brought forward. After the incident, she had taken a knock. Her respected reputation was torn for a while, and trust needed to be re-earned. She even lost her husband over it. He died due to a heart attack, maybe from the stress. Plus, she watched Saffron become the leading lady in the world of elite women, overtaking her, and never since that day did she manage to repair herself 100%.

Mindy was gobsmacked; the tears poured matching the amount of rainfall that month, re-reading the words and hoping that when she re-read them they would change into words of joy, happiness, or the realisation that it was all just a sad joke.

Mindy had had the pleasure of meeting Mabel when she was four. She remembered big hair, a big mouth, a big aura, and a big white dead bear around her shoulders. Baring his teeth, he was pleased he had been skinned to have the honour of being worn around her shoulders. Mabel was like an Aunt to her sending birthday cards, Christmas goodies, and even helping her find a place when she had worked for a year in New York. So, to lose a great influential woman in her life like that was a bitter blow to her current confidence. Slowly but surely each strong woman in her life was slowly exiting, leaving her. It made her queasy with grief, making her refill her glass more than three bottle's worth. You never know when life is going to throw a spanner in the works.

Peaceful Palace

Last night's bombshell was still ringing in Mindy's head alongside the minor hangover, both fighting for space like territory birds as a small man played a boom blaster in the little space left in her head. Pushing through the unusually crowded Reception, her head was down, not really in the mood for talking – plus, her red swollen eyes would probably set off a domino effect of tears amongst the grievers. Maud was busy answering phones, in need of another pair of hands, while sweat beads glistened on her head like Indian bridal headgear. Maud - worked into a sweat for once - failed to notice Mindy slip past.

The stillness of her sanctuary, the solace of her studio soothed her saddened soul. Stevie Wonder sang *Isn't She Lovely* in the background, making Mindy open the floodgates again. Such an appropriate song for Mabel, she thought, repeating the classic track five times with a few sniffs of the antiseptic cleaner. Setting up her table of transformational tricks, her make-up tools tapped impatiently ready to do their magic. Mindy did not know whether to leave. She tried to call Eric, but his phone was off; she knew sitting at home would be no help anyway. She thought about visiting her mother as she had yet to tell her, not wanting to upset her fragile mind by filling it with thoughts of a loved one lost. So, she decided that when Sunday came she may tell her - if she did not already know. Stevie Wonder was now battling to out-sing a Blackberry ringtone.

"Oh Alex" Mindy burst into a whine again. "Forgot to phone you so sorry, just I got sloshed on sadness." Mindy was mortified that she had forgot to call her friend.

"Wouldn't have been able to answer anyway girl, got bloody arrested, didn't I" Alex calmly told a tear stung Mindy. She had been arrested a few times before, so it was nothing to speed her voice up for.

"Arrested? Did you kill Mabel?" Mindy's voice raised a bar, shocked at the revelation; she gripped the steel table to stabilise herself, ready for the confession.

Why would Alex murder Mabel?

Was it because her second cousin had married an Italian?

Was she sent to befriend Mindy, to get inside access to Mabel - like a spy, but a lot more fashionable?

"Murder Mabel, fuck off Moo. Depriving your body of oxygen again?" Once Mindy had convinced herself that oxygen made you fat - she was naïve when younger.

"If am murdering anyone it's that bloody bitch of a receptionist and that fuckin' loopy cat!" Alex announced while she was in the police reception waiting for Troy to be released. She feared that confession might get her more than a night's stay in the cells.

"Well, what then?" Mindy sounded ashamed at her murderous accusation at her close friend.

"Well, was only waiting for you to call me in Chan's Chinese, so Troy, bless him, was starving as no point ordering 'til you phoned, or the food would go cold. So, the waiter must have fancied Troy, or me, as they kept saying 'you red dee to orrda?'" Her attempt at a Chinese accent made the police receptionist laugh. "So, as he came over again I knew you were not going to call, so I threw my phone on the table, which flipped a plate, which hit the stalker waiter, bursting his nose into blood. The woman next to us screamed, so I jumped - shitting myself fell backwards knocking over the big vase housing a tree that I'm sure Jack climbed up. Well, that timbered into a bloody aquarium that could house flipper, sending orange oversized fish flying. Water rushed onto the floor, short circuited the restaurant, which resulted in me being nicked for GBH and criminal damage." Alex spoke this as if it was the normal thing for a gal to do on a dinner date, using one breath.

"Oh my God Ape you ok? What about Troy?"

"Well, he jumped up to help me as I wrestled around in Evian on the floor with a fish opening its giant mouth as if it was either going to eat me or give me the best suck on me tits ever." This again made the eavesdropping police officer laugh. "He slipped head first and butted the owner who was trying to pick me up, just as some offbeat police officers came in for a birthday dinner." Alex needed him to hurry up; she had been in these clothes for too long. "Luckily, I know my laws, and the fact that those fish were illegally brought into the country meant that I managed to blackmail them into dropping the charges!" She was chuffed that she had read her Granddad Joe's fish keeping books as a child to cure her insomnia.

"Ape how funny." The tears now morphed into tears of laughter, descending down her hangover-coloured face. The images of a giant fish fighting Alex for freedom while debating whether to suck her to death was just the tonic she needed, minus the vodka though, as her head ached from the spontaneous wine binge.

"Got to go here's Troy. I've been waiting ages for you. Bye Moo." The drone of the phone call ending let Mindy know that Alex had gone.

*

Alex's little scene of comedy channel gold gave Mindy a step up on the ladder out of her hungover depression pit, giving her the energy to cope with today's client. Pottering around the studio with half an hour to spare, she washed the already pristine make-up palettes. Mindy suddenly found herself thinking of that Irish lovely, filling her with grasshopper glee. He was a lush vision of a man. She could feel his hands that could build an ark around her arm. With a black eye coming on, he looked attractive in a quirky way. Sunday's visit couldn't come fast enough - Mindy seriously needed to have sex soon. Whistling along to the only man in her life, she did not notice Earl the young lad wheel in with the trolley. Her client lay underneath the thin cloth, dead and ready for make-up.

"Hi Earl" Mindy jumped, not noticing him coming like a creeping Jesus. Mindy always thought that he should be an assassin he was so stealthy, but his strong body odour was his downfall, probably his killer weapon too. Earl was about twenty-seven; he was a lanky, skinny guy with zero posture. His limbs gave the impression that they grew and shortened on movement. Adult acne was chipping away at his face, and his skin forever looked as though he never seemed to wash it, stained with sweat. A Mexican wave of follicles in all directions was his greasy brown hair. The turn in his eye made it difficult at staff Christmas parties to know who he was talking too. Maud cruelly nicknamed him *Quasi* - as in hunchback. Despite the flaws in his unfortunate looking self and personal hygiene – never being up close and personal with a bar of soap - Earl was quiet, polite, and hardworking, even if Mindy felt he longed at her breasts a little unhealthily with his lazy eye.

"Hi Mindy." This was interrupted by a thick blue asthma inhaler and Darth Vader breathing.

"Hi Earl place the trolley over there please. Busy today, isn't it Earl? Have we got an offer on?" recoiling at how crude this sounded, she had meant like as a double funeral (which they nicknamed offers). She scrubbed up, putting her lab coat on that to this day did not have an ounce of make-up stained on it five years on.

"Ok Mindy."

Mindy filled her deep pockets with a number of brushes, changing Stevie Wonder to disc two of his greatest hits and tying her red hair securely up out of the way with a shoelace. Feeling she was not alone and sharing the oxygen, she turned to see Earl still standing there. "Can I help ya, Earl?" Mindy was familiar with this scene; eerie Earl was stood with a look like he was waiting for a tip.

"Sorry Mindy" With a blast of his blue whale inhaler he was gone, with only two-day-old sweat lingering as a legacy that he had been there. Mindy laughed; Earl was a sweet person, but was forever tormented by Maud who bullied him day in, day out, spraying him with air freshener and asking what Notre Dame was like to a bemused Earl from Clapham. Even though she was helping the situation, Maud could be a bit cruel.

Eric hadn't yet shown his face. Normally he popped in to brief Mindy on her clients like a kind of voiceover on a Bio channel. She didn't need him to brief her - she knew that they had died and that was all she needed to know. "Right, let's see what we've got here..." She knew nothing grotesque laid in wait under the sheet, no Freddie Kruger or Pete Burns. Having this solo client, she was impressed that the work day would be finished in about two hours, leaving enough time for her to change for her Bootcamp class down in Hoxton.

Mixing the foundation up to match skin tone, looking as real as possible and knowing that the client was a white female, Mindy hummed along to the music. She was loaded up and ready to go. Popping a mint into her mouth as she pulled back the thin white cloth, the next thing she knew, everything went black.

"Mindy, you ok? Wake up dear". A sweet voice started to wake her from her spontaneous faint, and the cold floor compressed against her cheek felt comforting. A peach fragrance smelling like a freshly cut peach held under her nose brought her around. Blinking open her eyes like a newborn into the lights she could make out a face she knew, yet it made her scream.

"Shhhhhh Jesus Christ girl, you're going to attract attention!" An aged hand clasped over her mouth feeling icy, yet velvety. A jewel the size of the moon threatened to block the light out and knock a tooth out. Mindy was horrified. Her sweet eyes bulged with disbelief at this ghostly greeting. Her hangover traded places with shock, and trickery must have something to do with this – like that fatal incident all those years ago in the woods?

Mindy only seven back then, wearing an oversized sparkly jumper and a pair of battered neon yellow jelly sandals passed over by cool Rebecca next door. She wore a pair of Poppy's vintage oval sunglasses and thought she looked so sophisticated, fashionable and cool. Out walking with Bessie, her elderly rescued Great Dane. A tri-colour horse-looking dog sniffing through the overgrowth with ease, dry twigs snapped under her jelly soled shoes as she followed Bessie on their treasure hunt. Bessie was her best friend, as animals tend to be. The afternoon sun darted through the opening in the treetops, beaming laser lengths on the leaf litter below. Poppy was well aware that Mindy was in the forest, so slowly walked out of sight behind her giving her a sense of freedom and the confidence to go it alone. Mindy was unaware that Poppy followed behind; she thought she was a big girl and felt so grown up. Bessie was mimicking a bloodhound, nose to the ground as she followed an invisible spaghetti junction of snail trails of smells, zig zagging across the rustling floor of the woods like the crossed ribbon on a corset. Mindy skipped behind humming a Disney song, spotting a panic-stricken rabbit diving down a hole in fear of being Bessie's dinner, and a lone buzzard shadowing above. Feeling like Snow White with images of animals skipping alongside her, like friends for life - she wasn't boy crazy at that age and would not have fallen victim to the seven dwarves' entrapment of becoming a live-in cook and cleaner. Back in reality, Bessie was barking furiously; her strong tail was wagging so powerfully that it blew the top layer of leaves off the ground.

"What is it, Bess? Have you found treasure?" Her vast imagination was running wild with the idea of the treasure that Bessie might have found, and how she would spend it on a new scooter with light up wheels. Skipping over, she ignored her small foot sliding around inside her shoe like a learner driver stalling on their first lesson, the shoes being a size too big. "Thank you. She will grow into them." she had heard Poppy saying that morning, thanking Rebecca's mum.

Mindy stopped in her tracks. No treasure, but face down in the mud with a few leaves trying to cover the evidence, unsuccessfully, was a man. His neck looked broken judging by the uncomfortable angle it was positioned at. Cold and blue, his upturned hands were poking stiff from the shallow dirt pit. A gash on the back of his head matted with hair and dried blood looked deadly; not understanding murder or death at this age, she sensed that it was murder that brought death to this man. She understood, witnessing it first-hand. She looked at the torso dressed only in a jumper, brown pants and one shoe. She knew that this man was dead, felt that he was dead and distressed at meeting his untimely end from blunt force trauma at the hand of jealousy and greed. The tense stormy air that lay around his body whispered to her. An eerie feeling told her that he was murdered; she felt an energy from this soul; it was tormented, cut short of his life by a good thirty years, his cancer denied the chance to take him - and this vicious death a lot more heart-breaking for his family. Turning to go tell Poppy calmly about the dead man in the woods, a feeling that someone may experience something like this again - like a sign of things to come washed around her stomach.

Poppy was worried, Mindy was acting normal. She thought that she would be scared, that she'd have nightmares attacking her in her sleep, or would start displaying bad behaviour to attract attention. She was a bit disappointed that her daughter carried on as normal, telling Mabel and Dolly how the dead man had told her that he had been murdered by his wife's lover. Forthcoming enquiries from the local police turned out that he was murdered by his wife's lover. Mabel asked Poppy if maybe she was gifted, but Poppy took it no further and no more had happened since. Now déjà vu was cashing in its 'get out of jail free' card, coming back with such a force that she contemplated whether to drink the cleaning fluid on the shelf to calm her shock.

"Come on now, sit down sweetness. My back's going to crack if I don't sit." The figure stood up, the hospital gown falling just about the blue lined legs.

"You're meant to be dead!" Mindy whimpered weakly, battling with bewilderment to overcome a mixture of nausea and faintness.

"Am I? Shit," Mabel pouted, passing over to the mirror and fixing her silver blue hair. The bags under her eyes were darker than normal and her lips were tinted blue.

"Yeah" Mindy was wondering that if she was a ghost would her hand go through her, stretching her hand out like E.T did to Elliott and hoping it did - how cool would that be? Shock is a wonderful thing to corrupt the sane mind. Mabel turned around from looking in the mirror and slapped away her turtle slow hand, and Mindy gasped. Could ghosts physically touch you?

"Oh, behave there's no pockets on this so I'm not carrying any money. Little Artful Dodger wannabe," cheered up by her friend's daughter's actions. She picked up a few lipsticks and rolled out their colourful necks of balm the way a tortoise appears from its shell; a few licked the back of her hand. Mabel was gutted that she was wearing a paper gown; if she passed wind it would certainly rip. Mindy wondered if she was psychic - able to communicate with the dead - afraid and star-struck at the possibility.

Now the big question stirring the air with a giant wooden spoon was, *is Mabel dead or alive*? Mabel, who was drunk at the time of her possible death, was extremely sad - but at least she would not age, could walk through walls, would pay no more tax and could haunt her bitch of a sister. Which famous ghoul should she take after on her reign of terror she wondered, laughing, not taking in Mindy's frazzled fear in her eyes at the sudden combustion of laughter. Mabel handled her champagne better than ducklings handle their first venture into a pond, and drank vodka like she had Polish heritage - so she may have also been alive. The plan had worked if she was still alive, but she famously suffered from a fragile dodgy ticker. Feeling her feeble pulse, she was not able to trace one but felt a puny tremor somewhere - so, fifty-fifty, she guessed. To the world she was dead; according to the media she was hugely missed, much loved, and seeing the front page of a paper on Mindy's small side table, she was rumoured to be gaining a day's celebration for the city - so she wasn't fussed either way.

"Love that picture of me," picking up said paper, opening it up on the middle spread.

"Mabel, what's going on?" Any fluid drinking thoughts were now dispelled from her concerned head. Slowly composing herself, *this cannot be real*, she thought. Or was it? Answers needed collecting, or Mindy needed a stiff drink.

"Not a clue sunshine. Your guess is as good as mine. And I'm shit at guessing - remember that sponge cake I tried to bake?" Mabel's dusty chuckle made Mindy smile, watching as she placed the paper and lipsticks down and exchanged it for the purple eyeshadow set out under the ceiling's spotlights. Her brassy chortling echoed in the sterile studio.

"You were not thinking about putting that on me, were you? God, the shame! Fucking kill me. I'll shut the cast myself! Didn't know Barney the dinosaur was the 'in' look," her loud Texan voice echoed again as if Mindy was stuck in a time loop, her hearing sensitive to noise. Mabel had never been brave enough to experiment with colour. Her slim hand - looking like it would crack if she clicked her fingers - picked up a midnight cat black powder.

"That's more me, morbid, moody and Mabel-line. Do you get it? No? Youth is wasted on the young!" Mabel took Mindy's blank canvas stares and her not catching on to the mock famous make-up brand joke as enough to tell her that Mindy was still in shock.

"Sugar, I've not got a clue if my plan has worked out or not, but I will tell you why I'm here... breathing or not!" Mabel wondered if she had popped her Louboutin clogs or if she had lowered her heart rate enough to just look dead. She was no good at measuring. Her apple pie would rise too much in the oven due to her using a pound of flour - not an ounce - and she'd have to phone the fire brigade to get it out for a slice. So, maybe the sleeping tablet dose had been too much.

"Right, where do I start?" she said locking the studio, allowing no entrance or exit. There was a rustling sound of the paper gown flapping as she waded over towards the stool, climbing up on a stool so tall that it must have been inspired by the empire building - probably as tall as Mabel. On her third attempt, Mabel finally sat on her perch. Catching her breath, she had at least thought in death that she would have more energy. But things felt just like when she was alive: slow, running low, taking forever to warm up. She was seriously in a land of limbo with this. "This bloody paper gown, found dead in Dior, bloody dressed in a brown bag. Come into the world naked - go out wishing you were naked." The creases in the gown matched her skin. Mindy was frozen on the floor where she had sunk to in disbelief of this sick wind up. She was exhausted with trying to figure out why Mabel was now sitting facing her, alive - or as a ghost - watching Mabel trying to pleat the paper gown to give it some sort of style. Was it a new trick for a TV show? Maybe Eric had allowed them to use the parlour as their set.

"Ok, Mabel. I'm ready." Gathering a paper bag and breathing into it to regain her breathing rate from running away and giving her a heart attack, hoping her heart had returned to its normal place, back out of her throat.

"Right, here goes." Mabel was pleased that her pleating resembled a Chanel dress she had owned in the 70's.

"Ok. Well, first of all I actually don't know if I'm here talking to you alive or if I'm a zombie - is that what a dead person is called? Anyway, as you know I've lived a fruitful life full of parties, scandal, and the infamous horse napping era," she normally craved a cigarette, but was waiting to feel the urge. She must be dead - the thought freaked her out.

"Mabel, what's that on your arm?" Mindy hoped the transparent patch was not evidence missed if it was an assassination on the mad crazy broad.

"Oh my nicotine patch," said Mabel. Glad she was still in with a chance of being alive; she carried on with her monologue. "So, as you know, the big event stayed with me for the whole entire remaining life I had. I slowly started losing my wealth as people didn't trust me, so they thought my charities were scams. Arthur died in debt, and I started to slip down the hierarchy of the social circuit. Yeah, I still had my humour, my aura in a sense - but that does not keep you living the life of Riley. I lost a lot of so-called friends' respect and contacts." She became uneasy at the thought of all those years of being a social outcast she had experienced. Even when she had been diagnosed with breast cancer, even with the chemo eating away at her, the mastectomy didn't bring any sympathy or help as people rumoured that it was all an act of desperation. "So, I found myself in a hole of despair, deeper than any fugitive could hide from the Americans in. My sister Saffron was the Queen Bee after back stabbing her way up, sleeping her way through the beds of power men. She was a mischievous madam, stirring her cauldron and creating a media murder of anyone who was in her way, including me," sighing, she remembered her failed battle with the top bitch.

"What do you mean Mabel? You were forever being photographed together at showbiz functions." Mindy thought that Saffron was the more glamorous, mature sister of her and Mabel, but stiffer yet, she was incredibly wealthy, never seemed to have a function or job, and enough husbands to give Elizabeth Taylor a run for her money.

"That was just an act to keep the mill sweet darling. You see, back in the beginning, Saffron was just a 'Plain Jane'. The guys used to call her Suck-fron - she was a bit loose with her lips in more ways than one." Mabel shifted to get comfortable on the stool that had started to iron her arse flat, ready to spill her sister's sordid secrets. "Her hunger for fortune, fame and free riding life like a flower needs the rain to live was uncontrollable. She was going to get it one way or another. I'm convinced she needs mental help. She was dating a non-looker investment banker who was besotted with Saffy, but she was just using him as a launching pad to gain access to the banking community, later marrying his boss. She needed to be involved in something big, something to throw her to the lions of luxury." Mabel noticed how clean the whole studio was. The place gleamed with shininess; she needed sunglasses and it made her feel like she was dirty and in need of a bath. It was hard to understand since Poppy was a ball of mess, a clutter collector and a hoarder. "Oh, how is your mother doing?" Always fond of Poppy, she was a tornado of fun and a great trustee in her life. Mabel broke from the path of explanation and took a slight detour with the question.

"She's ok, still in the home. Not deteriorating too much." Mindy felt bad saying she was in a home closed her eyes expecting to be scolded by Mabel for the act. She automatically thought that people would think that she was a horrible daughter, which once her mother needed help she had palmed her off in a car to the nearest nursing home – well, a manor. Even thought it was Britain's most luxurious one, it still didn't dampen the depressing thought.

"Sugar don't beat yourself up. Your mother decided she would prefer a home, with people all around her, spending her days doing whatever. Plus, you know how boring she said you can be to live with." Mabel smiled. Mindy was the mother in that relationship, but it had done her no harm; smart, clever, talented to boot, and a beautiful woman, Mabel saw. Mindy was certainly a rarity among the youth nowadays.

"So, how is Saffron connected in all this?" Mindy recapped it in her mind, catching up for part two. The paper bag was holding out.

"She stole the damn horse, didn't she" Mabel felt a huge weight lifted off her shoulders; the moody, massive cloud of depression that had stalked her for all those years vanished without a goodbye or an apology. What a waste of pills, alternative therapy, and fortune tellers that she had wasted both money and time on. If she had known that all it would take was her telling someone the truth, she would have done it when she was wearing Dior, alive, and not a pleated paper bag, dead.

"WHAT?" Mindy started hyperventilating in the paper bag, the bag pleased that it was being used for more than just carrying shopping, or hiding Earl's whiskey bottle. The revelation of one of the great unsolved horseracing crimes embarked Mindy into a flap. Sweat drenched her body, sucking her clothes and hair flat to her. Anyone looking in on this scene might think Mindy was in a sauna.

"Yeah, she stole Ballet Foot. Hid him on her vast estate" Mabel was on a roll; her tongue had longed for the day to spill the juicy beans. "She kidnapped him but he suffered a heart attack while being transported. Now, a live horse is difficult, but a dead one is a fucking nightmare," picking up a can of hairspray and choking her white curls with the mist. "So, God knows what she did with it. But, I know that a certain piece of jewellery never to be seen in public is the clue. I feel it in my guts, and many fortune tellers kept saying about a blue ring." During the height of the trail Mabel went through fortune tellers faster than Hugh Hefner goes through bunnies. "She was never in the picture as she dropped me into it with the earring." Sighing, she was quite hoarse from her monologue of truth. Revealing the truth was something Mabel did not ever think the day would come for - but, the truth needed to be told. It was a pity that it was only in death that she finally felt free to speak.

"She had an affair with my husband, Arthur, blackmailing him too. She stole the earring from my dressing table - loved those darn earrings too. Anyway, she planted it and she framed me to cover the affair. She knew that if I told people they would say I was trying to cover up the crime, and she also knew that I couldn't leave my husband due to him being the breadwinner." The image of young, naked Saffron entwined in her bed with her husband, Saffron's brother-in-law, wearing nothing but her birthday suit - which was a lot baggier than Saffron made out - was one image that had refused to dull, fade or age over her lifetime. It was still strong and clear as if it had only happened yesterday, not six decades ago.

"So, I took the reputational beating for the crime to keep me and Arthur from going broke." Deflated from this revelation, she had suffered years of hiding this inside her and it had taken up most of the time in her life; no more love with another man, and the fear of failing to keep this to herself was a full-time occupation. Even in sleep she had not been free from the secret nightmares, eaten alive by horses, waking to the pillow soaked each morning. The sad part was what it truly boiled down to - the chunk too hard to chew and swallow, like blue steak on a pink, toothless gum, was the immense jealousy that Saffron soaked her soul with towards her baby sister. This part damaged her heart every day until it had weakened enough to present Mabel on the cold trolley of the parlour.

"You have got to be kidding!" The paper bag gave up and lost its battle, ripping in two. Mindy couldn't believe this. Basically, Saffron had framed Mabel, her baby sister, with the crime, so that she could dethrone Mabel, clearing the path of popularity and rising through the social ranks quicker than inflation on house costs rise, to reign as Queen of the movers and shakers of London and New York. Wasn't the sister bond supposed to be indestructible? Sisters 'doing it for themselves we Saffron certainly did, Mindy angered. To understand why a sister would bring so many traumas into a sister's life was unbelievable. Mindy was a single child and unqualified to comment or have any judgement on passing a comment so stayed quiet.

"But why would you be seen out with her, forging a public relationship with her when she ruined you? She was supposed to be your sister!" She didn't last long in keeping out of it. "Totally I should have skinned the bitch alive, wore her as a coat, and paraded her betrayal for all to heckle." Bravo pumped her voice up for a moment "But" her voice return to tone of a little girl frightened "I needed her to stay in my life of luxury since my husband died dirt poor and broke. He owed a huge debt to Saffron's second husband, you see. So, to clear the debt, I needed to stay in the public eye. She needed a mentor to help her keep control, help her build a solid foundation of social skills and loyalty from fundraisers. Also, the lady had - still has - no class, style or social awareness. With her fashion sense you get my drift; basically, I turned her into me, but a lot less pretty." Mabel worked her magic on Saffron, and in return, Saffron surprisingly kept her end of the bargain - keeping Mabel in circles and with funds. If Mabel had come clean about the affair or the kidnapping Saffron would have been jailed, jilted by her wealthy husband, bringing shame on the family. So, she kept Saffron sweet, knowing she would be worthless and bankrupt if she didn't. She knew about Mabel's money woes and the life of luxury that she was accustomed to, her secret past of being a sex escort, and that she knew where the dressing table of the late Valerie - make-up artist to the West End - was hiding the million-pound piece of royal art. The bitter sisters needed each other as much as a fish needs water, even if that water was a murky pond.

"So why are you dead, or tried to kill ya self? Or pretending to be dead?" standing to her feet a little shakily as her legs were numb from sitting on the cold floor throughout the Oscar winning script. Mindy needed to know this last part of the crazy plot, and how she had come to be here.

"Well," unsure, Mabel morphed her face into a confused state of deep thinking. "I could have died of natural causes, or the fact I took a few heavy sleeping pills to lower my heart rate to give an appearance of death. As you can see, I skipped a post mortem and I leaked my own death to the press. I had hoped to get the details sorted, so I came here to you." The pleating started to unfold much to Mabel's annoyance, who gave up turning the paper gown into something with class.

"Why would you wanna kill yourself and end up here? I mean, I know my skills are the best in the business…" Mindy didn't realise she was sounding big-headed, yet saying it out loud felt good. She had never said it to anyone, never mind herself. It was like complimenting yourself on weight loss or a new haircut. She was the best in the business. She had held her own at the top for her whole career, the head of her game bowing out with sadness and applause from the industry. "Sorry, I didn't mean to blow my own trumpet" blushing in the face.

"Why, you were, darling - and still are - the best!" Mabel lent over touching her arm forever a fan of praising talented women, and her hands felt cold on her arm. Was she dead? Or was it a fact that older women's hands are cold? Was the heating off again? The frail hand was bare, its skin a map of her time on earth. Or had she died in the long flight, stuffed into a body bag on the transatlantic flight to London? To be honest, the cargo pit was still more comfortable than economy.

"I had to fake my own death - fingers crossed - so I could come here and tell you about Saffron, clear my name, then go and live my new life with a new identity, free from Saffron to live my life out somewhere hot with a hot ass toy boy in a jock strap, knowing she got her just desserts." The thought of reading about Saffron's fall from grace in a little Spanish cottage among fruit trees, with a young hot Spaniard stallion (either male or foal), was the way to see out your days. If she hadn't overdone the sleeping pills already maybe vodka to wash them down with was not her smartest choice.

"What? How am I going to do that? Court?" Mindy was mortified at the idea of taking on the might of Saffron. Mindy felt her veins bulge in her head as her voice scaled higher, her lungs squeaking to push the words out of her mouth. Mabel was more of a spontaneous bird rather than thinking things through kind of bird, but she was also a quick on her feet kinda girl.

"Who said anything about court? My dear, there's more than one way to skin a rat. Or is it a cat? I never understood that saying. Come closer, I will tell you," she said with a naughty, but fabulous smile. Mindy moved forward a safe inch, her hesitance about what she was about to be told etched all over her face, did she want to know? Happily to live in the present of not knowing or walk into the future with whatever Mabel was intrusting her with? Mabel looked at Mindy, and despite the whole shenanigans, she just had to ask, "Mindy, what the fuck happened to your fringe?"

Apartment alongside the River Thames

Lounging face down, she was pinned by a force too strong to try and fight back as a pair of the hardest hands in London the size of shovels beat down on her with power and meaning. Slapping her naked skin, she feared she may snap and be found bollock naked in two halves on the ceramic tiled floor.

"How is that?" Tamas the mobile masseur whispered, as he untied the constricted knots that even Houdini would have struggled to untie, and escape from her naked, oiled back. His real name was Jim, but Tamas sounded sexier, foreign, and fitter than just Jim from Hendon. It was better for business among the lonely housewives that his client base was mainly made up of – and a few horny gay guys with the fantasy of seducing their masseur.

"Gorgeous Tamas. Keep going, rub me harder," Alex spoke from her dream state, as she lay there naked. The candles flickered to the sound of a waterfall rushing through her open plan apartment - the alternative therapy CD that Troy had received free in the daily paper.

"Harder. That's it, harder mmmmmmm." Poured like cream from spilt carton, Alex was in body orgasm heaven with each hand movement connecting on her back, while his smooth magical hands made a lap of honour on her bare, slim back. Alex was one of Tamas' best clients; she was sexy as fuck, funny, full of humour and a great tipper too.

Niagara Falls in the living room washed away any hint of the front door opening in her pebble drift grey lounge that gossiped with her ice blue leather couch. A huge snow leopard print rug flooded over half of the floor muted the footsteps of the intruder. The door went unnoticed as it opened, with Alex too busy indulging in being kneaded like bread dough, a human gingerbread woman, shaped spread-eagle on the portable masseur table, her skin soaked with exotic oils from around the world but picked up at the supermarket. Unaware that the other love in her fast-paced life was home, she carried on moaning with stress-free pleasure.

"Ello Troy." Tamas' fake accent was back on like lights after a power cut, just so that Troy would find him interesting - which he didn't. He'd gone to school with Jim's older brother and knew very well that Hungarian was not the nationality on Jim's passport.

"Hi Jim" placing the canvas grocery bag onto the *Russian Night* black granite worktop that stood proud in the middle of the kitchen like a knight on a horse - in this case, the horse being a sandstorm beige marble floor. The canvas bag had been a gift from Mindy - a lover of recycling and saving the planet.

"It's Tamas!" Alex called from her face down position.

"Tamas" Troy whispered. Working in the waste unit of the city as a bin man since the age of sixteen, now at thirty-five, he had never known any different nor understood the fads Londoners went through. Alex was the breadwinner, a reason they lived in a dock apartment overlooking the Thames. He still paid his way, though; the bag of groceries was evidence of this.

"Hello baby. Whoa, harder. Just there!" Alex was interrupted by the rubbing of a pleasure spot, and waved a hand in any direction to greet her fiancé.

"Hi baby," in a baby voice - but not his normal baby voice, since Jim was here. Troy felt a little emasculated using his baby voice in front of Jim, despite Jim speaking with a fake accent. At least Troy kept loyal to his own language.

"Did you get dinner in? I've nearly finished baby" her voice wispy and orgasmic. The waterfall started to fall a lot more forcefully. Tamas' hands moved harder in time with the CD, like a gym instructor in aerobics class.

Troy looked at his naked fiancée, her fine body jerking with each slap, the red, raw fossil hand prints visible on her back looking like a twisted map; he felt he should hit Tamas. Her skin stretched with the fear that it may not fit her any more. How she found this pleasurable was beyond him, but the moans, groans, and giggles coming from the love of his life, battered in an act of stress relief by a huge man, showed she was either enjoying it or becoming a sadist.

Water crashed around the whole place suddenly as loud as thunder. Troy hoped it was not the Thames rocking some freak weather waves; since he had nearly drowned as a child, water was not his best friend; he ducked in panic behind the granite island in the kitchen. The candles contributed to climate change as they helped to heat the earth up, thousands of them over the place close to all the expensive flammable interiors in the home. The waves crashed almightily, and Alex's moans increased to match each audio wave. Louder, bolder, more intense waves crashed high around.

Alex's sexually moaning repeated. Troy was terrified - was his fiancée possessed?

Tamas dripped with sweat as he pounded Alex's back, his face twisted with concentration, the pound of his bare fist sounding harder, huffing out of breath like he was going to cum. Was this a sexual turn-on for Tamas? Troy disliked thinking this way.

A clamped fist hit her skin, ripples booming to reach the whole width of her back as if he had dropped a stone into her oiled back like a puddle. Alex's pleasure echoed loudly in the air, producing tremors against Troy's skin; it felt uncomfortable seeing Alex beaten by another man. The waves on the CD crashed and smashed, faster and faster, the trio in sync becoming lost in the pleasurable chanting of '*harder, harder, faster, faster*' that Alex muffled into the white padded table. Troy was certain that a demonic ritual was happening and expected a hole to burn through the living room floor, Satan taking his life to hell - perhaps it was a pact that Alex had made for a new promotion or a new handbag. Troy grabbed a wooden spoon just in case to fend off the Devil's hot pitchfork. He feared that Alex had been embedded into the table like a sexy fossil. Tamas thudded, punching her back that looked so small against this heavyweight. Troy knowing very well not to interfere, all he could do was watch the massage taking on a maniacal characteristic.

Flinching, each slap shook his ear drums and Troy could only imagine the pain - yet Alex seemed to be in a state of pure pleasure. Tough as the love of his life was, and hard as nails too, you had to admit that a boxer taking one of these slaps to the face would scream in pain. Alex screamed more, '*faster, harder*'. Troy felt a little like he was being cheated on - she never called out like this in bed.

"Nearly there, nearly there. Harder, harder, that's it. More left, up, yeah there...NOW HARDER!" Alex shot her beautiful face up screaming out ahead, possessed like she was about to give birth to the Anti-Christ, her eyes bulging out raw, her oily face replacing sweat and her mouth seeming to foam.

Furniture flew across the room as the walls blew out - well, to Troy, that was what should have happened with the force. Troy knocked the canvas bag of shopping over frightened by the roar, terrifying a cucumber that rolled out wonkily trying to escape. Alex looked like she was a dragon, breathing hot fire out. Tamas, with a final huff, slapped down in slow motion it seemed, the fatal silence telling Troy that it was over. Alex lay motionless, not a movement flickered through her oiled body and her back ripped red. Could she be dead? Tamas' eyes closed tight with the completion of his massage, his head held up to the ceiling and his chest rising deep and high, catching his breath after the cardio workout on his hands.

The minutes passed, yet the two bodies had still not come back to life. Troy, sensing the silence was disturbing, was too afraid to speak and stood motionless. Despite being from the East End and built like a Spartan, and a local weight boxing champion, the deadly silence was overpowering, and he felt afraid, unsure what to do.

"What did I miss?" his fiancée's friend's voice pitched through the silence, cutting through like a hot knife in butter. Mindy had let herself into Ape's apartment with her spare key; the *Russian Velvet* feature wall made Mindy smile. Alex hated it, but the feng shui power that she had blagged Alex to believe made her keep it. She knew that Alex was having her meditation massage with Tamas, a faux foreigner. An intense, forceful masseur building up speed and hard pressure, he was quite a hit among the city slickers of high-powered stressful jobs. And being mobile was even better; it was like S&M - but using hands, not dog leads.

"Oops, sorry," Mindy whispered, planting a kiss on Troy's cheek. His male fragrance was masculine and strong, just like Troy. He looked strong seeing his bicep pushed out from under his orange polo shirt, his jaw square and unbreakable looking. His nose was pushed a bit closer to his face from his sparring days and his eyes - one green and one light blue - always had people commenting on how attractive they were, being odd. Troy was a tired-looking Jason Statham, yet a totally gentle giant. Seeing a naked Alex in her wound down state, oil slicked pleasurably all over her skinny-bitch body that Mindy envied more than the ability to do the splits, was the centrepiece of the whole living room - even the Tiffany chandeliers gave up. Her friend was naked, if not a little red looking, lying horizontally on the cushioned table, and was possibly dead. Mindy preferred Yoga and boot camp.

"Hi," Mindy mouthed to Troy. He knew Mindy to be a bit of a dreamer and a hopeless romantic too, but surely even she could see his naked fiancée red raw lying motionless and possibly dead, while a chubby masseur had his eyes shut, looking up like he was turning into a werewolf at a full moon, was a bit unnerving - or was that his cum face? Troy, being a man, was clueless.

"She finished yet?" The bulging goodies in the shopping bag got the better of Mindy as she started to unpack, snooping at the dinner delights. There was fudge cake with more layers than an arctic climber and thick chicken breasts that you would expect to be injected with silicone - not water, and chunky cod fillets that would have Greenpeace waving a banner outside the door. Mindy was looking forward to this dinner already.

"I'm not quite sure?" his reply came out slowly as if it was on the back of a snail.

Troy was the chef of the relationship, and also cleaner, maintenance man, decorator, spider catcher, and a culinary wizard in the kitchen. He longed to open his own restaurant or bistro, delivering mouth-watering delights to the bevy of people in London who would toast to his skills. He needed to win the lottery, as with London rents rising more aggressively than ISIS, it was a dream long off. Alex had funded a course to send him to chef school of an evening the previous Christmas, and it was the best present she had ever surprised him with. Mindy appeared by his side popping a grape into her mouth, taking in the island of two humans dead and a massage table in the middle of the living room.

"Is she ok? They've not moved for five minutes." The rare uncertainty in his strong voice made Mindy laugh.

"Shhhhhhhh!" an out of breath, very pleased, alive Alex and a heavy-breathing male voice said together, meaning business. Relief rushed over Troy, even if he was being told off by his fiancée. Mindy hid her laughter in the eight-foot fridge, grabbing more delicious grapes. The fridge certainly stopped Mindy from eating, as it reflected her reflection back at her.

Nervous was an understatement. The salt from the three bags of roasted nuts forced her to buy two bottles of overpriced wine with a hint of vinegar, not fruits. The date was over an hour late, her fourth that month. Maud's patience sat low, playing with the buckle on her Mary Janes, bored as she sat in the window watching people pass in activity. The bustling noise created by end of work conversations buzzed in the background of the trendy wine bar, forgetting to block out Maud's self-loathing thoughts.

Why was love dodging her all the time?

Surely the tragedy from her teenage years lacked the power to tarnish her life as an adult? Endured chat up lines with more cheese than a dirty foreskin on the numerous dating site in her war to find love, at least as a thank one date could least turn up. She knew the real reason love was abusing her heart it was punishing her for the stupidity of an incident that happened over two decades ago. The shadow clouding over her as hot as the fire that night, the guilt as strong as all eleven firefighters fighting until dawn to put it out, scaring away potential lovers. Was she void of love in her life? Skipped the part with a soulmate for a life of solitude and carbs? Self-diagnosing the ache in her heart as angina, heartbreak had no pills to heal it.

A passing waiter - it was rare for one to not be a struggling actor - took her empty wine bottle away, heavy with sadness. He ignored how the label had been torn off in sexual frustration sheared with anxiety, sheared with the skill of a sheep farmer. He also ignored the obvious fact that she was a little dressed-up to be sitting alone, drinking a bottle wine for the past three hours. He was finding love in the city hard, and knew it was a cold avenue to walk down - and for a woman over a certain age in London, extremely lonely.

"Sorry love, closing up soon." Gently touching her shoulder brought her back from whatever world she was visiting in her head. He had gone before Maud had a chance to apologise for her stay, but on the plus side, he would not see her Boy George inspired make-up or raw blue tears from being stood up on a date, again.

"This is delicious, oh my God" Creamy fish sauce dripped on her spot-free chin as a souvenir of the grilled cod dish. Alex adored Troy's cooking among other things she still loved about him. It made the mouth come alive with lust, each taste bud whipped into frenzy, exhausted with taste, thirsting for a drink to reenergize it, leaving you satisfied and wanting seconds, which in this case, was chocolate fudge cake with Bailey's flavoured ice cream – the saliva dripping from the mouth like pre-cum.

"Cheers baby," the original baby voice returned. Troy lent over the smashed effect dining table designed by one of Mindy's freelance designer friends - and discounted too - kissing Alex on her familiar lips, fitting like pieces of a puzzle in his life. Just like they had done many moons ago while both dressed as Smurfs at an illegal rave Alex was the only smurf to be painted purple - even then, she was not afraid of standing out.

Despite having a mouth full of swede and garlic mash, the passionate kiss of paired for life love birds lingered in the moment. Still, after all these years, they were like young love's dream. A comically over-the-top cough spoiled the love fuelled kiss reminding them that a guest, a very single guest, was in the presence of them.

"Sorry Moo. He just can't get enough of me" Alex teased, pushing a fork full of steamed spicy broccoli inside the dental haven that was her mouth.

"No problem, Ape. Just want to eat this food, not bring it up!" teasing her friend, as Troy refilled the ladies' glasses up with more wine. Tuesday evening was not normally a night that Mindy would go to Ape's for dinner; usually a power pump class followed by a microwave meal for one was on the fridge day planner. Also, like every night, she said she'd start that novel, but the day's events with Mad Mabel had left her exhausted, freaked out, and in need of a confidante who had the same love for wine as she did. So she forced Alex to force Troy - who never needed an excuse, nor disliked Mindy's company - to cook for them.

Mabel was still rioting on her mind as she poured the wine down her throat without taking a break. She still didn't know if Mabel was dead, telling her these stories like a kind of crossover into the other side, as if Mindy was a physic sitting off in a flimsy tent at a seaside resort. Mindy had read about tortured souls with unfinished business, trapped in limbo and visiting people to help them. She was sure Mabel must know some policemen or a hitman - even Beyoncé could help her more than Mindy could. Another possibility was that she had successfully faked her own death and needed to finish the rest of her plan to be able to lead her new life, perhaps?

Leaving Mabel in the studio and watching her climb back under the cloth on the table was a little disturbing; Mindy drank a bottle of wine on the tube, for once not worried about the stares even if they were from the stalker/murderer type. She felt like she was in a dream, but she got Maud to pinch her, who was delighted with the offer and drew blood with her pinch.

An hour passed in the stylish, designer waterside home overlooking part of the Thames - the poor end, Alex would say - hoping to hit a big, bad court case to fund a move to the posh part, further up. The evening flowed like the Thames (but cleaner though), as fun flirted with laughter, the wine bottle repeated many a rosé refill, a second helping of cake for Mindy who promised Alex she would drop ten extra squats to burn it off. Troy told the girls about the time a body was found in a bin, again. They never bored of this story, and each time it was told always different than the last, more gruesome than the truth and more over the top than a drag queen's wedding.

Mindy felt nervous; she gulped her wine in one.

"Whoa Mindy, you're knocking them back tonight," said Troy, collecting the empty licked-clean plates, pleased his two biggest critics had given his dessert the lick of approval.

"Just very thirsty." Her reply far from dry, her eyes avoided diverted from his face. "Think I'm coming down with something." Her medium brown tinted eyebrows started to jig as Mindy lied, hating herself for lying to her best friend after that fine feast too.

Alex looked at her lovely - but lying - friend, ignoring the chocolate smudge on her friend's chin that looked like a birthmark from dessert. Her raised eyebrows were a sure sign that Mindy was telling porky pies - big, fat, heart attack inducing ones. All their friendship Alex could always point out when Mindy was lying. Where some people diverted their eye contact to the ceiling or the floor, Mindy's giveaway was her eyebrows coming alive voluntarily, as if she had been giving head and caught pubic lice. Alex needed to talk to her friend and find out what was going on before she made her forehead look like a Shar Pei.

"Hey baby, you get off to bed. Mindy will do the dishes." Mindy shot Alex a look that she knew Alex knew something was up. This made Mindy move her eyebrows even more; she feared they would vanish entirely with the exercise, even falling off possibly. Hitting the fourth bottle of wine too, she thought damn the dishes being done with her one-day-old manicure. She prayed it was only a joke.

Troy had been yawning throughout the meal - not due to the gossip of who was humping who, or what new eyeshadow had made Mindy drop dead with excitement, or the fact that Alex was thinking of getting a pubic wig – it was mainly due to Troy being up before the sun, lifting tonnes of wheelie bins full of the city's grime, which showed in his bulging biceps. Even though London was meant to be promoting recycling, he was still yet to see a recycling bin being used for exactly that instead of a flowerpot or a drunk's stool. Looking at Mindy, who seemed to have her neat head in the wine glass, he was relieved that she would do the dishes.

"You sure Moo?" praying that she was. An early night was just what he needed, plus his new book on Jamie Oliver was coming up to the bit where he had first gotten media interest.

"Yeah," Mindy spoke into her glass. The glassed steamed up with her hot, swallowed, lying breath.

"Cheers you're the best" flicking an ice cube her way, planting a kiss on her head as he moved from his seat to pick up the out of place ice cube off the floor.

Putting his tongue in Alex's mouth, he could feel himself getting aroused. Alex rubbed on his swollen groin, feeling underneath for the most perfect penis she had ever seen and accommodated - and she had seen a few in Law School, some between the legs but mostly on the heads of pretentious, rich males. His cock swelled in response to the rub, like a river bursting its bank as it filled up to its full eight heavy inches. He had to go before he had sex with her right there on the table. Mindy, being a sweetheart, would be mortified, but would refuse to say anything and hide behind her blunt fringe, which didn't really suit her. So, he pulled himself off his sexy fiancée and headed towards the bedroom, thanking God that his tight Levi's kept his throbbing hard-on strapped to his rugby muscular leg.

"Spill!" pouncing on Mindy like a cat on a mouse once Troy had left the living room, free from hearing Mindy's confession. Alex locked eyes with Mindy in a strict stare that Mindy couldn't hide from, or out stare - the infamous 'scouse stare' was its name. If Alex hit you with this stare, you were helpless against it. Its death glaze sucked the truth from you the way a vampire drew blood - fast and painful, with results. In court it was her weapon of destruction, brought out in the final hour when nobody could deter themselves from dishing out the truth. The stare could back off starving feral dogs, break glass, or make Mindy tell Alex the most ridiculous story that she would hear in a long time.

"So, I'm hoping by getting pissed you will just think I made it up" Mindy found herself in tears; the wine had gone to her head. She held it in a wrestling move until it became emotional and pleaded to be free. It sloped from side to side, not knowing which side it would be better off on. Relaying the whole event to Alex who for once sat speechless, no interruptions or dissecting questions asked, and not even a bored roll of the eyes as she sat in her dining chair in the shape of a throne.

"And she wants you and me to find this ring?" The wine glass was filling up with tears, and through her blurred, mascara-stained eyes Mindy tried to work out Ape's face. Still, sober, cold and expressionless, but beautiful as normal - not the positive look she had prayed for.

She rose from her vintage pop art inspired dining throne, which had a supermodel's face stencilled on to it…a bit off putting when eating something unhealthy. Alex stood to her feet, losing about a foot of height with being barefoot. She still had supermodel height, just no clouds hanging around her head as if she had a fluffy white afro. Striding over to the eight-foot stainless steel fridge in two elegant steps, Alex was happy with her gym-controlled reflection of herself in it as normal. A chilled bottle of Moet saved normally for celebrations like a work promotion, tax rebate, or weight loss - not deluded tales of dead women and horses - accompanied her back to the long table. She needed a drink seeing as there was no wine left - Mindy had seen to that - to take in the tale that Mindy had come out of out the blue with. Mindy should start that novel Alex decided, if this tale was anything to go by. With that, she needed a stiff drink.

She took her seat in the way that a Queen takes her throne ready to address her servants, but instead of wearing a gown, satin smooth pyjamas in a blood ruby red were the attire. She sat with pose-perfect posture. Mindy was tear-free for a moment, and took the silence as a bad sign; Alex was never silent, not even in her sleep.

"Ape, are you ok? Speak to me. I know it sounds crazy - believe me, it took me four bottles of wine to understand it a bit." Clear tears hijacked her eyes again. Alex fixed her stern face to Mindy's. God Mindy was an ugly crier, slowly unscrewing the foil cap of the magnum bottle. Chilled droplets fled along the neck of the bottle, in panic maybe.

"Please Alex, say something." Pleading was something new to Mindy; she hoped she had not lost her friend through this out of the world story, which was the main reason that her tears showed up. Plus, Mindy was an emotional drunk. If she accidentally swallowed her mouthwash in her morning rush she would feel suicidal. Dragging Alex - without her permission - into this secret could be something that Alex did not want to be in on. A few tense moments hung between the friends like a bad smell. A six-foot heavy brick wall wearing a crown of barbed wire would be a friendlier greeting than what she had at present, Mindy thought.

The woodchip cork popped in the mute air, banged out like a bullet; the first gunshot of a war killing the silence stone dead. The stem flutes of champagne filled up fast, exploding over. The silence settled once the pop of champagne lost all its potential - never to be a celebrating pop, the silence lingered hell too long to celebrate.

"CONGRATULATIONS!" Alex flung her slim arms around Mindy's neck, nearly choking her with shock as the satin sleeves stroked her cheeks.

"What?" Mindy must have been misunderstanding her friend's strange behaviour for something like an early sign of a breakdown for Alex, perhaps? Toasting her flute against hers, Alex returned to her throne, unlocking her toned arms before she got done for murder. With a huge smile plastered across her picture-perfect face like a rainbow after a storm, her body jerked with glee.

"Listen" leaning over her elbows on the table like an actor from those detective court dramas would do.

"This is just the case I need to kick arse, to get my solo career up and running. Of course I will represent the batty old bird if we are going to take it to court. I mean, she's a luxury icon, and it would slap Saffron down a peg or two - the grumpy old goat - if it comes to going to court." Alex was secretly gobsmacked at the thought of it, but chuffed that she had personally been handpicked by Mad Mabel, dead or alive, to represent her in court.

"What are we congratulating?" His red striped pyjamas aged him by twenty years, yet they were adorable and cute; too tired to care, Troy walked in like a zombie but a zombie you wanted to bite. The book was as addictive to him as cocaine, each page littered with lines keeping him awake and wanting more. The two friends looked at each other hoping the other one would answer, and luckily, Alex came through like a trooper.

"Mindy's got a Brazilian." Mindy nearly swallowed up in the room. Troy was now probably picturing a ginger afro in her knickers the size of a clown's wig, thinking '*hmmm, very seventies - so that's why she's single*'

Alex knew women's issues like heavy periods, leaking breasts or girl crushes made Troy feel uncomfortable, and on cue, he retreated into the chocolate-inspired decorated safety of the bedroom. Embarrassed, his face matched the red of his nightwear. The door slammed behind him - not in an aggressive way, just in a way how he forgot sometimes how strong he actually was. Troy muttered something about '*crazy bitches*'. The two friends raised a toast: "To crazy bitches, dead or alive!" The cool evening witnessed two lifelong friends bonding even stronger, coming together to help another woman in her revenge who had called in help from friends.

New York

Finding out that Delia had decided to fall from her balcony - and not from grace - wearing skimpy underwear, crushing her tarty body on the streets of New York for pervy cannibal pigeons to peck at had freaked him out to the point where he needed fresh air and a distraction. Central Park offered both.

Grief made people act in strange ways; shock hijacked common sense and rode it bareback across the meadows of your normal, sane way of thinking. Chad Rise rode his grief bareback right into the fanny of Celeste, a blonde leggy-creature fan he had bumped into in Central Park, asking for an autograph using the back of her *Vogue* magazine. She was so hot that his rule of two condoms was forgotten in their rushed strip.

The soft blonde strip left by her beautician bore softness; he imagined the down on a gosling as it nuzzled the base of his cock. She wore a petite frame as if it was starved of male attention, naive to what the female body could achieve with more curves and bigger tits, feeling her rib cage underneath.

Her skin was new; it shivered with each stroke of his hands with the ill feeling that it was the first time a naked man's body had weighed down on it. Not a mark, sun damage, or a crease under his hands gave any indication of wear, like the expensive animal skin bags in his Atlanta closet belonging to Maria that she dreamt to achieve. Her tightness was that of a virgin, yet her accommodation of his cock was confident, and she reported back with groans of 'don't stop'. She vowed in the park that she was seventeen, and that her navy blazer was from a cool boutique in the Meat District – a prep trend. Chad was blind to the fashion trends of women so took her word coming out of her rose tinted lips. The same lips pressed against his smooth head.

Sex made Chad forget - it made him feel special, powerful, and for however long his ejaculation took to release his build up, he felt important. Once he had sown his seed, the time it took for him to get dressed and leave beat his cock to swell down, he had returned to feeling numb.

Now back in his hotel on the cosy bed, the pristine white sheets were crumpled and wrinkled beneath naked him fucking Celeste, encouraging him. It was just what he needed to pump out Delia from his head, lying broken and smashed, leaking blood into the grey concrete like a bottle of red wine. His arse did the whip and nae, back and forth. He caught Celeste's greens eyes staring at him in admiration - for his fuck or for fear, he couldn't decide. Her eyes were full as if not believing what they were seeing, as if a dream had come true for the beauty.

Sweat from his forehead dripped onto her neck. As if her body longed to drink it, she arched her back with the touch of sweat as if she was trying to feed the whole length of his penis into her. She looked him deep in his eyes. Oh, his eyes sucked her in, hypnotising her to behave as what her mother referred to as a slag. That irresistible look pierced right into her fantasy while his cock pierced into her novice fanny. She always thought on the TV soap that they added contacts to create the eyes that deemed you powerless, yet in the flesh, his eyes were bluer than the whole career of Linda Lovelace.

"Are you sure you're seventeen?" Concerned his fat cock may be tucked inside a minor created no dent in his firmness or cut in the strength of his fast thrusting. Celeste pushed up and took to riding him on top the way she did with Diddy, her horse at riding school. Watching Chad lean back in delight, she took control just as they did in the erotic films she secretly watched, upping the gear into the last leg of the fuck, and kicking out his illegal thought.

"Yeah I'm sure," whipping her relaxed hair back, her roots dampened by sweat, face glistened highlighted her virginal beauty. Bouncing deep, her trivial tits hit up and down cheering her on, each bounced on Chads dick educated her. Digging the sensation of him inside her felt amazing, out of this world, and anything important in her life vanished like an exorcism from her body with each gasp. The compressed ache between her legs tomorrow would be a reminder of today that she would often daydream about with wetness. She was about to add a little extra to the white lie she told him in Central Park, yet her mother had always said: *don't talk with your mouth full, you're a lady.*

Feeling far from a lady and a little put off that her strict boring mother was in her mind as she felt the wet slip of Chad pulling out, he turned to force her young mouth to take his wet dick as he unloaded his sweet offering. She declined to add '*seventeen in two years*' to her reply.

London

Eric greeted Mindy outside the door on the grey goose pavement like a bouncer on the door at a swanky club at nine in the morning. Before Mindy stepped foot inside Peaceful Palace he jumped at her, grabbing her arm and looking both ways as if someone was spying on him - or hoping nobody had seen him snatching Mindy off the street like a bag snatcher.

The weather was overcast and coughed with heavy clouds, forming a barrier under the sun in disbelief. Mindy was wrapped in a camel mac, a little fragile from Alex's two bottles of champagne. She couldn't believe that Alex had taken it with such joy; she should have known that Alex would be game for anything. She was an adrenaline junkie at heart, and 'it's exciting to try anything once' was a familiar statement for Alex. She always joked that she was Poppy's real daughter.

"Mindy, quick!" pulling her off her feet and into the reception before she had finished her thoughts on the night before, nearly losing a satin pump in the process on the damp, down looking pavement. She was like a modern day Cinderella, only no one would be returning the pump – they would be selling it on, since it was Christian Dior.

"Eric, what's up?!" Her arm socket luckily held out, keeping her arm in place. Reception was stone silent like a surprise party hiding among the furniture, ready to pounce out singing 'Surprise!' in a medley of tones and pitch. It was strange that Maud was not sat like an overfed vulture on a bare branch, straining from snapping, behind reception. "Where's Maud?" listening out for the tea urn boiling, the biscuit tin opening, heavy breathing, and the smell of cheap perfume that reminded her of de-icer. There was not a sound to indicate the lump.

"Gave her the day off, she refused at first, but I promised to pay her double if she took the day off." Eric bolted the front door behind while Mindy rolled down the wooden blinds to create privacy. A slight darkness to the pleasant reception area fell around. He had physically pushed Maud out of the door this morning while she muttered something about GBH and suing.

Mindy bitterly thought that Maud had got the good deal - double pay and a day off - while she got whiplash to her arm. But whatever had Eric acting like he was paranoid from a dodgy acid tablet had her worried.

"Eric what's up?" The episode of Mabel alive like Frankenstein skipped her memory in this bizarre moment. Eric was acting weird; he was not at all his calm, collected self. Edgy, he was nervously whispering as he rushed her through to the corridor heading to his office. Had he finally lost his mind? The *Sicilian Summer* pale white wall blurred past like sheep in a field as you drive past in a Ferrari.

"Eric stop! What the hell is wrong with you?" Maybe all that time sat alone in fields watching birds had cracked him like an egg.

"Well Mindy. There has been a fuss over Mabel staying here. The media are offering a bucket load of money for details on the funeral." The large sum of money rattled around in his head, but he was loyal to his self-respect and declined invitations of ridiculous amounts of money - even the gasp of shock from the reporter on the phone signalled that he was crazy to turn it down.

"What's with all this urgency?" she said, using her body weight to ground him to a halt and bring sense to his peculiar behaviour this morning. She felt a little betrayed by her weight when it worked, and Eric stopped.

Shiftily loosening his plain coal satin tie to let out the heat of the rush, Eric couldn't believe the shock this morning when she had turned up. "Come I'll show you" Creaking open the office door in a gear next to slow, it looked still. He was standing behind Mindy like he was about to push her into whatever grim thing lurked behind it with disregard, like a bloodthirsty Roman threw his slaves to the lions and their death when his pots weren't clean or his toga wasn't ironed properly. Eric nodded forward with his head in an indication for Mindy to enter into the unknown. Curiosity took over her nerves as Mindy strolled in to see a beehive of aged blonde hair facing her. The back of a lady, a little hunched, sat facing the front looking at the many awards in the cabinet facing. She didn't look like anyone she knew - well not from behind anyway - or in fact a killer/debt collector/journalist or any reason for Eric to act crazy. She was facing Eric with a look like she was just as confused, as a hint for what he was acting odd about.

His pale face was looking tired with day-old stubble growing through his podgy chin. His wispy hair seemed to have had a wind dry instead of blow dry, and showed evidence that his hands had been running through it all morning with stress. Mindy couldn't figure out which direction it was brushed over in.

This was probably the biggest funeral Eric had ever dealt with, media-wise, for sure. Mindy looked at Eric; her face was a picture displaying her uncertainty about what the deal was. A husky cough interrupted – technically, it tapped Mindy on her cute shoulders. Mindy turned on her most customer-friendly, professional smile, outdoing the smile that a hooker flashes to a stressed businessman as he lowers his car window. She turned around to greet the stranger responsible for startling Eric, like Abba does - his long haired tortoiseshell cat - with the shabby starlings off his lawn. The next thing she knew it went black, again.

Ireland

Joe-Ryan whistled a childhood rhyme, collecting up freshly cut grass into the battered, loyal wheelbarrow to put onto the impressive compost heap at the back of the long lawn. A man of limited education by government standards, nevertheless, Joe-Ryan was highly educated in the teachings of life, and had been brought up to make family important.

He flew to Ireland once a month to tend to his Granny C's garden. Ireland was his birth country, born last into siblings of six, and they had moved to England when he was three - not due to a shortage of potatoes, but to their gypsy lifestyle. Each year passed, and they travelled more south in their luxury caravan pinballing across England, excited for yet another new start. Yet the prejudice of the gypsy lifestyle never changed with each city they lived in. The abuse about their lack of education, the invasive stares, the Johnny Big Balls mocking absorbed into him, and the only way to show that he was not to be pushed over was to bare knuckle fight and to fight against the stereotypical life of a gypsy.

Joe-Ryan wanted a different lifestyle than what his crazy mother and absent father had followed. Tired of modern media-fed prejudice and having to prove himself, life was more than grabbing and legally poaching, and terrorising councils; like Ariel from *The Little Mermaid*, he wanted more.

Joe-Ryan wanted a proper home and a decent job to learn about the world he lived in, to be educated beyond the expectations of the community. He wanted a house to call home - not a static caravan that even Domino's refused to deliver to. So, he decided that London was the big city in which he would carve out a new life for himself, the city that would teach him ways to become a better man, all in the hope of landing that one big dream - a wife.

Joe-Ryan adored the countryside; he missed it greatly to the point where it physically tore at his heart. England's countryside was nice, but nothing could beat the authentic, pure green of his homeland. England was simply a poor man's version. Coming back regularly kept his Granny C sweet, and gave the family - who all returned to

Ireland once their cautions had been lifted - the joy of mocking his London life, all secretly missing him when he left and glad when he came back.

Being green-fingered was something he fell into from knee high while helping his grandad rid the lawn of weeds and pests. He loved outdoor manual labour, and feeling natural with nature; he longed to open a wildlife rescue centre one day in the future. A man of the land, a modern-day Tarzan his sisters mocked, with his long hair and toned, pale body. He was a hit with the local ladies, Mother Nature being his personal trainer. His love of nature nicknamed him Tarzan in birthday cards, and he made sure they could read and write - which gave them added sexiness among the community. No bling could out-bling education. His sister Maureen used spelling out sexual favours as a form of foreplay.

He loved the fact that you could take an overgrown mess of a garden, and with dedicated hard work and sheer patience turn it into a space of beauty, accomplishment and pride. He became an intelligent force where nature was concerned. The clear blue skies above matched his eyes, and a flock of crows with feathers matching his hair called out in excited noise as they flew over. The corpse of a sheep would be their meal for a few days. The smell of cut grass lingered around him. The fresh smell was provoking memories and a homely feeling burrowing up through his nose, incensing into his mind like a tapeworm, but without the joy of a severe weight loss; all of this made him relax and think of his hectic, yet empty life in London.

London had kicked his head harder than any bully when he arrived. It mugged him of any memory of a slower pace of life, tossing his tranquil way of life into a stir fry. The internet pace left him with a constant stitch, where other Irish folk might say it was liver disease from drinking. It killed him to keep up in the beginning and Joe-Ryan was a fit man - his six pack wowed people every summer. A collective diversity of the world living in one place, where no minority suffered being outcast or prejudiced against was overwhelming and made him invisible. Everyone simply thought he was Irish, not a traveller. Work was plentiful and blessed him to be able to start to save, and send money home to his Granny C. The fact that everyone in London fed on their dreams and pushed themselves on with hope to achieve them was infectious, and his bite wound from the city was deep.

Joe-Ryan fell deep in love with chaotic London intensely, feeling like he was betraying his beloved home with his affair. Yet, this was the longest he had ever been faithful to a city. London - for the moment - became an affair; fresh, addictive, and catering to every kink that he wished or wanted to make up.

Five years had flown by without a care, and Joe-Ryan had luckily managed to get a steady job he enjoyed doing and buy a small flat in Hertfordshire. He needed to be near green grass and nature the way that a stressed pregnant woman on the tube needs a free seat. Compared to the latest hot clubs, raving restaurants and concrete parks in Central London, Hertfordshire was the complete contrast. A promiscuous sex life was frowned upon in his community, but luckily, London lacked community and stern morals and so Joe-Ryan got his five-a-day in a forbidden fruit kind of way. A hit with the women, his lush locks, dreamy accent and stable, hard body made his sex life easy pickings. Yet that was dissolving and becoming more of a chore, and with each strange bed he woke in, or boring date he paid for, gave distance enough for him to watch his dream of a wife drift away. To stop him living a life of commitment-free sex he needed to take the other steps in life - to marry and have children.

Finishing the last heap of cut grass, he tossed it onto the compost heap he sold locally to the gardens of the village for a few quid per bag. He parked up the rusty wheelbarrow, orange rust covering its metal body like eczema, decaying its body. It was trustworthy and embedded in his life from his earliest memory of being pushed in it like a pram, as Charlene, his older, bossy, baby-mad sister dressed him up as her doll. Now it longed to retire, its wheels thin and bearing thread as if it was starving, and reminding him of those working donkeys in India pushed to work until they eventually collapsed and died. He smiled and closed the shed door, returning to the annex that he had built for Granny C.

Granny C was traditional, and so Catholic that she was called on to perform exorcisms among the community - many evil spirits left just from her abusive swearing. Extremely popular among mothers who would threaten their wayward children with her name if they misbehaved, the children feared Granny C more than the bogeyman. Granny C liked comfort, showing off her good fortune from her years of psychic readings - so the three-bedroom annex with an en-suite and open fire would be a welcome relief from the common caravans, especially in the grips of wild winters where snowmen begged to be built indoors.

"Wipe ya shagging wellies before you come in here" you would hear Granny C say before you saw her or smelled her.

The smell was a mixture of incense joss sticks burning away all over the home, becoming a kind of laser protection system like what you see in spy films, twisting your body around them so as not to suffer a hot poke. Dead animal fur lazed around the home; most retiring grannies knitted as a hobby, but Granny C was far from retiring, a massive fan of taxidermy and her skills were par to none. One year she had sewed the head of a boar onto the body of a deer and added a pair of swan wings - she left it in the forest to scare the walkers. Local police cautioned her, and now it came out at Christmas as a terrifying alternative to Rudolph.

Joe-Ryan smiled; his favourite noise was that of his Granny C swearing. It has been the soundtrack to his childhood, and transitioning from his teenager years into manhood Joe-Ryan favourited 'fuck this' and 'fuck that'.

She swore without aggression or confrontation, and to look at her you would think that she lacked the energy to do anything but sleep. *"Here he is, the fucking Biblical son of a bastard."* His Granny C never hid her disgust in his father doing a runner and leaving her daughter with a number of offspring that would out-do a rabbit. Joe-Ryan entered into the warm living room heated by the log fire. It flickered with flames of different lengths and colours, and it reminded him of the girl's hair from the nursing home he had butted without fear of an injunction due to domestic violence. *I wonder how she's doing.* The question stayed put, placing a nice feeling in his head and planting a seed to fruit plenty of sweet daydreams, touching his eye which was now free of bruising. Something about that woman stayed with him long after the bruising had healed. She had an aura of calm and positivity; he felt like he could walk into it and be among a cloud, with her as the angel.

The weirdest thing that was unsettling him of a night was that normally his first thought would be how hot they would be in the bedroom together with her on his dick - but this was not the case with her. He simply wanted to protect her and wake up every morning to her face being in his life - not just his bed - the face being the sunshine to his day. He had heard fables of love at first sight; I mean, most Irish folksingers sang about love at first sight or of love lost. If Joe-Ryan had been a singer/songwriter he could have a smash hit on his hands based on what he was feeling towards the redhead.

Granny C's living room resembled a junk shop. Every available space was filled with something useful, but mostly useless. There were communal collections of amusement arcade games broken, with stuffed roadkill animals hanging on top waiting for a win. There was a huge pirate (from the front of a ship) of a woman with shells covering her breasts working a halo of Christmas lights, left out five years too late, and with her nose missing she had been nicknamed Jacko.

His Granny C's quirky and unique taste explained the working water fountain in the living room with real goldfish - his Granny C loved the sound of running water, and fobbed off the common joke of just letting the tap run. The ventriloquist doll sitting on top of a lampshade gave him the creeps still, while the head of a deer nailed to the wall chatted with a shelf full of mammal skulls.

Heavy, dominant floral curtains restricted the light into the square room so that it always felt like dusk. The small ray of sunshine breaking through the floral curtains made it look like it was the canopy of the rainforest, while a single moth was trying to bump and grind against the hot bulb. Despite the clutter, it was clean and felt like home.

Granny C was like a chameleon in this living room. She blended well into the surroundings in her thick, earth hued cardigans, and being the height of a garden gnome didn't help, so you always heard her before you saw her.

"Granny C" he called, tossing another cut log into the fire. Granny C liked it hot, and she told anyone who melted in this heat that it was preparation for when she went to live in hell. He didn't know where the 'C' came from; he faintly remembered that his absent father used to say it was for *crusty old cunt*. Everyone called her Granny C, even if they were of no relation.

"I'm fucking busy ya eejit" It sounded aggressive, but Granny C had one of those voices you could listen to all day. She sounded informative like David Attenborough, educated and posh like Joanna Lumley, and high pitched like Alan Carr.

"Sorry Granny C," he replied, taking a pew on an actual church pew with 'Jesus smokes wee' scratched into it next to him, the intended 'd' missing. A few moments of silence passed. The beaded curtain separating the living room from the dining room - Joe-Ryan planned to put the door on every month he visited - drew his attention and revealed human action through the thin smoke screen of eight burning incense sticks in jam jars. He was expecting the person behind to say, *'Tonight Matthew, I'm going to be...'*.

"Thanks you so much Granny C. I do hope it all comes true - it did last time." A large, Irish old lady walked through, the oval wooden beads beating her chubby face as if punishing her for eating, trying to smash her teeth and stop her from overeating.

"Joe-Ryan, I wish you would put this fucking door up! The bastard thing is a fucking torture merchant, beating poor Josie's face like a bloody drum." Granny C appeared from thin air. Although she was only four feet tall she demanded all the attention in the room among the nit bits of the wonderful, the curious and the complete crap. "Sorry Josie. Bloody lazy arse grandchild, I knew he'd be bone idle coming out the womb backwards, cursed with those fucking eyes of his father. He'd rather fucking stalk frogs to the safety of their pond than put up this wooden door for his old, frail Granny C!" kicking said wooden door, which was leaning against the wall.

"Watch how you go Josie dear. Remember to sleep with amber under ya bed and a knife. Karma will get that cheating scum bag, but if you get to him first the knife will be fucking handy. Love the new bob!" Josie left, heading down the small path wobbling like a pissed penguin, fifty quid lighter for her reading, but confident about her pending fourth divorce. Granny C stood at the door, and then closed the door, turning to Joe-Ryan.

"That fat bitch fucking bored the living Jesus out of me. I prayed that God would interfere and kill her, or me. Moreover, did you see that bob? It looked like she was wearing a fucking sixties helmet! That Chinese bob and that fat face is an awful combination." She enveloped her beautiful grandson in a hug. She only came up to his waist. He bent down two feet with the grace of a giraffe reaching for a watering hole, lending his cheek as she planted a dozen kisses. She smelled of lavender, and her thick, mustard coloured cardigan gave a peek showing of her navy blouse underneath through a hole in the shoulder.

She shuffled to her armchair - not due to aching bones, but to her shag pile which was so thick that it slowed you down. Joe-Ryan laughed; his Granny C was so two faced she was literally a coin. Yet she was adorable all over, and he literally thanked god that she was his Granny.

"How's that bloody garden looking? There were bloody potholes the size of a crater last weekend, I feared for me life hanging out me knickers." Picking up her cup of tea, the cold, thick skin formed on top broke as she pushed her thin lips in. Colder the tea the better, ignoring the black dog hair simmering on top like a pond skater, an escapee from Chip dipping his grey dip-dyed muzzle in.

"Those bastard kids you'd think they were at a fucking festival. You would think a flipping dinosaur buried underneath, the amount of soil they tossed. I've seen wild dogs dig with more grace than that scruffy riff raff." The thick skin fell into her mouth and she swallowed it. Joe-Ryan loved when Granny C went wild about her great-grandchildren - his nieces and nephews. She never held back.

"All filled in, grass cut, and the compost heap is looking impressive," stroking Chip the skeletal Yorkshire terrier, who was eating fresh chicken every day but never ever seemed to fill out. Eileen, his second eldest sister, was forever on a diet and forever jealous that the dog was skinnier than she was.

"Fucking compost heap looks impressive? What kind of bullshit is that? Is that London talk, grandson? 'Oh, my compost heap is looking impressive'," with a perfect mock cockney accent and slapping her bony knees with jest, her thick tights softening the blow. "Fucking impressive Jesus, I've heard it all now." She laughed husky and loud, winking at Joe-Ryan who felt like a whopper of an eejit using the word 'impressive', but laughed. A moment of peace sieved the soothing noise of the wood crackling in the fire and Chip's gentle snoring on his lap, encouraged by Joe-Ryan's stroking ability to relax him.

"Oh aye, forgot to tell you didn't I?" Placing the cup of arctic cold tea down on a log stump, she leaned forward. Granny C was famous in the family for forever forgetting to tell you something - forgetting to tell his Uncle Ronan who his real father was, that was one. Forgetting to tell Maureen down at the swimming club that she had put her costume on back to front, and poor Kian, her grandson, she had forgotten to tell him that the fence was electrified on one of their walks, letting the little eejit touch it.

"I'm going to your neck of the woods next week." She was looking forward to her little trip; it had been a while since she had been to a big city.

"My neck of the woods?" His bushy eyebrows lifted a confused inch, failing to figure out what the code word for neck of the woods meant. Staring at his Granny C, her snow-white hair was hidden under an Irish flag tea towel that she used as a headscarf. His Granny C, like most women in his family, was blessed to keep a good head of hair. It was Granny C's miracle that she had kept her hair - her skull had been ragged more times than a mop across a kitchen floor.

"Yeah you deaf twit. I'm going to London with your mammy. God fucking help me." She didn't give a fuck if she had given birth to Aoife in a cold stone stable with only a litre of homebrew cider to be used to wash the newborn down with after a twelve-hour labour in a thunderstorm. Aoife, her only daughter, was cursed with the pregnancy skill of house mice, and was a massive pain in the fucking arse. She always wondered if it had been wise *not* to give her away to the nunnery. Aoife would look fetching in a habit. Joe-Ryan felt a cold sweat descend over his pale skin, like a cloud passing the sun. The fact that his mother Aoife was coming blew it across.

Peaceful Palace

"Oh dear Mindy you ok?" A concerned, monotone male voice stirred Mindy from her black out. Feeling weak, she felt the softness of being on one of Eric's chesterfield chairs. The cool material cooling her hot head down, Eric was afraid that Mindy had suffered a head injury, hitting the floor and table like a clumsy baby chick just out of a nest kneeling beside her.

"What happened?" Mindy weakly whispered with uncertainly made a mental note to get her iron levels tested or to take to drinking a pint of Guinness a morning instead of her probiotic yogurt drink. Fainting was now taking over her life, though it was understandable based on the shocks she had received lately - like the one responsible for this fainting act.

Sitting in the chair opposite with a yellow tweed cape that added a few extra pounds was a woman, her blonde beehive making her head look small and her make-up vibrant - in the sense that Ru-Paul was her make-up artist. She looked like a giant lemon. Rubbing her eyes to bring enough focus to be able to do a double check, Mindy tried to remove anything alien in them that disfigured the sight she was seeing.

There, bold as brass and as alive as Elvis was rumoured to be, was Mabel. Well, it looked like Mabel, but she was more alive-looking, with her make-up done too and blonde.

"This is Madeline. Mabel's sister, twin sister." Eric was unsure if he believed what he was saying, his deep voice pitching at 'twin'. Madeline smiled. That morning Eric was convinced he had seen a ghost, but before she had called to see him, he had checked in on Mabel. She was flat out as dead as an openly gay footballer's career. Yet her sister...He knew that twins looked alike, identical - but her sister was a ringer.

The other factor playing on his mind was that he never ever knew, heard of, or had seen Mabel's sister. Yes, Saffron the older sister, but no twin. Mindy sat up, her head sore from a hangover adding concussion into the headache blender – she just wanted to lie in a dark room with a whiskey. What the hell was going on? Looking at the sister, the peach fragrance familiarly floated towards Mindy, encasing her with the sense that this was another part of the plan. Mabel or Madeline smiled coyly at Mindy, then bloody winked, which made Mindy's head blow up. *What the fuck!* Mindys head spun questioning. "My poor, deceased, fabulous, beautiful, generous, marvellous icon..." Mindy kicked Madeline/Mabel under the chair who was getting a wee bit carried away with the five-minute description of Mabel, her dead 'twin sister'.

"Sorry" pulling at her skirt "my sister would prefer to be cremated, please, closed casket, champagne reception, a band playing Cabaret, and a film playing of all her fabulous times, you know," the peroxide blonde dyed hair told a bemused Eric exactly, with the flare of someone who had organized a party plenty of times before. Eric was nodding as if his neck was suffering an earthquake, while her voice picked up pace with each new idea popping into her head. The only thing that was different with this lady was that she was not dripping in diamonds.

Now either Madeline, as herself, or Mabel playing Madeline, was here to sort out funeral arrangements as fast as possible. This could be due to the fact that she wanted her sister at peace, or it could be that the villa that Mabel had her eye on would be bought soon if she didn't hurry up and buy it.

"Ok, Miss...?" Eric scribbled down the random facts looking at the list - glitter, topless waiters, a white tiger and a pink coffin. Looking up at the lady and repeating his question, "Miss?" He had forgotten to be a gentleman asking her name for the records. Madeline/Mabel looked stunned; her shoulders jumped a foot high up her neck. Whoever she was, she had either forgotten her name, or did not know the second name of her character.

"Cookson. Never married did I. Huge lesbian I am." Her shoulders dropped, returning to their hunched position, either relieved for not slipping up, or relieved at remembering her own name. Mindy sat silently staring at Eric, lost with this crazy situation. Her eyebrows came to life as they wiggled about on her Botox-levelled forehead. Mindy did not know if Mabel was dead or alive, or on the other hand, if Madeline was her real sister, if Madeline was Mabel in disguise, if Madeline was real in on it the revenge for

Saffron. Madeline playing dead Mabel was so confusing, like British dress sizes. She could murder a vodka at the end of all this like she'd be in rehab for a drink problem; she couldn't wait.

Suddenly, Madeline stood shaking Eric's well-lived hand, the conversation carrying on as Mindy daydreamed about this extraordinary situation. The thought of being caught, flung in prison living with women who ate their husbands had Mindy all freaked out. Saved by Madeline's sudden movement, she returned to reality.

"Would you like to see Mabel?" Eric transformed back into the collected businessman that he was respected for, retrieving his waxed jacket from his swivel chair. Madeline stopped in her tracks.

"Sorry what did you say?" Her heart started to speed up.

"Would you like to see Mabel?" Eric understood elderly people could find it hard to hear, not realizing that this could blow Mabel's cover. Or could it be that the shock of seeing her twin sister dead would be too much for Madeline? Madeline/Mabel needed a diversion from this scenario. Just like her sister she needed a plan - and it had to be a good one.

"Eric - is that an encyclopaedia on the birds of the British Isles?!" She was impressed that she had pronounced the word on the book. She could be as thick as Saffron's make-up at times but it worked, and made enough of a distraction to allow an escape.

"Well Madeline." The dusty book was a favourite of Eric's. It was an old vintage collection, with real paintings of British birds - not the photoshopped images many books nowadays palmed you off with due to laziness. He was like a little boy on Christmas Day when Madeline showed an interest, excited to relive the joy of reading through this book. Mindy helped him get the book off the shelf; his back was still not fully fixed from his falling out of a tree. *'Glimpse of a woodpecker'* on his A&E forms made the nurse on duty chuckle, and Eric blush.

Red-faced and straining under the mini ton of paper, the pair managed to thump it down on the desk as a cloud of dust blew out. Facing Madeline to be met with an open door and the fragrance of cut peaches teasing the stuffy office air, the split-personality lady had vanished.

Mindy knew that she was in with a chance of catching 'dead' Mabel in the act of still being Madeline, and it would help her to make sense of all this. Mabel would have to get changed, change her hair, wipe her make-up off, climb back on the cold table, as well as trying to make her breathing slow down. Making excuses to Eric, his face was etched with sadness at being unable to show Madeline a painted picture of a puffin. Calmly leaving the office in silence, she dashed down the dainty corridor with the speed of a burglar being chased by police, ignoring the rule of no running, pushing through the studio door and nearly taking it down as it flung open.

Greeted with silence, there was not a creak, not a peep, and not even the squeak of a mouse - only Mindy's unfit body made noise as she tried to catch her breath back. The studio was lifeless. There wasn't an ounce of anything that would make a noise; it was spotless, so sanitized it stung the eyes. Not a thing moved out of place, nor had been touched. Her make-up mountain was still in one piece, with no foundation or powder on the floor, no brush in the wrong holder, no scent of any hairspray laid out on the table. The biggest clue was that nothing had changed in this clean-freak scene and no evidence of anything strange or out of place on the table gave anything away.

A lump formed under the cloth making not even a microscopic movement, and no breathing underneath to raise the emaciated fabric solid evidence someone was underneath, dead. Surely the noise Mindy created bashing through the door like a wrecking ball would have shocked Mabel into movement? Mabel would have stirred if she was alive, Mindy pondered in her aching head, in the tiny space not affected by her hangover-induced migraine. The body laid there exactly as it had been left, like a sack of rubbish that no foxes had investigated. Mabel must have passed over, her last breath taken alone, unable to see the falling of Saffron. Saddened by the thought, Mindy was drawn to the body, peeling back the lightweight cover and revealing Mabel. Her cold body had aged with years of good partying, and it was etched on her face. Looking at peace with the present, unfortunately the past had escaped without any comfort. Maybe this was for the best in case Saffron survived the whole ordeal and her status remained unaffected at all, with Mabel's name being blackened even more.

Looking at the face of the family friend she had loved, now missed forever like Bessie - her dog friend from childhood, Bessie the rabbit, and Bessie the snail. At that age Mindy's favourite name was Bessie; she blamed the Yorkshire puddings that Poppy fed her daily, to the point where she would tell her school friends that the fat lady on the packaging was her aunt. Mindy started to drip tears. One day she would be here looking at her own mother, the thought so strong that it pushed through the hangover, the guilt for not going to Zumba, and the guilt for not starting the novel or returning her Avon form. It was powerful, blowing anything in its path away like a leaf blower in autumn.

Working with the dead had helped her to build a defence mechanism to deal with death in a positive way, and not be affected by the negative. The thought of her mother leaving her for a better world was something closed up in the back of her mind, along with stealing a KitKat when she was eight from the corner shop and a snog with a girl on a hen night in Amsterdam. It pushed right to the front, like police kicking the door open and pouring in, taking full advantage of Mindy's tired, emotional frame of mind at that moment.

Deep down she had prepared for the loss and had subconsciously started to pack all her memories up, and ideas for funeral preparations took place in her head. Seeing Mabel lying on the table, the shell of her lifeless body that had inhabited her soul left behind like luggage at an airport let her grieve for the terrible waste of life that death brings. Wiping sad tears away and pulling herself together, she collected herself before she broke. Mindy knew it was time to say her unwanted goodbyes to Mabel for the last time, hopefully bringing her justice and clearance to her name, and give Mindy time to go to rehab. Leaning down she stroked her head and felt the frostbite etched onto her brain - the cold, sure sign of death.

"Goodbye old friend, sleep tight." Mindy lowered to kiss her forehead, and the smell of peaches fluttered away like butterflies with her kiss long and full of love. She returned to standing, looking down. She stared at her face intensely; she wanted to take in every detail while she stood staring, the room draping silence on her shoulders for comfort.

"BOOOOOOOOOOOOOOOOO!"

Mindy roared, the bottom pit of her stomach filled with fright, cracking a few of the eggs in her ovaries as she jumped into the air at the scream of the dead corpse as it rose up, knocking over her make-up tray as she fell backwards. Her scream was of the purest fright that a soul could create; Mindy feared that a white streak of hair had appeared both on her head and on her fanny.

Never in all her life had she been so scared, not even the first time she had lost her virginity - fortunately his name had been Bernard, not Bessie. Collapsing to the floor like a demolished building was inspired to fall as well, colourful tubs of pots rained down and she screamed again as they littered around her, spilling colour and mess all over the Cinderella-scrubbed and polished floor.

Mabel sat up with droplets of laughter leaking down her famous face in danger of drowning her.

"I always wanted to do that." She was referring to the sight of Mindy falling on the floor; legs sprawled out like a new born deer on ice. God the girl could scream, making Mabel find the whole trick even more hilarious. Poor Mindy's heart needed rebooting before it failed her. Mabel sat up on the table bent over in joy at the successful scare.

Mindy had forgotten how she loved to play wind-ups on people - like the time she had dressed up as a man, pretending to be Poppy's new boyfriend to a thirteen-year-old, gullible Mindy. You would think that the batty old bird would take in the circumstances, the environment and the stress that Mindy was going through. Mindy burst out crying. She didn't know if it was due to the fact that she had pissed herself, or that Mabel was alive, or a ghost, or if it was looking at the mess of make-up.

"You bloody crazy old bat! How the hell is that funny? You gave me a heart attack. I could have been on that table next you!" Mindy regained her breathing, and the serious tone told Mabel that she was not impressed as she wiped away tears and snot.

"Chill lax! Or whatever they say on Twatter," she said, getting the social media site's name wrong. Mabel preferred to write letters of thanks rather than tag.

"God, a girl's got to make her own fun round here. Not exactly buzzing with life is it?" Mabel knew that it had been cruel to play that frightening trick. She loved pranks and wind-ups, and she had always been a practical joker. It had been so hard to avoid - it's not every day that you can jump up from playing dead. Mindy's reaction was priceless; it been worth the wait. Mabel knew that it would be the highlight of her stay here. Oh, and having her make-up done by the award-winning Mindy. Her final act was to get Mindy to agree to fly to New York. Mabel knew that Mindy would find it extremely hard to take time off from work. She put more hours in than Hitler. Leaving her mother added pressure. Convincing Mindy to fly to New York was going to be hard, to find the ring made from Ballet Foot even harder. Mabel's last act was going to be the hardest; she needed to pull out all her acting stops for this.

Los Angeles

Working the seedy streets and strip clubs of the infamous strip was not what Sally had imagined she would be doing when aged seven and Miss Cause had asked what she would like to be when she grew up in Kindergarten. Ok, so writing *'a Princess'* in purple crayon certainly was far off, seeing as she was yet to meet an actual Prince - but playboys were plentiful. Engaging in sexual acts for cut price money with horny bastard men in cars, cheap hotels or shady corners of alleyways was not the career she had thought that she would end up in or excel at.

Sally was one of the most popular whores on the strip. Deep-throating a local legend, and an honour for would-be eighteen-year-old virgins to lose their mighty V to, it was easy money for Sally. *You're Not a Real Man Until Sally's Sucked You Off* had been sprayed inside the subway tunnel by a graffiti artist in honour of her blow jobs. She could take a cock in every orifice in her body and still paint her nails without a smudge.

She was a rare one. She had never been hooked on hard-core drugs or lost her personal hygiene. Her hair roots were never on show, her nails were painted, she was clean, and regular facials - both sperm and salon - kept her skin healthy. But drink, she liked. If you lived in Los Angles then a drink problem was the norm, either if that was alcoholic or celebrity juicing. Due to resisting hard drugs she had managed to drag her pretty looks out longer, giving regular fucks to her personal trainer, a failed actor born too late to rely on his Adonis body to cover his wooden acting...Arnie had already taken that role. She worked a healthy L.A lean, sun-kissed body. Her long, tanned limbs and a slender stomach curved in all the correct places. She looked athletic, with just enough rib bones on show for people to maybe question if she was a sports model. She was average height and had blonde hair down to her mid back that hid her profession as a prostitute well, and tulip-pointed lips that opened wide into a friendly smile.

Sally was at the local grocery store on the corner of her street picking up some diet cola, chorizo and a can of tuna for Pepe, her

Siamese cat. Cats were independent, survivors and care-free, just like Sally. Sally walked the sunny ten minutes back to her small studio, ignoring the beeps of approval from passing cars driven by men and the jealous stares from women lunching outside the bistro on the main street - their salads bought without sucking cock, yet these women lived off their husbands, just as Sally did. Who was worse, the hooker or the housewife?

Sally was independent. Sally walked on, ignoring the fact that walking to the shop in a neon-yellow bikini was an everyday sighting in L.A. Yes, men and women stared at her cute arse, yet the stares were not anything to do with the bikini or her pert arse today. Her cute arse was on a break, and her face was the real reason for the prolonged stares. What had happened?

Sally closed the thin door of her home behind her using her long legs, shutting out the afternoon heat from the Californian hot sun as she headed into her tiny, air conditioned flat. The stench of cat piss days old choked the air with the dangers of chloroform. Flies took a pilgrimage to her poxy flat as if it was food aid, but even they couldn't handle the smell.

She tossed the groceries onto the spare available space amongst the dirty dishes and empty bottles of vodka, slumped between the dozen ashtrays complete with the Olympic endurance of holding the most dirty cigarette stubs. A weak eighties born fan circulated above, recycling stale air, spewing it out, disgusted that the pungent smell coated its wooden fans of beauty. The thing was, Sally held personal hygiene very highly, had regular dental check-ups, attended the sexual health clinic each month, had weekly beauty visits, but lacked it within her small home. This obsession stemmed from her moving around many times as a child, never staying long enough for a mop bucket to become more than just a pretend helmet to fight her younger stepbrother. She would go to sleep in one state, and wake in another. You could shout out zip codes from all over America like bingo numbers and Sally would be able to name which city and state it was without pausing to think - it was a nick knack talent to have.

Her Daddy, a major crime lord, kept on his size eleven feet all his life from haters, the Feds and rivals, kept his only daughter safe through his midnight migrations across America. Her father doted on her. She was the only precious thing in his life, until shot point blank in his head on this very porch two days after she had moved in six years ago. The thump from his dead body echoed throughout the street. The blood looked like an abstract painting across the whole flat that day covering all four walls, painted by a shotgun, with membrane and parts of his head fused into the floorboards. It was a horror scene, and once the investigator had left, Sally was forced to sleep among the smell of her daddy's blood.

Sally, from that dreadful day, had never picked up a washing cloth, mop or brush. The killer never found, so he must have left DNA. This nightmare nagged at her every night. She read about cold cases being re-opened all the time, and she longed for the day her Daddy's did - so she refused to clean just in case she washed away any evidence to nail the son of a bitch who killed him. The saddest part was that Sally shared the same DNA as his killer...she often wondered where Regan, her stepbrother was; she missed him terribly.

Pepe jumped up onto the table waving his sleek tail for attention, pleading for food, knowing that the best tuna the shop offered was going to be his brunch. Pepe did not do normal cat food. Tinned cat food was for the common alley cats of the neighbourhood, and he was a pure breed and prize winner. Pepe was forced to suffer agoraphobia. The poor cat didn't know what outside was, never felt grass beneath his paws, or had the pleasure of killing a mouse to bring as a gift for her. Fresh air blew teasingly on his oval face through a small vent. It was Sally's way of being certain that Pepe stayed, not leaving her like most people she had loved in her life had - for some reason, people always left her. Sally emptied the oily fish into the only clean bowl in the flat, humming a popular TV tune. Her sweet humming hypnotised Pepe as he purred in the duet. Sally sat on a beanbag and opened the local paper, which would not be used as cat litter but was tossed aside to join the neglected mass of newspapers and crime magazines yellowing and decaying in the flat. There, on the second page, was a man who deserved to have his head spread all over the walls with a shotgun. His cheesy grin made her sun-kissed skin prick with heated irritation and the desire for revenge.

She sparked up a cigarette and poured a large straight vodka into a mug. Both vices helped with the sickness on seeing his fucking smug, famous face. Chad Rise was grinning from ear to ear, chuffed that he had been announced as the new star in *Cop Gone Bad* - he was the reason she was plotting revenge with each pull on the cigarette. Bruce Willis was on one side aging well. He was an actor whose looks and acting got better with age, she thought. Victoria's Secret supermodel, fiery Kitten Minx stood angelic looking on the other side in her first feature film. A slit in her dress showed the lucrative length of her famous black legs. She knew that they had probably already fucked hard. Chad Rise was irresistible, handsome and ripped, remembering his massive cock and cut muscles. A drop of jealousy watered her vengeful roots. Kitten Minx was a slut.

Sally read the small paragraph accompanying the glossy picture. She pulled on the cigarette with annoyance on reading how well Chad was doing since the hotel fire incident. She reached for the small pot of Aloe Vera gel, twisted the plastic lid off, and scooped the cool gel onto her fingers. She prayed that it worked, costing at least two dick sucks. She read on, hearing how Chad Rise and his beautiful fiancée Maria were set to live in New York when filming started. Sally massaged the gel onto the side of her face that had gotten the diners asking her what had happened. With each smug picture of Chad Rise, she rubbed it in firmer and harder. How that cunt had survived the fire, then gone on to land the biggest gig of his career was some kind of cruel joke, or a fucking demonic gift. '*Time for payback, sweetheart,*' her father's voice spoke as if he was coming through the front door, as if he had just been to the shops and not dead for several years. She shot her head up, greeted only by the empty front door and the mob of flies trying to get out. All in her head still and from beyond the grave, he was looking out for his baby girl.

Sally rubbed a little too hard for her tender scars on her burnt face for it to heal properly. Chad Rise might be about to start his new life, but Sally wanted revenge for the fact that Chad Rise was the reason why people stared in shock at the side of her face, hiding beneath her hair. Scarred, burnt like melting plastic and disfigured, on the whole side only half an ear remained. Chad was about to have his career disfigured as Sally stubbed out her cigarette onto his handsome face.

"Time for a little vacation," she told Pepe, who was staring with his amber oval eyes from by the sink. New York was the unlucky destination.

Peaceful Palace

"You missed it this morning Mindy." The tone in Maud's voice told Mindy with great glee that Maud was knowledgeable about something that Mindy was in the cold on.

"Oh right what's that?" Mindy placed down the bunch of sunflowers which were this time sprayed pink; a funky, creative symbol to celebrate their fundraising for Cancer Research. She was not really interested in whether Maud had groped the postman, again.

"Yeah, it's all happening today." Maud looked like the cat that got the cream - cream cakes, that was. Mindy was not bothered about playing games this morning. She had not slept her full eight hours since the whole Mabel/Madeline incident. So, being behind on sleep and stressed about having to become a criminal to jail one, she was still thinking of that Irish hunk, and him devouring her in her sleep like a cannibal was another welcome factor in her abnormal sleep pattern.

Mindy silently displayed the sunflowers in the vase on the desk. Maud's tiny eyes were burnt bare into Mindy's back, fuming that the gossip she had over Mindy was not interesting her at all. Mindy heard Maud's strong smoker's cough, which if you did not know it was Maud, you might have thought that a man was the owner of it.

"Sorry Maud" she paused fed up at this routine of rudeness from the receptionist "would you like a cup of tea?" Mindy knew very well Maud was hinting and waiting to be asked, but she refused to. If Maud had something to say, she should just say it instead of using it to gain control and power. Maud refused to answer her about the tea, and her twitching from holding on to the information was starting to build up to a dangerous level. If she did not spill soon, her coroner's report might read *spontaneous combustion* and there would be a huge fleshy mess left for the cleaner.

"Two sugars." Missing an opportunity for a free cup of tea was like missing a free smear test for a woman whose fanny had not felt the touch of a hand for decades or seen a face. It was not on Maud's agenda this morning. "Anyway, have I got news for you? Sit." Maud grabbed Mindy's arm, ignoring how the slenderness of her arm highlighted how big her arms really were. Both sat down on the floral couch.

"So, I came in this morning, a little worse for the wear from another date," chuffed as she told Mindy - another point scored on the imaginary scoreboard that she mentally kept. Mindy shuddered at the vision of her make-up last time, and twirled the beading on one of the cushions in her fingers. "Anyway, I was a little early. You know me, like to get in, go that extra mile," she said smiling, as Mindy thought to herself that Maud could do with walking an extra mile. "Well, doing me daily routine checks." *Routinely nosing around, you mean* - Mindy bit her lip before she could say it. "So, I went into the toilet and there in the waste bin was a bag. Didn't think anything of it, until I noticed a yellow-looking thing like a shrug you get down Shepard's bush market. Well, you know these recent terror attacks - was not taking any chances." *Because planning a terrorist attack at a quiet funeral parlour already full of dead people does seem to be quite the ideal spot to attack...*Mindy yet again bit her beautiful lip to stop her from saying this. "So, I got the bag out and looked through it. Well, the shrug."

"Was that the explosive one?" The resistance got the better of Mindy as she interrupted Maud. If looks could kill, Mindy would be on that cold table with Maud doing her make-up.

"No, actually, it was a wig. Like a bob but with more height, a suit, and a pair of low heeled cheap looking things" Mindy's heart stopped. Was that not Madeline, Mabel's twin sister? Maud was delighted by Mindy's shocked face and knew that she was thinking the same as her - she found the inch and took it to a mile. "I know, I was shocked too but not surprised. I mean, being alone you must need something to spice ya life up."

"Maud, I enjoy being alone if that was a hint at me?" Mindy felt defensive towards the crude comment from the lump of lard of a woman who was speaking a tiny bit of truth.

"Not you, Eric! He's a cross-dresser. Totally understand now why he's so interested in where I shop. Our boss is a tranny," slurping her tea she smirked from her eyes, knowing she had the ultimate gossip, and the inventor of the word tranny. It would be easy to twist this to her benefit, which was normally called blackmail. Maud had already chosen a gorgeous blue leather bag from the catalogue to buy with her forced pay rise.

"Eric? A cross-dresser? I don't see that Maud." Mindy spoke slowly, unsure, looking at Maud's smug smile not knowing what to say.

"So he's like a perv or something." The slurp of Maud drinking her hot tea echoed loud and menacingly. Eric was far from a cross-dresser and a perv. Knowing Maud, she would probably tell all the remaining staff this. Gloating about their cross-dressing boss was something that kind Eric could do without, but that would be the rumour that Maud was to spread.

"Maud, I doubt they're Eric's." Maud cut in with a childish immature giggle. "I know Eric's not a cross-dresser!" Mindy continued.

"You would say that, kiss arse. Mindy, you're so wet," Maud said with a digestive in her mouth, which was in danger of soaking Mindy as she spat crumb spittle like bullets as she spoke. Mindy was hurt at this outlandish comment. Mindy felt attacked for being a good worker, a kind person, and a woman who saw the good in people - and recycled. Mindy, unlike Alex, would take the remark like a vitamin each morning. Mindy didn't like confrontation, and she was starting to feel like she would clam up. Maud chewed away at her second biscuit, crumbs falling towards the floor like confetti over her findings on Eric, only they never got that far as they hit her wide cleavage, mimicking seabirds jumping from sea cliffs.

"For your information, Maud, the clothes you found belong to someone else." Mindy's feeble comeback embarrassed her immensely, despite it being true. Why could she not be like her mother who would just knock Maud down to the floor with a chair? She should stand up for herself a little more, and maybe even pepper spray Maud. A strange sense came over Mindy, and she felt that if she did not stand up for herself she was letting her mother down. "Well I would, erm, rather, erm, rather kiss his arse than your arse! Looking at the size of it, it would kiss me back." Not seeing Maud's face reddened with rage, she fled before Maud could eat her.

Twisting her ankle as she sped away could not dampen the proud feeling that she felt inside. Just to be on the safe side Mindy bolted her studio door behind her, suddenly bursting out laughing with bravery - and fear that Maud would be waiting for her after work like schoolchildren did for their school fights. Wow, it felt good to shout Maud down, as she texted Alex to tell her what had happened. She now understood Poppy's high when she won over the corrupted on behalf of the weak.

*

Maud couldn't believe that meek, little Mindy had grown the big balls to say her arse was fat. It was cuddly, maybe. But fat, gosh no! *Was it?* Sat behind her unorganised desk among unopened letters, thank you cards and at least two tins of chocolates open, gobsmacked, she crammed chocolate into her mouth to choke back the uninvited tears. Maud forgot the remark quickly as she pulled out a chocolate the size of her computer keyboard; many skinny bitches hated her curvaceous, womanly body. Even her diabetes had failed to make her adopt a healthier diet. Her grey-black cardigan sleeve, bitty from too many wears and washes, wiped away the spill of tea from her chin - her second one. Food had always comforted her like a hug from a loved one. Reliable, comforting and always available was Maud's stash of junk food. The rock sized chunk of chocolate was melting over Mindy's misjudged mistake about the size of her arse, and brought her counterfeit happiness. Mindy and her short fringe could fuck off; Maud celebrated by chucking another chunk of chocolate in her mouth.

Logging on to the computer, her heart started to flutter away without the grace of a butterfly, but a beetle - and just as black, riding Mindy's rude comment bareback. Lately, each time she logged on she felt tension with the thrill of the unknown, of what was - or more importantly, who was - waiting for her, lighting her up. The cheap nylon blouse restricted any air between the material and body, and with the hot weather and the air-conditioning down, it made Maud a little hot. A familiar, welcome page popped on the screen with the effect of a happy pill, and Maud silently cheered. The tacky icon flicked a glittering love heart. She placed the arrow cursor on it and clicked on the glowing *enter* button. *Single2 Mingle* was her favourite dating site of the five where she was a member. This site was yet to send her a warning email for over-threatening and borderline stalking messaging. Joining this site was a drunken night casualty after another failed single ad's meet in the local standard, circling enough potential boyfriends that her pen ran out.

Why she was still single, looking at her Boy George inspired make-up, was beyond her. Un-dateable how? This was something she wondered daily. However, she was not a quitter. Well, apart from dropping out of *Weight Woes* slimming club, *Banish the Blubber* boot camp and *Skinny Sarah's Aerobics*; she would find her puff pastry prince if it killed her.

A profile popped up with a ping like a comedy cockerel, as the profile picture lifted Maud's mood up until it hit the cloud white ceiling. The dating site encouraged meets based on personality, shared interests and hobbies, matching you to a potential profile. A picture was not required but it would help to attract more potential dates if it had one. Maud had tried to take a photo - ignoring a comment that she looked like Rose West when she had asked Earl to take a picture on her phone - but couldn't find a way to place a photograph on her profile, not knowing that uploading in pixel form was the way, and not to post as a negative. She felt like it was her birthday every time she logged on, waiting to see what was inside her surprise present - but this present was in inbox form. '*You have three new messages*' the highlighted icon flashed excitedly. This made Maud scream with delirious delight. Lately she had been cyber-chatting with one guy who made her feel like the only user on the site, made her forget about all the other messages she had received, including the rare nice ones, the weird ones, and the warning ones stating she'd be blocked if she messaged them again. Fixing her hair as if she was meeting this guy in person - not cyber space - she spritzed her neck with her lavender scent. She wanted to ask Mindy what the perfume was that she had let her use, but decided against it knowing that she would never be able to afford it. Hand sanitizer was extremely cheap, Mindy would have told her.

There nestled between a '*you've been blocked*' message and an admin message about her membership needing renewing, was the prized envelope waiting to be opened, Boredcockerl1. She smiled a genuine smile that had been vacant for years, last seen when she was seven when she had been given a rabbit by her beloved, now deceased grandfather. Maud clicked on the message, the 207th one that month since they had begun chatting and typing away to each other.

"Hello MysteryM, how have you been? Missed our chatting recently, work crazy busy! Cannot tell as I would have to kill you! Cock a doodle do x x" Oh my God, he had put a kiss. Not just one kiss, but two! Maud was beside herself with glee. Ok, she vaguely realised that they were not real ones, but it was still a sign that their relationship had stepped up and affection was being shown. Maud's fat fingers tapped back shakily with speed, *"I have been good thank you! Sorry for late reply-"* checking and seeing that his message was sent two days ago after midnight. *"I had a random day off so had no computer access,"* with a sad face symbol, to show she was sad she had missed him. *"How have you been? M* x" Asking how he had been left her email open for a reply. Plus, her one kiss felt more personal than the two he had sent. Hitting send, it was sent, followed by the winking icon wishing her luck and showing that it had been delivered.

"What's that you on Maud?" said a man's voice she recognized as belonging to the man that paid her wage.

"Erica mean Eric" flustered by the surprise of him standing there. Her skin pinked slightly, automatically closing the tab of the dating site down fast. Eric, with his aging hair and thick glasses enlarging his blue eyes, smiled his polite smile. She noticed how handsome - in a cuddly way - his face was when he smiled.

"You internet shopping again? I must be paying you too much" he sweetly chuckled loudly to himself. He did not really know how to speak to Maud. She came across too unfiltered and bossy, so he asked about her shopping habits mainly to keep it safe; most women loved to talk about fashion in his experience. Today's make-up was bold and black; it was well-suited within the funeral parlour. Maud was a lady who piled make-up on with a shovel, completely the opposite of his late wife's *less is more* method. Still, Maud was always smart, presentable at work, and loyal to turning up. Eric, being a gentleman, gave a compliment when one was due - a good rule for any boss to promote a feel good attitude among his staff.

"Like your make-up today, Maud." Picking up the small pile of letters for him, he paused to check through them. Maud felt her cheeks heat up. She had never told anyone about her internet dating hobby - or obsession, to anyone who found out. No one would understand it, preferring to think that she was sad, desperate and friendless. Each home truth slapped her harder than the one before. She managed to toss the feeling in the mental bin inside her head, along with the diet. Wearing a size too small skirt, the pinch of the waist band brought her back and retrieved the tears making their way to her eyes.

"Something like that. Would you like me to find you a dress?" she asked, remembering Eric's cotton evidence of his cross-dressing secret. Maud was uneducated with transgender issues and thought to become a great supporter of the unfortunate and the freaky. She was planning on telling BoredCocker11! all about her cross-dressing boss if they went on a date. The question of '*if*' boomed around in the silence of her mind.

"I doubt I have the legs for a dress Maud. But thank you anyway, very kind of you to offer." Eric, being forever polite walked off puzzled by Maud's fashion offer, but not before he noticed how pretty her eyes were beneath the black and white bricklaying of her make-up.

Canary Wharf

She was pacing her ventilated skyscraper office the way a lioness does its grassy territory searching for weak prey. She liked the chill of the office; for a person entering it was a warning sign, like a head on a spear, cold metal piercing deadly into you. The heel on her designer shoes was in danger of filing down, turning into a designer flip-flop. She untied her shiny hair from its face-lift inducing ponytail. Her face relaxed as her argan oil drinking hair flowed down, shimmering under the ceiling light. This Mabel case was a tough one. There was zero evidence apart from a dead woman's confession, who when alive had more visits to rehab than Alex had facials - so it was not a solid block to build from.

Cold hard evidence was needed to start gaining the strength to take down Saffron; it would be a modern day tale of David and Goliath, both fabulously dressed, and was what Alex needed. Taking a seat in her plush, cold leather swivel chair, she kicked off her shoes under the chunky desk. Stretching out her perfectly painted roasted red toes, they clicked with the new found freedom from the torturous triangle-toed Louboutins; she half expected to land in Munchkin Land.

Looking out from the wall of windows she noticed the top of the city she adored and called home. Below the smog of pollution, people weaved among the buildings like water through the hills. She sighed. She loved being a tough-ass solicitor, and this was the case she needed to go from small time ass-kicking, to kicking ass into next week. But how was she going to get it started?

The picture of her and Troy caught her eye, and she immediately reacted with a love-filled smile. His handsome face resting on her head as she leaned on his strong shoulder, he was the most important possession in her life. It had been taken in Thailand as they trekked through on an adventure holiday, capturing the love between the two of them. She remembered going through three pairs of stilettos on that mountain climb - Alex didn't do flats - and Troy shitting his kecks after catching a bug. The sunny memory hugged her heart tightly. She stroked the picture with the softness of a kiss on a newborn head; she would kill for this man. Another reason to get this case going was so that she could buy a plot for Troy to open his own bistro. The guy was a whizz in the kitchen, as well as in other rooms, remembering the hot, quick sex this morning as her smoothie blender whizzed with excitement. The fast, deep sex, orgasmic on the smooth island top beat any yoga position. A knock on the glass door engraved with Alex's name stopped her lust from rising and calling Troy for bit of phone fun.

Debbie the temporary worker was holding some brown files close to her inflated chest like poker card, looking smug did she have a straight flush? She entered the plush office before Alex motioned for her to enter. Debbie pushed the door with her large chest, and her skirt - or belt, Alex didn't know what to call the flimsy PVC material covering her lady bits - rose up the only spare inch it could. The tiny skirt was totally wasted on Alex, but not the males of the office, knowing very well that Karim the financial accountant wanked in the toilet during most dinner breaks. The office cleaner rudely asked Alex if she was eating the toilet tissue for her eating disorder, as she replaced it numerous times a day.

"Here are the files on the Arthur vs. Arthur case," she said, approaching the large desk with the walk of a lioness in heat - only this lioness wasted no time in waiting for a mating male to come to her. She was curvy, with the secret help of a waist trainer, a coke habit and a carb-ban stricter than France's ban on the burka. She wore a thin white blouse with three buttons undone, too low to be respectful and more see-through than a jellyfish. She had yellow home-dyed hair cut to shoulder length, with a few feathered layers gently hiding her average face which added the hint of a salon job. Her mascara was thick and shadowed the ruthlessness Debbie had seen in her life. Her plump lips were glossed with venom, but Alex was no fool.

Alex declined to smile. Noticing how Debbie thought she was someone in this firm unnerved her for a reason she couldn't place. She had worked big balls as only a temp for three months, only employed until Joseph from tribunals was due to come back as a Julie. She was always sashaying her way through the office as if she was the head cheerleader in an American high school - not expensive London tower buildings. Her heels high, her skirt higher, and her confidence blew smoke from the roof. The other females disliked her enormously, and it wasn't due to the fact that she was young, or had tits like balloons or legs like Tina Turner. She was rude, sneaky and so disrespectful that it overpowered whatever perfume sample she was wearing that morning. Debbie gave the impression that she wiped her arse weekly on the girl code. The male colleagues liked her enormously, the way wolves love howling or brothel madams love a light bulb sale. With her blow-up chest, tiny waist, short, choppy mixture of blond bob and swollen blow job lips so big that you could advertise billboards. She was the image of a cheap American porn star. Today her red lips were wet-looking as if Debbie had just sucked the blood from a dying man two shades too deep for a professional law firm. Alex agreed to herself that she was pretty - anyone with eyes in their head could see - but in a hooker-looking way; a cheap one with an obsession for the more make-up the better.

"Thanks," not looking up as a sure sign that they didn't have to interact, yet keeping it professional. Alex flicked through the notes on a case between neighbours and their garden fence; garden fences were in the top ten reasons for a case. The smell of a cosmetic catalogue's perfume tapped Alex on her nose, telling her that Debbie, unwelcome like a bad smell, was present.

"Can I help you Debbie?" She nearly jumped out of her luxury leather chair to rip Debbie's head off and throw it out of the high rise window. The reason for this violent thought to end Debbie's life was that Debbie was holding the picture frame in her hands of her and Troy. This little action fired up Alex like a rocket launching; she clenched her fists under the table and counted to ten in her head in English, French and Arabic.

"No" Debbie pouted, replacing the frame down slowly and raising her bright eyes to line up with Alex's stare. If both females had been dogs, then a vicious fight to the death would have commenced.

Who would come out on top? Both matched well. Debbie changed her blow-up red pout into a small smile, and turning, she poured out of the sleek office like a lethal gas leak. Alex felt a warning chill cover her body, and it was not because the air conditioning had kicked into full power.

"MINDY! OVER HERE! HERE, OVER HERE! OI!" A straw hat the size of a satellite shaded the almighty voice pounding from underneath. An aged hand acted like an antenna waving above. The whole gathering of elderly folk in the common room looked over.

Mindy reddened at the attention, dodging elderly folks who seemed to be on a stand still mid movement this visit. The chess pieces of chairs dotted across like wooden land mines made Mindy weave in-between, stepping over Alfred as he mimicked a seal on the floor. A sleep deprived nurse hit the alarm button; he was having a fit.

"Saved you a chair" pulling her flowery wedges off the common green coloured chair.

"Thanks Mum" kissing the soft cheek which was shaded by the oversized hat. Mindy did not comment that the hat was not needed indoors. The chaos of Alfred's fit as a dozen purple rinsed residents all insisted on helping, even though the nurse was quite able and qualified to do so, gathered ringside seats as all the other residents sat and watched like it was an afternoon play. A dozen residents flocked to Alfred like pigeons on a pasty, but something stabbed her heart distracting her away from the drama of the frail bodies, all now tripping over each other landing on top of poor Alfred like an adult game of pile-on. The straw hat was sadly a giveaway that today may not be a good visit.

"How are you dear?" Poppy pecked her daughter on her cheek. The softness of Mindy's skin provoked memories of Mindy's soft skin as a child. The fresh smell of white lilies made Poppy smile. Having a daughter like Mindy was the biggest achievement in her life; it gave her immense pleasure, like rich, low fat chocolate to a dieter. Poppy knew that she was ill. Not physical, but mentally. Some days it was distant and stayed away as if it owed you money. Poppy described her illness as a boomerang you could throw it away, but like fucking garden weeds, it always came back.

She passed over a cool glass of lemonade, with a chunky slice of lemon floating like a lilo in the cool refreshment. "Homemade. Home in more ways than one" she winked a colourful wink.

"Thank you," Mindy said as she took the glass from her crazy mother, confused by more ways than one. Her dash through the grounds had worked up a thirst inside her, last seen when she had sprinted to catch an Elizabeth Taylor film at the open-air cinema showing in Victoria Park. The fuel - the real reason for her quick dash - was that she didn't want to risk bumping into the handsome gardener that after meeting Mindy had left with the reminder of a black eye. Mindy, for most nights since, had dreamed of him in a variety of sexy scenarios and stages of undress, including a pint of Guinness as fancy dress. She was hoping that his cock was like the one she dreamt. This week, reminders of Ireland appeared everywhere. On the tube she had sat next to a hen party from Dublin. She had received an email for speed dating for next year on Paddy's Day, and had come across a lone potato in the supermarket as Boyzone's *Love Me for a Reason* blurred on the in-store radio. The encounter had left her bruised with the possibility that it was a sign from somewhere, or someone, to move on, and for her to open her heart to the wonders of love. It had been such a long time since 'Him' had betrayed her. She had simply packed her ruined heart onto a first class express train, evacuee style, and sent it to live with her strict, more rational, take-no-bullshit, hater brain. Sending her sensitive soul into fury, the blueprint of her future was in its ruthless hands screaming that there is no such thing as love, and tore it up, watching it fall to the cold floor in a thousand pieces.

    Her father had left her mother without leaving a name. Her first port of love by a male sailed away, leaving a hugely absent gap in her early life. She thought that Father Christmas was her real dad until she was seven years old, and he didn't always deliver what she wanted on her crayon-written list. Finding her fiancée beneath two naked bimbos killed any chance of her believing in a Prince Charming, but something about bumping into that gardener - call it faith, call it concussion - gently knocked on the door to her closed-up heart, waiting patiently for her to open.

    The glass touched her plump lips, and the cool summertime flavoured drink washed away the dust in her dry mouth. Her parched tongue automatically moistened and became alive again, moving like a beached dolphin with the strength to finally move back into the ocean.

"Eeurrrghhhh!" Remembering where she was, and with manners drummed into her, there was nowhere to spit out the salty tasting lemon liquid except maybe into Hector's lap next to her. Hector was snoring away. She could tell that Hector had pissed himself in his sleep. Unfortunately, she was a kind girl, so she had to swallow it.

"Mother this is not lemonade." Tears stung her pretty eyes feeling the salt attacking her throat distastefully and coating her truthful tongue. She hated it when a visit was going wrong. The demolition of her Mother's mind was evident by this event, and the cause was invisible. It was heartbreakingly visible to loved ones watching like an audience.

"Mindy. So sorry." Poppy hated the upset that she had caused her daughter over her inability to remember. Tears formed. Mindy was upset at the distress in her Mother's kind eyes, producing clear tears. A nurse approached on hearing Mindy's noise of disgust, and she was glad of the break from holding back the residents interfering with Alfred who thought that watching one episode of Holby City qualified them as nurses.

"Good morning Poppy. Everything ok?" asked Julia, who was the Matron for the afternoon. Poppy was dabbing her eyes with a napkin in upset, which was an uncommon sight for the nurse.

"Sorry Nurse," embarrassed at crying in public. It was a rare thing for Poppy to do, tissue dabbed tears away

"Mindy how can you drink that? It's vile!" she said chuckling at the state of Mindy's face, twisting in disgust at the cloudy drink for all to see. "I told Poppy that too much salt in it would make it taste horrible!" laughing, the gold pin watch bobbing on her uniform slapping her right breast like the perverted hand of a politician, applauding Mindy's bravery for drinking it. Mindy wondered if her mother was looked after by carers whose minds functioned less than Poppy's, or as the BBC news reported, many nurses were taking unprescribed drugs to get through their slavery shifts. The puzzlement of the lava red haired daughter of Poppy's - who the nurse always found herself looking at, with the perfect complexion of her skin, a milky tone highlighting the green of her eyes, resembling Henry Dooley - provoked the nurse to give the answer to her questioning gaze.

"The homemade mouthwash to clean out the mouth - she complained she had toothache," she said slowly, like she was trying to diffuse a bomb. The nurse looked between the two eye-locked people. She jumped back in shock as the mother and daughter burst into an eruption of loud laughs. Poor Alfred looked up from his stretcher as he was carried out, and one resident pocketing his loose change sprawled across the floor as he dropped it all in a panic.

"So sorry Mum, it's really nice." Mindy was mocking her mother's general mix up of the two glasses, pretending to take another delightful swig. The right glass on the table had sliced lemon floating in it, waiting to be drunk and explode the taste buds; it waved.

"Here's the glass I meant to give you." Her slim hand picked up the correct glass of homemade lemonade, handing it to Mindy. "I must have mixed them up with the distraction of Alfred." She had tears now of joy and laughter. "YOUR FAULT, ALFRED!" she shouted, not waiting for Alfred to reply - oxygen masks make it hard to hear anyway. Mindy relished in the fruit flavoured fizz like animals of the desert do with long awaited floods to the bone-dry plains after a life-threatening drought. Her body selfishly soaked it all up. She had childhood memories of caravan trips away, washed past in the freak flood on the plain that was her mind. Her eyes shut tight acting like a dam lock, allowing no light to penetrate and dry up the flood. Each memory played out on a plasma screen against her closed eyelids; it was utter heaven in a moment of someone's life slowly turning to hell.

"Mmmmmmmmm..." purred from her rosy pink lips. The pleasure of taste rolling with the magic of memories, her purr showing pure pleasure in audio form for all to hear, and she didn't care.

"Ay, that even before ya see me?" An Irish voice housing a black eye that Muhammad Ali would've high-fived rushed into the freak flood like a dam. It abruptly broke into her flashbacks, cutting the charming film short. Midway down her throat, she choked on the lemonade fluid and her shocked eyes shot open as she coughed, trying to catch her breath - maybe her last one ever.

'Now is not the time to choke,' was all she could think, echoing with the thunderous power of a storm inside her head. She prayed that this was not the end of her life. For one, she had mismatching underwear on - a huge fashion faux-pas. The distraught look on her mother's face if she choked to death was something that she did not want to be the last face she saw before it all went black. Too embarrassed to signal for help, she politely coughed again a bit more forcefully, with added aggression. It failed to budge. She thought, *'this is it'*. This is how my life is to end. Choking to death in a nursing home in front of the sexy Irish man whose penis looks like a pink aubergine, while a dozen old folk pile on top like human Jenga blocks, with a few men having a little grope of my shy tits for a pleasurable kick in their dull day. She found herself siding with Poppy's illness, to make sure her mother forgot her only child choking to death. The thought of being her only daughter - dead in front of her eyes - tortured her, and brought her determination to dislodge the watery blockage soon. Questions lined up like mourning at an open coffin. Who would look after E.T? Alex certainly would put him down painfully with a homemade toxic injection, administering it with the smile of a Disney villain. Her boss Eric would be left in the shit, and would have to find another mortuary beautician as good as herself before the weekend came out to take victims.

This rare self-praise passed its sympathy on. She thought of Maud's delight at becoming the reigning female supreme in the Peaceful Palace - for that reason, Mindy needed to live. Suddenly, before she blacked out, a huge slap to her back made her jolt forward like learner driver. Through her watering eyes, the blur of a shadowed figure stepped closer. Was this the angel of death? Or maybe it was a dark spirit to drag her away, like the demon from Paranormal Activity does with its victims out of the bed? The shadowy figure was either repeating the backslapping to kill her or save her. She prayed on the last breath that it was the latter.

"Joe-Ryan, hit harder!" Poppy's voice called in the fading distance.

"Smack her like a piñata!" another called.

"Whack her like a mole!" another person yelled.

"Leg drop her!" grumbled someone.

"I'm great at mouth to mouth!" said another; his slurping told Mindy that this man didn't possess a tooth in his whole head.

"Tanvier, your gums are as dry as a sandpit. Not a chance you're kissing my daughter, you dirty old dog!" Poppy laughed clapping her hands. Mindy was glad that her mother had her back in a crisis, silently mocking. The gathering of many voices told her that the whole room had diverted attention from Alfred to focus on this redhead being man-slapped by the sexy Irish gardener with the gorgeous eyes and kooky smile. Mindy wondered if she should just choke to death to save face, to get out of seeing Joe-Ryan, and to avoid the stares of the show watchers. Poppy would be retelling the story to everyone in her own over-the-top gypsy style version at her funeral. One last lifesaving cough and slap finally diffused the citrus blockage. Her breathing returned to normal as if it had not been on the missing list, showing up without even an apology. Hearing the elderly mutters along the lines of attention seekers, Mindy slowly opened her wet eyes. The 'waterproof' claim on her mascara had broken its promise.

Poppy was mimicking a straw-eating animal with the thin brim of the hat in her mouth, the first view to come back to Mindy as she regained vision. Her shaking told Mindy that her Mother was laughing, and did not have severe Parkinson's. The once blurred shadow was now next to her and smelled divine, a mixture of cut grass with an outdoors freshness clinging to his clothing. Lifting her head up, the tickling of the mascara trailing down her cheeks seemed to be in excitement for what she was about to witness. Taking in the washed-out denim of his jeans, she caught a glimpse of his knee through a peep-show rip, looking manly. The bottom of his t-shirt was un-tucked in a roughed up way. Further up, the red uniform widened out covering a raised chest. A slim neck gently dashed with shaving rash showed that he was not overly vain. Her stomach flipped over, landing like a perfectly tossed pancake; the reason for this was his face. Oh, what a face. The infamous black eye highlighted his cheeky wink, and his green eyes gleamed against the purple backdrop of bruising. His smile was genuine and wide, with black stubble cut in half and his eyebrows - strong, just like his arms

- were raised. Instead of producing hunger noises for once, her stomach mumbled with delight at the tasty treat.

"Hi," she said, trying to show that she was calm - well, as calm as you can be when you have just started your descent into dying, and calm as you can be when you've been choking in a room full of people who looked pissed off that you jumped the queue to die. Then throw into it that she had been saved by the man she had head butted - and had many a sexy dream over - you could understand why her 'hi' came out shy and sounding all girly. Joe-Ryan laughed, and his Adam's apple vibrated. It was a manly size; if he had been transgender it would have taken him to bankruptcy to shave it down.

"No worries. It was my pleasure, seeing as you gave me yours last time." He pointed to the black eye with his strong finger. She noticed two doors down that there was no wedding ring - unless he took it off for work, her lack of confidence shouted at her from inside her head. The eye with its mash up of blue, black and yellowing made Mindy apologize again. Ignoring everyone's - including Poppy's - stares, who were all at an age where wisdom outdid youth, and most had experienced love, they knew that this was love at first sight for the two strangers. Mindy blushed, thinking '*God, this man is having a strange effect on me. No one ever since 'Him' has*'. But unlike 'Him', this effect was promising and positive.

"Some things happen for a reason," Hector muttered, asleep through all the commotion. In his deep sleep he sucked his dentures back in from his chin.

*

Mindy jumped into her Mini just as the first droplet of thunderous rain hit the windscreen with a threatening splash. Her choking fit had flicked her curvy body with the delighted embarrassment of meeting Joe-Ryan. Damn he was handsome as hell, Mindy thought as she hit play on the CD player. Poppy had given Mindy some motherly advice on their parting hug - 'Climb him like a tree!' - reducing her to a blushing child as happens whenever parents mention sexual related comments.

The rest of the visit had gone without a hitch, choke or a salt flavoured drink. Mindy had decided not to tell her mother about Mabel just yet; she did not need to spoil the visit or cause her any major upset now. Sounding horrible, she wondered if she should tell her when her mother was having a bad spell - that way the pain would be less of a blow during the battle. Mindy wiped the solitary tear sliding down her pretty face that appeared every time she left the nursing manor. Starting the car slowly, she left the gravel carpeted car park and started heading home. The grand manor evaporated in the rear mirror, but the depression stayed clear and strong in her heart.

The long drive down the skinny lane became slow due to the unexpected downpour falling from the grey sky, creating mischievous mud for the wheels to plough through. The Weatherman had forgotten to mention this downpour on the weather report this morning. Mindy tutted, as she had wanted to spend the lovely evening planting some summer bulbs. The angry grey clouds were ganging up on the once clear sky and it darkened; this late afternoon put that idea to bed.

She hitched up the volume on the radio a notch to drown out the window wipers that were working furiously to keep a clear screen for Mindy. Their OCD obsession was keeping the rain off, she admired. Something caught Mindy's eye. A lone, drenched figure was hunched over as a flimsy sports jacket stuck to his body as he pushed through the wall of rain. His black hair was slapped to his head like a bathing cap. The rain was so dense that she could see droplets air bombing off his jacket. Mindy panicked; with the wet driving conditions she feared she might hit a pothole and knock the poor man down dead.

The wet guy turned around and stepped out off the road to the safety of the grass bank on hearing the car approaching behind. Before Mindy had been warned by her common sense of asking wet strangers with maybe a hobby of killing or raping into her car, or even asking his rates in case he was a prostitute, she pulled over and wound her window down.

"GET IN."

"Thank you very much, I'm soaked through. Even my bones are wet!" rubbing his black hair with a picnic blanket that Mindy kept in the back seat. His sleek hair resembled a thick oil slick that every bird in the land would happily roll around in like a pig in shit, just for the chance to feel him. His bare bicep boldly shimmered with the rainwater.

"No worries. Thanks for saving my life back there. This means we're even" making light of the choking event; Joe-Ryan smiled. His teeth made an appearance slight wonky, clean and cute - Mindy had read in a body language book that this meant it was genuine. His face glossed with the rain shone with cleansed freshness. His midnight black hair was messed up from the drying with the wool blanket, making it wild like Dennis the Menace, just asking to be stroked. She smiled back, declining the offer for now.

Mindy felt herself blush again. '*For fuck's sake Mindy, get a grip. You are over thirty, not a schoolgirl!*' her interior mirror snapped at her. She looked into it distracted, her stalking eyes pulling away from him and cheekily checking that her make-up was good. He was so close that his manly aftershave floated over to her teasingly, giving her a coy feeling and the temptation to look at him. Being so close she was acting as if she had stumbled in on him naked by accident, not knowing where to look. If only this scenario in her head was true. *Imagine his big dick and hard body, there for the taking.* The shock of this sexy thought jolted the car forward, and she flushed a hot sweat from her toned, clean pores.

"Wow" His hand hit the dashboard, bracing him from going forward and smashing through the windscreen.

"Sorry!" she pleaded. She glanced briefly at him, and then her eyes focused back toward the washed-out road ahead. *Calm down, Mindy. Why am I acting like this?* She looked back at him for the answer, and there it was. He was so beautiful, calm and cool despite being wetter than a fish. Mindy had worked in the industry, so she knew that his sharp look and black hair would be a sure hit on women in London. He seemed blind to how good-looking he was. Where other men would strut like a peacock, all tail feathers flared, Joe-Ryan seemed happy to blend in like a pigeon - this was an attraction in itself. *Do not kill him, Mindy. But if you do, you could do his make-up and see him naked*! Her humour was starting to get kinky and deluded with her drought from sex and her closeness to Joe-Ryan.

"Women drivers" he said, nudging her side with his elbow to show humour. She smiled beautifully, he noticed. She felt real; not starved thin to the point where her main meal was the swift lick of a low fat yogurt lid - she actually ate. She was captivating to him, like a rare species to a zoologist. She oozed class, success and confidence; she would not look at him twice. A gypsy gardener paid buttons like him stood more chance of winning the lottery than winning this woman. Still, at least she was friendly enough to help him out in this freak downpour, he thought as he dried his hair.

Mindy turned up the heating, aiming it in his direction after noticing him failing to dry himself with the wool blanket that had cost Alex an arm and a leg that Christmas.

'You never know, Mindy - he may strip with the heat!' her normally sane head - now turned pervert - said. This made Mindy contemplate cheekily whether she should lower the heat or turn it up. *'Oh lord, now I'm turning into a dirty old woman,'* finding it hard to resist imagining what she would do if he did take his top off. Joe-Ryan soaked up the benefit of being air-dried; giving up with the blanket he rested his head back and smiled. Mindy wondered what his girlfriend was like. He had to have a girlfriend. If he did not then he was gay, a massive mummy's boy or a serial killer. On the plus side, if he was a serial killer at least he would have to touch her when he chopped her up.

Back on the motorway the heavyweight rain was undeterred and not running out of steam, belting down from the upset sky like a waterfall, tapping hard on the window screen and trying - but failing - to break up the animated conversation going on in the car between Mindy and Joe-Ryan. For the evening, the motorway was eerily quiet. Only a few brave motorists took the fast lane, a horsebox took up the slow lane, and a caravan lead the way, so Mindy braved it and went in the middle. The tar had another fresh coat on, all shiny and clean-looking as the rain washed away tyre marks, exhaust fumes and road kill blood stains. It was as if it was a modern day Noah's ark flood, but with no animals needing to board a rickety wooden

Titanic - WWF would have placed them all on a luxury all-inclusive cruise liner.

Mindy and Joe-Ryan gabbed on like there was no tomorrow, eating the oxygen like candy floss. Their conversation ranged from cats versus dogs, childhood memories, to celebrities that they liked and disliked, game would you rather. They talked of corrupt politics through to the price of buying in mortgage-robbing London. Joe-Ryan was in awe of Mindy. He took her in every time he looked at her, finding something new and attractive on each visit to her face. Her smile lit up the whole of her face. Her cute nose wrinkled with each laugh that was feel-good and infectious. The way her beautiful eyes focused when he spoke made him feel important; he felt as if she looked beyond his handsome face and looked deeper.

She was a proper woman with intelligence about the world - not like the waifs that he seemed to attract. They were all lip liner and short skirts, or the loud brassy ones with a pint in one hand, a baby in the other and a three-berth caravan. Mindy was a sensitive, caring person - her aura was soaked with it. *Ask her out.*

Mindy loved her job; she was animated as she spoke showing her passion, and it all added to the list of what he wanted in a woman as his wife. *Did I just say wife? You just said wife.* Asking the entire range of familiar questions about her job he asked: 'Do you ever get scared?', 'Don't ya get lonely?', and 'Do you ever think that they might jump up?' She was going to mention the time that Mabel had, but she forgot that Joe-Ryan did not know about that. It was a bit early to tell him yet, but she felt at ease enough that she could. She didn't want him thinking that she was any stranger than she was, so she refrained for now. Imagine if they got married them saying to the guests 'I knew she was the one when she mentioned a dead woman had jumped up at her!' - She laughed to herself suddenly. *Oh my god, am I thinking about marriage?* This made Mindy swerve the car a wee bit. Joe-Ryan just looked at her, his thick eyebrows raised, screaming *women drivers.*

They engaged in deep talk over blooms, gardening tips and secret tricks to help plants grow as Mother Nature intended. The windows steamed up over the conversation, allowing no one else to look in on this moment in their lives. He was flabbergasted when she mentioned that she had never visited Ireland, and he mocked that it was the biggest insult to his day. He did a pretend 'don't talk to the hand' gesture and was glad it made her laugh, and promised to take her one day if she was lucky chased up with a bold wink.

He was useful as well as delicious, handsome, manly and perfect. He probably had a girlfriend at home, an outgoing fun type that could holds a room full with her wonderful personality and perfect hair. This girl would be a girl that his best mates treated like one of the lads, with a welcoming slap on her toned back returning from building wells in Africa and a pint ready for her to down. She bet that she was athletic running marathons, daring, spontaneous, jumping out of planes, and good in bed along with a cellulite-free waist you could wrap your hands around like a human tortilla wrap. Her dress sense would be up-to-date, and any female in her company would be envious.

Mindy did not want to deliver questions about his love life - she would prefer to have no more heartache today. What would happen if he sensed her crush on him? What if he said that he did have a sexy, gorgeous girlfriend? It would crush her, and the developing crush would send her into a kebab binge. She was only four pounds away from her two stone loss certificate at Slimming World - it would not be worth the greasy guilt. Therefore, she simply didn't bother asking.

Enjoying the relaxed banter that was like a squash ball bouncing between them, inspired by the raindrops bouncing off the car roof, she thanked the rain for the wet conditions reducing her speed and prolonging the time they spent together. Would Mindy ever be immensely in love with a man again? She was starting to sound like a bitter spinster on her way to adopt another stray killer cat.

The pleasant journey started to shorten, and Mindy was grateful for the company while it lasted. It had helped to push away the normal negative thoughts about leaving her mother there along with the unhealthy thought of her mother slowly wasting away, blocking the gut feeling of hot guilt that she was helpless to help.

"Ay, your mother's a crazy one." Joe-Ryan jumped onto her thoughts as if he could read her mind. "Oh, I mean not crazy like that," correcting his mistake before Mindy could register any slight comparison of the 'crazy' that Joe-Ryan thought this sounded like.

"No she is crazy. Bloody bonkers before she got ill!" she said good hearted, liking that someone saw her mother for the crazy woman she was, Mindy smiled, her face forever lit up when she smiled.

"Yeah she's a good laugh. She brightens the day up really, has everyone smiling." Stretching his arms above his head, Mindy was eye-jacked by his tennis ball biceps. "Hey, just the one lane" Mindy straightened the car back up, touching Joe-Ryan's thigh as she slipped the gear. She burnt up hoping that Joe-Ryan hadn't noticed the accidental slip, and then an image of his manly thighs raced naked around her head, wrapping her up in them. She imagined her head buried in between his muscular thighs, imagining his big cock in her mouth. She imagined it big and grinding in her throat, feeling his heavy balls hanging at her chin. She gripped the wheel tight as if gripping his back as he pushed deep, exploring into her, just before the car verged out of the lane again. The rude image knocked her concentration away from road safety as Mindy's imagination awoke from its dormant sleep, mouthing 'sorry' to the caravan owner whose dream of a holiday up north was nearly ruined as a beautiful looking redhead tried to crash into his lane. Joe-Ryan laughed again.

"Women drivers ay?" Mindy said, opening her window to cool her body from its sudden lustful hot spell, oblivious that this could be an early warning sign of premature menopause. Approaching the first train station to come into view, this was unfortunately the one that Joe-Ryan would be bunking on to get home.

"Light at the end of the tunnel," Mindy joked, turning off the car because she hated waste of any kind.

"You saying that being stuck in a car with you were a bad thing?" showing the evidence of the rain holding up the damp, wet woollen blanket, grinning childishly waiting to see how Mindy would get out of this wind up.

"God no, oh, I meant, oh God, I…" before more 'sorrys 'could fly out, she was silenced by his lips. His warm lips pressed with the gentle pressure an exhausted mother lands on her children when they sleep - a sign of love, and worth the nine month wait. The sudden kiss lasted a lifetime as she enjoyed the life changing, heart-celebrating kiss. Her adultery-scathed past melted away and she was surprised she didn't piss herself with the melting iceberg inside. She imagined a version of her future blessed with amazing things, until he pulled away and jumped out of the car in a flash.

The rest of the short journey home Mindy was on cloud nine, rocking with angels who were giving her relationship advice. Unexpected kisses are always the best, and Joe-Ryan had taken her on a magical journey to the land of *What If.* Unexpected, it came matching the joy of a lottery win and dreaming of what you could do with it. Mindy digressed, with multiple scenarios stemming from the seed of the kiss - a few were realistic, but most were deluded. After the kiss stopped, Joe-Ryan had got out of the car a bit too quickly for Mindy's liking.

Was he ashamed?

Was he regretting it?

Maybe the kiss was simply him thanking her for the kindness of the lift to the train station in good will?

Was he aiming for her cheek and she threw her lips onto him?

She thought this, but the passion that had passed between them was pure. The lingering length of the kiss had left a tingle, that if she had not experienced the kiss, she might have mistaken it for a cold sore coming. Mindy did not know what to believe, but she believed that kiss was the best kiss she had ever had. Or maybe it was that she hadn't had a kiss in so long, wondering whether she should donate her lips to medical science that morning. The way that kiss had ignited her sad heart with hope would keep her company all evening and delivering a hot dream to her that night. The skies cleared away the black angry clouds to reveal the most spectacular rainbow, slicing its colour of pride with ease. Mindy slowed down. It was beautiful; a slither of hope at the end of a bad day. Now, if she was Sabrina, her goddaughter, she might think that this was a sign of good to come after the storm of 'Him'. The rainbow was so beautiful it became the number one trending item on Instagram that day.

Joe-Ryan kicked the plastic waste bin used sometimes as a seat when the train station was full. *Feck, Feck*, he repeated out loud in his warm Irish voice. Why had he jumped out of the car like he was a jack-in-the-box with a rocket up his arse? He had never meant to kiss Mindy, but seeing her look as sweet as she struggled to explain herself and the fact that her hand slipped and touched his thigh earlier, so tender and tense, exploded electricity in his body like a party popper too loud to ignore. Hibernation was over for his tired heart bursting into cheery song, very appropriately.

His slow tired grey train approached the busy platform, crawling on its last route of the long overworked day, its wheels burnt on the track lines. The moody rain was not giving up and pounded down, each raindrop hitting him was like a punch - why had he not asked for her number? Better still, why had he not kissed her a second time? A few people paused looking to the grey sky before boarding, and Joe-Ryan followed suit. There across the clear sky previously battered by blackness was the brightest rainbow he had ever seen. Instantly, the lipstick Mother Nature was wearing brought him to smile, and his smile lasted longer with the thought of Mindy. Was this a sign? Granny C was forever saying *'If two people see the same rainbow, they become the ends of the rainbow and the colours become their love'*. If only, he sighed.

Climbing on to the rammed evening train among stressed-out suits, his mind took inspiration and rammed a dozen questions into his head all shouting loudly for an answer from him. His clothes were damp and heavy on him, and his mind matched. If Mindy liked him back, why hadn't she called him back into the car? Did she have a boyfriend already? The thought horrified him that he might have just made a pass at her and she was too polite to brush him off. Riddled with guilt at the kiss, was he a kiss rapist? Thinking that he was some sort of predator to women, Joe-Ryan found himself racing with insecure feelings of self-doubt and worthlessness. To make matters worse, the train conductor was on his way down checking tickets - adding to Joe-Ryan kicking himself in the confused cake mix in his head. A fifty-pound fine for not producing a ticket was the cherry on top.

Beverley Hills

The black, long legs famous for walking the polished catwalks of the fashion world had swapped the runway this afternoon to grip around his hard waist, like a human harness holding onto him. Cut calves were drawing him in closer and she needed him to be inside her, all his body - not just his pumping cock - without an inch of air between them, her jealous streak. Her entertaining entrance soaked his pubes.

She was a Venus fly trap and he was her juicy prey. Droplets of sweet sweat travelled from her smooth forehead all the way down her slender, sensual body suggestively, prolonging the teasing sensation and sliding shockingly slow between her fake tits, sloping into the concave of her food-starved stomach, touring the landscape of her lean body like hikers, and finally lubricating his cock as he entered her.

His firm butt moved up and down, up and down in a delayed rhythmic wave, propelling him into her tight pussy, with her wetness soaking his swollen cock. His teeth gently gnawed on her big nipples while an eager tongue investigated his pink hole. The wetness on the smooth skin was unsurprisingly turning him on.

Kitten Minx was a world famous supermodel, but damn if you were fooled by the sweet nature of her first name. She was a fiery, black, six foot tall Kenyan supermodel who had taken the modelling world by storm and men by their balls. She was a dream on fashion covers, but a complete nightmare in real-life. She had been nicknamed 'The Beautiful Nightmare' by the media. Olive eyes illuminated brightly from her black feline face. She was naked and on her back, working up a bubble of pure lust that needed popping by this dick deep inside her searching for it.

She was a highly in demand supermodel; clothes simply came alive on her. She was a fashion muse with the power of the likes that Cindy and co demanded in their heyday. Kitten Minx was sensational in clothes, but volcanic dynamite out of them. The elite supermodel of the day was applauded for her striking looks, and could sell transgender surgery to the butchest of men and make cocaine look cool. No angle displayed a bad picture of her ever, and she was now sashaying into the world of film and expanding brand 'Minx'.

She was feared for her volcanic attitude and anger - you were fucked if she threw a shoe and you were in the way. The granddaughter of a world iconic Politician, while her other grandfather was a blood diamond criminal. The polar opposites between her heritages generated plenty of media interest and respect from the good, the bad and the fashionistas.

Kitten was a living legend. She was born to wear delicate eye-wateringly priced clothes, fused with a promiscuous, open minded sexual attitude competing with a drug addiction just as hungry as global news. The bitch was an icon. The lines of coke on her neat breast gave the appearance of a taper. Sharing the big screen in the new Bruce Willis film, their first scene together had been filmed and was in the bag. She was now sharing a hotel bed and her pussy with her co-star since the filming had wrapped up five hours ago. Only her pink Westwood patent heels gave a clue that she had been dressed today, as they waved in the air screaming in pleasure above her head in protest for more.

"Deeper, push into me deeper you fucking punk!" Her husky voice was low due to her breath being beat out of the rhythm of his thrusting, demanding more. She was a diva who was true to the title.

Chad Rise was sweating. The hurricane of sexual heat failed to escape the hotel room, and rising heavy, was caged by the room and fell damply. The moans were heavy as if oxygen was lacking in the room, eaten by the frantic, energetic bodies on the bed, egged on as if there was a live audience watching.

Kitten Minx was a woman whose sex drive was high and only fed with a cock or two. The third guest into the sex party rubbed his pink bullhead flirtatiously on Chad's pink bum hole. Tense, each wet touch of the cock was suggesting entering into his arse. The sensitive sensation felt appetising and teasing, and it gave more lead to his hard on. Looking Kitten deep in her sensational eyes, he noticed how dark they became, as if you could walk down them like tunnels into the unknown. Chad was balls deep in Kitten already - did he need to risk it and go further?

The three naked bodies glistened with sweat and hands were everywhere, playing instruments of different levels of pitch in pleasure, moaning loudly in the hotel room. Kitten Minx saw men as pleasure where others saw a mortgage payer, baby daddy and father figure. Men equalled sex. Kitten Minx preferred the gentleness of a lesbian relationship, but she adored cock - dildos just never hit the spot. This afternoon was just what she needed to take her mind off a looming court case.

Chad could smell the cocoa butter on Kitten Minx's skin. He licked it and it was as if she was made of the finest chocolate, delicious, delicate and raw, yet poisonous. It made him hungry for more hearing her gasp with his deeper thrusts. He reached for her lips, taking her long tongue into his mouth. She was mesmerising, built strong like a warrior. The masculinity of her was a turn on for Chad, feeling it was inspiring the intrusion from Si Ling - the costume designer on set - with his petite cock poking its head against his butt for permission to penetrate. Chad hoovered up three lines from Kitten's tits. They raced to relax his tension building from the guy intrigued and hinting to investigate further in his forbidden rear, feeling Si Ling pre cum lubricating between his arse cheeks.

Chad had never taken a cock before. Fingers, yes, and he agreed that the male G-spot was explosive when touched. In the heated moment, reality was numbed by scotch and comforted by cocaine, and he was being egged on by an inquisitive Si Ling. He wondered, *could he?* He looked at Kitten who gave him a look of "well?" raising her fleek eyebrows, her forehead twinkling as if there were diamonds on her and not sweat. Was she daring him on? Chad was one who was forever looking for the next thrill to find the next high in sex. Would this mmf threesome be his first? He threw all caution out and decided to rid himself of his cock virginity from his lavish life, pushing back and indicating permission for Si Ling to enter. After all, Chad was an Alpha male.

The searing pain of the trendy, kooky designer's five-inch cock breaking entry into Chad's exit hole gave an all-new dimension to his sexual high. Chad indicated after few moments of pounding pain that he wanted more by pushing back his compact arse built by lunges, it swallowed Si Ling's tiny cock in one. Si Ling's breath on his neck told him that he was inside fully. The pain took his breath away; as quickly as the penis brought pain, it became pleasure, high pleasure pushing for more, the new sensation sent a fire thought out Chads naked body. The cement mixer of drink and drugs gave a blurred fantasy to it all, as if it was only imagination. It felt so good.

"Feels good, doesn't it?" purred Kitten, who was a massive fan of anal, latching her vast lips onto his muting his weak moaning. The pleasurable pain was only a fraction of the pain to come that he was about to experience in his lavish, selfish life.

London

"You have a visitor" Maud shouted rowdily across the small reception, her small eyes taking in the visitor just in case he was a murderer. Maud would love to write to a teatime chat magazine for a thousand pounds; how ironic it would be for a murder at funeral parlour. If Maud wrote about her past she would earn more than a thousand - but that was behind police tape, like the tragic incident was itself.

Her blunt voice raced like a pack of foxhounds thirsty to kill, finding their unfortunate prey coming out of the staff toilet. Mindy rubbed her Molten Brown hand conditioner on, replacing the tin back in her pocket.

"Who would visit me at work?" Talking to herself was a hobby. Maud was a nightmare for not letting anyone but the staff past reception, even if people had tear stained eyes and the white face of sorrow, she still wanted proof that they were related to the deceased - in Maud's eyes, a DNA test was the only thing acceptable. Maud really would benefit the country's safety by retraining for border control instead of working on reception; not a fucking bride with a rucksack wannabe or a sun-kissed drug mule would get past her.

Mindy walked down the slim corridor with a game of Guess Who playing inside her head. Definitely could not be her mother - she did not know the address. Alex was too busy to take time off to venture this far from Central. Oh, God no Joe-Ryan maybe? Mindy stopped. Shit if it was, Mindy thought as she caught her reflection in the stainless steel door. She really should have done her hair this morning, but the snooze button was more alluring than blow drying.

"Mindy are you deaf? You have a visitorrrrr!" Her feeling of being fed-up soaked through the sentence. Mindy ignored her ruffled reflection and rushed on. Please don't be Joe-Ryan, she repeated like a mantra as she headed to reception.

Mindy purposely walked with the speed of a zombie with arthritis in its hips. Who the hell would visit her at work? Joe-Ryan, she feared - and secretly also wished. Why would he visit her? Would it be a romantic gesture or a potential stalking? Another male entered her head washing her skin with a cold sweat...'Him'. The idea flirted in her mind. Would he be here begging for her forgiveness to take him back? Before she digressed with this scenario the image of Alex burying her alive in a shallow grave outside of Zone Three for being a fool brought Mindy back to reality. She had no idea who it was, and there was only one way to find out.

Mindy walked on, running her fingers through her sunset coloured hair and tying it back up, while all her thinking rattled inside her head. The slim corridor finally brought her slowly to reception as if she was fit to hang, ready to push her out and reveal her presence to her visitor. The bright lights from the large bay windows hit her sight, and she shielded her eyes as she heard a voice.

"Hello Mindy." Oh fuck, it was a male. Mindy squinted and failed to see him, and she replied "Hello?" quizzically. Her sight reduced as the sun beamed on her pretty face made it hard to see his face. The sun swiped left as if it was on Tinder, disliking the male suitor already, and Mindy could see.

"Mindy," an incredibly soft and cold hand shook hers. Mindy could see her visitor now. Yes, a male, an extremely odd looking male - quite feminine, or maybe an old transvestite. His brown suit three sizes too big swamped his frame as if he was slowly shrinking by the second, like that scene from the witch film where everyone turned into mice.

"Hi. What can I do for you?" she said taking in the appearance of this man, who reminded her of someone, but she could not pin point it yet.

"I come with an envelope for you from the marvellous, beautiful, extremely talented Mabel." It clicked - he looked like Mabel if she was an emaciated man. The over-the-top description was very Mabel-ish. Mindy stiffened.

"An envelope?" she said taking the crisp envelope, noticing how clean and polished the man's hands were. "For me? Why?" Mindy stared intensely, wondering if she stared any longer would the man combust. Maud spoke to break the stare.

"Mindy, why are you looking at Mr Manning like you're trying to burst him into flames?" Maud quizzed as Mindy carried on with the intense staring.

"I'm sorry. Thank you," taking hold of the white envelope after Maud hit her with a custard cream to snap her out of it. Was this Mabel in disguise as another one of her characters, a man called Mr Manning? Mindy felt the tension of a headache coming on.

"Well? Open it then!" Maud rudely interrupted; being a nosy bitch she wanted to know why this strange man was giving Mindy the posh looking envelope delivered personally and what was in it. It was too thin to contain money, or a bomb; she had worked that out already.

Mindy didn't know what to do.

This reminded her of when she was younger and it was her birthday, when someone had given her a card and she had hoped that money was in it – showing an excited face was a hell of a lot easier than trying not to show a disappointed face.

"I think I will open it in private if you don't mind, Maud," turning to Maud, who was pushing a whole ginger nut into her mouth - if Mindy had been a male, she would have had a hard on. Maud pulled a face and swivelled her red chair back rudely to face her small filing cabinet, her back fat waving for someone to unclip the tight bra strap. Mindy turned back around to thank Mr Manning, but the mini looking man had gone. A peach-smelling aftershave lingered to apologise for his abrupt, silent departure. *What the fuck is going on?* Mindy wondered as she stood looking at the crisp envelope what on earth was inside it? Did Mindy want to know?

New York, JFK Airport

Landing at JFK airport, Maria Dieppe lowered the gold designer sunglasses, placed her well-photographed head down and prayed for an easy run. It was hard being who she was, and who she was engaged to. Thick raven hair tied tight pulled her face tighter, giving her more youth and firmness causing gossipmongers to circulate rumours of a facelift. She wrapped her cow skin Burberry trench rope belt tight for protection. The tight fit felt like armour - expensive armour at that. It constricted her, putting more shape into her hourglass figure. She took one deep breath, popped a Prozac and took a deep breath, pushing through out into the overcrowded airport.

The flashing of the dozen or more picture hungry paparazzi dimmed behind her oval glasses. Her famous name echoed all over the airport deafeningly, outdoing any important announcement over the tannoy as the scrum of flashing wolves chanted, calling her name like some cult. She was like the pied piper as she gained more attention from the celebrity-hunting public, who all ran over wanting a picture of the Mexican bombshell, joining in the football rant loudly shouting. She wished she could change her name, ignoring the fact that she was named after her great grandma - a famous women's rights campaigner in Mexico, and BFF of the late Mother Theresa.

The reason that Maria had landed at the airport like a Salem witch, fit to burn by a gang of finger happy paparazzi falling over themselves to capture a reaction from Maria - or a peek under her trench coat - and risked death by being trampled, was for two very public reasons. One was that Delia Von Grouse, New York's richest divorcée had been found dead on the pavement below her expensive penthouse suite apartment - shock horror, without her fur coat. This fact upset people more than the actual death. Maria was no stranger to telling the media what she thought of the fur-wearing whore after finding Chad finger-blasting her vagina at a posh dinner.

Secondly, Chad Rise - her fiancé - had been announced as a lead in the new Bruce Willis film alongside the volcano-blowing supermodel whose legs so long that her fanny gets tickled by angels, Kitten Minx. It would be taking his handsome, chiselled face from every TV screen in America to every cinema screen in the world, and probably to Kitten's bed. The sickness returned. World exposure would certainly blow up his profile and blow up his ruthless ego; sadness shivered through her sexy body despite the heat of the airport.

Maria pushed on like a pro; she refused to comment or slur. Her grandma had always said not to speak ill of the dead. She walked fast, her Christian heels striking the polished floor with a precise point of contact, giving her poise; sparks flinted with each touch.

Maria wanted to get out of the airport, into the limousine waiting and get to the hotel to her man, fast. More importantly, she wanted to get the fucking dog back to Chad. Roxy was panting, loving the attention like a true dumb blonde. Roxy wagged her tail like a social media slut, pulling on her pink rope lead. The dog was more famous than Maria - well, according to Instagram, where Roxy held two hundred thousand more followers over Maria, and even Lady Gaga was a follower. The glossy door of the limousine slammed, the lighting flashes ricocheting off in protection. The sleek limo sped off, and the distance between the popular airport grew longer trading distance with the trendy hotel. The distance housing her man grew shorter and Maria's plan of revenge grew stronger.

Roxy stared at Maria; her glossy brown eyes never flinched nor grew smaller in envy at her insane beauty. Roxy was the only living thing immune to Maria's ravishing beauty. Roxy's thick, pink tongue hung out of her meaty mouth as if it was a clutch bag, and her yellow fur gave a shine in the early sun. Maria stared at the loyal dog. She fucking hated this dog. She knew Roxy felt the same about her, and she knew Roxy knew about her plans concerning Chad.

London Camden Town

Debbie Marque had never been the type of woman to fuck other women's husbands, or have one-night stands, or nosh off drunken men in nightclub toilets. Nor would she get in situations where she was at risk at the hands of men who failed to register the word 'no', or have three abortions under her belt. Yet that meek, intelligent Debbie Marque was long gone.

This man-eater did not care anymore for the old Debbie who loved gardening and horse riding - that miserable bitch was dead and buried back in Wigan, where the only time she had inserted a rabbit was into a hutch, not her vagina, and had been buried alive by the new transformation of peroxide, fillers, Botox and a gym body. Betrayed by men all her life since her father had walked out on her at two years old as she screamed with stinging tears over her tiny, cute face, from a cot in a nappy hanging filthy by her tiny ankles. He left her literally hanging with shit, and the stench never left Debbie or the hate for men. She finally cracked the comfortable cocoon with a pickaxe, and instead of a butterfly emerging, a Black Widow binge-eating spider crawled out.

Verbal abuse and being disrespectful replaced paying compliments, as she passed through each damaging relationship like a 'pass the parcel', planting the self-destructive seed. Those boyfriends cheating with other women...the disloyalty dug into the relationship and started to water that seed. The cracking of her confidence with each cock of her 'then' boyfriends she found in the clit of another was the sun to the seed of self-hatred, and it all finally created a human with big blonde hair, enchanted tits and lips built for blow jobs, and a gym-trained body built for sexual satisfaction – it was all part of her trap of torture. This black widow spider was spinning its web, hungrier than a Muslim was during Ramadan.

She used men to show women that they did not have to put up with it any longer. No longer just a baby bank or a housewife, women had power, brains - it was just that Debbie's were all in her designer vagina. The game of seducing, fucking and leaving men in a cloud of confusion when she dropped them, and heartbroken with an ache in their cocks from her appetite for hot, hard sex, beat any Sudoku puzzle to keep her mind healthy. Resentment and anger were hard for Debbie to let go of, no matter how fucked over she left the men. Dropping her knickers was easy, but dropping the past matched the difficulty of trying to pull off a chastity belt. Debbie's deluded idea was to empower women; it was just that Debbie's method was yet to win a Noble Peace Prize. Had Debbie been born in the era of The Suffragettes, they would have pushed her in front of the King's horse. She wanted to save other women from heartache, even if it meant she received a few black eyes and was named and shamed across the town on social media for fucking their partners as a thank you instead of chocolates.

Debbie was in her cramped, but well-decorated studio flat above the butcher's, sitting by the open window. Make-up free with her blonde hair wild and loosely free, she worked an innocent and sexy look of an American girl-next-door - it was a rare look that only she ever saw. Anyone who lived in London tended to add 'cramped' into the description of their home. Yet today it was more cramped as another male victim of hers lay sleeping naked in her double bed, exhausted from her poison of sucking his energy through sex. James-John or Joe-Ryan - she failed to remember, not fucking caring as she would not be seeing him again - was fast asleep. His pale white torso did wonders for his dark body hair. He reminded her of a vampire, an extremely sexy vampire who bit more than her neck, feeling her lips tender from his nipping as they had kissed. His jet black hair fell limp covering his starved-looking face, and long lashes gently tickled his sun protected skin. He was a nice little night cap from last night's antics with Janina, her pal who had left with his mate - it was a lot healthier for her than Abu's donner kebab, anyway. His slim, athletic body worked well with the shade of pale to actually glow, kept fit from gardening at the nursing home, boring her with details of nature. His abundant cock with its dense, curly pubes fitted her enough to enjoy the ride, while his Irish tongue had flicked with free lease on her wet clit and lips, making her cum more than once and exhausting her to sleep well. She wanted him to go home now. OK, maybe she would get a full English out of him down at the greasy spoon first, since she had fuck all in the cupboards. She prayed he got her name right this morning - who in their right fucking mind calls their child Mindy?

Camden High Street killed any noise of songbirds of a morning with its flood of traffic and swarm of tourists travelling through like cattle off to market, or in this case, horses to the stables. The afternoon sun was high and promised another glorious day, lunch in a beer garden style. The weird, wacky and wonderful of the local zombies were entranced walking towards the pubs. Debbie lit another Marlboro up as she sat on the window ledge, blowing the smoke into the air of London. It filtered up into the air, adding to the pollution level. She felt old school smoking Marlboro; the great love rats of film had smoked them. Feeling like she was one of them, she would do anything to empower herself over the opposite sex, to have what they craved more than anything - sex. Her flimsy dressing gown was gentle on her skin and made her feel empowered.

Debbie thought of nothing in particular as she looked over the bustling street like a Princess trapped in a pollution-painted tower, waiting for her Prince to arrive in an Uber. A pigeon working grease and car oil into its feathers like the next big beauty fix, feeding a combination of fast-food and human vomit carbs to a podgy, fat, disgusting chick, gave her light entertainment but no maternal urges. The fresh air came in off the street, airing out the smell of smoke and sweaty sex from the studio flat, disgusted to see yet another man asleep in her open to all bed.

She was a rare woman, Debbie. She was a woman without dreams or ambition that simply just enjoyed being alive, enjoyed fashion and enjoyed her hobby of promiscuous sex. Her job as a temporary worker down in Canary Wharf in a hot law firm would do for now, until she got bored or was caught fucking an employee on paid time.

Debbie needed something to work towards, a challenge to test her ability to get cock. This idea digressed now as the pigeon bonding started to bore her. She had seen the picture of that rich bitch Alex's fiancé. He was hot, old school cockney looking, broad and big, and dim-looking. Bitches like Alex thought that girls like Debbie were nothing but dirt on their shiny red Louboutin soles. Debbie pulled long and thoughtfully on her cigarette as the idea of fucking her fiancé grew real and realistic, a challenge to really see if Debbie had what it took.

She released the cancer-friendly smoke, watching its whitey-grey smoke rise upwards like a white flag, as if Alex's fiancé was already surrendering to Debbie's offer. If Alex could read smoke signals instead of Braille, she would have known that her relationship was in danger.

Manhattan

Maria pulled her dove-grey silk Givenchy dressing gown up from the lush beige carpeted floor. The expensive material was limp and looked like a glamorous ghost rising up out of the floorboards to haunt. Maria was haunted, but her ghosts were never visible to the public eye - well, only the demon sleeping next to her. The dark hotel room played the perfect scenery if it was to be a horror film. Only a shimmer of moonlight sneaked in from a gap in the curtains, giving silhouettes to the room and minor comfort.

She got out of the enormous bed, ignoring its pull of comfort for her to stay among its thick duvet cover. She celebrated the fact that she had not woken Chad, whose high sex drive would have him ready for round two, his dick standing to attention inside her before she could say no. The unfamiliar scent of cocoa butter turned Maria's stomach with nausea, feeling sore below from his rough penetration as she placed her legs out of the bed. Sometimes when they made love Maria wondered if Chad thought he was fucking a hooker, with his rough, crude attitude and zero signs of any affection. Wrapping her tender skin on its come down from an orgasm in the silk dove-grey Givenchy gown, she sought sanctuary in the en-suite bathroom, clinking on the lights, and she finally felt safe.

Maria was one of those women who glowed after sex. Her skin looked younger, her eyes shone, and her soul was a little lighter - so why was her heart heavy? Her thoughts were becoming dangerous, drowning her in severe depression, its dark hand tight on her glamorous life. The darkness blinded her in every waking moment, following on the shoulders of her shadow. One of the world's most photographed women, her pain never transcended in her pictures, so no one offered her help for the hurricane of turmoil inside.

Would the feeling ever leave?

Would what happened that night dissolve, be forgotten, and be replaced by good memories?

The cold chill was nothing to do with her splashing her face with cold water in the bathroom. Chad Rise did give her good sex - most of L.A knew this. She had heard a few bitter rumours around the tables of lazy-arsed ladies who lunched, living off their partners and sharing gossip for dessert. Maria swatted rumours away with disrespect like hungry flies around a corpse - it was easier than letting them settle to feast.

Chad had been delighted when she had turned up. He greeted her second after Roxy, who rolled onto her back like a slut to have her belly tickled by Chad, who showered her with sweet affection. Praising her loyalty he repeated the chant *'who's been a good girl?'* which seemed directed to insult Maria. Yet Chad was an actor who had just landed a main role in a film that was already buzzing with box office success, so maybe he was just acting like he was delighted, the reflection in the mirror asked Maria as she dried her sensational face.

Maria had decided she was going to sleep with him on the first press of his thick lips against hers. She had missed him this week, relieved to see him half-dressed and waiting in the hotel room with a wet magnum of champagne and a dozen red roses. All his let downs over the weeks disappeared as she smelled the roses, the power of memory erased. His firm torso worthy of underwear modelling and perfect to stroke took over her brain and held her hands hostage to touch them. His washed-out Levi's sagged on his waist all hip and sexy, inviting as if helping to pull them down for her; it was an instant invitation for her to drag them down, and with no underwear beneath, she glimpsed his trimmed pubes above the worn waistline. His dick stood pink and solid, ready to please and please it did as it disappeared into her willing mouth.

Chad's secret weapon was his kiss. His stocky cock was good, but his kiss was better. It was like he used Rohypnol as lip balm. Once his velvety lips touched yours, your will power and clothes raced to drop first. Your body pleaded for you to allow him to go further as if you had never experienced sex, deprived of the male touch for your complete existence, ignoring your seven children and stretch marks. His lips took you to a world of all your firsts in your lifetime - sleeping with Chad Rise being the number one.

She stared into the mirror, its immense size giving the impression that you could step right through it. Maria felt dirty; she just wanted the shower to rid the presence of a penis having been inside her.

Droplets of sperm were trapped in her pubic hair and the touch made her gag; her empty stomach had nothing to give but just the noise of desperation and bile, but why? The power shower burned her skin as it rained down, stripping away the sensitivity from her skin. The smell of sex left by her fiancé swirled around the plug, trying to prolong its stay and torment her, for punishment for what she had done?

She could not decide which burned her skin more - the shower or the furious scrubbing. She just wanted to be clean, free from any sexual evidence that a man had taken his fancy with her. She loved Chad, she really did, but she despised him even more since that night in Vegas. What woman in the world gets engaged, but the first cock in her vagina is not that of her fiancé? Half an hour passed, and she felt able to stop scrubbing and get out the burning shower.

Standing in front of the impressive mirror again in just her fluffy towel covering her modesty, in talks of being displayed in Playboy, she looked at the beautiful reflection that she was. On the outside, she was still the same - striking looks and a body blessed to be curvy yet delicate. On the inside was a completely different matter. So much had changed; inside was the carnage of a smashed soul rampaging with a pickaxe, not giving a fuck about the damage, with the autopsy an impossible puzzle to complete.

The recollection of that sordid, sickening night made her rush back into the power shower. The shower wept tears in horror as she turned the heat to scolding, as Maria scrubbed her raw skin with hate for Chad Rise.

London, Canary Wharf

She sat on the black leather sofa that dominated the office like an anaconda would among worms. Its designer style won no awards for comfort as Mindy shifted, trying and failing to get the ache from her back out. Maybe she had lost weight on her arse, hence the discomfort. She swallowed a painkiller found at the bottom of her patent Mulberry bag, and killed the idea of a weight loss.

Alex's slick city office was a skyscraper of a building that planes dodged on their flight path, grown in Canary Wharf. It was set among the swanky buildings, grouped together like supermodels at a show. Tall sculptures of human design and constructive genius were fighting for dominance and supremacy in the financial area that made the area more expensive. Mindy sat watching the office, full of smart suited people racing around like headless chickens outside the wall of window. The pace in this office matched London - fast, non-stop, a human blur, and an array of phones vibrating on the wooden sleek tables, home to these human whizz toys. It reminded her of those old toys that you would wind up and they would jump all over the place. Each of them had a phone glued to their ear. Mindy wished her already perfect skin would shine like the desks.

A photograph of Alex and Troy captured in a stone frame shared a memory on the glossy desk. Each were in a look of pure love, and Mindy's heart twanged with envious hope. There was a glass vase with the bloodiest red roses fanned out, each the size of an egg. Her laptop was nestled next to a phone designed like a shoe - *this girl keeps it real*, Mindy smiled.

"Sorry, girl," she heard her best friend first, and smelled her sweet perfume second. Alex busted in, a Stella McCartney suited whirlwind as if she was on a police raid. The glass door did not hide the envious stares of the female colleagues or the horny looks from the males.

"Ignore those bitches," she said unworried, her voice filtering through the open office and rolling her mile-long roller-blind down with a remote to create instant privacy. Alex had arranged for Mindy to meet her in her office to sort out this crazy idea of Mabel's, and to hear Mindy's other confession that Mindy couldn't tell her over the phone. Mindy double-checked that the envelope was in her handbag.

Alex had tossed and turned all night in her Egyptian cotton sheets. As excitement was dispensed through her limbs, they were coming to life on their own, moving with the excitement taking control like they were the strings similar to a puppet. Troy woke up thinking she was having a seizure of some sort. She was so excited she pounced on him, shagged him, and then his phone call at five am from his friend waiting to pick him up broke the fun. Troy's cock was tender all day due to Alex bouncing on it like she was at a keep-fit class involving a trampoline - yet each time it rubbed on his jeans and made him tense with sensitivity, he smiled.

"Right, business!" Her long runway limbs folded over perfectly like a page on a book. She perched on the side of the desk, her voice booming an octave lower than normal. Alex looked fierce, powerful and quite intimidating. Mindy felt like she was in trouble and started to sweat in her cream polo neck, her hands clasped shut fidgeting with nervous energy.

"Oh, sorry Moo!" Alex realised her alpha female pose was not needed for this case, and took to her leather swivel chair as she relaxed her Olympic pose, taking her hair from its hair grip, and her locks flowed catching the light reflecting off it. "Got carried away," she said, shredding documents in a shredder that appeared from under the table, menacingly like a guard dog. Ripping the paper with ease, it made Mindy uncomfortable.

"I'm not really sure how this is going to work?" Mindy had no evidence - only the word of a dead person that was maybe alive. She would never be believed, she could not testify, and she couldn't say that she was told previously because the police would ask her why she had not spilled earlier. Nor did she have a clue what this Saffron was like in person, nor the power she had in circles. She needed proof; a tip-off was not strong enough, as any tip-off would be leaked back to her due to her having connections to the chief of police. Now Mabel wanted Mindy to go to New York in two days and find a ring.

Mindy only knew how to bring colour to her client's cheekbones with blusher. Gaining evidence by looking for a horse that had disappeared years ago and had now been turned into a ring was a different story. She wished that Bessie was still alive...that dog was great at finding anything dead. Mindy was truly out of her depth. The despair of the unknown rattled her bones; other folk might say she was in the shit. Alex only really knew the legal stuff. She knew how to hot wire a car, but trespassing, collecting invisible criminal evidence, or bringing a case to the court over a dead woman's word? She must have skipped that lecture at university for a hungover day in bed. Plus, Alex dreaded flights, so how could she convince Alex to come New York?

"How are we going to manage this one, Ape?" The thought of this made Mindy sick with anxiety. The fact that they were lacking any strength on their side left her vulnerable. She feared that if it fell flat on its face people would start pointing the finger, saying she was losing her mind like her mother. They would say that she was crazy, just like her mum. It hurt her heart every time she thought about it. Poppy was perfect to Mindy, despite her frail, degrading mind and wacky in-your-face fashion. "Another thing is, we need to get New York in two days."

"New York? Why?" Alex's reply was fast, tinged with fast shock at Mindy's newest revelation.

"Well, there's a big Gala for a fundraising which Saffron will be attending, which then gives us the chance to root in her home for the ring." As each word that Mabel had told her in the note in the crisp envelope left her mouth, the ridiculousness of it somehow finally made sense.

"Evidence is needed," Alex declared strongly. "And if it means going to New York, then New York it is." Alex was rather excited; she wanted to pick up some Christmas decorations ignoring the fact that it was early spring - it was a hobby of hers to collect Christmas tree decorations from her travels, and not an illness like she had done in Africa. She would deal with her slight phobia of flying at the airport with the help of champagne, and plenty of it. Alex pulled out a black book with a list of things she needed. "We need any type of evidence of Ballet Foot, like a bone or something - which would be cool. Or a head!" Her dark side was starting to come through like root regrowth on a blonde. She loved gruesome films; getting reality mixed up with make believe, her biro tapped at the pad awaiting instruction.

"A HEAD?" Mindy didn't like gruesome things at all. She gagged just eating liver, and felt sick watching people swallow sushi.

"Sorry, I was getting carried away. If that happens again, please tell me! Or we need a confession from the old bitch, since Mabel is dead." Mindy diverted her eyes while Alex placed the biro end between her teeth, a sign of concentrated thinking. "She can't stand up in court or find an eyewitness, which I doubt because trying to get an eyewitness is like trying to find a bikini wax that won't hurt!" This was not a case that Alex was used to taking on. First, she had a lack of evidence for a start, not an eyewitness alive, and a confession would take Chinese torture methods just for Saffron to consider it.

"How the hell will I get anything on her?" The thought of playing Miss Marple being a look that Mindy could not pull off played on her tired mind. When she wore woolly tights Maud teased that she looked like a librarian, so never mind her trying to wear a hat. She was not her mother - strong, confident, forward and pushy who could bring down a government if her mind had not decided to reverse. She loved a bit of role-play.

"Well, we need a plan." Suddenly, Alex's receptionist called through. Alex was annoyed as the red light flickered for her attention, and she debated whether to answer it.

"One moment, Moo. Jean, what part of 'don't disturb me' did you miss? Oh, ok, put him through." Alex mouthed to Mindy that it was Troy. "Hey baby, what's up? This is not the time to do phone sex, if that's what this call is," laughing as Mindy turned crimson, looking through the high-end interior design magazine. "Oh my God! That is amazing baby, well done. When is it?" Silence simmered between Alex and the phone, and Mindy looked up. "In four days? Oh, erm, ok. Yes, of course I will be there. And yes, Mindy too." The colour drained from Alex's face. She ended the call with her lover, replaced the receiver, put both hands on the table and let out a deep fat sigh. Attempting to bring justice to clear Mabel's name - the plan of the century - meant that Alex now had to get to New York to find evidence and back to London to see Troy's cooking debut at a pop up restaurant within three days, and more importantly find a killer outfit to wear. This pushed her designer-clad back into a make-believe state, and Alex started to cackle like an evil witch - but with amazing hair and perfect teeth. Louder she went. An interruption cut in just before she could call her flying monkeys.

"Ape, you're doing it again!" Mindy was grateful for the one strong woman in her life, and smiled.

*

Already standing in his underwear when she arrived home, he pounced on her ripping her sexy body free from the restricted Stella suit. It was a cause for celebration, and him and his cock wanted to celebrate with sex. Speechless and shocked, she did not resist his sexy welcoming at all. His tree trunk solid thighs made the tight briefs look miniature; he had one thing on his mind and one thing covering his dense cock. Beneath the cotton briefs his hard cock pushed an outline, rigid and ready, and it would take more than a wank to rid.

His hard, defined abs pressed hard against her own defined abs, and his strong arms brought her in close in a grip of love and wanting. She slipped her hand underneath the waistband of the underwear and felt the heat of his cock, hot with longing, hot to touch like a freshly baked bread roll ready to eat - which she intended too.

Taking hold of his girth in her gentle clasp, she never got used to the shock of its thickness and was already looking forward to it inside her. Slowly she rode the length of his penis in slow motion, up and down with her hand.

Their lips hit, held hard for a moment while his broad hands unclasped her pink bra exposing her breasts. Swiftly cupping one, he fed it towards his mouth. Her nipple was hard in his mouth and growing for more, wet from his eager tongue rolling around it, making her raise her head in a hallelujah. Her hair fell. Lifting her up in one effortless move onto the granite kitchen island, he lowered her down with grace, passionately kissing her and rubbing his hands against her smooth vagina. Her knickers were soft and teased him with dampness. She lowered her back down so that her face was further away from him, her eyes closed with the effect of being blindfolded, wondering where he would lay his hungry touch next.

He stroked her stomach, feeling the soft skin beneath. Her tits parted slightly with gravity, exposing her slim neck; he climbed his lips from her navel all the way up to her neck.

"That feels so good," she whispered. The touch of his lips was familiar, regular - yet each kiss felt new, scary and exciting for what might happen next. She lifted up her long legs in assisting the pleasure, feeling left out from the planted kisses along the line of her leg. Every part of her body he wanted to kiss. "Stop with the kissing and just fuck me." He let out a gentle laugh. He loved knowing that she wanted him as much as he did her.

Resting her sexy legs on his broad shoulders, he dragged her down towards his waist as a lion would with his juicy prey. She hit the hardness of his cock in under three seconds, which was still held behind his briefs. She slipped a leg from his shoulders proceeding to pull down his briefs with her leg, his heavy balls smoothly dropping out, breathing in the air of sex anticipation, pushing her foot against them, soft and full how she liked them. The hardness literally jumped at the base of her knickers, banging, begging to get in.

"Your turn. Take them off," she begged. With the soft cotton of her knickers damp, he did as he was told. When she was demanding he found it horny as fuck, foreplay at its best. Pushing herself onto his cock, she let out a gasp with each penetrating push of him, digging deeper into her. She had never been one for religion, but this didn't stop her repeating '*oh, God*'. It sent shockwaves of lust throughout her stressed body, leaving the stress of work on the floor with each moan of '*more*'. With the banging of his muscular legs against hers and her eyes closed, she felt the powerful thighs and brick solid arse, looking divine in his thrusting.

Nothing could ruin this moment of ecstasy, nothing at all. If the neighbours ran in with a gun, she would enjoy the bang. If the block was collapsing or her annoying mother popped up outside the window as a window cleaner, with all the family taking selfies with them, she would still ride the wave inside until she hit the shore that was long off. She wanted to drown in his juice.

"That feel good?" he asked as his face came closer to hers. His breath was tinted with protein shake, warmly reassuring her he was enjoying it too and needing no reply to his question. Her slender legs were wrapped around his strong back and locked tight, in an invitation to fuck her further.

Suddenly he brought himself onto the marble kitchen island and fucked her with a depth she did not think existed. She half expected to become a unicorn, imagining his dick drilling out of her forehead he was that deep, investigating still after all these years feeling him wanting to explore all of her. She wondered where he had learnt this, but was in no rush to waste any energy asking.

"It feels like the first night I ever made love to you," she said grabbing his face to kiss him; his lips, as always, belonged to her own. Dragging his Adonis body down on to her, for his build and muscle he laid gently on top of her like a sheet of snow. His packed pecs pushed her tits flat. The weight of him made her feel anchored and safe. They wanted to be as close together as possible; their closeness never seemed believable, they felt they could get even closer.

The two naked, gym-fed bodies on the kitchen island fucked away without a care in the world. They were blind to the small flock of seagulls on the balcony and their neighbours who were forever pestering them with swinger invitations, stretching their necks around the balcony at this moment as if they were giraffes.

She decided nothing could ruin this horny moment. This was the best sex they had had in a long time. She wanted every inch of him, feeling his tongue in her mouth competing with his cock for who could go the deepest. Not even if her IBS decided to let rip an almighty cloud of toxic gas and an abrupt noise - nor her mobile ringing berserk in the living room - nothing was worth stopping this moment of two people making love.

"I love you so much baby," she said. As he thrusted deeper she arched her back to accompany every inch of it.

"I want to make our own baby. Let's have a baby," his hot breath delivered each word into her ear with desperation, longing and hope. She felt his meaty dick tense and ready to unload inside, about to deliver the said baby riding on a stampede of determined sperm. Alex opened her eyes in shock, and stared in true horror at Troy's face twisted in pleasure. Nothing could ruin this moment, apart from fucking that.

Manhattan

The mink coat was the elite, most luxurious of animal furs at its best. Constructed with sheer elegance, its scent was vintage Chanel and the weight of it screamed real fur and skin. The rare mink skin was grateful for the offer of being wrapped around the shoulders of one of New York's most fabulous high society names, leaving the battery council living cage conditions as nothing to protest about.

The purple grey-mink coat was an iconic piece of fashion captured by the mass media of the eighties. Splashed all over the television screens as one of the most talked about court cases ever in America, the coat was as loyal as Mabel's lawyer. Saffron agreed that Mabel did look amazing in it as she came out of the court, found innocent of any involvement in the disappearance of the famous Italian racehorse. Saffron still felt resentful that her plan had failed.

Lady Saffron Sapphire was New York's richest socialite, and an influential mover and shaker in the circles of celebrity and charity. She had finally found time to go visit Mabel's apartment since her sudden death. Saffron was shocked about the death of her baby sister but raised a toast, *'about time'*.

The faking of a short illness had to end before people thought she was sick for real, stalked her and made up numerous rumours about her failing health - Cher style. Her popular sister was dead. She now understood the pressure on the Queen around Princess Diana's death. She replaced the heavy fur back over the small chaise knowing very well it would not fit. Saffron was always on a water and ice cube diet, while skinny Mabel stayed a true Texan and ate live cows. Their weight difference was just one of the many that the sisters had.

She walked further into the expensive, tasteless living room, grimacing at the trashy furnishings, and cringing at the lack of coordinated taste of Mabel's interior design skills. Mabel seemed to have popped acid, blindfolded herself and tuned into her inner Drag Queen, painting as she tripped. In addition, to show good face to keep the gossip down, she made sure the paparazzi caught her entering her dead sister's apartment block. Her black Dior two-piece suit was ideal as a test run for the funeral, to be held in London of all fucking places. Saffron hated London; the outfit would certainly be talked about among the Fashion Police.

The vast apartment screamed of Mabel's gypsy-style taste from the flamingo print wallpaper to the checkerboard marble floor. Big trashy fittings in gold and glitter dominated most of the space. A zoological catalogue of fur laid everywhere. How she and her were from the same womb of a washer mother was a mystery. Saffron wondered if Mabel had stashed the exclusive coat of Bigfoot the hermit as a rug, seeing a fur the size of a football pitch laid out exhausted on the marble floor. The giant head of a brown bear was attached snarling his dagger length teeth, and Saffron knew that if it was alive it would have ripped her jugular straight out for what she did to Mabel, and chew her up. Saffron kicked its big head as she passed.

"You so would not think this place would look like this. It's so bloody fabulous I could die, and Cher could finally sing at my funeral. I so wish I could Instagram this swag. Oh my God how fucking gorgeous is this lampshade honey?" The fabulous drawn-out camp shriek of delight cut the air as Lucas Desmond raced over to a gold lampshade with feathers as tassels as if he was a kid at Disneyland and had just seen Mickey, dramatically clapping his bony hands like a sea lion. It made Saffron shudder. Queer men annoyed Saffron.

Lucas Desmond was a flamboyant, orange skinned, emaciated gay interior designer from the Meat District recommended by Ewan her stylist, who was now fingering a pearl beaded cushion - he probably thought that the firmness of the pearl was the G-spot in the anus of a Grindr fuck. His fitted tartan blazer and white shirt with its dramatic collar made his long, horsy orange head glow. His diet consisted of champagne, idle gossip and cheap cocaine from a Brazilian dealer in the rough arse area of Brooklyn. In his early days he paid for his habit using his mouth on the dealer's cock, hence his ability to fit into a woman's size zero jeans - this accomplishment meant more to him than his fashion degree. The only straight thing about Lucas was his sideburns. He had been recommended to accompany Saffron as she toured Mabel's Manhattan apartment, a few streets too far from Fifth Avenue and too common for her to take up residence in.

Saffron was at Mabel's place for a few reasons. She obviously was saddened by the death of her only crazy baby sister, but was relieved more. She was intending on buying the place to leave everything inside to rot, and not have the pleasure of being lived in. The main reason she had rushed over from her manor in the Hamptons was to get the dressing table, yet it was not here. This pissed Saffron off immensely.

Saffron searched every over-decorated room for the dressing table, using Lucas as a sniffer dog. His excitement fuelled him on - it was more draining than a marathon. He had done most of the footwork in his Dolce patent cowboy boots, as he looked in every room and cupboard with the awe of being in the socialite's home and unaware that he was being used. Only a gay man in interior design could cover the apartment space of a famous lady in less than fifteen minutes. It was as exciting and unreal as his first visit to a gay sauna had been when he was eighteen, his first spit roast of many. His friends were so jealous when he told them that one of them deleted him from Instagram.

All she found was fur, fur and more fucking fur. She took seven anti-allergy tablets to combat her allergic reactions. Mabel always did love fur; when they were younger and they had come across a mountain lion dead, their father had skinned it and made Mabel an adorable cape from its wasted fur. Saffron had again been pushed aside for her sister. Lucas pranced around in his cowboy boots acting as if this place was his, distracting her from the memory.

Everything was *'fabulous'*, *'gorgeous'*, *'wonderful'*, and he threw his skeletal hand to his glossy lips in shock at anything fitting this limited vocabulary of description. Saffron had told him to lose the phone; the constant flashing was driving her insane, and so did his camp and overwhelming smell of aftershave. Saffron had nothing against queers, but she preferred to mention her support for gay rights in interviews rather than practise it in reality. The gay community were all queens and queers to her, and she was the only Queen of New York ridding any contenders to her imaginary crown...Delia Von-Grouse could vouch for that.

"Oh, this is so wonderful, being in the home of Mad Mabel! She was such an icon. And a great supporter of the gay community, ya know. Oh my God, the amount of drag queens using her as a foundation is amaziiinnngggg. I can even smell her." Lucas preened himself in a mirror framed by jade, the way a lone budgie does to a cheap plastic mirror in its tiny cage. Checking his drawn on black eyebrows had not smudged into his fake tan, nor his bleached blonde hair lost any more strands, he was hiding his bald patch with a purple trilby. His eyebrows were as thin as his arms. Seeing a small comb on the table beside him he made a mental note to pocket it as a souvenir, a story to tell Coco and Chanel - his identical twin surrogate children born from the womb of a virgin in years to come.

Saffron politely forced a smile. "What a sweet thing to say Luke," using the incorrect name on purpose to show that she held the power in this grand flashy room. One thing she loathed about Mabel between her celebrated fashion sense and talent for making people laugh was her popularity. Ever since they were both out of diapers, Mabel had been everyone's favourite. No one directly said it, but Saffron knew she was. It was the first seed of loathing for her sister; it rooted and grew inside her body with the destruction of Japanese Knotweed. It suffocated any love she had felt for her sister, and no therapy could have trimmed and cut it back to allow a little to flourish.

No matter what designer Saffron wore, or exquisite jewel hung around her neck, Mabel could be wearing a rabbit sack and still steal all the attention at any party they attended. The rumour, Mabel the inspiration for the country-western superstar global smash, based on a hoe called Jolene. People would queue to talk to her, a human attraction of honour. Lucas was too engrossed in his heavily made-up reflection to notice the sly smirk on Saffron's face. Could she kill Lucas and blame it on Mabel with the blood spilt of her recent death? The idea took hold of her hand as she picked up a letter opening knife.

Where had the stupid old bitch hid that fucking dressing table? Saffron needed to find it; its beauty was to be sold at Christie's and what it was worth would be record-breaking, making Elizabeth Taylor's jewels price tag seem like a bargain. Saffron needed a stiff drink and to get rid of lanky Lucas. The faggot was doing her nut in, teasing the sharpness of the knife. Noticing him wrapping himself up in a piebald fur throw he declared he looked '*fugly fabulous*', clapping his hands in gay delight. Saffron debated whether to throw a kipper at him. He looked ugly like a skinny Chewbacca. She placed the knife down, for now.

"What is fugly, Lennon?" Saffron liked to be in the lingo of the young, so she would at least get an education from the flamboyant breadstick - it was the only slight bonus of having his camp company. Lucas ignored the incorrect name and decided against battling with the Queen of New York; there had been many battles he had won with Queens on the scene, but this one was very old, and had dementia maybe.

"Oh my God! 'Fugly' means so ugly that it's fabulous, darling," he said twirling in the dead fur, pouting in a way that would turn Marilyn Monroe in her snug grave. Saffron huffed and left the living room with expensive smell of vanilla and jasmine oil fresh from any interference from human modification in the air. Those believing in after life may say Mabel was waiting on earth in limbo for revenge as Saffron slammed the heavy door behind her.

London, Heathrow Airport

Duty-free and champagne - a jovial mix that gave access to an exultant mood, and one that Mindy loved. Once her bags had left on the conveyor belt, they got checked through security. There was a nice little pat down for Alex from the hunky black guy, his smile matching the width of his strong body. Mindy got the short guy with additional facial hair. His search on her body for the culprit setting off the alarm made her feel like he was a plastic surgeon checking which parts to suck away with lipo. After that, their holiday started. This trip was not really a holiday, it was a mission. It was a mission set by Agent Mabel, the flute of champagne already massaging deluded ideas over their brains.

"Oh, these glasses were a steal!" she said, appearing like a supermodel from behind the screen at the beginning of a runaway. Alex covered half of her beautiful face with oversized floral designer shades. She gained a few looks from other duty-free loving people all thinking she was actually a star; Alex certainly could pass for a top model. Her lean body was wrapped up inside a gorgeous grey cashmere jumpsuit, ultra-comfortable and sheer class for the long flight. A few dozen duty-free bags hung at her side confidently showing she loved a bargain, and her compact lips were painted in seductive red.

Heathrow airport, strangely diluted of holidaymakers, gave the impression that there had been a human apocalypse outside. Inside, only survivors made Mindy volunteer her womb to help repopulate. The oval UFO bright lights made moths congregate at the Niagara Falls tall window like immigrants seeking safe refuge. The vast space of the airport strangely brought a feeling of calm after the last few days.

Their flight to New York was the first of the early morning, so duty-free, a full English and a magnum of champagne was for breakfast. Mindy sat in the VIP lounge allowing her body to relax and set sail to the previous week's stress on the river of champagne. What was happening? She should be getting up to an alarm clock to feed E.T before work, who was boarding at a cattery. *'God help you,'*

Alex had said to the receptionist as they had left him. Sipping champagne before the morning came and waiting for a flight to New York to try and find evidence that Saffron had kidnapped Ballet Foot was not a normal morning.

Alex sat, pulled out her iPad and googled Saffron's name. Thousands of images multiplied with the simple click on *search* of the famous high society lady of New York. Couture fashion clothed her body, and jewels dripped and hung off her body like ripe fruits from a tree. Coiffed hair was whisked up onto her head and held with a mouth-watering piece of jewellery. She oozed confidence, class and power. She was a powerful woman, great friends with Oprah and Hilary, and had once dated a semi-warlord. She was a colossal aid giver and held a few prestigious addresses in America, but something in her eyes gave away that Saffron was far from a pushover. Mindy gulped her champagne fast.

"Wow girl, you're going to get kicked off the flight before you even get on it!" she said taking the flute away from Mindy's lips as Mindy's heart shaped lips chased it.

"Alex, do you think we've got ourselves in at the deep end? I mean, do you think me and you can break into her apartment and root for evidence?" Mindy popped a complimentary chocolate into her mouth, glad that it was brandy flavoured.

"Sweetheart, listen," Alex redressed her long legs and leant in, Basic Instincts style. A pair of random aged executives looked on from their seats hoping that the redhead and brunette were prostitutes, or at least good fun-time girls, waving for a bottle of champagne to be sent over.

"We just need connections. And darling, I'm a scouser. I'd hotwired a car before I could walk," Alex said chuckling. Mindy laughed, another chocolate entered her mouth.

Alex was right as usual - it was just connections that they needed. Each brandy truffle she ate diluted the madness of it all into something achievable. They just had to break into Saffron's apartment, find the ring and leave.

'*Simple! What are you worried about?*' the fourth brandy flavoured complimentary truffle said before she devoured it.

New York City

Fucking livid was an understatement. A woman of class and sophistication, Maria slammed the hotel door in such force that she set off a fire alarm in the corridor. She did not give a flying fuck, throwing her Tom Ford shoes at the wall.

The lilac silk halter neck Versace gown cooked against her fired up skin, and any crease in the flimsy gown was literally ironed out. Her eyes turned black with anger, fuelled with her embarrassment. She scratched her wrist vigorously until her shellac nails ached, and the pain became a sedative to her phoenix anger, not noticing droplets of clean blood soaking the cream carpet.

Slamming the bathroom door, she ignored the harsh crack of the wood splitting in sheer shock, locking herself in. She launched her ceramic clutch solid into the glass sink, ignoring the contents of expense spilling out from its open wound, afraid of the kick off.

"Chad, you're such a fucking prick at times!" she screamed into the solace and silence of the shiny bathroom mirror; it remained mute without a reply, afraid. Maria unhooked the ruby red earrings, throwing them onto the side in fury and letting out a hate-filled cry.

The snide comment that Chad had mentioned which had rallied Maria's anger to rattle on her skeleton inside like a prisoner on bars, was: *"Roxy will forever be my number one girl in my life, she just had to come to the preview,"* in a tone that was sickeningly sweet and borderline bestiality sounding. Maria had stood demurely and sexily hooked on his leather-dressed arm like a human charm, with a wide pearly white smile hiding her public dissing. The pretty reporter had laughed, but her eyes had screamed that she felt pity for Maria on behalf of the entire female audience at home watching.

Roxy wore a glittering red bow in her long fringe matching her painted pink claws. She was the star of the premiere invited to generate publicity for Chad and his new upcoming film. A Kardashian had claimed a selfie with the dog, and Bruce had saluted the dog as if she was the First Lady of the fucking country; it made Maria twist her perfect lips with jealousy. Chad's sleazy agent had got them the invite; Greg Locust was a cockroach as far as Maria was concerned. The mutt got all the media attention on the red carpet, and every reporter acted like Roxy was the fucking star as she played dead, hi-fived with her paw, and rolled over on command like a hooker - minus the fifty dollars. If Maria had been standing in her birthday suit she still would not have won the battle of the bitches for Chad's attention.

Chad made Maria keep hold of her pink lead. Maria did not get to pose once in her fabulous frock, with the thick pink lead tangled around her clutch bag and her legs as if Roxy was working to bring her down. Ignoring the mocking and careless jesting, she simply smiled as heavy tears filled her eyes. Never in her life had she been so degraded by her fiancé - second best to a fucking mutt. Maria had been beaten black and blue by her drunken father as a child; despite this disrespect not being physical, it hurt more than any punch her father had delivered to her body for her own good, in his words. The worst was to come.

Finding out that Roxy had been seated next to Chad in the picture house while Maria had to do with not one, but two rows behind at the screening next to an aging fashion designer whose skin needed a stitch or two, was the tortilla wrap that broke the Mexican's back. Maria was fuming. Volcanic anger raced from her Tom Ford soles right up her sexy body, and she had clamped down hard on her tongue to stop the eruption of verbal hot lava from coming out. It was also due to the fact that the miscarriage had fucked her up three days before now, and her fiancé had relegated her to the third row and put a fucking dog before her, whose only one talent she had over Maria was that she could lick her own fanny. Maria found this mildly humorous, and the only consolation was that at least Roxy was a pedigree.

Maria hadn't always felt this fury of destructive internal fire towards Chad, burning every positive emotion she felt for him leaving ashes of hate. Every time a thought or memory of him entered her mind she tossed it onto the bonfire, revelling in its heightened heated roar. Once that fire burned bright and strong, the flames flickered passionately, lit by love for all to stand and warm themselves in the glow.

Meeting him on the set of the hit soap *Sunset Dawn,* his aura had been addictive and drew her in like a sale at Cartier. He had staggeringly beautiful looks, with his eyes of gems and flirtatious flicking of his lush eyelashes. Every time he blinked, you would hold your breath until he opened his eyes to give you that look. It was a look that dissolved everything around you, a look of protection, love and promise. Maria was a woman who did not drop at the hat of a gorgeous looking man or leave her heels on a doormat worn down by a stampede of heels. She was herself, one of the top three most beautiful women in Mexico; she felled men to her feet wherever she went. At the time she was being wooed by a young Saudi Prince, yet with Chad, she had dropped her guard, her heart and her skimpy knickers in the toilets of the studio within a day. Attentive, romantic and caring, he was the whole package. He had been a gentleman - chairs pulled out, flowers delivered, doors opened, and so many notes littered her hotel room that she worried they were a fire hazard. She had given a donation to a tree planting charity to cover her sweet guilt. He had treated her as if she was the most sought after leading lady in life, the only female left on the planet. It was pure ecstasy for her and Maria became a hardcore addict - she needed to suck, blow and have more of this drug. Earth-shattering bottomless visits to hidden orgasms within her racy body floored her with amazement. He had flooded her soul instantly on his first penetration, with his desirable, sharp indulgence entering her and making her gasp in gratification with short breaths and moans. She would howl in hedonism, craving his cock acknowledging her soft sides. The only time she would ever shout *'Oh, God'* was when she was on her back and he was inside her.

He took her so dangerously low, holding her body on the brink of collapse. She felt like it was the end of her body if he didn't push that inch more to release her body under her own building lust inside. Yearning to drown her in the teasing trance his cock had her in, it would will her to give in to the pleasure. One swift turn of position or speed would release enough line for her to soar high like a kite, higher than she had ever been before, leaving her past lovers as mere dots on the ground; she expected angels to push her back down to earth. Her grateful moans matched a soprano. She watched herself having sex - and damn, the diet was working - like an out of body experience, drowning herself with her own wetness and that kiss. Heaven simply opened when his lips touched hers, and any care or worries fell away with each item of extravagant clothing he slipped off her.

That night, that one encounter on the happiest night of her life changed everything with no hope of return. The buxom diamond ring, only a few hours old and yet to reveal its beauty to all her family, friends and the fans, was tarnished all on his uninvited touch. The strange touch gave her a sickness, not a seduction, and the kiss was the giveaway that things were about to go horrifically wrong for Maria. The kiss was not the familiar softness, but abrupt, hard pressure forced onto her lips. She hurt her neck twisting to get away from it, yet the stranger did not leave. His musky breath soaked in scotch and Cuban cigars scorched her face. She caught Chad watching on in glee, caked in the finest cocaine and naked, his eager erection hard and entertained in his moving hand. He was spread-eagled in the chair in the far corner like some fucking Playboy centrefold. Through her wet eyes she knew she had met the devil, and this devil had sadly taken two for the price of one - her heart and soul.

What happened next in that hotel room on her engagement night ran full force into her non-dairy, no carb, sugar-free juice loving stomach, knocking her fairy-tale future face flat, letting the start of the nightmare stampede over it all, football hooligan style. The pain from the uninvited forced itself inside her. The pain in her head brought on by her tightened eyes closed burned. The pain threw a deadly spear through her Princess idealism of love. With this ugly memory pushing its disgusting face back, her body reacted gagging, and dry sick brought her back to the bathroom mirror. Catching her reflection, it made her sick. She started to wipe off her perfect make-up abruptly, alone in the bathroom.

Each wipe ripped through her expensive make-up. She wiped away the colourful mask that Maria wore for the adoring public, a facial disguise that was praised in the media and beauty magazines. She ripped through her make-up with the venom of a cheated wife let loose on her bastard of a husband's shirt collection.

Each wipe revealed more of the real Maria that only she saw. An onion wore fewer layers, covering its heart, Maria's heart was dead. A sensitive Maria longed to be just a mother and a faithful wife, to have a happy home environment without worrying about guns, gangs or drugs. She wanted to show that not all Mexicans were destined to become gardeners or maids. She peeled off her extensions of luxe lashes and ripped off her fancy nails in one. She pulled out her hair extensions that had been grown by an orphaned child on a mountain top in India, and lastly, she ripped out of the designer dress with one tear, enough to make the mirror cry.

The marble bathroom was lit low, afraid to offer brightness and afraid of what it would reveal was standing in the bathroom naked, panting like a wild dog. The mosaic tap dripped single tears, the lone drip menacing and loud like a sinister clap of *well done*. Here was the real Maria, beautiful but raw. She was naked and at breaking point; unless something changed, Maria would die a broken woman.

Maria stared at her new reflection, the red lips smeared across her face like blood from a slap to the nose. The purple eyeshadow gave the impression that she had taken a punch from Ali. Her hair was wild and showed no evidence of a salon blow-dry, and one finger bled from where she had ripped her nail off. Her stomach was slightly swollen from the pain that the miscarriage had left, as a cruel reminder of the short life that had lived in her womb. She knew that the searing pain had been brought on by the kick Chad had delivered to her stomach in his drunken rage; of late this had been appearing more often and lasting longer. This was the reason that no child occupied her womb.

To anyone looking in she looked like a battered wife - not a fashion muse - and they might plead with her to leave the violent man instead of praising their loving relationship over social media. Maria wanted revenge. Since Chad had robbed her of the chance to be a mummy, then she would rob his baby and his chance of a hotshot film career. It was simple.

One question lingered, and unafraid of the whirlwind of self-aggression it came to comfort her: *What revenge could ultimately destroy Chad Rise, the cunt?* it whispered. It bounced inside her head in directions she was unable to catch. Cheating on him would make her look bad - he was turned on by the thought of another man fucking her and would want to join in anyway. She needed something dangerous to ruin his life, and end him finally, forever.

Murder? But no, she wanted to watch Chad suffer as he watched her career take off. If he was murdered his star-status would be cemented, James Dean style. *Come on, Maria. Dig deeper. What is the one thing Chad adores most in life?* Revenge asked her.

"Himself!" she said slowly, as it echoed around the empty bathroom telling everything in the bathroom. An acid attack would only bring sympathy for his melted looks, and an accident to cripple him might result in a huge endorsement for a mobility company, she laughed.

A sex-related illness like AIDS? She darkened at the idea of infecting him with it. With today's medication to manage it and a less aggressive stigma, it would become an ally to him. No, Maria needed something life destroying and untreatable, a type of revenge there would be no return from, to cripple Chad into a helpless mess for the world to laugh at for the rest of his life. Presently, like her womb, her mind was vacant. Not one idea of revenge presented the right CV to take the acclaimed position. The saying that '*good things come to those who wait*' rang loud.

Maria's newest role was to bring 'Storm Revenge' to his perfect life, giving light to the tight darkness around Maria's life that she wore like a Prada cape coat. The smile on her inflamed beautiful face became the most genuine thing that she had worn all night.

Beginning of the End for Some Bastards and Bitches

Central Park was one of Mindy's favourite places in the whole world, beating the Maldives and whale watching in the Atlantic with 'Him'. She licked the tri-flavoured ice cream with gusto. A new bitch to a litter licking them free of their little bubble of protection from the womb would take inspiration. The park amazed her with natural beauty. The only time Mindy played promiscuous was when it came to ice cream flavours. The more the merrier for her, dragging her taste buds into an organic orgy, distracting her from taking a trip down memory lane with 'Him'. A few passing gents felt a twinge below watching the licking of the mesmerising redhead.

Alex played monogamous to ice cream and kept it safe with vanilla but flirted with a few chocolate chips, drawing admiring gazes from most of the men in the park - *was she a Victoria's Angel model?* The question of Troy wanting a baby played on her mind since that passionate evening of sex to celebrate his place at the Pop up restaurant. *Why are you so uptight about having a baby?* he had roared as she slammed the bedroom door that night leaving him to take the sofa. Alex's reason was strong, something she for once could not argue to win. Troy wanted a baby. She had seen how he smiled when couples with a toddler passed, or how he kept dropping suitable baby names. Troy was obsessed with Greek mythology; Hercules, Zeus and even Hades were names that Alex had thrown her resting bitch face at.

Alex didn't want a baby, plain and simple. Ignoring any urges of broodiness with out of control shopping sprees or dragging Troy on adventure-adrenaline holidays, he had been hoping that if a child came along all of this would be in the past. She caught Troy's Amazon history once and he'd been looking at a baby harness and mini crash helmets; she had smiled as she closed the tab down.

Did this mean their relationship was over? Was she cruel to clip Troy's chance of fatherhood? Honestly, it was time to take the relationship into the next stage and a baby was part of that, but could they not just get a cat and turn it into a social media star? It was the reason her mother had taken up knitting and knitted enough white, lemon and pale cardigans to clothe the next human race of babies. She longed for Alex to get pregnant to point she thought about drugging Alex and artificially inseminating her. Alex's long awaited pregnancy was top of the prayer list at Carol's church.

Accidents happen. *But what if the accident repeats itself?* she silently questioned. Was it an omen for what was to come? Was the past, two decades old, ready to forgive and let her forget? Or was karma painting her talons, ready to balance out the accident by taking something valuable in her life, such as her own child? Alternatively, it could torment her conscience for the rest of her life in the same way that the loss would with her forgiving aunt.

On the other hand, the pain of Troy wanting a baby she could never deliver would be a punishment and a stabbing reminder of her carelessness forever. The memory of it made her shiver, but the realisation that she may lose Troy iced her soul more. Surely the memory of the drowning of her baby cousin under her ten year old watchful eye would know that she had been helpless to save little Selby that day?

"Bloody hell, Mindy, when was the last time you put a penis in your mouth?" The pink tongue of Mindy blurred like a hummingbird's wing, tasting the sweet nectar of the dairy dessert. Alex was grateful for the distraction from being reminded of Selby's tiny, lifeless pale white body, drenched on the pier with her favourite wellies missing on that terrible morning, and mocked her best friend, upset that she had left Troy on a bad note when leaving for New York.

"If cock tasted this good I would lick it every day." Her tongue washed away the escapee ice cream on her lip, singing back the banter to Alex and unafraid of speaking about sexual goings on in public.

"Burn in hell you whore!" an elderly, high-pitched voice cut in across the private conversation. Mindy spun around feeling like she did in school when Mrs Dully caught her bunking from her religious education class in the toilets.

Sister Mary Manger was notorious for attacking women who lived their life in any shade of red; the New York Post had run an article about her back in the eighties. She lifted up her loyal wooden crucifix, her sidekick through her years of hard-core worship of religion, storming away from the pretty redhead declaring she would suck cock every day. Alex erupted with laughter, her abrupt noise spooking nearby pigeons to take flight.

"I'm going to hell, aren't I?" The green bench appeared as if by magic just when the girls needed a seat, for Alex to catch her breath, and Mindy to sulk. She hated to upset anyone, yet Poppy the anarchist would have flashed her tits to the old nun, ignoring the fact that they sagged below her belly button.

"Well if you go to hell, save me a seat," sitting down next to Mindy. A fortune-teller with a glass eye and a hairy mole - failing to add the sexiness of Cindy Crawford - on her left cheek had told Alex for a fiver that she was to live a long life of sin.

"And why would you be going to hell?" Mindy laughed, knowing very well Alex would be on a first class Concorde to hell with her carrot oil already packed.

"Troy wants a baby; I don't." Why did a lump catch in her throat?
You really want a baby, said her loving heart.
You would kill it, her logical head reminded her.

"That's wonderful news Alex." Mindy sensed it was for Troy, not Alex.

"Is it?" she questioned. She had kept Mindy in the dark about the drowning of her cousin on New Brighton Pier. The paper cutting, yellowing and decaying still kept strength in the tragedy she kept in a file hidden away.

The bench was peacefully placed back from the busy path, solid in structure as if it wanted to hold them up strong no matter what made them sit. A huge tree lent its branches to offer shade from the sun. A few tender, shy leaves sprouting gave an inventory of colour to show that the weather was warming up. The tree was gearing up, ready to blossom natural beauty to wow the entire park, cemented in a thousand selfies in one summer hit. Mindy and Alex stared in content silence with their delicious gelato ice cream.

The park's power to comfort and calm played. Mindy noticed the bench wearing the in-trend brooches for benches, a rectangular gold plaque inscribed with *'Edna, back where she belongs with her beloved Barney'.* The smooth, cold metal kissed her fingers and the engraved writing deep and italic, written with love. But sadly, Edna was never to read it. She hoped that Edna was back with Barney. The touch of the plaque touched her heart. Would she ever reunite with a husband if she was to die before them? '*Mindy, back with Joe-Ryan*' had a beautiful ring to it she thought, and a sweet smile appeared. If Mindy had turned up last week when the police tape had forbidden anyone to sit on the bench, she would have seen the body of a frozen elderly woman, making it difficult to put into the body bag. Edna had become just another dead body from suicide in the glorious hotspot of death in the park, revenge on her ailing sick body. Mindy would have cried, and offered her card for make-up services to the grieving relatives.

Clouds sailed past gently with the speed of a snail, and birds and squirrels gave energy to the park. Mums and dads chased after their offspring, and dogs became sleigh dogs pulling their owners or paid walkers in the direction of squirrels. Joggers passed in speed. One chubby kid was trying to hit a pigeon with a stick. It was probably trying to kill it to eat it, Alex thought - she hated obesity in children. A moment passed.

"Alex, how the hell are we going to break into Saffron's, steal a ring, and get back to London without getting caught? Access to Saffron's I doubt is an open house for all." Once Mindy had been asked by Miss Carey, the old dear next-door with more pussy than a brothel, with her seven ASBO cats running riot around the council estate, rumours they ate Elmina Harris who went missing, if she would kindly climb through the window and let her in. Miss Carey had forgotten to take the house key when she changed her M&S mac, declaring herself a dozy mare. She had always been brought up to help the unfortunate, so Mindy had agreed. Being twelve years old she felt that she could tackle any crisis, knowing that the pound tip from Miss Carey paid the bonus, which had been the driving force into her accepting the request. Unfortunately, Mindy had ended up getting her arse stuck as her zip caught onto the latch. She had banged her head against the window, her head heavy as if she was a wrecking ball. The window had cracked. Frank from down the road had to cut the window frame in half for Mindy to get out, and cost Miss Carey two hundred pounds to fix. It brought endless joy to the whole street, out in community force like it was the fucking Queen's jubilee to watch, with cups of tea and everything. Poppy had been delighted. That little episode had given her the lifelong phobia of trying to get into someone's house. It was impossible for Mindy, unless invited, handed a key or kidnapped and held there by ransom. Being a lawyer, you had to have answers, hard cold facts and solid evidence - Alex could score a hat trick.

"Well, luckily for us, you are good friends with her neighbour." Saffron's tower block housed one of the world's most famous women ever to live, more renowned than the Virgin Mary, googled more than Kim K, and with enough of a temper to make Miss Piggy volunteer herself into a pork scratching.

"Who?" Her puzzlement showed. Mindy was roll calling a list in her head. Most people she knew in New York lived in the cheaper parts where police tape worked like picket fencing. Alex smiled, turning her phone screen slowly to show the sell-out Vogue cover of said friend. "Oh, fuck." Her last bit of ice cream fell off the crunchy cone in shock.

*

Gloria kneeled on her square knees, slighting rocking in her black outfit of fitted white shirt and stiff black jacket - a family funeral favourite, or borrowed court couture for criminal family members. Stroking the smooth wood of the demure front door tenderly, she ignored the sharp ache building up in her bended knees, having been in this position for the last hour. Tears blurred her vision, using up much of her water retention - she could have sworn her ankles felt slimmer.

She was crying, whaling better than a hormonal banshee needing her roots doing, as if it was her lover dying in her manly arms and not a tacky door needing to be replaced. A fed-up carpenter stuffed tissue into his ears. She even went as far as saying an Irish prayer fast and repeating in a trance. Her battered rosary beads were rolling between her fingers like cardio for her chunky fingers, ignoring the fact that Gloria worked as the biggest sin that the Irish church loathed. The poor joiner adopted the idea that maybe Gloria was a tree hugger, or a well-dressed psychopath. Alternatively, she might have belonged to a new cult - this was New York after all.

"Gloria, give it a fucking rest will you!" The sweet voice purred from inside the grand penthouse suite. The honey tones made the crude explicit word seem sweet, belonging to one of the richest women in the world. Fed up listening to this audio of woe from her personal assistant for the past hour, she wondered if the joiner would put a lock on Gloria's cracked lips.

The owner of the voice did not give a fuck if the wooden door had been carved by the legendary Angelo Catalo, the blind one-armed artist from the 1920s, a timeless masterpiece, or two flying fucks if the door was part of history, and a remaining survivor of the Titanic. Simone Delvin wanted the nice glass door engraved with a huge 'SD' in pink diamonds. Simone loved modern and expensive, not old and historic. The bible-thick petition that the rich residents of the well sought after block had court delivered cured her insomnia when she had read it.

"I hope you're this upset if I ever die!" said Simone Delvin, global superstar, built entirely on her God-given beauty and wild behaviour, one of the biggest exports that Britain had offered to the world - bigger than Adele and tea. She was the granddaughter of the late Dame Rose Delvin, superstar of film and theatre. There was nothing and no one that Simone was afraid of, nothing she could not afford. Her wealth made her more powerful than a few countries combined. She was so famous that she was a member of the exclusive celebrity club known by just her first name.

Sitting at the smashed effect glass table with a lukewarm herbal tea in one hand and a carrot stick in the other with all the glossy magazines that Gloria's loyal, hardworking, slightly alcoholic lesbian P.A had fetched from the newsstand on the corner, lay wide open. The thin pages were like a willing weekend lover, ready to finger and turn over.

Tonight was the night of the fundraising Gala *Golden Halo*, the biggest charity ball in America, hence Simone being in the insomniac city. Each magazine confessed her celebrated arrival with a dozen glamorous pictures of the sexy star and her gorgeous model husband, Leon Jaxon. He still gave her butterflies after three years together, and the mere sight of him sent shockwaves to her waxed fanny. Each day she woke with him she felt blessed and thanked Mary Magdalene, her favourite saint, each night when she slept.

A ruby encrusted mobile flashed a number that was not recognised. Instantly she wondered which Hollywood hunk it was this time, trying to whisk her away. They all knew she was married, but her infamous bed-hopping reputation of past stalked her relentlessly. Orlando, Leo, maybe Jared…she prayed it was not Charlie since his recent revelation - the virus did not bother her, but his debt did. It could be a bloodthirsty journalist willing to give up their poor mother to ISIS, knowing that the terrorist group would take anyone for a bride, who would do anything for an exclusive interview with the super beauty Simone. It would be certain to break the internet if there was a feature of Simone in the issue, making Kim K break into a tantrum and Kayne slate her in a hit rap, again. Simone harboured the power to make the Pope break his vow of celibacy with her heavenly looks and killer body - so a male calling was her number one suspicion. Maybe it was Donatella; she had not worn Versace in a week.

The caller was determined and rang on. It could be a stalker; Simone was afraid of no one. Simone picked it up and pressed the green phone icon, pursing her juicy lips she spoke "Hello?" nibbling a carrot stick, bored already as she waited for a reply. The name on the other end of the phone made her scream in sheer joy. "Get your fucking sexy arse over here!" The joiner wished she was referring to him. The chubby Irish woman reminded him of his ex-wife, chubby and constantly wailing. The only difference was that his ex-wife never went on her knees. He could do with the break.

Logging on to her favourite dating site out of the unlucky seven that she had signed up to, *Single2mingle*, Maud nibbled a shortbread biscuit, and in three visits to her mouth it was gone. The crumbs fell into the Grand Canyon known as her cleavage, and were grinded to dust. The afternoon had been low on activity. Mindy was in New York, so Maud had not actually spoken to anyone all day, and boredom pestered her like a boil on the arse.

Maud secretly liked Mindy - it was hard not to. She knew she was hard on her and tormented her, but that was Maud's way of coping through life. She had to get in there first with the abrupt attitude and forceful opinions, and create a ballsy barrier for protection from cruel comments about her weight or her dowdy appearance before they did. The target of her gob would be burned alive by the fire-hot remarks she breathed.

Throughout her young life and much of her early adult life, Maud started and ended most days with negative comments - not always said in a rude way, but someone like family, friend or a stranger would mutter to her about the benefits of losing weight. Healthy cookbooks were the favourite Christmas gift from her small circle of friends, stocked high in the kitchen. She actually used them as a stool to sit on when she ate a carb carnival plate of food.

When she was young, aged around eight, was when the weight started to appear over the months sticking to her like moss. Her childhood was happy; she had plenty of friends in the community-promoting street, but slowly she walked where the others ran. She would sit beneath the tree while her cousins climbed it, and sat on the side of the swimming pool on her holidays abroad knowing that if she got into the rubber ring, she wouldn't be getting out of it. Her appetite was never huge, nor was she forever sneaking food to eat to help with negative feelings or to comfort. It was just down to good old-fashioned great portions that her mummy - who never a beanpole herself - had cooked. Maud was cuckoo fed on her mother's love, who just happened to be an award-winning baker. It did not help that her mum and loving dad, skinny as a rake, ran a popular bakery store. The shop fed the whole range of celebrations of the idyllic Cornish village, and any occasion, her mother Patsy would bake a mouth-watering cake fit for the purpose.

Popular and delicious, the homemade cakes and pastries were celebrities. People travelled from other towns just to purchase them. The only child in her family was the downfall and leftovers became second nature, replacing siblings made from the oven of the kitchen and not a womb. It made Maud popular among the school yard when she would take in cream buns, strawberry tarts, chocolate-chocker cakes and meat filled pies, selling them for a few pence and spending the profits on plastic nudist-loving toy trolls with crazy hair.

The event that took the weight gain from stubborn puppy fat into a full pack of wild food-consuming wolves was when her beloved parents had perished in the horrific house fire when she was sixteen. Food became comfort. Cakes, sugar, and fat alleviated memories of her lovely parents. Pies were perfect to cry with every night. They were the edible equivalent of a favourite song of a loved one. Each photograph of happy times captured forever, never to age or to be forgotten, pushed her into a food binge. With each piece of their clothing to smell, or wearing her heart low and cold over the loss egged her on to lose the pain in hot apple pie and chunky custard.

Every time she ate the catalogue of cream cakes, she felt close to her parents who had been taken too early. Each taste became a kind of engaging conversation with them. No one knew about the horrific fire that charcoaled her parents as they slept after a busy day - not even a bomb would have woken them. It was only when thick smoke choked the clear night air, the red glow coming from the direction of the high street where the bakery lived that brought the illusion that the sunrise had risen earlier to the whole beach of youths illegally raving and underage drinking. Most knew that something bad had happened to Maud's family, in their state of substance over-indulgence.

When the community woke the next day to the burnt skeleton of the cottage smouldering in a pile into the fresh air, it was bad news. Two bodies were lead out covered up; it broke the whole of the village's hearts when the devastation was confirmed. It broke Maud's once positive outlook on life forever. They all rallied around to support Maud. Collections that burst with money put Maud up in a rented cottage for three months. Stews, soups and food hampers kept her company at night, and so did the guilt. The burning blame, the stark reason why the killer fire had happened in the first place egged her on to eat. It was torture for her stupidity, and why her parents were now baked deep six feet under in a grave bare from any flowers from their own daughter for over twenty-two years; it latched on when she ran away to London and abused herself with the one thing that gave her happy memories of her childhood - food.

Living in London, she had hoped the chaos and fast pace of the city would speed her through life like Sandra Bullock did on that bus, with no time to be reminded of the fatal fire, and no time to stop and think. She was getting fat to bury the physical pain, the bright make-up was to distract, and the rudeness was to scare off anyone who dared to get too close and enquire about her childhood and life before London. If Maud were a parent herself, she would know that parents forgive their children for anything - even something as devastating as being burned asleep in their own bed. Maud had told no one the real reason that the fire started. Only the investigating fire officer knew, but he had died three years later from a heart attack. Working at the parlour was a reminder of their deaths and punishment for the person responsible for the fire - Maud. The fat became heavy and vulgar; a constant reflection and punishment, death row rolls of fat for Maud the murderer.

Maud may have been a fat girl on the outside, but she was a fat girl with a personality and her confidence had grown over the years until the point where nobody could ever imagine Maud being skinny. Fat was a part of her just like breathing; fat became her suit of armour. Maud, like most young girls had dreamt of falling in love, having the dream white wedding like the entire beautiful princesses did in the bedtime stories her caring dad had read. If only Maud had run back to check if she had turned off the iron from ironing her new dungarees she wanted to wear to the beach party then her parents would still be alive today, the bakery would not have been sold and she could possibly have had that wedding.

Maud was lonely, and the only time she forgot the trauma was when she was on her dating site. Logging on, the cheesy ping excited her and made her forget the guilt she was yet to address and put to bed, but she wanted to put something to bed first and that was to meet up with BoredCockerell. She saw that he had not replied to her last message two days ago. Feeling brave from the memory of what her dad always told her, '*Anything is possible, my magical Maud. Just take the bloody bull by the horns,*' she took the keyboard by its keys and typed out '*Let's arrange a date*'. She celebrated her burst of confidence with a creamy chocolate éclair.

*

Oscar De La Renta never failed to make her look anything less than a million dollars. The curve of the sheer material took in her slim waist, which unlike her second husband had never left her. Sparse tiny diamonds covered the chest and arm area and twinkled with the light, giving Saffron a heavenly glow.

"Fabulous" expressed Cindy, the make-up artist with one eyebrow tinted purple, cementing it with a clap.

"Wonderful" declared all seven feet of Ewan.

"You look very regal, Ms. Saffron," Helena the maid said, as she went about dusting the Tiffany chandeliers on a portable ladder on wheels, wondering if she cut the chain would it kill all three below her.

"That's because she is the Queen of New York, darling," said Ewan, one of New York's most in-demand stylists, failing to give the maid his attention. His unique selling point was that he was a metrosexual straight Welsh guy, who had fucked Saffron a few times like the rumours his hometown folk did sheep. Ewan crowned Saffron with the unclaimed title for the added brownies points; to be honest, he spoke the truth with Mabel gone.

Oscar was her favourite - classic, couture and demure, everything Saffron worked for as a legend. The Gala was the hottest ticket in town, knocking a world-class boxer's comeback fight out in round one of ticket sales. Being the hostess, she needed to be flawless - pure perfection, a vision of demureness to show that the older lady could wow just as much as the tit baring, leg flashing, bed hopping, coke sniffing bimbos clogging up the fame business nowadays.

Saffron was in the league of women such as Meryl, Julianne, Angelina and the gorgeous Sophia Loren - women of power, success and lasting inspiration whom certainly stood behind no man in the stuffy kitchen chopping onions, preferring for their men to carry their famous surnames. Ewan and his Asian-looking P.A started to zip up the losing gowns as Cindy packed away her make-up and Helena was lighting candles around the apartment to create Feng Sui. Really, it was to disguise the smell of sex in the room, hoping the flammable curtain made from butterfly wings would blow onto the naked flames and engulf the posh suite.

Saffron was timeless and graceful, yet she was a total slut. She would be known as a GILF if she had grandchildren - a Granny I'd like to fuck, that is. Air kisses dismissed all from the room leaving Saffron alone in the living room. Helena was busy running the bath for her, thinking of maybe throwing in a starved piranha instead of bath salts. Saffron took her glass of champagne and walked over with slow grace to her grand bedroom closing the posh door behind her. The door reminded her of hating Simone Delvin for going ahead with the gross glass door installation next door. The noise was quite disturbing to the peace, and whoever was howling like a failed dieter on weigh-in day was annoying her.

She had closed doors on many things in her life, in reality and in theory. Alone in the room she took off the fine dress, tossed it to the shiny floor where it crumpled with disbelief as she sat at the dressing table. There she picked up a piece of jewellery with exquisite beauty; it was heavy in her palm and majestic in her touch. The deep blue stone caught the light and flickered as if it was alive - like an eye, not a stone. The ring slipped on with ease as it had done for decades, but for decades it had never seen outside of this room. It had never been complimented, never been papped, hostage to this room like a genie for all its life, but why?

Its construction was that of rare skill. Cemented among the craftsmanship a dark secret of torture and theft hid. It was a ring so dangerous in the wrong hands that she kept it under lock and key. The ring came off back into its cushion box. It seemed heavier of late, as if she weakened each day. Was it heavy with the illegal jewel, or heavy with the secret? Or was she just getting plain weak as she aged? This ring was Saffron's kryptonite; if it was ever to fall into the hands of the law or an enemy, she would be sentenced to spend the rest of her short life behind bars - and not gold bars in a vault. She had already committed murder for the ring. Killing the maker of the fine ring, his slit throat had shocked the small French village where his workshop was. Secrets always felt safer in death than in a weak handshake or a feeble vocal promise. Just before she had time to lock it anyway, she was disturbed.

"The bath is ready, Ms. Saffron." The gentle knocking had broken her reminiscing about the past. Thankfully, it was to stay in the past. The last remaining doorway to the secret of the ring was dead. Seeing Mabel's face framed in a wedding picture, her smile turned slightly at the corners as if twisted into a loser's pout.

"As normal, you lose," she said, turning the picture frame around to divert Mabel's haunting stare away from her. Only she and Mabel knew the real truth.

Saffron disappeared into the marble bathroom to soak like a Queen before she needed to be ready in the Bentley to take her over to the Gala in under two hours. Unbeknown to Saffron, Mabel had sent secret agents to get the ring from beyond the grave. Saffron - for the first time in fifty years - forgot to lock the deadly ring away.

*

"Well, well, look who it is, Mindy the fucking hermit" Simone was a vision of goddess beauty as usual, and as usual nearly naked; only pair of angel white lace knickers covered her modesty, her voice soft, honey coated and sexy greeted them as she opened the door.

Her famous tits that had been captured in Playboy and Vogue front covers were exposed, and stayed pert and positioned in their welcoming, little studs of pink flesh dotting the centre. Mindy felt her tits and wanted to book a boob job or a mastectomy.

"Fucking hell, Mindy! I can see why you're in hiding. What's that growing from your forehead?" she said, stepping back and touching said fringe with the distaste of touching a dead rat. Simone shivered on touching it.

"How have you been?" landing a soft kiss on both of Simone's cheeks. The softness was still there, the same as their first meeting twenty years ago.

"Oh, you're too fucking gorgeous you." Simone had dabbled a little with girl on girl action back in the days of drugs, but preferred dick over fanny any day. But, Mindy's friend was hot. Alex had heard this comment plenty of times, but to come from Simone Delvin - the biggest wet dream for all humanity - was surreal. She was the reason puberty-suffering horny teenage boys bought extra socks. She blushed for the first time ever, ignoring the tongue-in-mouth kiss that Simone planted. Alex tasted cherries, strawberries and a hint of carrot on Simone's tender lips; she knew that if Troy had been here it would have been a tick off his bucket list, *thank you.*

"I'm good, thank you Sisi. Apart from the fact that my fringe looks like an overgrown bikini line," flicking the midget fringe away from her smooth forehead. The nickname showed a personal touch with Simone, a secret code word for only her loyal circle of close friends to call her - which amounted to about three. Not that Mindy disliked Simone - she was very fond of the heir, it was just that Simone possessed the power to make any woman flood envy and jealousy out of their pores. The Virgin Mary would stab out her own eyes with a loose rusty nail from the crucifix she would feel so inadequate compared to her beauty. Eve would have bashed her head in with the apple - never mind let it be eaten, jealous of the star's aura that reeked of super wealth.

Simone had once been brought in by MI5 as a useful tool in getting terrorists and spies to speak; her Sharon Stone leg crossing could provoke a confession in fifteen seconds flat. She had breathtaking beauty, captured by sell out calendars. She had pre-sales for the next decade already making it an Amazon bestseller before the pictures had even been taken. Simone's looks helped a fertility clinic collect a record amount of sperm samples by having her pose semi-naked in a video talking dirty to help potential invisible baby-daddies wank. The queues outdid any food bank in Africa; the 'Simone sperm boom', the tabloids named it.

Simone curled her bare feet under sinking into her velvet mink fur couch and pushing her golden hair behind her shoulders. "Gloria, please come here. Girls, we need champagne to celebrate!" Gloria failed to materialise. Simone rolled her aqua blue eyes to the ceiling to show her annoyance. The million-pound chandelier draped in hand cut diamonds did not even get a smile from her. "One moment." She rose, leaving the sofa as if she was a grand swan in a lake; she took the living room in three supermodel steps. Alex and Mindy sat in stunned silence. They were stunned and in awe looking at the interior of one of the wealthiest women in the world's residence, in one of the wealthiest addresses in New York. Not a single item was a replica of an idea. Everything was the original, a one off. If Alex had still been fourteen and in her phase of petty shoplifting, just taking a cushion could have sent her to the Caribbean on a private plane.

"That bloody Gloria is playing fucking Juliet out there to that door," she said, appearing with a huge magnum of Bollinger and three crystal flutes in a gold ice bucket. With the famous tits beneath an oversized Bronx basketball jersey, she looked catwalk ready. "So, are you ladies coming to the Gala tonight?" filling up two flutes and leaving her own empty.

"You not drinking Simone? What's up, are you sick?" it sounded rude, but Mindy knew that Simone not drinking was equal to Jesus refusing to be crucified due to a fear of heights. Mindy was concerned for her fabulous friend.

"I'm trying for a baby, so cutting down on alcohol to one bottle a week."

"Congratulations, that's wonderful news." Mindy said, delighted and hugging Simone. Alex plastered a forced smile and hid the vomit rising; fucking baby-making was stalking her.

"Which - the baby bit, or one bottle a week?" Simone pouted her lips turned shade of red associated with danger. The silence shimmed, teasing the fear of an argument. Simone was infamous for blowing a fuse and had once butted the Dalai Lama. All three women popped the tension with their laughter.

"What's so funny?" A male voice cut in from over the far side of the open plan living room. Alex froze with the voice. Was it the voice of Bert Doodle, the infamous Bolton serial killer - her first famous trial case? He was infamous for strangling women with a Jennifer Aniston bob, who had called out maliciously in court that she was his next victim, spitting his evil promise as he was led down. Alex, ever since that day, always made sure her hair was immaculately done. Luckily - and non-life threateningly - this husky voice belonged to Alex's celebrity crush fuck of all time. Both she and Troy each allowed one celebrity fuck, that if they ever met their crush they could fuck them without fear of their belongings being sacrificed to a bonfire on the front garden. Alex had no competition - not due to her ravenous beauty, but more to the fact that if Troy met his celebrity crush fuck he would need to have a kink for necrophilia and be handy with a spade. Marilyn had been dead for decades; '*no threat*', Alex had coolly claimed one night while painting her nails victory red.

Leon walked into his huge living room competing to be just as beautiful as Simone. He was the most beautiful thing in the flesh - all polished, stylish and perfect. "Hey, Mindy what a great surprise" kissing Mindy. Alex was next, and his aftershave stroked her skin; she felt the threat of infidelity just smelling it. It stained her skin the way a whore's lipstick would on a man's crisp white collar, and he finally landed his winning kiss on his world, Simone. As always, once their lips touched nothing else mattered; it all just faded into the lavish background of the penthouse suite. They were a once in a lifetime pairing, loyal as swans, and their future fixed to be in each other's arms. It was a huge draw for the media. To look at Simone and Leon in their embrace was televisual, as if all war was over and love was greater. If Simone was cut open, she would bleed love.

Does it count as cheating if you imagine another man's body in your bed? What about the fact that you may have to change your knickers as your lust for this man just kicked out your tampon? Alex had no answers to these infidelity questions in her head, but was glad that she was not blind. Leon Jaxon was everything she could wish for and more. Nothing could kill her admiration for this male model. If she had been single and handy with a knife, she would have slashed Simone and taken Leon for herself, tied him up just to look at him every day like some human porcelain doll. Leon was perfect; nothing could kill this moment, nothing at all. Noticing Leon as he cocked his manly bare leg up, his hamstring competing with his bicep for being more cut and worked-out got Alex's stomach twisting better than a corkscrew in a wine cork. She wondered if his cock would slip out, touching her phone maybe get camera ready? Suddenly a horrific noise was let out from something under his seat, gassing

Alex's digressing thoughts of her kinky Leon based fantasies. One thing that Alex hated in men was their public display of affection for a fart.

"Shit, sorry girls. This bloody protein diet is lethal," he said, laughing it off as if it was the normal way to greet guests all way from England. It was typical the way some men thought a fart was like some sort of achievement. "I'm upping my protein to help build up strength in my sperm to get this one pregnant." The thought of Simone and Leon having sex jumped into Alex's head, and she had to sit on her hands to stop herself from fingering herself, wet. The smell was vile, like wet, dead meat. Simone, blinded by love, laughed with awe like it was a baby doing a raspberry.

"That stinks" Mindy held a mink cushion to her nose, while Alex debated whether to collect it in a jar. But, she joined Mindy in holding a cushion to her nose. Leon laughed out loud, "Sorry! Are you two attending the Gala tonight?" Leon repeated Simone's unanswered question about the Gala.

"No, we're going to see a show," Alex lied. Had this ring business not been so important, Alex would have sold all her organs - and Mindy's without permission - just to go.

"Wonderful! Gloria, ring every show on Broadway and get them front row seats, meet the cast, the works."

"Oh no, please, no need for that Sisi, we're perfectly happy sitting back row with a restricted view" laughing, Mindy enjoying the poverty of it. Simone thought 'restricted view' was a boy band.

"You a dyke or something? Back row?" Simone looked at Alex and Mindy to see if it could be possible. I mean, after what 'Him' had done to Mindy it would be a perfectly good excuse to carpet munch. Simone remembered handing Mindy the card of a hit man.

Alex wondered if they had been dykes if people would think they were a couple. They did everything together. They were each other's plus ones for distant relatives' weddings, attended wedding shows on boring Sundays together, and went dining together at romantic, expensive restaurants. They even held hands during each other's cervical smears. Alex preferred something more masculine, while Mindy would prefer someone uglier than herself - probably a lesbian whose carpet shag pile had a healthy bounce due to having had no visitors. This was the first time self-doubt had reared its ugly head since they had landed, and it hurt.

"I prefer the politically correct term of 'homosexual', please." Gloria finally left the dying door. Well, the maintenance man of the building arrived with two couriers from Christie's Auction House, peeling a grieving Gloria off the door as if she was one of those guard dog stickers.

"Not on about you, ya big lezzer. It's great that you decided to come back - how's Pinocchio?" Simone gave a look to Leon that said she would tell him later. Gloria's eye make-up was smudged all around her eyes as if it was trying to eclipse her eyes; it was the result of her terrible ability to put make-up on, and nothing to do with the two hour upset protest at the door. Gloria was a typical old school Irish woman fed strict religion and carbs. It gave her a cotton wool lifestyle, content and comfortable, with a bowl hair cut sharp and chunky. The first time she had put lipstick on in the shade that 'only whores wore' it went all over her chin and cheeks as she applied it, saying 'Our Father' prayers six times for forgiveness, which didn't help in trying to apply it to moving lips. She blamed being a lesbian on spending all her childhood surrounded by frigid man-hating Nuns; being a lesbian was her revenge against her parents and religion. Noticing Alex, she gave a cheeky wink. "Ok, well you are to stay here for your time - no buts! I will have Gloria send for your belongings at the hotel." Gloria let out a sigh. Gloria overlooked the fact that the point of being a personal assistant was to personally assist her famous employer.

"So, do you live on this whole floor alone?" Mindy repeated the question that she and Alex had practised in the lift. It came out much less convincing than Alex had hoped, shooting Mindy a look.

"I tried, but the old battle axe next door wouldn't shift. Think the old bitch laid the first brick, she's that old." The half billion price tag, made Simone think it was a bargain; her wealth in the multibillion brackets.

"Why, who's your neighbour?" Again, Mindy's rehearsed question came out staged. Alex looked to the ceiling in frustration, wishing she hadn't. The ceiling mural of Simone and Leon naked was hand painted above, while sparkles of diamonds, she presumed, added a twinkle like stars and made her want to cry out.

"Saffron thinks she's fucking queen of New York. Complete and utter slut if you ask me." She had no respect for the elderly, and calling her famous neighbour a slut was like the kettle - and all the other appliances in the kitchen - screaming at the pot black. "Wrong sister died if you ask me. Mabel was a bloody diamond, a fabulous woman out for a good time. Saffron? Well, there's just something about her I don't like."

"What the fucking hell is that horrific smell?" Her Irish voice made Mindy give Joe-Ryan a walk on part in her head. *Maybe get him a fridge magnet,* her inner voice encouraged, cutting into Simone's description of her neighbour while Gloria was holding her hand to her nose in horror.

"Sorry" Leon erupted with laughter, waving his beautiful hand traffic police style over the foul smell. All the girls screamed a chorus of disgust.

Over on the Poor Side of New York, But Hip Enough to Say Aloud in Public

Standing spread-eagle naked as the first day he was born, the sun from the open studio window dried his thin body with a gentle blow; if he was a vampire, he would be glitter dust. On his knees in front of the naked him, Jude rubbed vigorously up and down, working up a minor sweat. His tongue hurt from concentrating for the past half hour on that area. His biceps repeating the up and down action started to burn with lactic acid, but Jude was not giving up until he was covered in the sticky solution. Hoping for perfection for his boyfriend, hearing him moaning with pleasure at each stroke gave him the indication that the job was going well.

Lucas was getting ready for tonight's *Golden Halo Gala* - it was unbelievable that it was happening. He felt like Maria in Sound of Music, minus the most unflattering costume ever in a musical, when she is released free from her chores of minding those un-cool brats, and races up the hill like Rocky Balboa. Receiving the call this morning while dying his blonde locks and an egg and banana facemask was filling in his temperamental pores, Lucas was low on patience for one of Jude's weekly pranks. The realisation that Jude was not winding him up on his popular radio show *Gay Gossip,* after his seventh '*fuck off, Jude'* hanging up of the phone sank in, the truth was that he was going to the Golden Halo Gala. Jude was forever roping in gullible Lucas for pranks on his radio chat show - certainly if it involved celebs or fashion. Lucas screamed so loud with sheer glee when the P.A to Saffron asked if he was available to personally accompany her to the A-list celebrity crammed party tonight. He must have left a lasting impression on the old broad, he thought. So loud was his camp scream of joy rupturing the whole apartment block that Ms Aronowitz, with an uncharacteristically short nose, knocked in concern asking, "Are you gays ok?"

"Baby, your hands feel so good. You're getting better, firmer and faster."

"Thank you," Jude replied not looking up, the sweat gathering at the barrier of his eyebrows with the power to push through the dense hair giving the impression they'd slip and land on his top lip. Lucas liked it perfect, and if it took more than one stroke, he would give as many strokes as it took to get Lucas happy. After all, Lucas made him happy beyond he ever believed he could be. Jude's knees started to ache, and he had to stand in defeat - but satisfied.

Years of rugby had aged his bones quicker than most thirty-three years old, even if they had osteoporosis. Jude's hands were covered in his commitment to his boyfriend's happiness, sticky with satisfaction, and plenty of fluid from fulfilling the deed. The tan mitt was caked in the history of many fake tan applications that Jude had helped with, and held it in the air like a trophy. Jude wished his knees were sore from giving Lucas oral, but Lucas refused the offer of Jude trying to lick his cock into arousal and stiffness saying, "It will ruin me tan, babe!" in his best put on English accent.

A typical, textbook gay couple the world sees, each one represented far wide scale of gay man evolution. Lucas flew the pink glittering flag for the camp queens; he had the fashion, celebrity diets, christened all his luxury man bags with real human names, and was Team Aniston.

Jude waved the pink flag for the straight-acting sporty hunk in a straight way; he did not have a clue who Karl or Anna were, and he was Team Jolie. Yet opposites attract - look at Kermit and Miss Piggy. And for the past four years the relationship had grown in strength allowing love to flourish, and they were moulded together by memories of holidays, glued by good. The relationship had survived many savage attacks by jealous gay guys who thought nothing of bumping and grinding up against Jude, like dogs did to lampposts, in full view of Lucas who was known on the gay scene as a diva. In the world of fast sex and faster STI's, a simple swipe on Grindr guaranteed your place in an orgy - like a deposit on a house, but the house normally came free with a mattress and herpes replaced a free goodie bag. In the fickle world of the gay community, they were more vicious than a sale stampede on Fifth Avenue. If you did not fit a stereotype, or were cursed with a normal body lacking zero percent fat and abs, or had an addiction to Krispy Kremes, the chance of you ever being just a top was a faint dream. *'Who wants to fuck a fatty?'* Lucas had told one ex-boyfriend; you were doomed. STI's and party drugs ran rife among the gay community, just as the gangs of Mexico did causing chaos and terror. You were either addicted to liquid G every twenty minutes, or religiously visiting a GUM clinic and confessing your sins to an underpaid nurse rather than a priest; it was the norm. God forbid if you didn't like Beyoncé. Lucas and Jude were proof that love conquers all in a sometimes harsh and pressured community.

Jude Waters was built like a rugby player; broad and six foot three tall, he was a giant specimen of a man. He was extremely pale, which was an instant attraction for many orange gay vultures on the gay scene. He had brown hair that was forever brushed back over his head in an English gent way, showing his hunky face while his deep blue eyes - perfect to look into for the rest of your life - shone. His smile was slightly not as straight as people expected he was, that gave cuteness when he smiled. He was laid back and nothing really rattled him, whereas Lucas was one caution away from jail for threatening behaviour towards any twink who thought they could take his man. His aim with a petrol bomb was as spot-on as a sniper. His distant blue blood gave Jude a high education, and his British ways lent him James Bond sexiness - like when he had asked what brunch was. In the age where you could pick up sex on Grindr faster than a cold sore, most gays wondered if the grass was greener on the other side - even if that grass was fake. Everything about Jude was real. They were now content and comfortable and fell into a harmony of happiness.

Lucas spent all morning in manic preparation for his glamorous celebrity-filled evening, and now into the early afternoon, he was getting ready in a rush. God help him when it was his own wedding, knowing very well that Jude had purchased a ring. Betty Big Balls the drag from Brooklyn had told him, *'and not a cock ring, my dear!'* she had finished, with a neon orange wink.

Vodka and energy drink was his petrol to push him on in his grooming military regime, taking up most of his morning. Running the length of a Beyoncé album and wearing cling film as the latest fitness wear on his treadmill in six-inch heels, sweating like Hillary Clinton on her second election to drop a pound. He had rushed over to his designer friend Mattel in the Meat District to pick up his outfit of a fitted purple tartan suit, teamed with a McQueen white shirt and finishing off with his whore shoes - red patent Prada loafers. He had bleached his teeth, wallpapered a glycolic peel on his bony face, tinted his thick black eyebrows and coloured them in with black marker, and now his tan, four orange layers deep, was drying. The fake tan gave the impression that his emaciated frame had shrunk to a size zero, the rubbing of Jude's thick hands sanding him away. Lucas had first realised he had an eating disorder when he had started licking tea bags; he knew he needed help. Weight was the only thing he could control in his unpleasant upbringing. Some days he never ate due to being so poor, and being thin was his stark reminder of the past. So, if he stayed in control of his skeletal self, his past could never come back to hurt him. His revenge on his awful abusive upbringing was to be in a loving relationship.

Jude gently encouraged Lucas to put weight on, but Lucas snapped, *"You fell in love with me skinny, not fat"*. It was hard for Lucas at first, but he did manage to put half a pound on. Incorporating whey protein powder into their kinky foreplay was a eureka moment. Jude dipped his generous dick into it and Lucas sucked it off - it made it fun to fatten up. Anything that made Jude happy Lucas tried, apart from a threesome. Lucas' jealous streak was not worth the eighteen years for the murder of a Brooklyn power bottom.

Interior design was the newest career rising from the ashes of many that Lucas had set fire to. All the rich people of New York attending financed all the daydreams developing in his head made him thirsty with the glory of attending the Golden Halo Gala, as no other than the host's plus one. If Lucas liked fanny he would have given Saffron a complimentary fuck. His good friend Ewan filled in their sexy shenanigans over a happy hour prosecco, so Lucas sent a candle instead.

"Bae, will you get me a drink please?" facing the large window, allowing the natural drying of his tan and the opportunity for him to search his body like a bloodhound for any patches. Jude had really learned a lot at the fake tan class he had enrolled on; not one patch of pale skin broke through the orange coat not even on his penis. Jude returned with a cosmopolitan cocktail in a can.

"Here you go, a class-in-a-can trash cocktail," knowing Fiona - his uptight, posh mother - would be mortified that his common (her words) boyfriend was drinking a cocktail from a can, cutting short his small allowance before Lucas finished the can. The pink straw in the shape of a penis went into his boyfriend's mouth; his lip filler had finally calmed down enough to look real. Jude was going commando and felt a twinge beneath his grey joggers watching Lucas' prolonged suck of the straw. "So, you excited for tonight?" Jude returned to the grey sofa at last to finish off the sport magazine article on the upcoming Olympics in Brazil, hiding the swelling in his pants. He was genuinely interested in his boyfriend's evening - it was rare to witness this in long-term relationships.

"Excited! Babe excited is an understatement; I'm over the fucking moon. I now know what it felt like for Julia Roberts to land on her feet in Pretty Woman, or for Monica Lewinsky to wear that skirt to the office that day. I feel like I could die, and Cher could sing at my funeral." He was a massive Cher fan, managing to get Jude to play her on his dance based radio show.

Jude laughed. "I forgot to tell you - I had a meeting with my agent." Jude was excited about his career change. Radio was great but it paid slowly, and there were not many promotions to achieve. Modelling seemed fun, and acting was a passion of his; for it to materialise into anything would be a dream.

"How did it go bae?" Lucas asked.

Jude paused.

If Lucas was not so concerned with his tan drying, he would have noticed Jude's nervous twitch. He was always honest with Lucas, but telling him about the little spontaneous photoshoot involving a thong - that Jude first thought was a mask - would go down as well as a swimmer wearing concrete flippers in the Hudson River. Jude Waters could be tad naïve in life - it was part of his attraction, and the downfall of a cotton-wool boarding school education.

"It went really well, some good ideas and a few castings soon." Greg's enthusiasm had come across as genuine.

"What's his name bae?" His jealousy and insecurity made Lucas want to know the inside and out of everything to do with his man. Some days, Jude wondered whether to wear a blindfold.

"Greg Locust," he said, picking up an apple from the glass bowl shaped like a skull. The name was cemented in his memory like handprints are on the Walk of Fame in Lucas brain. Only Greg had left an imprint in another part on Lucas, what he had made Lucas do on that wet afternoon when he was barely sixteen and looking for something solid in New York to start afresh - he would look bitter, and all he wanted for Jude was for him to be happy. He wanted him to achieve his new dream of becoming a model and an actor, and cross it off the bucket list post-it note on the fridge. Therefore, if Lucas had to keep the pain of what happened at that casting years previously to him, then he would. Lucas would do anything for love, including gritting his white teeth and speaking past the trauma that happened at the hands of that perverted rapist bastard.

"Named after an insect? That's strange. If he dares to get you to pose in skimpy underwear, you know I'm bringing out my gasoline and burning the bitch." Jude knew the look. He knew he was serious. Jude laughed uncomfortably. Jude loved Lucas to death. The thousands of grooming products lining up the bathroom like landmines made the bathroom a hazardous zone, the designer clothes taking up the main room like squatters while they slept in the box room, his Disney-esque outlook on life, and the never-ending dreams all made Lucas. Lucas was kind, funny, ambitious, and loved Jude Waters for the good, the bad and the HIV positive.

He had become HIV positive six years ago. The stigma of the illness was not as propaganda powerful back in the day - some celebrities living life on the harsh medication gave it a worldwide platform for funding. Jude was still selective about whom he told, and certainly kept this part of his life away from the media. When he had told Lucas the real reason he had prolonged sleeping with him, Lucas was convinced that Jude was fucking that muscle Mary, Ged from Staten Island who wore platforms behind his bony back. Lucas knew deep down Jude was not the cheating type.

Lucas had asked so many questions: how, when, who, if he was going to die, and what hymn to sing at his wake. He asked all the normal questions that HIV attached in its invisible leaflet. A hunky man of his workout build, riddled with an invisible illness - it reduced him to tears simply thinking of it back in the early days of diagnosis. Jude explained about his drug addiction over the short period of a month. Coming to New York and working as a bit-part model, invited to all the hip places, he had felt invincible and rode high on life, caught up in the modelling scene of never-ending parties. It was a new beginning from a sheltered life back in the English countryside. Released in the Big Apple he went crazy, and this craziness involved sharing a needle. It infected him with a simple prick; he humoured the idea that he wouldn't have minded if it was through sex - at least there would have been some enjoyment in getting it. Despite having a fitness diploma and a degree in communications from Oxford, he could now add HIV positive to his many credentials in his life. Sadly, it would be the one that most people would mention over a tuna sandwich at his funeral when he died. Even if hit by an airplane and filmed live - people would spread the rumour that his disease was from his homosexuality, and that made him ashes. Fiona, his own mother, was in the dark about his illness. Sadly, being in the dark to the illness was no longer being the life sentence that it was. The sympathy that Lucas gave him matched as if Jude had just told him he had terminal cancer. Jude lay awake wondering; the only plus side was that HIV had a survival rate higher than cancer, and there was no risk of having to wear a dodgy wig. The gay scene was ruthless if it wasn't 100% real hair promoted by a Kardashian.

Humour was just as powerful as medicine. "Will you be a star and walk Moonlight pretty please, before you become a big star and think it's beneath you to do?" blowing kisses, trying to grab the pink lead with his thin feet off the side table and successfully tossing it to Jude, laughing. Lucas liked things big, including his dog. Moonlight entered on hearing her Oscar winning name.

Moonlight weighed more than Lucas did. An Old English mastiff, she was the size of a small car but possessed more grace than a cat with arthritis. The huge dog walked as if she was a supermodel on the runway, and not a dog on the sidewalk. Jude clipped on the pink lead. Moonlight shook her old body in excitement, warming it up for a stroll and disposing a hailstorm of dog hair for OCD Jude to hoover up; she was ready to roll. For a big dog she was extremely lazy -

once around the block and she was done. Jude left the room with Moonlight huffing and panting already behind him.

Lucas absolutely adored Jude. Standing naked and alone with his daydreaming thoughts and crazy scenarios at the Golden Halo Gala tonight, he felt a calm fall around him that he regularly felt with Jude in his life. One thing Lucas dreamt of since birth from an alcoholic mother who sold him on for drugs. Pinballing from one bad home to another, Jude gave Lucas the ultimate prize in life that he wanted more than any Prada shoes or lip fillers or celebrity following him on Instagram - Jude gave him love. It was something that Lucas had believed only existed in fairy tales and movies before Jude came along.

Tonight was going to be so special. Tonight, to mingle with icons of screen, song and fashion, to get a taste of celebrity pumped a high around his body faster than heroin. Tonight, he would get Bette's reclusive autograph, and he would be papped for all social media sites, his name dropped in context to his self-promotion of brand 'Lucas'. Unknown to him, this wonderful cloud of make-believe wore a dark lining under its silver tux jacket. Tonight, he would show himself just how much he loved Jude. Tonight, he would do this by getting deadly revenge on Jude's behalf.

The Golden Halo Gala

The lush red carpet parted the way between the drowning screaming crowds on either side, like Moses walking the celebrities and power players, not Israelites to the safety of the grand museum hosting the Golden Halo Gala. Snipers lay on the nearby buildings blending in with the dark night, ready to shoot any eager fan or killer stalker just for insurance purposes - it was cheaper to kill a civilian than be sued by a star. Much loved faces from film, fashion and politics mingled on the red carpet. Well-rehearsed smiles were lit up by a million flashbulbs lighting up the city, captured by all of New York's hungry paps. The noise of screaming fans deafened the traffic noise of New York.

Saffron stepped out from her sleek limousine in one smooth move. Her painstakingly glorious, hand-sewn frock gathered flashbulbs like a light bulb does with moths. She looked elegant; if America had a Queen, this was she. Saffron looked like the part, gently waving and smiling generously to the screaming fan hungry crowds gathering to witness the glitz of the Golden Halo Gala. The combined wealth of the guest list could wipe out third world poverty on all planets in the solar system, but not one of them was foolish enough to bankrupt him or herself for the world.

Saffron proceeded up the red aisle like a bride, age slowing her walking. Her classy gown drew gasps, eyeing up the reporters on the side-lines who were tempting her with positive words to snare an interview. They were like anglers on the banks of lakes, casting their hungry line to hook using microphones and compliments instead of juicy fat worms. Seeing as half of the actresses had not eaten since last year's Oscar nominations, worms would be extremely useful tonight as the world's biggest and rarest fish were all fighting in this lake for one night.

Waving and acknowledging the ones from the biggest TV stations, she played the game well. The skinny blonde from a prolific fashion show was giving her critical opinion on every woman walking past, despite being dressed as if after this stint she was going to work a corner. Her collarbones jaunted out - maybe the bitch was on the coke diet, again. *Avoid*, whispered Mabel, spinning her head fast to face a Latina sex bomb and her backing dancer toy boy, who lacked the pulling power as her rapper ex. Mabel had been her secret weapon on affairs like tonight. She knew who to talk to, who to be pictured with, and what to say to gain popularity and columns inches. For the first time since hearing about the death of her sister, Saffron felt the void and a spittle of sadness left by Mabel's departure to heaven. She needed to get in and get a gin down her, hearing one reporter mentioning Mabel's name as she entered.

*

Was this heaven's waiting room? *'Am I dreaming?'* he thought pinching himself, bruising his bone. Lucas was in his wildest dream living it out, happily retired from life. Icons from his childhood straight through to his Instagram account were gathered in one amazing room decorated like an abstract version of Alice in Wonderland. Whoopi Goldberg was chatting animatedly to Bette Midler, and Goldie Hawn was by a huge fountain where the water was changing colour and a live mermaid sat on top playing a gold harp. Orlando Bloom rested his hand on the small of the back of Katy Perry, and Kami Jarrod and sisters, hottest American family since the Walton all worked a gothic leather look. Poor Koolin-J the eldest sister would be mercilessly vented tomorrow as pregnant in the media. She was minus her hot rapper boyfriend, Tail who was probably at the bar trying to turn the water into champagne to outdo Jesus.

Walking the room with his champagne flute as company, he became a microphone each time he spoke, his awe slowed him down. I t was like being at Madame Tussauds, but instead of wax they had upped their game and got in the real-life celebrities; this was New York after all. Puff Daddy was speaking using the language of back slaps seeing Snoop Dog and Busta Rhymes using the same sign language, a bored hip-hop honey sulked into her enchanted tits, overshadowed by Jane Fonda in a green sequin disco jumpsuit.

Meryl Streep worked her best *'I'm interested in hearing all about how I made you want to become an actress'* poker face, as a gaggle of younger actresses pecked her for advice flashing more flesh than a pig in a butcher's window. Britney Spears looked fresh and capable of being trusted with an umbrella as she chatted to Elton John, and Ryan Reynolds, in a cute sequin mini dress taking a glass of champagne from a bare-chested Minotaur. Rihanna - wearing a bear on her back, gold heels and nothing else - was scanning the room like a CCTV camera. Would she leave with Chris or Leo?

Chad Rise was unbelievably more handsome in real life, a real Hollywood hunk. Lucas prayed that his adopted child would look like Chad. Chad Rise stood leaning sexily against the bar with his drop-dead gorgeous fiancée, the Mexican sex bomb Maria Dieppe. They looked cute wearing matching purple Dolce, chatting away to Doris Kreme the legendary food critic. Mariah Carey flashed a rock on her fingers as big as her tits disguised as a knuckle-duster, making over in the direction of J.Lo. Courtney Love was being stepped over as she played dead. Beyoncé and Jay-Z had brought a human wall of entourage with them, including Chris Martin, Pattie LaBelle, and the fiery Kitten Minx towering over them all in a white plunging dress, her chocolate smooth skin twinkling with diamond dust. Lucas toyed with signing his name on one of the mean looking security men looking like the Berlin wall and refrained from approaching, noticing slap-happy Solange standing nearby.

The Brits were not to be outdone and had sent over their biggest gift to the world of late in the fight, Adele, who was mouthing off saying how shit the canapés were to Ellen DeGeneres and Simon Cowell.

Simone Delvin looked out of this world in her backless baby pink Versace sheer gown. It became her skin. Sex sold her beauty to be the best dressed, as every male and a few closet lesbos glanced her way as she chatted to British film legend Henry Dooley, oblivious to her nipples shadowing under the sensational gown.

The Gala received the stamp of royalty in the form of the fittest ginger ever born, Prince Harry, working a slim beard as he spoke to Saffron looking stunning in her Oscar gown. Ruddick St. David was still fat in his dapper suit, and the bankroll of the Gala looked proud as punch surrounded by a gaggle of pretty, identical Asian girls.

Ms Campbell and Ms Moss were dropping moves on the dance floor showing their competition how it's done, as Cindy clapped and gave the 'V' sign to the young pretenders. Paul McCartney chatted with his daughter Stella, while Mick Jagger moved closer to Cara who engaged in a selfie with Miley - who, shock horror, was dressed. No Cher yet; the strain in his neck asked him to give up looking for now.

No matter where Lucas turned, a huge celebrity figure stood within arm's reach. It was a safari of exotic, endangered celebrities from all walks of creativity and power. Hilary Clinton was chin-wagging with Oprah and Donald Trump. It was all just so unreal, yet he felt comfortable as if he was part of this world. He was wondering whether to break into the acapella version of the Disney hit like Ariel had when she got her pair of hot legs, but there was no receipt to take them back. The gala was the event of the year after the snooze fest that was the Oscars; this was hailed the party of all parties.

Scanning the lavish room exchanging brief smiles and compliments of '*you look gorgeous*', he noticed one of his favourite ever icons, so exclusive to autographs and pictures that they had been nicknamed the Human Loch Ness. He froze. Once thawed, he decided on throwing out the caution to keep a little class and not be a typical gay - YOLO, and all that jazz. He didn't care, placing his empty glass on a passing waiter and taking a refill. His targeted guest was famous for leaving within ten minutes, so he had to make his move now.

"Anna, darling!" he said, marching over towards the Vogue matriarch. The black glasses hid the rolling of her eyes.

*

Over on the other side of the city, attempted burglary was being undertaken on the balcony of Simone Delvin's three million pound penthouse suite.

"You sure this is going to work?" The wind blew dangerously. Never one for mounting anything, Mindy sat on the wall dividing the two balconies with her legs dangling impatiently either side.

"Yes, you will be sound. Right, masks on." Alex loved a bit of danger in her life, peeling down her mask the same as Mindy made from a misshaped pair of cut nylon tights. New York was breathtaking at night she thought, forgetting their act of burglary for a moment and distracted by the lights that were spectacular enough to give the Northern lights a break.

"So straight in and straight out you understand?" Alex made it sound so easy, so spy film, coming back to the job in hand. She made it sound as if it was a hobby of hers, a normal thing to do on a Saturday night - she was from Liverpool, after all. Mindy stepped over and tip-toed towards the glass door. The nylon tight was pushing her nose flat to her face, her breathing becoming that of a pug. Her fringe poked through the web-thin material wanting to see what was going on, heart raced and pit-stopped in her dry mouth. Knowing very well Saffron was gone, it still made Mindy insecure thinking that someone may be home. Alex had pounded on the door like a bailiff before and no one had answered; the place was empty. She turned seeing Alex stepping over the balcony wall, waving Mindy to carry on and give her confidence - '*go on*'. The balcony door leading to the bedroom slid open with the ease of a hot knife through butter. Why it was not locked? It worried Mindy to think that Saffron somehow knew they were coming, and Mindy stopped in her tracks.

"Why have you stopped?" Alex said, turning to face her friend wearing a pair of nylon tights as a burka - but the only flesh on show was her neck and not her eyelids.

"It's not locked. What happens if there's a laser beam or something? Or when I walk in it triggers a gun?" Plenty of spy films worked the kind of security Mindy was preaching. Both friends stood for a moment to think, staring into the darkness of the bedroom teasing them with easy access to raid and root.

"Only one way to find out Mindy..." Alex broke the silence.

Mindy gasped. "Alex! You can't! What happens if you die?" Suddenly, Mindy didn't have time to think about picking up the charcoal pieces of Alex and putting them into her hand luggage to take home to a heartbroken Troy to put together like a 3D puzzle. Alex pushed her into the bedroom without any count to three, and

Mindy screamed. "Oh, you bitch I cannot believe you just did that!" panic squeaked her voice.

Joining the bedroom laughing, Alex replied, "At least there'd be an excuse for your fringe."

Mindy playfully slapped Alex and joined in laughing, despite her heart racing like a greyhound. The bedroom was dark; only the moonlight and a sole balcony light lifted the darkness enough so that Mindy and Alex gained enough sight. A few insomniac heat junkie moths made shadows as they bounced off the hot bulb. Admiring their willingness to not give up, it spurned them on.

"Right, what are we actually looking for again?" Her face hid her blank expression.

"A ring" loving car boot sales when she was younger, Mindy developed an eye for the unusual and alien, racoon-rooting with gusto. Something unusual about the bedroom stopped Mindy for a moment. It was decorated quite masculine, and a musky sweat choked the air. Was it a security trap gassing them?

"Mindy, I thought she was single?" A pair of white big man's briefs blocked her face, and broke her rational thinking of gassing.

"Jesus, the size of those" Whoever wore them was a big guy - in waist and bugle. The baggy front was fossil imprinted. She wondered if Joe-Ryan's penis left a fossil of that size in his underwear, the thought kinkily creeping in. The nylon hid Mindy's pink face.

"And why is there a naked picture of Jackson Nikko on the wall?" What was the trend of famous people having portraits of themselves banning their clothes, adorning their homes with their genitals on display? Mindy understood her overweight picture of past on her fridge, but not a naked one. Before they could discuss the generous length of the famous Hollywood lothario - a huge star of gangster films - another knob caught their attention...the creaking doorknob to the bedroom. Mindy froze.

Fight or flight were the two choices for Alex and she chose flight, scaling the balcony wall like a cat chased by a dog. Mindy was shit in situations like this, so her spontaneous sidekick jumped in to help her before she was caught. Mindy's leg disappeared under the bed just as the bedroom gained light and noise.

Reggie lit another smoke up in the side alley. The harsh inhale calmed his jumping nerves, releasing the thick smoke into the night air ignoring the fact that its illegal smell would attract attention. Immune to its effect, he pulled another quick pull. The expensive Ozzie Boateng suit Saffron had sent over worked his sporty body very well, while the manmade artwork of his life and beliefs tattooed on his neck and hands added a little edgy street style, keeping it real.

Reggie had been invited to the Gala. His Grandma - rest her soul - would have been over the moon. It beat going to prison. Planning to make some extra dollars knowing that most of the party, especially the insecure white actors, would need a little confidence boost in the form of white powder, he felt his bundle strapped to his thigh. Extremely fitting, he would easily have passed as a rapper or an actor on a grimy programme, especially when he smiled. His savvy smile was broken by two gold teeth, adding naughtiness to his thug look, showing a time when business had been flush. The tight trousers wrapped around his gym-addicted legs like a lover refusing to believe you have split. The outline of his meaty cock resting against his thigh rubbed commando each time he walked, causing shocks of pleasure up into his body. Each shot of sensitivity on his purple head reminded him to try and fuck a sexy model, maybe that crazy Kitten Minx. Maybe tonight he would get papped in her famous company. Things with Saffron of late had been working well and regular. Reggie knew that if he was to up his game he would be mentioned as a toy boy to a wealthy broad and it would be easier than actually auditioning for roles. His spliff finally drew the heat closer to his lips as a clue that its end was up and time to go in; he tossed it to the floor and smashed it dead with his black velvet shoe.

Tonight, Reggie had the pleasure of mingling with the stars of the world heading towards the side entrance to the party. All the wrong he had done in his life, people hurt by him, and his thieving and battery all walked silently behind him, ready to witness the perfect party for his last day on earth.

*

The party was in full swing. Ruddick St. David was as pleased as the alcoholic punch being served.

Ruddick St. David was a legendary and powerful film director with enough Oscars under his belt that he could host his own. His name was breathed in the same breath as Spielberg and Allen. *Saints Productions*, his film studio financing the Gala, was the best investment to add a little youth and glamour to his studio. In this room was at least fifty years of Oscar winning talent. Mariah Carey wowed everyone with her voice showing that Whitney's little slip in the bath was not due to no bath mat; their feud was finally over, Mariah was the ultimate diva. Black suited womanisers womanised, gold diggers dug deep like moles, and paranoid actors networked with the speed of fire ants.

Maria Dieppe looked phenomenal in her gown, standing by her man and giving him a clear visual of fucking her. Chad Rise's star rising interested Ruddick St. David and the new gritty film he was about to direct. Chad was the ideal actor for the drug-using, child-abusing priest on the run. Chad possessed a kind of darkness Ruddick St. David liked in his actors. His killer looks would certainly be a winner with the ladies and the fags.

Ruddick St. David wanted something in return if Chad was to audition.

Chad Rise caught the hungry look of Ruddick St. David, a dream of a director to list on your CV. This party was out of this world. Networking came with canapés and potential jobs passed with champagne. If 'celebrity' were a jungle, then Chad was in the lion's den. The look Ruddick St. David passed across the crowded room was alluring and tempting; if Ruddick St. David was gay, then the casting couch it was. He would do anything to get the perfect life - Chad would be no fool to turn down a film with the great director. Chad raised his scotch in his direction, and was shocked to find Ruddick St. David waving him over in his powerful direction.

"Maria, let's go," he said, rudely cutting the conversation between her and a Brazilian Angel, pulling her arm hard in the direction to change his career and give Maria a brush with death.

Saffron walked the room like the pro, parading around as if she was a show pony. Diamonds glittered from her neck, ears and fingers. Her sheer dress gathered gasps and compliments like sticky fly paper on the back door of a greasy kebab shop. Every one of influence, wealth and modern popularity were all in one room. If Saffron was the jealous, career-driven, bitter type, she would blow the whole place up and kill all the competition. There was one face that Saffron was yet to see in the couture crowd of celebrity. She noticed Ruddick St. David avid chatting to the young actor making headlines from hotel fire, Chad something. His look was clean and sexual, and she mentally made a note to introduce herself. It was time for a new toy boy she told nobody but herself, and his dumb fiancée looked bored and in need of a female. It was a charitable idea to go over and talk to the buxom bombshell to pass the time until she found the face she was looking for, Reggie.

Lucas thanked God he did not suffer from asthma or he would be on his fifth attack mincing around the glamorous ballroom; he was in heaven. Poor Jude had been stalked with selfies all night, and he had managed to get a few cheeky autographs too. Anna wasn't as friendly as he had liked; she didn't speak a word, so Lucas guessed she was either stoned or dead standing up. His body started to collapse with the champagne flooding inside and for once he could do with food - it was a rare idea for him to think. A waiter weaving in and out with a tray of canapés like a lion on the hunt a few hundred feet away caught his eye, so Lucas started to follow his penguin-tailed prey.

The fishy canapé was delicious, dissolving away his hunger and creating a solid anchor to keep his body from becoming shamefully drunk and ending up on ENews - he wished. He went to take another one and felt his hand collide with another hungry guest's. He looked over to apologise hoping it was an actress famous for yo-yo dieting so he could tell Jude that they were falling off the wagon, knowing that they would have a fitness DVD out by Christmas. However, the face to greet Lucas, a life changing face from Jude's past, was the last face that a shocked Lucas saw before he became a murderer.

A ritual started to form in the evenings for Eric, and it was a ritual as common as brushing his teeth before bed - but a ritual that had him thinking of it all day. His little dating site was reeling in small interest from the pond of single women in the city. *Single2Mingle* alerted him to a new message on his profile. Recently he had struck up a boomerang conversation with one profile and they had sent messages between them - nothing of a sexual nature, Eric was a gentleman. No hint of madness, just general questions like *'how was your day?'*, and *'how have you been?'* He clicked on the flashing mail icon in the shape of a letter - very original, Eric was amused.

It opened, asking him a question that brought the reality of the site home...an actual date. Eric flushed. It was a compliment in his lonely life, but the guilt stopped him from typing out a reply, so he closed the lid. *Let me sleep on it and give a decision in the morning,* Eric thought. Staying loyal to his deceased wife, he held back the spontaneous side rugby-tackling him to immediately give a reply. Fortunately, that same night when he dreamt, instead of dreaming about birds, his dead wife visited and gave her approval for Eric's heart to finally move on.

*

Distracted by the glamour and the smell of divine fruits of the world, Alex forgot for a moment her purpose for breaking into the bedroom of Queen Sociable Saffron. The bedroom was fit for a Queen, and it took all of her will power not to go all Goldilocks and dive onto the giant bed in the middle, sleeping like a bear. The fur cover gave the appearance that it breathed. She witnessed Mindy being sucked under the bed as the three naked bodies fell onto the bed, rumbling around and mating as if it was a race; the experience told her that Mindy was in no fit state to be breaking into anything, so it was down to Alex.

The bedroom was demurely lit like an elliptical lamppost, and it was the space of her whole apartment back in London. The décor was as if a hooker lived here; if Simone's stories were true of Saffron, a slut did live here. Feeling like a superhero on a mission to stop the world ending, to find the ring, to stop all destruction of humanity, she started to creep towards a dressing table - most women kept their jewellery there. A thought that Saffron maybe kept it in a hidden vault somewhere in the room gave doubt to Alex as she approached the vast dressing table with thousands upon thousands of jewels. Alex gasped in awe.

Women of all income love jewellery from a young age to pretending to have a crown made of plastic to mark life events. A woman on child benefit might work a 'MUM' ring on her fingers from the catalogue shop, but the pride would outweigh any blood diamond. A woman in the top five richest women in the world held a ring collection with precious stones that would outdo a mine in Africa. Staring at the line-up of potential rings Mabel wanted back, Alex was stuck, distracted and attempted to steal.

Ruby stones grew in a lavender velvet box as big as rosebuds. Emeralds of pure bulk ran like a border in a rectangular silk box. Sapphires sprung up in size and height in a pyramid display box, while diamonds threatened to attack her like an army of killer ants keen on human flesh.

"Fuck," she said to no one, just herself - a dead end. *Maybe I should just wait and attack Saffron, and force her to give the ring over.* During late night research Alex had watched a small video of a charity boxing match Saffron had taken part in and won last year; Alex liked her nose so declined on ambushing the legend for information on the ring. She let out a sigh of complete frustration, picking each ring up to guess becoming time consuming. She needed a clue, yet the room stayed quiet out of loyalty or fear. She sat at the dressing table far from as elegant as Mindy's treasured dressing table at home. Noticing a picture turned away like a naughty school kid, she found it hard to resist the nosey scouser in her - Alex would look in a suspicious rucksack left on the tube. She turned it around and it was of Mabel. The smile, immense across her soft, adored face, made Alex smile. With classic beauty, her eyes sparkled like the gems on the table. She placed the picture frame down; it suddenly fell forward as if Mabel had lost her balance, tumbling towards a small box and hitting it hard. The force knocked it wide open, and there blinking shocked at its rescue was the ring, her gut screamed. Taking the ring in triumph, the mission successful, Alex rushed out and back over the ledge, vanishing into the night. The wonderful ring possessed another power, a power of destruction and revenge, sending out a secret signal for deadly revenge to come their way.

The combination of cocktails, an orgy of spirits, prestige champagne with a free pass and the free line of coke all rushed to give cheerleader confidence in his little plan of revenge. The studio flat was small but tidy, a bit like Tom Cruise. He felt a little disheartened, more than the time that he had gone to his first Gay Pride thinking that it would match a Disney parade. The only thing in common was that it had a lot of princesses and wicked queens. He had always imagined crack dens to be littered with drug paraphernalia, with maybe a hooker or a bone skinny junkie lying comatose on the floor spaced out, and a gun lying around just in case – well, on CSI they did. He had been expecting crack den chic.

Reggie was either promoting a new type of crack den or suffered from OCD, seeing a lavender plug in air freshener letting out a fragrant sigh every fifth minute or so. Maybe he was gay? A holy picture of the Pope in his cute matching outfit hung on the wall; it was the only privileged picture with the other walls bare, not even displaying a Tupac poster. Lucas's drunken imagination told him that it was to hide a bullet hole and bits of brain, when really Reggie was just after some protection from above. Certainly, if the Pope offered more than just cheap wine at communion and gave homosexuality a free pass from sin, the church's career revival would be better than any dramatic weight loss on an actor would. The bare pews dressed like fashion week. A limp plant in the corner wilted as if it had seen too much or was afraid of what it was going to see. Part one of Lucas's plan had worked.

He had introduced himself to Reggie asking if he knew somewhere for drugs and a chill with a cheeky wink. Reggie knew that the gays loved to spend their pink pound on drugs and this flamboyant, camp guy seemed to have the dollar to deliver, his expensive shiny shoes and thick watch being the giveaway. Why was it that all the white folk always asked the black dude at a party where the drugs where at? Ignoring the minor racism in the queer's question, Reggie was very happy to oblige to make a dollar. The star filled party of the year started to die down as the overrated egos left in their identical limousines to go back to whatever hotel in the sleep deprived city was putting them up for free. Reggie started to bore of the entire pretentious crowd. Saffron had avoided him for a reason he did not know; she could go fuck herself. Kitten Minx throwing a kick off and being escorted out by security had killed his plan of a fuck. Lucas became the runner up for an ideal nightcap in many ways.

Lucas started to make himself comfortable with his dangerous idea to teach Reggie a lesson. Gay men were notorious for revenge. They adored a challenge when it came to men, especially straight men. Lucas had grown up in an unstable childhood, moved around so many times that he did not need to learn his address, and failed to make friends to last into adulthood. Raised on social services due to an absent mother boomeranging in and out of his broken life before her suicide from jumping off the bridge wearing socks and sandals, Lucas knew she wasn't of right mind just on that fashion no-no.

Abuse had rained down from more than one foster parent. Each undeserving punch he received battered down his self-esteem and hopes for a good life. Starved of affection growing up, he had also been deprived of food as punishment for simply making a noise or not cleaning the toilet properly. Fashion was his only love and escape from reality, and being gay was his destiny; it killed the idea of being married with 2.5 children, giving Lucas a road ahead of him free from being tied down by the normal way of living - unless it was bondage in the bedroom.

Lucas did whatever to survive, and survive he did. Quite confident around violence, he had learned not to let men hurt him, and that misery was just a common occurrence in his life. Petty thieving, sexual favours and good old solid studying to better his adult life had left his broken childhood in a heap in the past where it belonged; in hindsight, his troubled upbringing was his saviour. Jude was the love of his life and came into Lucas's life all beautiful and hunky at a time where he was losing faith in love and human kindness was merely a distant memory. Jude made Lucas happy and gave him the confidence to become the gay he was today. Jude even joined in his obsession of Cher just to show him how much he loved him.

Thinking of his boyfriend made him smile wide, glazed daydreaming into the distance thinking of their future, church bells, children, an Oscar for Jude acting. He would do anything for Jude, and if that involved murder, then murder it was. The nasty mixed up coke cranked up his confidence in the harsh culling of Reggie. Reggie came back into the room from the small toilet drying his hands on a white hand cloth, and Lucas's smile evaporated. Lucas played a blind eye to the crashed out junkie in the bathtub with her saggy tits exposed and her make-up days old; she looked dead as her long limbs peeled over the bath tub looking as if she had tried to escape. Lucas was glad that Reggie kept some tradition of a crack den and wanted to get a selfie with the passed out girl.

Reggie was handsome - there was no denying the mixture of street toughness, ripped muscles, and maps of tattoos covering him was a porno turn-on for Lucas. Black skin of the rawness of the night failed to show any age and highlighted his athletic build. Pillow-thick equal lips that had rested on many women's lips in the city, and pressed against many clits in the bedroom became inviting. His amber eyes glowed from his face and a six inch scar shrieked noticeably across his lower abs - a gift from a crazed ex-girlfriend with a carving knife furious to cut his cock off when she had found him in the arms of another. Yet his exterior was all Lucas could see. Unfortunately dominant, abusive, and used to getting what he wanted, was something that Lucas would find out the hard way a little later into the deadly night.

Reggie changed from his restricted posh suit that gave him the designer swag he lacked in his baggy jeans and oversized tees into just a pair of nylon starved of length shorts. His package was on show looking inviting and pleasurable, if you were to receive the invite to pleasure and accommodate it; Lucas had tried black in the past and even went back a few times too.

"What you after? Coke, smack, crack, weed or liquid G?" The gays love liquid G the way a herd of elephants love scarce watering holes in the African dead heat, gays just like elephants would travel the peril distance of the city jut to buy it. Reggie rolled off the list of his illegal products with the ease of a teacher calling a register, fixing up a cigarette to his thick lips, his gold tooth resting on his bottom lip. Lucas played with the idea of asking if he had any hair gel, knowing that his blonde locks had lost some structure; Lucas was such a hair gay.

His voice was deep, lacking any joy. He slouched on a small wooden chair deprived of a cushion or comfort. His black toned thighs raised the shorts a little higher for a better view of his open legs. His fat-free cut six-pack didn't vanish, and his belly button was an outie. He could easily be an underwear model with the pose and his tantalising black cock dangerously close to poking out for a preview.

"Make yourself comfortable."

Lucas in his stiff boa tight outfit sat straight with perfect posture. Lucas always sat extremely straight; it stopped his imagery roll of fat on his stomach hanging over his pants like a peak on a baseball cap. The real reason was that one foster father had beaten a phobia so blue that it had formed him never to slouch. He had looked sexy and quite entertaining at the party, working the glamorous room better than paracetamol works on pain. Lucas had popped out dance moves like he was a Gayoncé - gay Beyoncé. Reggie saw that he was extremely thin, like supermodel hungry slim. His body was feminine and delicate, and slightly turned him on. Reggie was a try-sexual - he would try anything once, and back in the day had received oral for payment. Male or female, it was sex - no matter what the sex. Reggie liked to force his conquests into being submissive; he loved the power and control, and the more they feared him the harder his erection became. Thinking about how Saffron loved a little S&M when she was high, he wondered if she had gone home with that stud Chad Rise. His jealousy fired up a little inside.

Lucas slowly took off his fitted jacket in fear of it ripping, and his patent shoes, revealing pedicured toes polished to perfection, followed by his white shirt. His tiny nipples were erect while his belly button ring was purple to match his underwear. He wouldn't sleep with Reggie; he knew that on the taxi ride back. Nevertheless, if he had to use sex to get his way then he would. He had done it before in his old life, but normally was paid for it.

The small place was screaming for the help of an interior designer. It was all just bland, painted in the knotweed of the paint world, magnolia. This distracted Lucas a tad to not notice Reggie beside him holding out a fat rolled up spliff. Lucas lit it up, took a macho pull and thought that it was him who would be dying in this crack den from the strength of it provoking his chesty, deep cough. Reggie laughed, his cut fine face showing how handsome he really was. The slight musky smell of male sweat mixed with a woody manly aftershave was what Reggie wore, and being alone with the drug dealer was a gay fantasy turn-on. Lucas felt like he was in a rap video minus a big booty, he was saving up for a Brazilian bum. The champagne was freely flooding his confidence, diluting the dangerousness of the situation that Lucas had stupidly purposefully put himself in. He didn't feel like celebrating just yet.

He passed over the obese spliff to Reggie who leaned back a little on to his bed, resting on his elbows. His boxer-fit black body with his smooth raised chest made Lucas think about what a waste his sexy body would become after his death; maybe a body transplant was possible. It would beat having to add protein powder to anything that went in his mouth. Jude's cock wore a coat of protein powder instead of a condom; there were carb-free flavours available on the market that they used in the hope that it would help when he put Jude's cock in his mouth, and he would gain weight. Lucas knew that Jude wished he would put some weight on and be body proud, not shamed. This thought created a smile, a tiny glimmer of light in this dark situation.

"Any glasses?" he asked, producing the stolen champagne bottle he had taken from the party that was hidden in his Vuitton, knowing very well that Reggie was not a man who would be harbouring a glass set of slim flutes from Bloomingdales or know what a Luis Vuitton was. Reggie pointed to a single cupboard, its handle missing, letting out a thick veil of smoke.

"In there, man. Take off your pants if you want." A cloud of dense smoke filtered slowly from his mouth with the sexy suggestion. Smoking weed always made him horny; Lucas's tiny, tidy arse in his purple jock strap sparked a rush of blood to his cock as he removed his pants, folding them up and putting them over his expensive bag. It dirtily reminding him of a school girl he used to fuck before her dad had found out and given him a beating with six of his brothers; the metal plate in his jaw was his proud war wound.

Lucas found a cup with a hazardous broken handle and a pint glass that were both smeared with suds marks, but they would do.

Being gay, Lucas had put worse in his mouth. Taking both glasses and the empty champagne bottle with him, he knew it would be wise not to leave any evidence of him being here. Pouring for himself in the broken cup and the pint glass for Reggie, he stirred in the sleeping powder that he had bought from a late-night chemist on the taxi ride over with a butter knife, making sure that Reggie was busy tying a rubber band around his forearm and could not see.

Returning to the double bed that was also a sofa with a few illicit stains streaked across, he saw that Reggie was slightly aroused in his lightweight shorts, his cock far from famine. It did not take much to notice his fat cock beneath the flimsy material - it was like trying to cover your face with a stamp. His cock matched the pumped vein in his arm that was building from the dam of blood building up behind the rubber band. Lucas handed Reggie the pint glass; the smell of heroin always made Lucas nauseous, stopping himself from gagging by drinking his stolen champagne.

"Cheers." He toasted his cup against Reggie's pint, watching as he drank the champagne and then pierced his skin with the ease and experience of doing this many times before with a thin, deadly needle to shoot up, the gateway for the street drug to surf in his blood stream. Lucas was to play this cool for however long it took - he would wait. Reggie needed to be weak and easy to overpower. Lucas was good at waiting; he had waited three days in a snowstorm for a sale at Macy's department store and ten years to finally see the hermit Cher in concert.

Reggie finished his liquid hit, offering Lucas the used needle as he started to untie the cord, allowing the blood to flow freely back. The needle slid a tiny drop of blood down onto his finger. Lucas hated heroin more than rubber croc shoes - it was the only thing in his life that his addictive personality had failed to latch on to. Even the promise of weight loss could not get him on board.

Looking at the needle looking so weak and fragile, he wondered how the fuck one prick passing on a prick could change your life. *Was this how it had happened with Jude?* Had Jude and Reggie engaged in a sexual act that night? These questions twisted around his dry brain, choking any warning of getting out of the place and running to safety. Lucas was deaf to the pleas of his worried head.

He wondered if Reggie had the vile virus running riot in his body. Nowadays HIV was not the death sentence that the eighties had promoted, or the killer disease that heterosexuals scared their naïve, impressionable children with, giving the bogeyman a hiatus, and failing to tell them that it had been a horny arsed straight male with a monkey kink for the spread of the illness in the first place. Reggie did not need infecting as payback - he needed his life cut short to stop his ruthless reign of drug dealing and sexual terror in the neighbourhood's demise.

Lucas panicked; he had to distract Reggie into having another deadly hit, weakened for his attack, idea bowled to the front knocking all the sane safe options to the floors like skittles, strike hit. *Jude fucking murder you if he ever found out* small sense left in his head screamed, but fuck it - needs must and all. Slowly reaching under the thin elasticated band of Reggie's shorts, uninvited, his manicure fingertips touched the sensitive head of Reggie's smooth purple head, wetness licked at his intruding fingertips. Reggie tensed; he was either tense with fear or tense with the invitation to carry on. Lucas gathered that since no fist had hit him that it was the latter.

Waistband slip down with ease, Reggie worked a bald look in his manscaping, making the length of his cock look longer. Being pubeless never was a turn-on for Lucas - he felt like a perv if there was no hair to show maturity and being of legal consent age, unless maybe Reggie suffered from alopecia. His black mamba snake dense cock stiffened automatically, accepting the invitation, the chilled air blowing on his exposed cock like a blowjob, rising like king cobra ready for spitting salty semen, not poison.

He re-tied the rubber band. Reggie loved shooting-up while being sucked off, so Lucas was relieved. Lucas hoped that his fatal plan would work. Lowering his head for revenge on the person who had given Jude HIV, Reggie placed his hand on his descending head. "Suck it, gay boy, and suck it good."

Lucas stopped and lifted his head, paused, pouted and said, "Off the hair, bitch." This made Reggie laugh and lean back, offering Lucas his massive cock to feast on. Part two of Lucas's plan for revenge started with the first contact of his glossy painted lips on Reggie's hard cock.

Cramp plagued her neck and all four of her limbs from lying in the same position, like a person found dead at a crime scene or a person paralysed by a freak accident, for the past six hours. Mindy needed the toilet badly; her temperamental bladder was threatening her with pissing herself as it pushed in protest, and she had certainly been put off sex forever. It had been worse than hearing Poppy that time in the garden shed with the window cleaner one Sunday afternoon; poor Bunny, the rabbit who lived in the shed, thought that rabbits got a bad reputation. She had not eaten either, which was a miracle. She decided that if Eric ever sacked her, she would start a diet plan where you hide under a bed while skinny people fuck above you. She knew that they had been skinny; famous people only fuck skinny people.

The peeping morning seeped into the bedroom of debauchery offering hope and light. In the last six hours Mindy had heard most of the karma sutra in pornographic audio, and stuffing her nylon tights mask into her ears had failed to dim the noises of rampant sex. She was now fluent in verbal foreplay.

Being under the bed for six hours, she could not remember the last time she had spent six hours in her own bed. In these six hours she had pleaded with every God, promised to change her life, had seven mental clean outs, picked enough fluff from the carpet to make a fleece, and had managed a two-hour nap where she married Joe-Ryan in her short dream. She wondered what he was doing.

How one encounter with one man could stretch out so long affecting her dreams and mind puzzled her. Why was she longing to see him? She decided that the mind must be going mad to distract itself from the pounding above. If she had had a mop, she would have banged up on the mattress with it shouting, 'keep the fucking noise down!'. If she ever got out, she promised herself she would ask Joe-Ryan out for a date. The idea gave her butterflies, while her self-doubt tried to capture them and pull their wings off.

The sex had started off wild, carefree, and noisy like a pack of chimpanzees going wild at feeding time, downing multiple cans of energy drink with their fruit salad. With each minute morphing into an hour, it died down as if Storm Threesome was losing power, hearing gentle snoring from the women who were knackered from the marathon fucking, cheered on from the side line by the purple pill, supporters of their stamina. Mindy remembered lasting three hours once with an ex-boyfriend in the sack. Ok, he technically fell asleep for an hour, but she had stayed naked until he woke and finished her off.

Abrupt snores came from the famous Latin Lothario, who must have suffered weight gain judging by his thunder-like snores. Mindy looked on in a new light at the very famous movie star, applauded his sexual stamina and appetite. Mindy needed to get out; Alex would be going spare and Mindy's poor bladder begged for release as if on parole. It was courage she needed, and courage was something she managed to find. Her joints creaked as she started to put to use her army crawl, a favourite at Bootcamp.

Mindy's head popped out from underneath the bed, the bed being her quilted luxury shell. Her misfit fringe was stuck to her forehead from fright of the light. She was greeted by the sweaty air exhausted from the trio of naked bodies, thick with the scent of stale sex and cum weighing her down. Drink and a faint smell of weed tinted the magnificent room disrespectfully. Each army crawl brought more of Mindy into the bedroom, the heavy snoring still ongoing. Luckily, the trio had not closed the balcony door, preferring to let the view of New York Manhattan look in like a peep show.

The fresh breeze was encouraging on Mindy's face like a new bitch licking the sack from a new born encouraging it to breathe. Free from the nylon makeshift balaclava, relief washed over her as if she was glimpsing fresh air for the first time since being buried alive in a landslide. A pigeon landed on the ledge, twisting its little oval head as the wind ruffled against its grey blue feathers; Mindy dramatically wondered if she would ever be free like the pigeon. She would have preferred a dove to be honest, since they were symbol of hope and peace - but a pigeon represented…well, she didn't know what pigeons represented, but she did know that the Pope had never tossed one from the Vatican.

Each crawl towards the open balcony door to escape became closer, and freedom, and the possibility of making it out became a reality. Maybe pigeons were sick and tired of being the black sheep of the family, and were the new symbol of hope. Suddenly, the bed moved; Mindy froze dead holding her breath in, and positive that she felt a rib bone, she felt joy at last. She sensed someone turning over in the bed. She stayed flat to the floor hoping to be mistaken for a human rug, maybe; this was a celebrity's bedroom, after all, so it was a new interior trend possibility.

A few moments passed; Mindy felt safe that nobody had woken and proceeded to crawl with more speed, ignoring the carpet burns branding her elbows. It was worth the small amount of pain, and she would ignore Alex's accusations of doing it doggy-style.

She crawled faster, and accidentally she knocked the bed leg. Something thin and moist fell onto her face as a result, and the smell of banana slapped her face. She wondered if they had included a banana in their orgy - it was one way to get your five-a-day, she mused. The faint aroma of sex and lube told Mindy that she doubted it was the popular fruit, grabbing it from her forehead and ignoring the soaking it had given her redneck wild fringe, only to find it to be a yellow, transparent condom filled with cottage cheese thick spunk. She could not scream in disgust as she had not spoken for the last six hours and lacked the energy. Disbelieving that this was actually happening, she humoured the idea of putting it in her pocket and donating it to a sperm bank on seeing enough of the chalky white fluid from the famous man to populate a small island. Wondering how much she would get for it on eBay, she escaped at last. The pigeon cooed its congratulations before it flew off and disappeared into the iconic skyline of New York.

Her body was not as firm as usual, nor was she as young as his normal conquests or his fiancée, but she accommodated him well and moved with the flexibility of a Barbie doll. Saffron oozed her powerful placing in New York worked it as a skill, it became a tool in her attraction to men; she was a living legend, wealthy like a Saudi Prince and full of surprises. She had left Chad exhausted, hungry and tender with her impressive sexual stamina for an old broad. The session had ended with her wearing a pearl necklace with the sheer grace she would have if it had been made of real pearls, not spunk. She was a great bang.

Now, waking up in her bed alone, the decor was spacious and dressed in vintage glamour, and the expensive view delighted him. Silk sheets slipped with ease off his hairless chest as he sat up, prolonging their stroke of his young torso. Last night at the Gala was everything he had expected and more. He had mingled with the millionaire stars, talked deep with potential directors, had made a grand impression and impact on Ruddick St. David with talks of an open audition for a gritty thriller, and lastly, had landed the hot shag with Saffron, the Queen Bee of the New York elite social hierarchy.

Said woman was not in the bed beside him. A stab of gut-wrenching guilt repeatedly plunged into him for not waking up with Maria, knowing that the crushing guilt nothing to do with his cheating but more to do with his devious career promotion proposal with Ruddick St. David; little did he know that his betrayal of Maria was powerful enough to end life.

The morning light bled into the majestic bedroom as he checked his Rolex - his second in the space of a month. It was two hours away from noon, and he felt surprisingly fresh. Just a lingering headache, but he knew that was from the fact that he needed to eat since he had been fucking all night, seeing his expensive suit folded perfectly over the throne-looking chair facing the bed, patient and glad of the free show.

Chad slipped the remaining cool sheets off, stretched his toned, naked body out, and said, "thank you" out loud into the room. His flaccid cock tenderly hit his toned thigh in applause for his fucking of the rich bitch, his velvety balls were drained, and his purple pill sexual appetite fed. If he had been into his interior design, he would know that these sheets were the rarest silk ever to be spun. Cleopatra rumoured to have been enveloped with the same silk; the spunk stains had ruined them. The grand bedroom was inspirational for what his wealth could allow if his acting career went from strength to strength with the few potential offers from last night. His sordid secret with Ruddick St. David meant that in a film or two he would be able to own the whole apartment - not just the bedroom.

The white curtains drawn back gave the panoramic view a spellbinding touch. It was the perfect excuse to get out of the gigantic bed, and he was excited like a child on Christmas morning. The whole of New York was beneath him as he looked down - it had never lost any of its golden glow of opportunity since he had arrived for the first time five years ago to study; it owned his breath every time. The sheer height of the apartment made him feel like he was God in the heavens - a naked God standing in his birthday suit, looking down on his world.

"Good morning," a sweet voice interrupted his naked stance towards the view of the city. His smooth arse was firm and tight; it was a great view. It beat the view of the subway, she thought. He turned to see the maid stripping the bed with precision and speed.

"Good morning." He ignored the etiquette of covering his meaty modesty. Chad enjoyed displaying his sexual prowess in the company of women" and this woman, pretty, surprised his cock with the energy to twinge with the hint of hardening.

Helena carried on stripping the bed, ignoring the stains and stray pubic hairs. She knew that Saffron was a slut and sold a few stories to keep her mortgage payments paid each month. She would put these sheets on eBay - she had a super fan, so for anything Saffron-related, she was dollars in. Helena was over forty but easily passed for her early thirties; the physical work of being a maid kept her a trim size ten, and her skin cancer scare at seventeen meant that she kept a vigorous skin regime which had thankfully paid off. She had seen many cocks. Truth be told, none had been as impressive as Chad Rise's thick member that was dangling knackered, yet Helena was a devoted married woman, and she was happy with Ivan's average penis. Helena was luckily immune to star egos too, thank fuck.

"Can I get a cup of tea?" he asked. Helena stopped the stripping of the bed and stood upright, straightening the ache out of her back. "Sorry, Ms. Saffron left no memo to look after a" she paused "guest." She rolled her disapproving eyes over the fantastic naked man in the room, who happened to be Chad Rise, the infamous bad boy of soap. Maybe if he had said please she would have made him one. Chad wanted to slap the rude bitch down, with her disapproving look and the shade of calling him a guest. But, if he wanted to see Saffron again, beating her house cleaner was not going to work in his favour, relaxing his clenched fist.

Chad found Saffron to be nowhere present in the plush penthouse suite. After a one-man mini tour, he was ready to leave. He wondered why Helena had failed to give him information on Saffron's whereabouts as she held the door open wide for him to leave. Helena smelled divine as Chad breathed her in. "Shame...your loss," he hissed close in her ear; Helena refused to give a reaction as her brown eyes locked with his magnificent blue. Unbeknown to Chad, Saffron preferred to shag and shoot off - she had no time to stay for small talk. Plus, she had a huge interview to celebrate the successful Gala, a record breaker, over at Trump Tower.

Chad felt his ego brewing a bruise. Normally women wanted him to stay, stalked him or claimed that they were pregnant, ignoring the fact that Chad was a fan of pulling out and shooting off. Chad's worse outcome would be getting some money-hungry whore pregnant, famous or not. Chad sometimes even wore two condoms and carried the morning after pill as backup. Luckily, he knew that for women of Saffron's age an unexpected pregnancy was as rare as Britney having a successful marriage.

"What about a kiss, sweetheart before I leave?" he said flashing his killer smile and blue eyes hoping for a quick ego boost, trying to turn the charm back on. Helena smiled, turning down his charm and slammed the door in his face. "Fucking dyke" he said slamming his fist into the closed door in anger, running his hands through his hair at the blow out. Maybe his charm was fading, his looks losing the power of seduction if a poorly paid house cleaner could turn him down; he shuddered to think. *Time to go home stud,* his head told him.

Mindy was leaving Simone's penthouse suite to go and buy some keyrings for all her colleagues at the funeral parlour and heard a thud on a door in the corridor. She closed the jewelled glass door on Alex, Simone and Leon's prolonged, dynamic laughter brought on by her retelling of the story for the fifth time. She looked forward to the peace on the New York street.

Mindy turned herself into the posh hallway laughing at the believability of the indecent incident, trying her best not to steal a beautiful vase, bumping into someone as she fumbled in her handbag for a mint. Sometimes the past can be present but unrecognisable. Mindy's unrecognisable past had unfortunately caught her up.

*

The glare of the morning sun teamed with the fresh air landed overwhelming joy to Lucas, as he emerged on to the dirty street in a part of town where people carried knives instead of smiles; he imagined that Nelson Mandela had felt blessed with the same relief when he had been freed from his filthy cell.

Lucas needed to hail a cab to take him home, to take him to his Jude the sooner the better, feeling his emotions starting to thaw; his eyes welled thinking of Jude. He needed to distance himself from the trauma of the night, get miles away to forget, but the strange thing was Lucas felt unusually calm for a murderer. He noticed a small group of hooded youths taking an interest in him, nudging each other for a potential mugging. His leather bag heavy as an empty cup, pint glass and the empty magnum of champagne that would all be discarded in the Hudson River later that day, hid. Committing murder again if the youths tried to steal his Vuitton was not on his agenda this morning.

His lavish suit was crumpled, coated cruelly by the harsh smell of cigarettes and weed lost its star quality that it had possessed the night. Droplets of blood pebble-dashed the structured collar as slight starched marks on his neck stung when he sprayed aftershave, a cruel reminder of what he had done. This Cinderella had truly outstayed her twelve o'clock curfew, yet her shoes too expensive to leave behind, and he already had his Prince waiting for him at home.

Champagne soaked his shirt, and the dried blood to the slight cut on his lip gave the innocent impression that he was suffering from a cold sore. Reggie, true to his upbringing, was a fighter struggled for his wronged life, but Lucas fuelled on by revenge and love for Jude, and the fact that Reggie thought he had the right to force Lucas to take his monster cock with the aching pain as his arse torn tears glazed his eyes, won the battle to smother a drugged up, drunk Reggie dead.

His knight in daylight robbery fare yellow cab pulled over. Lucas was so relieved he wanted to cry. The driver knew that no one as excessively dressed as that was safe around this shady neighbourhood, where police tape acted like picket fences around many properties and corrugated iron was like double glazing. Even if he was a pimp or a schizophrenic, as a father himself he sensed that the skinny guy needed a bit of rare New Yorker kindness for breakfast, and not a bagel.

*

"So sorry wasn't looking where I was going" Mindy apologised first; it might not have even been her who was the one not looking, but she was polite.

"Me neither." His rogue, loving heart stopped. Shit, after all these years apart, standing in front of him was she. His throat was dry and constricted taking his breath as payback; his cold heart struggled to slow down. He nearly blurted out her name. He looked at her in utter astonishment, more gorgeous than he ever remembered her. He felt his skin sweat and his mouth open - did he want to kiss her? Tell her it was him? The flowing locks of red hair confidently established became a part of her huge attraction along with her eyes, her perfect face and friendly smile. When younger her red hair had always been the target of a tease and sunstroke, but once she found herself as a woman, her red hair became her best asset. Chad Rise stood in front of her speechless. Mindy was forever bumping into men but never bonking them, she mentally laughed to herself as she took in the handsome stranger. She knew Chad Rise was someone in America as she had seen him on a few pages of the magazines around Simone's penthouse suite and on ENews, rumoured to be linked to Delia Von Grouse, the socialite who had been found dead on the sidewalk.

He was extremely good-looking in typical American star gloss, his skin gauche smooth, his face free of stress, and stubble shaded, contoured his sharp face. Beautiful blue eyes sparkled fresh, longing at her she noticed, and the Hollywood typical gleaming straight smile opened his beautiful features more. Mindy wanted to jump out of the nearest window - she had had enough celebrity encounters working in the make-up industry. Mindy, like Helena, was blessed with immunity to star power. Chad could not believe that Mindy, his Mindy, was standing outside Simone Delvin's trashy glass door.

Was she a maid? Was she a hooker? Maybe Simone had become a fan of rug munching, fed up of cock after all these years. Was she here for long overdue revenge? Her resemblance to Henry Dooley, an acting idol of his, was prominent. Was it a sign of faith? Was she with that crazy, fist-happy friend of hers?

He was confused that her reaction was calm, not aggressive or spitting thousands of questions at him, knifing deep into him and exposing his sordid soul, as he had imagined many a time. Then it clicked - his saviour. He was beyond recognition of what she remembered him as thanks to the reconstruction of his movie-making looks. Mindy noticed Chad Rise's puzzled look at her.

"Yes, it's a fringe, and yes, it's cut shorter than funds to the NHS, and yes, it doesn't do anything for my face. But, I was doing a good deed," she started. "Bloody can't wait for this criminal fringe to grow to a length to be hair pinned, nor allow my goddaughter to use me as a guinea pig at hairdressing school ever again." It was like having bloody leprosy, the reactions she received.

"Fringe?" Chad, being a man, failed to notice the short fringe - only tits and arse - but now she mentioned it, it was quite short. It stuck out like a bamboo roof on a pool bar. He put his hand to his mouth to smother his laugh. Mindy was one of the few females who made him genuinely laugh, and one he actual regretted hurting. That is when Mindy saw it - the crooked little finger. 'Him' had one too from a motorbike accident. *It was a shame it wasn't his neck* she used to bellow back in the early days of despair, drunk on wine and a stone heavier thanks to Kalbi's kebabs. *How strange*, she thought, passing quickly through her thoughts of the adulterated past. If she had passed the strange thought through a Victorian mangle, she would have processed who he really was underneath his catalogue-chosen face.

Her memory gave her brain a sharp nudge but Mindy failed to notice, his handsome features fracking her normal, sane mind away, Chad held the power to break her immunity to famous faces. She smiled, feeling the conversation with the handsome actor staling. She was left wondering why he was leaving Saffron's classy place - Alex had filled her in on how glamorous it was. Alex had triumphed in retrieving the infamous ring. Mindy was dying for a nose around; she loved property programmes, and just getting the chance to have a look around someone's home made her kill the cat of curiosity. Could Chad be in on the ring too?

"Well, have a lovely day, nice to meet you." Turning, Mindy walked away hoping in her head that she sashayed like a model, trying to suck her curvy arse in. It took all of Chad's acting experience not to blurt out who he really was.

*

Ruddick St. David woke up in the huge bed in the black and white decorated penthouse suite in the award-winning famous hotel alone. The top hotel was gracious about his stay and had given it to him for free, ignoring the fact that they were losing thousands of dollars for the privilege. The publicity alone tripled the value of the room for frantic film fans who wanted to stay in it.

The star-studded gala had been a runaway success, but why wouldn't it be? The crème de la crème of celebrity had attended and brought the global attention that not even a terrorist attack could muster the coverage of. Chuffed all night, he was. His phone had alerted him on every single media platform that it was top news, and the papers laid out on his bedside table each showed an image from the wonderful night of celebrity fundraising. Saffron was draped with other star famous men and women of the evening, hitting the three-million-dollar target and more.

He felt a tad rough from his minor hangover. Naked, his fat belly was canopying his stumpy dick with the shadow cutting much-needed inches. He scratched his patch of dry skin on his belly letting snow skin flakes fall into his greying pubes, and let out a wet cough to clear the phlegm from his throat. Picking his nose free of obstruction, he sucked his finger free of what he found.

An empty, high-class bottle of champagne rested at the bottom of the bed like a loyal pampered pooch, while his underwear, half-mast on the bedpost, seemed in sorrow. Ah yes, it occurred to him - he had come home with the sensational Maria Dieppe, very drunk and legless, and quite lacklustre in the bed department for a Mexican sex bomb. She had been a sore let down but she was still cheaper than a hooker, and Chad had kept his side of the carnal deal. Ruddick St. David was a man of his word, and would certainly keep his.

He had fucked her, spunking twice in her, tasting her pussy on his rough tongue ignoring her weak pleas that were drenched in drink to stop. He gathered that she meant 'stop' as it was pleasurable; yeah, sure it was, he told himself. Plentiful breast meat slipped over his chubby hands as he teethed and nipped at her brown, hard nipples, like a puppy suckling from its mother. She was sensational naked - he wished he had filmed it. Now, in the bright morning light, she was not in the giant bed among the crumpled sheets of stained sexual activity. He didn't care much for women out-staying their welcome, quite glad she had upped and left like a good girl. As a bonus, it killed any awkwardness of Maria asking how she had got there. If only all whores were like her, he thought, sipping warm whiskey from the tumbler, the sole witness from last night.

He pulled off the silk white sheets from his bulky fast-food fed frame. Fortunately for him, his success and wealth were bulkier, and this was why most women he came into contact with went to bed with him in the first place. He put his foot down, feeling his ingrowing toenail hit his brogue and shooting a searing pain through his foot, feeling scolding him for something but what?

"All the fucking money in the world and still can't buy your health," he said talking out loud to himself, scrunching his round, red, fat face up in pain, cursing the new morning light. He proceeded over to the en-suite for a ritual shower to wake him up and wash the smell of sex from his dry skin before returning to his Suzie, his dull wife of thirty years back in Beverly Hills. She was a meek woman who knew better than to ask him questions of his whereabouts, but bought clothes as if they were going out of fashion. Her idea of being dirty in the bedroom was to wear her make-up to bed. He kept her dripping in diamonds, so he dipped his dick whenever.

The bathroom door was hard to open, something stubbornly refusing to allow him entry. Was it afraid to show him something? Had he trapped the bath mat under the door? Seeing it free from obstruction he pushed again and the bulk of his unhealthy size made the task easy. It opened enough for him to put his bald head through to see what refused the door to open and allow access. What he saw provoked him to push the door wide open in sheer panic, snapping the door; it hung on by its hinges in grief.

Maria Dieppe had failed to leave the penthouse suite, but had succeeded in slitting her wrists in the plush bathroom, floating in a puddle of blood naked, blood staining her sexy body of pleasure for him but immense pain for her. Ruddick St. David prayed that she was not dead. No PR stunt would save him from this if she died, and Suzie would certainly take him to the cleaners in the divorce; he was being selfish, as usual. He may have fucked Maria Dieppe, international sex symbol last night, but Maria had fucked him big style this morning.

New York

Strolling along Broadway under the artificial stars of all the glittering billboards of award winning shows advertised took the roles of the evening stars, all fighting for you to purchase a ticket glistening around them; the man-made light gave the impression that it was an Indian summer. They had one night left before they needed to return to London for Troy's Pop up debut.

Mindy could not wait to get home to see Poppy, hopefully Joe-Ryan too, and deliver the ring to the police, get all this poppycock finally out of her life. Mindy was gobsmacked by the size and sheer ugly beauty in the ring. It was so majestic that she half expected Elizabeth Taylor to rise from the dead to buy it and sign an autograph on her tits. Made from horse bone and the eye of a horse, it had beauty in its gruesomeness, but it was evidence, finally Mabel have her sweet revenge on her criminal sister.

Walking arm in arm the two best friends chatted about everything and anything. It was eight pm, and after a leisurely day of pampering at Simone's, the friends decided to grab a heart-attack inducing portion of famous New York food perfect excuse to break from the chilly air. Food had become the glue in their lifelong friendship. Simone had declined their offer to join; her sex chart said that tonight was ideal for shagging to conceive twins, so Leon's hotdog was on the menu.

New York was magical of a night. It lost none of its deafening noise or the chaotic drama of people it had during the day. Lights in their millions created perfect backdrops for pictures and gave a feeling that anything was possible, adding planet-destroying heat to the earth. Knowing that just a portion of American-sized fried chicken hid more sins than the Catholic Church, it would be the perfect end to the short trip.

"What a crazy bloody night," Alex spoke.

"For me, yeah, not you! Never again will I be able to watch him in those adventure films." Mindy chuckled hiding her face in Alex's shoulder. "Were you not tempted to join in?" Alex loved to wind her best friend up.

"To be honest I would rather have just sat and watched, and learned a few things." Truth in all her words, Mindy knew her boring, well-rehearsed doggy position would be laughed at by the experts of group fucking. Alex chuckled; her and Troy regularly had good sex and their bedroom had an open door to ideas policy - just not ideas involving anyone else, animals or whipped cream, since Troy was dairy intolerant. Remembering the way that Debbie had looked at their picture as if she was planning to have Troy to herself, the idea gave her shivers. Then the question of Troy wanting a baby jumped on the back of the shivers; Alex needed a drink.

"I so can't wait to go to Troy's pop-up restaurant. If he does really well he could land a job with the restaurant's chain promoting the event, and even have his dish selling in their restaurant." Alex voice full of praise prayed that Troy got noticed. His food was delicious, daring and made with love just like the man himself. Troy deserved his big break, and it would hopefully keep him busy enough to distract him from his wanting of a baby. Alex had already ordered a beautiful sequin jacket and restricting-any-wide-movement-of-the-legs leather pants on Net-a-Porter, and if she was pregnant she would never be able to shop on Net-a-Porter again - this thought alone was the best contraception.

"I can't wait to have a normal civilised evening involving no dead horse ring, or an orgy above my head acting like a kinky human halo." Alex stopped, and it stopped Mindy's stern plan of her evening. "Civilised? Us? Bitch please. When have we ever been civilised?" she asked in a faux American accent, flicking her lush black hair back.

They walked on chatting about life dreams, Poppy, Troy, and Mindy saying that she would start her long overdue novel as the cooling night airbrushed their bare faces. Alex felt it first. Being a hair model, she could sense the smell of rain like a dog can with a storm. "It's going to rain, Moo. Let's find somewhere to escape from it." Uneasiness pushed Alex few steps ahead of the potential downpour, Alex dared not go back to Simone's looking drenched. Leon already thought that she was a weirdo without looking like a drowned rat - although Alex knew she was far from being described as a rat.

"Oh God is it?" Mindy did what typical British people did when someone mentioned rain; they did one of two things - they either looked up to the sky, or held their hand out. Mindy did both. "My hair is going to get wet," protesting to the obvious wearing her Mulberry bag as a makeshift leather hat to protect her red locks from the coming drenching of the upset sky. The dumpy fringe she did not give a fuck about keeping dry. Dodging oncoming human traffic like a super fit zebra does with a pride of hungry lions in its way, she sped up to catch Alex a few feet in front.

"WITH ANY BLOODY LUCK THAT FRINGE WILL GROW!" Alex shouted mocking, running towards a hot food sign glowing like a beacon from the side of a building. Her red soles flashed with speed, happy for a safe haven from the sudden downpour that New York was about to be drenched in.

*

"Where the fuck is she?" he asked the hotel room short and aggressive, wearing the beige carpet thin from pacing up and down for half an hour, powered by the fact Maria was yet to materialise back at their hotel. It was gone eight in the evening; there was not a chance in hell that Maria, clothes fashionista would have stayed out in last night's clothes.

Chad was concerned. He realised now that it had been stupid to offer Maria as a token for an open audition for Ruddick St. David's new sci-fi film. Chad was an actor - not a pimp. There had been no offer to cast on the couch for Ruddick St. David himself. First of all, Ruddick St. David was a secret homophobe who would let actors go if he found out that they were gay, but, he had let Chad know that Maria was ideal for film bargaining.

Chad felt a prick for once in his shallow, self-absorbed life for treating Maria like a piece of meat for his own benefit. He prayed that Ruddick St. David had kept schtum about their sordid deal - Maria certainly leave him if she found out. Hopefully a trip to Tiffany's would keep her sweet and off the scent of deceit.

Roxy pined for some affection as she pawed at Chad's faded Levi's, and it was the distraction he needed as he sat stroking his loyal dog. Her soft fur relaxed his racing mind, giving room for insecurity to pop in with a hello. Had she decided to leave him for good, heading back to Mexico? Yet, her passport was here. On the other hand, he wondered if she was staying with Ruddick St. David to boost her ailing TV career. Most of Hollywood would give their fake left tit and first born child to land a role in one of his instant box office smash films. Rumours among the circle of film were that Ruddick St. David was a God in the bedroom with an organic stamina free from the purple pill, and as kinky as they cum - no pun intended.

Chad lit up another cigarette, his fourth in half an hour. It was his vice only when stressed or worried. He normally stressed over whether he looked good and worried about aging, yet he had failed to give up the cancer sticks - as his mother had named them. Both stressing and worrying was so abstract from his normal behaviour that he had booked to see his shrink on Monday.

Where the fuck was his fiancée? Roxy looked at him with her endless glossy eyes. He saw her disappointment in her handsome master, resting her golden head on his knee; but, like a mother he could do no wrong, as she loved him no matter what. He always relied on Roxy to cheer him up, stroking the pedigree pooch to distract him from his woodpecker guilt knocking a fat hole on his cold conscience, knowing he had gone too fucking far this time. Mindy popped into his head with his betrayal. *For fucksake*, he thought lighting another cigarette up. Women caused too much shit in his life. Chad needed a distraction; he left his hotel room, knowing that plenty of willing distraction lay on the streets.

Super Soup

A six-foot long heater blew artificial hot air on their entrance like a blowjob as Mindy shook her leather jacket free from rain like a sheepdog. Alex was virtually dry from the freak downpour outside that had vaporised Broadway of all human activity. She ran her hands into her own hair, and it fell with the precision of a favela house cleaner laying bed sheets. All the theatre shows had sold out within the first heavy drop of rain. Alex was first to notice that this restaurant seemed a little different from your typical restaurant; it took Mindy a few moments.

"Erm, Moo don't think we're not in a restaurant." Alex spoke slowly looking around the well light room unbuttoning her coat.

If they were, then they were certainly overdressed on seeing the attire of its guests, working a look of being unwashed and the more layers the better eating. Mindy looked around thinking that it was a new hip trend of restaurant, the way that London cooked up a new way to dine each day from paying a small mortgage for a bowl of cereal from your youth - minus the pencil topper - to beef from cows fed on champagne soaked hay. The two ladies were barged out of the way by an elderly gentleman as if he had read their minds at their snobbery, with three frayed rucksacks and a small Jack Russell strapped to his bent back. He joined a queue of similarly dressed customers; he had no time to wait – it had taken him eleven hours walking to get here, so this was his Bethlehem.

"It's not got a great dress code, I must admit, but each to their own." Forever being the non-judgemental, type, Mindy scanned the large, well-lit room with rows of benches and plain tables with a floor layout like being back at school. Mindy liked the minimalist look of the place.

Alex and Mindy were again pushed aside as a few mute people walked past, joining the growing queue. "Feel like a fucking penguin in a circle here" one guest that seemed to be wearing piss as aftershave muttered loudly and crass. Mindy pulled a discreet face in disgust, noticing that he was not even old. Alex pulled out her perfume, openly spraying the stranger in a CS gas flowery attack "take that stinky" she fired back.

Alex and Mindy started to disrobe their thick coats and scarves in unison; the heater had worked a treat in bringing on a hot flush. A young, bambi brown-eyed girl approached them wearing a blue plastic apron and a hair net that blocked out her eyebrows, giving her forehead more length. She was so timid and shy but free from smelling like piss, looked like she bathed daily, and was maybe a waitress - she was safe to approach into Alex's personal space, just.

"Evening ladies are you ok?" her voice sweet and faint of confidence. The two beautiful women were not the normal clientele that Super Soup served, but never judge a book by its cover - her Great Gran was famous for saying this; it was on her headstone. This was New York, so anything went. Maybe they were reporters from the snobbish, stuck-up weekly *New Gossip*, who had finally given in to their persistent requests to feature the place in its glossy to help boost its donations. She was excited to get this little place noticed in the big, careless city.

"Yes we've come in from the rain and for a bite to eat. I'm starving" said Mindy, with emphasis on the word 'starving'. The young girl knew starving since she had worked on building a well in Africa - Mindy was far from starving judging by her curvy, healthy hips, yet she smiled. Mindy smiled back smelling hot, fresh bread. Alex tried her best to avoid touching another scruffy man who was passing by a little too close for the couture dressed Alex. Adoring the English accent, Amelia pondered whether to curtsey before she replied to the gorgeous looking redhead who was working an extremely short fringe. Most British people she encountered said that they were related to the Queen or The Beatles.

"Well we offer shelter and hot food, so just join the queue and take a seat, ladies. Tonight, it's chicken and broccoli," she said smiling little confidence filled her voice on doing good, pointing towards the ever-growing queue as Mindy and Alex attached themselves to the end. They left a healthy gap between them and Grant, the walking petrol bomb, a regular who forever smelled of petrol; it was the best thing to sniff, he would say.

It was about time that this place got a bit of free publicity. Amelia rushed off to fix her make-up in case they needed a picture to accompany the article. The good that Super Soup did feeding the homeless of New York was something inspirational and positive to write about, not starved, paranoid celebrities fucking each other - even though Amelia would so ride that Chad Rise. Super Soup was the busiest soup kitchen in Manhattan.

"You should never let a man ruin you. You are a woman of brave soul, powerful beauty to benefit your life, and born to do better than this." The wise old voice belonged to her Grandma, and she was not finished with her inspirational speech. *"It's time for you to show the world who you are and what you can achieve for the women in the world living by the harsh hands of men. You are destined to use your beauty for the good of underprivileged women everywhere."* Maria could not see her; strong, bright light blinded her of sight, and she couldn't answer back. The medication was holding her body in a coma-style sleep.

"You will be an icon in women's rights. Carry on my work." Grandma disappeared, and only her faint smell of rich argan oil lingered, killing off the clinical smell that had surrounded her of late.

It could have been the high dose of morphine that was making Maria's broken mind hallucinate, but her Grandma's voice, deceased a decade ago, was vibrant and real. She came to Maria in the darkest hour in her life. A pioneer in women's rights in Mexico, she had refused to desert and abandon women in need, and even in her death, certainly not her favourite granddaughter. Maria needed the inner strength, and her Grandma was just the woman to awaken it.

She had been a fool to let a man put her in a dark enough place to try and kill herself. She couldn't even drum up the humour to wish that it had at least been a hot man and not fat, sweaty, rapist pig Ruddick St. David. Maria felt a gentle nurse changing the bandage on her wrist, checking the stitches as she drifted in and out of a heavy sleep. "You're going to be fine, my love. Just sleep the pain off and all will be better in the morning, I promise," she said tenderly, soothing her with kind words. Luckily, Maria hadn't cut too deep to cause conversation-starting scars. The sight of abundant blood and her lack of food for the past five days to fit into her sensational frock for the Gala had been the real reason why she had collapsed in the bathroom. Maria needed sleep to recover. Most people got their best ideas when they dreamt. Her long sleep had delivered the best idea for revenge against Ruddick St. David, the sexual predator who liked his hookers and drugs – a lethal combination for a heart attack survivor to be indulging in. Her bare eyelids were crushed under tiredness, forcing her to sleep. When she awoke from this cocoon of sleep the next morning, she emerged as a different woman - a woman hell bent on revenge.

*

Her tits were just as heavy and fleshy as they had been at their first meeting. Her nipples, deep brown hard in the tense clench of his white teeth, dissolved the little remaining distraction of his fiancée missing. Claudia was topless in the seedy toilets of the strip joint. The constricted space of the John made mobility hard, but his energetic tongue worked a fierce frenzy on her wet clit just as much as his fat dick would have if he offered her it, but he didn't. The shift had started quite quiet, punters few and far between, so to pass the time until the game finished, Claudia had indulged in drinks and a few lines of the white stuff. The mixture of drugs put Claudia into a dream state. Her bare back hit against the toilet door feeling him feeding her tit into his mouth. She felt safe, wanted and for once in a long time, loved - he had come back for her. Was this a sign for her happily ever after?

His smooth hand travelled up, roughly rubbing at her exposed skin. Claudia was eager to please like most hookers, and gave forced high moans of pleasure in the lone cubicle calling for more, ignoring the sore rubbing, knowing that this quick session could lead into something more full time like a relationship. His eagerness to find her had faked belonging in her sad life. A car key appeared under her nose, and looking at the expensive car logo, the image of her driving beside him on long drives to the beach drove her nose to land one sniff to remove the heap of cocaine. The rush made her flick her head back, offering her neck to him as a kind of sacrifice to touch more - big mistake.

Chad Rise wanted to squeeze away his anger from offering sweet Maria to dirty Ruddick St. David, and through bloodshot eyes, Claudia willingly offered her neck to be squeezed. It would be rude to say no, he thought, gripping hard.

*

Simone Delvin was not a woman who heard 'no' a lot in her privileged life. She took 'no' from no one, and certainly not kind Mindy or gorgeous Alex. Both of them pleaded with her that they were absolutely fine getting an economy flight back to Britain on their return from eating out. "Illegal, criminal immigrants complain about being flown on economy class!" Simone snapped back.

Simone rolled her sapphire blue, clear eyes to the ceilings, her painted as Ariel in an underwater scene. She clicked her powerful fingers ignoring Gloria's huff of annoyance, and the *Simone Star,* her pink private jet, was ready within an hour.

Darling Revenge is my Middle Name

London

Nerves kept Joe-Ryan company in the old cockney pub that was just off tourist trap Covent Garden, rumbling in his stomach nausea threated to erupt lava of vomit from his mouth. A pint of cold cask ale was stopping his hands from fidgeting, and some dull sports on a TV tackled his wandering mind from what mischief his mother would cause. Dressed in his Sunday best of white shirt and beige chinos church polished loafers, ignoring the fact that it was Tuesday, he looked very dapper in the quiet bar, the two barmaids competitively untied their hair allowed it to fall in hope to hook a look from the hot man at the bar, alone. He was waiting for his favourite woman in his world - and his most annoying.

It was the week that Granny C was terrorising London with her sidekick, Aoife, his over bearing, annoying, loud brass mother for the biannual psychic convention. Aoife looked like any other lady. She was pretty with blonde hair from a bottle and hoop earrings you could hula hoop in, that forever left a graffiti stain of green if worn for too long. She wore bright make-up in pinks and purples, and leopard print was her second skin. Joe-Ryan's relationship with Aoife was strained. Joe-Ryan knew that he was loved by his mother, but she flaunted her love for his sisters more than she did for him. She was forever mocking him for trying to better himself and for not giving her any grandchildren, like it was payback for giving life to him, ignoring the fact that she had been blessed with nine from her daughters. He wondered what Mindy would be like as a mum. He had not seen her at the weekend; he had developed a migraine thinking that she was away on a dirty weekend with a boyfriend. Next time he would try and find out if she was single, and if he was feeling brave he would ask her out on a date; the idea made him perspire.

He loved his mother even if she did abuse drink, wore a new man on her arm every second dole pay week, and went on the missing list a few times a year. The fact that she had forced him to dress as a girl when younger so that she could pimp them all out to the social clubs as a Nolan sisters tribute act hadn't dented his love for his promiscuous mum. It was just that his mother was draining and always hard work and demanding. He looked at his watch that he had saved up a year to buy; the achievement was worth every long arse day with it representing that with hard work anything is possible – the name of the watch was held in high regard in the world of jewellery. He could see it was twelve. In another hour they would arrive, and the whole pub and probably the local police station would know of Aoife's arrival. He had plenty of time to dilute his growing anxiety with a few more cask bitters, eyeing the busty barmaid over for a refill.

*

"What's the fucking fuss about London? I so prefer Dublin. That fucking tube was cramped worse than a dingy from Syria to Greece." Granny C loathed London, and immigrants, and anyone who was not Irish - the only bonus was that Joe-Ryan lived here, and they were off to meet her handsome grandson for bangers and mash. It brought a smile to her wrinkled face. "Got bloody tourists stopping and starting like it's some fucking game of human chess. Every cunt's got a fucking camera phone attached to a fucking lamppost, waving them about like they're fucking landing planes. Oh, I love your coat." Rare compliment passed to the surprised stranger.

Luckily, she was the height of a dwarf and rarely needed to bend down to avoid flying obstructions, walking under another selfie stick with ease.

"Look how hot these men are Mammy!" Aoife sang, trying to gate-crash the picture of a group of hot Chinese men that were here for a hockey tournament at the underused Olympic stadium, but, knowing what the Chinese are like, they rudely shoved her out of the away.

She loved her new bob cut that she had picked out of Hairstyling magazine; it had been a few months out of date, she wanted to get in as many uninvited photographs as possible show it off. Aoife's faux leopard print coat and beehive blonde hair towering on her head was paired with dramatic, coal-black Winehouse eyeliner that gained her a few looks like maybe she was Bette Lynch or a drag queen strolling from Soho.

Strutting down the human gridlock of Oxford Street in her pink, patent high heels lacking any grace of a supermodel, she loved London - if only she had a calling to stay. The average length of a man's penis long heel had been glued back on with No More Nails wobbled with her carb loving weight - she had optimistically vowed that she would not use shoes as a weapon no more. She thought she was a fashionista; Granny C labelled her a *fashionista fuck up* of a sight.

Granny C cursed as she walked on as if she was a born and bred Londoner; having the elbow push down to a T convinced people on the receiving end of her sharp, bony elbow that she was from East London. Her thick, navy cardigan offered no cushion to the elbow stabbing. Her loose dentures gave a kiss of the teeth warning as she kept sucking them to stop them from falling out.

Mother and daughter were hijacking the cosmopolitan capital for the convention for psychics, a biannual event that she looked forward to. She claimed it could be her last at her old age to family members who all refused to accompany her. Catching up with other psychics on the circuit who had not died, some she liked, but most she thought were frauds out to prey on the naive and grieving. In this day and privacy-weak age, social media made it piss easy to read people's lives – it was an open book that people plastered all over the internet. Baby bores were easier targets to defraud. Anyone wishing to make a fast fraud buck or two could see what they wished for the future, pick initials from their relatives in their friends list and describe their child and what they ate for breakfast, giving solid information as a backup for their dodgy mind reading skills.

Granny C had first realised that she had the gift aged seven, when her first boyfriend had been a deceased war solider riding a horse that no one else could see. Each year her gift had grown in strength like an oak tree. Her premonitions and dead spirits stalking her were ideal excuses to go on the sick long term. She specialised in auras and tarot, crystals, and reading the palms for the future. She had been called in a few times to solve top murder mysteries, a few Irish celebrities had her on speed dial, and one famous Irish jockey had her on her back, back in the day. She always predicted the truth, and her professionalism held her in high regard in the circles of such like. Walking down one of Britain's most crowded shopping streets, more so than immigration at Calais, spirits jumped out on her with every second person like a surprise fucking party with the good, bad and ugly outcomes of people's lives; she needed to swallow another pill.

Unfortunately, Granny C had failed to read her own future, her gift blind to the beautiful redhead that was coming towards her in a beautiful grey woollen coat with a matching beret. Indian sunset locks poured from both sides framing her pretty face, gleaming in the London sunshine, blissfully walking towards her future.

Mindy had taken an extra day off; jet lag refused to leave even after two days, unlike her birth father whom Poppy had never seen since that rampant sex night in the field, or the time she had headlice twice in one month. So tonight, the night of Troy's pop-up debut had arrived. Mindy needed something to wear. The tasty soup and homemade chunky bread had added a stone to her figure that showed no bones and made her three hundred pounds cheaper when she and Alex donated on their realisation that it had been a soup kitchen and not a kitsch little bistro. Simone disinfected them on their return. They had had a ball in that soup kitchen. All lifestyles had gathered sharing warmth and human kindness no one was better than the other despite who had a roof over their head and who didn't, each of them leading characters with life stories to tell; it would have made an ideal film or documentary, Mindy had told Leon.

Oxford Street was typical of its congestion of human flesh spilling off the kerb-side dam, bursting onto the road and causing havoc for tonne-heavy double decker buses reduced to a tortoise crawl, never knowing what second gear felt like. The tube exits were regurgitating people out with the force of projectile vomit, and the multinationals made it look like the entrances had a nut allergy, sick after eating a bag of mixed nuts. It was a bright, cheerful and promising day, which led a few people to dare to bare a little more with shorter hems and t-shirts and shorts as the trend of the tarmac runway. Why Oxford Street was not a traffic-free zone did not make sense to her, dodging left and right out of the way like a hip hop star doing a one-two step.

Her loyalty was to a few fashion labels that were all housed in an outlet on the busy street of shopping mecca destinations on her hit list for something wonderful to wear. London street fashion was more inspiring than any fashion magazine could offer using over paid stylists and celebrities to promote. Every fashion, style, trend and oddball decorated the streets of London in their quirky own sense of dress; the mixture of the fashion muse to the fashion madcap gave the street the best catwalk show on earth. Mindy was not shy in stopping people to comment or ask where they had bought their garment.

She walked on free from having to rush anywhere, given the leisure to stroll with a steady, content pace for window shopping that was rare in London. Ahead of her, quite a character dressed in an oversized fur coat and Eiffel tower high blonde beehive was chatting away to a cardigan-clad elderly woman hobbling beside her. Mother and daughter, she guessed; it pulled at her heartstrings knowing that her time to do things as such with Poppy was like a melting iceberg. Slowly, time would vanish and the emotions of losing a loved one would flood her. How would she cope without her mum when she's gone? This was a question that Mindy devoured no further, then told herself off for thinking such a thing. That is the thing with the truth - it has the power to sadden you and change your life. People all bang on about telling the truth, yet sometimes the truth is more painful than the lie.

The comedy couple got closer; Mindy knew that in contrast, Poppy would probably be dressed like a cavewoman lookalike, full of confidence and zest for life, as she looked on at the boring cardigan woman, safe and comfortable in the knitted cardigan. Mindy laughed to herself. Poppy had the gift of being able to make her laugh without being present, and she grew a smile until it stopped at her cheeks. The two women approached, deep in animated conversation in thick, fast accents as the morning gave their pale skin a healthy glow. The older woman looked up, her cardigan dense like a moth gimp suit turn-on, looking nearly as old as she. The old woman caught Mindy's eye. Mindy smiled; she was so cute, until the old woman muttered something very un-cute. "Oh fuck!" she said, as she collapsed right at Mindy's feet. The leopard screamed in sheer shock.

London

Debbie smiled her best smile ever. She fluttered her feathery eyelashes a dozen to the second, blurring black as if her life depended on the Max Factor. Her sheer blouse undid itself another button voluntarily, helping her out in seducing this hunky piece of a man. This was so easy. She was a Venus fly trap, and her dumb prey had come to her. He was completely irresistible in the flesh, a God-like human; her skin shivered thinking of his manly touch. Her fanny ached, trapped behind her folded legs, for him to penetrate her deeply like a mole in a tunnel.

Troy felt extremely uncomfortable sitting in the air-conditioned reception of Alex's workplace, the chill blew him to the core like a warning, too tired from his shift to pay full attention. The power and intelligence were displayed in bucketsful with awards along one wall; it intimidated him. Troy was not thick - it was just that his brains lived in his hands and not his head. But, living in London, if you didn't have a degree, or millions, or a famous relative, you fared better in gaining people's attention if you suffered from leprosy. The hungry stare of Debbie, the blonde receptionist, the main reason for his uncomfortable state.

Alex had asked him to pick up an important file at the end of his morning shift. Alex was being waxed, dyed, tinted, and glycolic peeled, seaweed wrapped, and beaten with bamboo sticks, all as she lay on a vibrating table in Mayfair with bee venom on her face. Tonight, his pop-up debut was on and Alex was going all out to look her usual fabulous self to support him.

Troy was feeling the pressure to cook for the elite culinary critics of London. Knowing that Alex was going to be there he knew he would be fearless with her by his side - he just prayed that nobody slated him in her presence; Alex was nifty with her fists. A few important publications of the city were attending to either call the event a grand cook off or a burn out. The excitement simmered like the boiled eggs he would be using for the starter. He could not wait for tonight.

"So, what do you do?" She purred applying her red gloss lipstick. Being a man - a straight man - the colour red failed to warn him of danger as Debbie layered it on like a builder building a wall.

"I work for the city's waste disposal." Politely answered, his orange uniform was like a red wine stain to the black and white of the slick reception. Debbie checked out his bulging biceps in his polo shirt. Could she bed a bin man? She had accidently slept with a homeless man once.

"Well, thank you for keeping the city clean." Flattery was a simple hook to snare a man, pouting her dense lips in applause. Man was a simple creature - they needed food and sex, and Debbie excelled in the latter.

Troy was shocked. Nobody ever said 'thank you' for keeping the city clean, but they complained if strikes were on or they could not take the extra rubbish they had piled up against their bin.

"Cheers." Smiling maybe this woman wasn't all bad, guilt gave him a judgemental kick, and Debbie flicked back her long blonde hair billowed like a cape from her pretty face. It was a simple movement that always got her noticed in the way of casting a fishing line or wolf whistles. Her blow-dry gave her a fifties look, while the fingers ran by Advil that morning gave her a bed-head look.

"What else do you do apart from keeping the city clean and working out?" Her sapphire eyes rolled all over his toned body in no rush like a derma roller, dropping the subtle compliment, another invisible trick she used, imaginarily raping him of any clothes. He would be a specimen to see naked. If his knob was as big as his bitch fiancée's gob she would be in heaven, his dick in her vagina acting like a vibrator, knowing that her clit could accommodate it very well. Debbie felt aroused and slightly damp. She leant forward on the reception desk showing the full exposure of her enchanting tits, the ceiling spotlights lending them a glow. If she was an angel, you might have mistaken it for her halo slipping off just as you wished her knickers would - if she had been wearing any. She knew that there would be a damp patch on her leather seat like the sweaty crack of a gym addict's arse left, hot from their work out on a machine seat. Troy was a man, so he noticed her tits and her hard nipples due to her wearing no bra.

"Erm well, I want to cook." He was unnerved at the receptionist laying it on better than Cathy down at the greasy spoon buttering thick toast. *Where is Jean with those files?* his fidgeting fingers signed. "Actually, tonight I'm showcasing in a pop-up event," blushing at his small accomplishment. Troy had told anyone and everyone this from the moment he had received the invitation. To get anywhere in this city it took hard work or a lucky break - in his case, it was a high recommendation from his highly admired chef at chef school.

"I love food," she lied. The last time Debbie had a carb it was a lasagne poured over her head.

"Really?" It was the best compliment for a budding chef to hear, he thought with a cheesy grin. "You should try out my chicken curry one time." It was his favourite dish, and was adored by anyone who tasted it - even his vegan aunt. The polite comment was mysterious and certainly said without invitation.

"Maybe I will," she said, taking out her perfume and spritzing it over her exposed chest acted like ryphonal to the male senses, honey to their stunted attention. It fell lightly, mimicking rain across a plain. The thin material became more see-through with the drenching, as she flicked her head back to elongate her bare neck as temptation for his broad lips to slide down all the way to her clit. "So where is this fabulous pop-up restaurant at?" She knew that her time to ensnare her prey was running out on smelling Jean coming from Alex's office with said file, lavender forever blooming off her flat chest and bright nylon blouses. Troy was blind to Debbie's plan of revengeful seduction to knock Alex down a perfect peg or two from her perfect perch, about to reveal the information.

"Here you go Troy, the file her majesty requested," handing the stud the brown file her boss had requested. Jean flirted in Troy's company - every woman did. It was hard not to, since he was this giant form of a hunky man. Debbie cursed the mousy jobsworth PA as she cut the reply of the location, almost as if Jean knew of her plans to fuck Troy. Debbie knew how to get rid of Jean. Looking at the clock, she had an hour to do it before they clocked off.

"Thanks Jean. Will I be seeing you tonight?" Troy loved Jean. She was sweet, funny, and the only colleague that he had met of

Alex's in fifteen years. She was stick-thin as a toothpick but ate like a pig, with mousy, long, straight hair that became too stiff to move as she ironed it every morning.

"I wouldn't miss it for the world! I've not had a night out for a while. Give me the exact address - you know Alex loves to wind me up, sending me to random places." She chuckled like a crow with a smoker's cough. Her little glasses steamed up due to her being a little unfit from the walk back as Troy told her the address. She remembered that Alex had once sent her to a GUM clinic on Dean Street for a bag of Wine Gums as a wind up. Jean was so loyal to her boss, hence her long employment with the successful company. A healthy bonus was being on good terms with her fiancé to the point where she would go on holiday with Troy, and Alex's lovely Mindy. She was looking forward to tonight. Unknown to her, she was the reason why Debbie now held the address written on a post-it note in red lipstick on her desk. She had helped Debbie with her plan of seduction of Troy, and her bid to destroy Alex.

"Goodbye Troy," purred pleasurably from Debbie's red pout, her famished eyes took all of him in, feeding her desire, giving energy to her plan. Already planning to wear the little red Prada dress, commando style "Nice to meet you, hopefully see you soon," pulling the soon long and sensual painting thick red lipstick across her pillow-fat lips the way she would the tip of his pre-cum penis. She smiled wide like the pussy that knew it was getting the cream and the cock – smearing blood wouldn't save Troy from this demon, Alex could only pray Troy had a God or Goddess on his side. Troy smiled out of politeness and rushed out.

Jean gave Debbie a disapproving look, snarling her disgust like a dog to another. "Bitch, please" Jean liked to think she was a ghetto gal sometimes, Jean walked away from the revengeful whore flicking her flat hair it didn't even lift an inch.

London

Where the hell is Granny C? Half an hour had passed, passing concern on to Joe-Ryan as he was vacant of family company in the cosy pub. He watched the less busty barmaid cleaning the brass due to boredom, giving it a vigorous rub; he pitied anyone getting a wank of her. Granny C knew London well and that this quaint pub was the meeting point - so, where were they? He had tried to call Aoife but to no avail, and Granny C preferred to send mail by pigeon - she was a technophobe to the point where she refused to turn the telly off by hand. Hear no tube attacks and check for delays on all public transport, all clear and for once running on time wondering, slightly borderline panicking, where the hell they were? The busty barmaid was joined by a less busty barmaid with a pixie cut. Both had filled his pint a few times and both were infatuated with his sleek look and warm Irish tone, playing a fantasy game using him as their fantasy husband. The less busty barmaid grabbed her chance to serve him another pint upon seeing his big gulp, and this time the conversation was to see if he was single. "Another sir?" flicking her eyelashes, Joe-Ryan wondered if she had something in it, a twitch or was having a fit, her smile wide, her teeth crooked and yellowing. "Please" half-mast smile.

Mindy cursed her iPhone, knowing it was deaf to any insult since the battery was dead. Covent Garden forever reminded her of being in a romantic European city. If only it had canals cutting through, people would say 'Venice who?'.

A few street entertainers pleased the growing crowds, hoping that the coins in their buckets matched their enthusiasm. The Royal Opera House was showing a matinee, and pigeons worked a glossier look than their typical cousins roughing it a zone away, too proud to neglect themselves and beg. Mindy needed a stiff drink. The old woman dropping at her feet faster than the BBC had with any involvement with Jimmy Savile had shook her up. The paramedic had diagnosed low iron and had taken them onwards to hospital for a check-up and to be safe. He didn't need another one being diagnosed wrongly.

The old woman had spoken frantically from behind her little oxygen mask, but Mindy had been oblivious to what she was trying to say due to the mask covering her face and the screaming from her daughter banshee crying "mammy don't die, mammy where ya purse?" Disrespectful beeps of passing traffic and the ambulance slowing down drowned her words out. Her daughter smoked a dozen cigarettes to calm her 'fucking nerves'.

Mindy prescribed herself a stiff drink to self-medicate on her walk, so she came to a small pub that she visited frequently in the summer whenever Poppy visited. On the entrance it had old stained windows that told colourful stories, and hanging baskets that brought beautiful blooms. It had an old thatched black beams and white walls suited and booted for the Tudor period. Her favourite thing about this little pub was that the old booze smell hit her strong, as if the pub worked as a fragrance counter. It was a familiar lover that no matter how long the gap was, once it hit, it was familiar and gave her a sense of belonging. Despite it being stale ale soaked into the carpets over years it was a welcoming smell, a smell of memories past and a smell of memories to come in years when she would be asked about her love story that she was about to make an appearance in.

The small pub was a rare breed of pub that was slowly becoming extinct to wine bars and champagne clubs with free Wi-Fi, lacking in character and charisma due to people being too busy posting and tagging their fat pouts rather than participating in actual conversation. This pub sold British brewed real ale and served good old conversation that saturated the place instead of fancy cocktails and gourmet burgers, and a battered jukebox watched over the dance floor. She started to pull out her charger. Not looking as she pushed open the heavy door, she felt it hit someone and heard them fall to the floor with a thump.

"Shit!" She rushed inside to help out victim number two of the day, Florence Nightingale who? Faith produced another knockout. Faith, the hit woman, crossed out another hit on her bucket list.

Having been a bare-knuckle boxer back in his younger days he had taken a few knockouts in his time, but this one had floored him good and proper. He counted to ten feeling his anger spurned on by his worrying about his absent mother and Granny C, and the rudeness of the person not looking as they had opened, no flung, flung was the correct word he thought, the pub door. The busty barmaid and less busty barmaid were by his side in a split second helping him to his feet, with Busty trying to bury his head into her blown-up bosom. Joe-Ryan came face to face with his hitter once he had regained his height.

"You need to fucking look where you're going mate!" Checking the slight cut on his lip, blood painted his finger and his Irish accent was fast and aggressive like fire. The hitter hit more than his face, and was no bloke but a woman, beautiful This woman hit his heart hard, showing in his smile as if the pain needed out. He could feel another black eye - the second that month - already colouring. It was a shame he was not a fan of Guinness, with his iron levels low for sudden bruising. "Apologies for my abrupt remark," he said, brushing his black hair off his face and blushing. Revealing his sexy looks made her silently thank someone above somewhere for destiny, thank Mother Nature for being off her period.

"Sorry again for hitting you" She spoke shy, smiled softy, skin blustered her cheeks pink, and this man was so divine. Joe-Ryan forgot all about his crazy lost family, smiling at beautiful woman, the beautiful Mindy.

RUDDICK ST. DAVID FOUND DEAD. THE MOGUL SUPER DIRECTOR FOUND DEAD AT HIS PLUSH HOTEL RESIDENCE. HEART ATTACK BROUGHT ON BY HIGH DOSE OF VIAGRA AND COCAINE FOUND IN HIS SYSTEM.

Saffron spent the morning in sorrow at the loss of her good friend. Champagne eased her sympathy.

Chad was distraught to the point where he hit the bottle. His big chance to star in his new film was over before it had even begun. He snorted four lines chased by a bottle of gin, and finished with a blow job off a hotel maid.

Suzie St. David wore black. She always did anyway, but this time she accessorised it with her new billion-dollar fortune on her private jet to Hawaii with her secret toy boy, whose pool cleaning days were over, only thing he needed to fill was her.

Maria was as happy as a pig in organic shit on a Jewish farm. Her dormant acting skills deserved an Oscar that night, raising the Calypso liqueur coffee at the cute bistro, toast to her. She read the breaking news gripping America with a wave of shock with biggest smile on her face, the waiter never seen such a beautiful smile in his life watching from the counter. A cigarette balanced perfectly on her thick lips, releasing a small line of smoke into the air, on par of a satisfying smoke after good sex. "One bastard man down, and one bastard man to go" confidence floated her voice as if the words filled with helium, she didn't give a fuck who was listening or heard. An image of the deceased film director and her hot, up-and-coming movie star fiancé, her next victim, smug at the Golden Halo Gala, was featured in the four-page special on the death of Ruddick St. David. Chad's good-looking face burned away as she stubbed her hot cigarette out on it with a killer smile; revenge is a bitch.

The hospital canteen tea reflected most of the elderly patients - too weak and smelling of piss - while the biscuit reflected their bones, crumbling off before you dipped them as if they took the dipping as torture. Granny C was hooked up to a drip while Aoife was hooked up to a junior doctor. Joe-Ryan was grateful to have Mindy here, and chatted away.

After Mindy had explained, he was the second person to drop at her feet that morning. Joe-Ryan knew that Mindy had meant his Granny C when describing a woman accompanying her plastered in make-up and leopard print. Mindy knew where they had taken Granny C and paid the black cab fare. Now they sat on the little plastic table with its plastic hard chairs. With the NHS saving funds by cutting down on luxury, Mindy was glad her arse wasn't just bone, and was part of Bupa.

The little canteen was busy mid-afternoon as most hospitals would be. Mindy looked stunning. She simply shone with beauty and goodness, where some women shone with Botox and fakeness. Her grey coat and matching hat looked cute. Joe-Ryan had managed to ask her for a drink, but he doubted that Mindy would take the tea in a plastic cup as a 'drink'. Still, sitting here with her, who knew where today would go. Mindy prayed to God that her barren, misbehaved fringe stayed hidden under her beret, and her thin tea stayed in the cup and not spilled down her front. She was here sitting with the man who had reintroduced her to masturbation and was forever the bridegroom in her wacky wedding that she had been dreaming of constantly since head-butting him at the nursing home. She could not forget her vow of asking Joe-Ryan out for a date if she ever escaped that bed in New York.

The setting of the hospital canteen was not the most romantic place she would have liked to have a drink in, but it was memorable. *That's if it is that type of drink, you saddo. He's just being polite because you paid a taxi fare that you could sponsor a whole rice field of orphanages with.* Her inner voice was forever putting her down.

"What are your plans tonight, Mindy?" he said, sipping his tea. The tea was vile - the six sugars could not sweeten it up.

To ask you out for a date! her mind wanted to scream. "Tonight, I'm going to my best friend's fiancé's debut at a pop-up restaurant. He's an amazing cook - that's why I work this look of 'is she pregnant?'" *Nevertheless, if you want to ravish me and have sex right here and impregnate me, feel free.* She would have loved to have the balls of her mother to say this, smiling.

"Aye, nothing's wrong with ya! You're a great specimen of the ideal woman." Joe-Ryan dipped another suicidal shortbread biscuit into his weak tea. It snapped off and sank to the bottom, just to get the drowning over and done with.

"Specimen? A compliment or a sly remark that I resemble a mammal?"

"I mean, oh shit." His Irish words fell over each other as they raced out to correct what he meant, they fell clumsy and cute, his panic turn on for her. Mindy laughed; she was glad he thought she was fit. '*No sweetheart, he said a specimen.*' '*It is my compliment, I will call it what I fucking like!*' she snapped back at self-doubt, who shut up for the moment.

The piss-thin tea tasted a tiny bit sweeter with his compliment. Silence cooled Joe-Ryan's pink cheeks. He was so beautiful with a face that even aging couldn't hide his handsomeness behind wrinkles. His eyes sparkled of honesty, and as a rarity for a man, kept his focus on her. The way he dunked and tried to catch the wet biscuit dropping off was cute and it made her smile. Something about this man made her want to take the present into her future. Mindy grew brave enough to try a ginger nut in her tea, and Lady Luck was on her side for once as she dunked it and retrieved it all in one piece. It gave her courage; if she could scale a wall top of one of New York highest blocks and had been held kidnapped under a bed for eight hours without food, then a simple question would be easy, wouldn't it?

"*What's the worst that could happen?*" Poppy was championing loud and clear in her tangled head.

"*You did fucking what?*" Alex would screech later, opening champagne in celebration.

"A date? You? Really? Is he blind though?" Maud's predicted jealousy, failing to believe that she had done it couldn't dampen the idea on the tip of her daring tongue.

In this modern day, women fought for their rights - so she decided to do one for feminism and take charge of her life. She decided to catch her destiny and walk into her future with her head high. *'You can do this, you are Mindy the Marvellous! You go girl!'* With that small pep talk, she was ready.

"Would you like to go out one night for a meal? Like an, erm, sort of date, with, erm, me?" A red flush swamped her face. The 'date' bit whispered out as if Mindy was on her deathbed in Ward 17.

She got an answer - just not an answer she could understand - but a nodding of his head either in agreement, or in trying to dislodge a biscuit as he choked. Joe-Ryan was so flabbergasted that Mindy wanted a date with him that he choked on shortbread in delight and fell off his plastic chair.

*

Hot sweat drenched his lined forehead. The back of his rough hand visited his forehead more often than a bhindi dot, exfoliating away a layer, window-wiping away the beads that were dripping into his eyes. The kitchen a stirring pot of a sauna of sweat, stress and swear words represented by more than one country like a Eurovision song swear contest made the air thick.

Tonight, the debut pop-up restaurant *Hot Chop* was open to the public for them to savour the students of the cooking course that Troy had been attending for the past ten weeks, to showcase their skills of seduction with food. Therefore, an art gallery had loaned its space out to host the event which was a sell-out. London loved anything new and loved anyone trying to achieve a dream. The critics loved to tear any such soul who tried, leaving them hanging in a noose of their harsh words, making many budding chefs want to stab themselves with a steak knife. Troy was making a starter and a main- the only student to being doing both. The steaks, if you pardon the pun, were high and needed to be well done.

Tonight, Troy was about to become a hot toast in the city or crash and burn; his new future depended on him becoming a hit, or going back to stir fry daydreams. Alex and Mindy took to their reserved seats. "isn't this so posh?" Mindy politely whispered "thank you" as the waiter held her chair out smiled and left. "Fabulous" Alex replied looking around at the grand turn out, all the starving males looked at her, perfect starter. The round table seated a few other invited guests who all smiled as they sat passed common small dinner talk such as l hello, good evening, good weather like cheap after dinner mints. Alex looked amazing; she was wearing a black fitted Stella tux suit, and a leather bra underneath that was slightly on show. Her hair was pulled back into a high, glossy dressage ponytail, with crystal clear skin and purple lips - she looked fierce and dominant. Mindy had gone for a simple grey cat suit with electric blue shoes and a matching patent clutch, her red locks up in a bun, and for once, the short fringe worked the in-trend fashion of a blunt cut. Both girls looked amazing.

"I couldn't get hold of Jean?" Alex started the conversation once they had sat, accepting a glass of cold champagne from a young-looking waiter with a fine beard. Jean had failed to answer any of the twenty calls. The vacant seat was proof that Jean had not answered or turned up; it worried her, but the champagne helped calm her.

"Maybe she's stuck on the tube?" Anyone travelling on the tube to an event and running late were a match made in hell - delays, strikes, suicides and terrorist bombs meant that there were hundreds of valid reasons. Mindy had no alerts on her phone about a bomb going off, so that was not the reason for Jean's absence. She sipped her champagne, feeling her best friend's worry. Alex was concerned. Jean, being her PA, prided herself on punctuality and had not shut up all week about how excited she was to be coming that Alex gave her a day off just for the peace. Alex knew that Jean harboured a crush on Troy - most women who came into his contact did. What was keeping Jean from this fine free food event presenting her man crush's food? Or, more importantly, who?

Heads turned in no order of fashion towards the entrance of the pop-up restaurant. Male heads fell like dominos doing a double-take, while females - unless they were fans of licking minge - turned in disgust and fear. Debbie soaked up the reaction she had made on her fine arrival. It was like heroin to her soul - addictive, powerful and easy to come by. Attention from males was her daily lover - she gathered them in every city she visited like tacky fridge magnets. She was never short of it, just short of hemlines. Tonight, the effort had been worth it.

Her red PVC Prada dress was seductive, a second skin on her curvy silhouette. The tightness as if she wore a human size condom showed not a bump or a lump to disfigure her sexy silhouette allowed no fault to be attracted to herm turn on she loved, most males in the room matched it with their hard cocks in their pants. Her tits, high pert under her chin, perfect weapon in the braless dress, the peep show of her smooth back in the backless dress waved to all the women wearing mummy bras under their dresses, a finger salute to them all . Her blonde hair fell in dramatic, soft curls itching to be brushed aside by a hand, and the walk was feline-inspired, like a panther. She looked like Pamela Anderson - if Pammy walked on the beach instead of running.

She walked towards the table, bouncing back every hungry male look with the ease of a ping-pong ball. She ignored any jealous bitches, leaving her sexy perfume lingering as a warning to the females and an aphrodisiac to the horny males. She was here for one meal, and one meal only: Troy.

Alex did a double take - not because she was afraid, nor a lesbian, but because Debbie, the dick-loving receptionist, was here and coming closer in her direction. Suddenly, the blonde bombshell took the empty seat next to Alex before she could hide behind the menu, smiling her dense red lips. Her poisonous perfume choked Alex - it was Debbie's first weapon of attack, and her second weapon was in her clutch bag.

"Good evening," her red lips parted, showing a gleaming smile. Alex stared for a moment. Why the fuck was Debbie here sitting in Jean's chair? Debbie held her faux smile, waiting for Alex to acknowledge her. She didn't. "Jean sends her apologies," she said, accepting a wine off the bearded waiter. He got hard in his briefs just seeing her, and would wank at least three times in the staff toilets, ignoring his mother's future questioning of what the hell this stain was on his apron in the washing basket. "She fainted at work, so I took her home," shaking her blonde mane around and it was as if each individual strand of hair casted out hooked attention from all the hot blooded males on the surrounding tables, another layer of lipstick laid wet across her lips where many men at the table wished their knobs laid, gave impression she was a she wolf finished her feast of a man already, used their fresh blood as lipstick. "She told me to come here as a 'thank you'. I refused at first, knowing she had been looking forward to it all day." Debbie waved her hand in motion of battering the idea away. Alex knew this bit was true. "Didn't have anything to wear, and had like an hour to spare" This she knew was full of shit. Debbie raised her high voice for this last part, to show the men on the table her distress at the situation and to show the envious women that it didn't take her long to look this fantastic. Debbie was certainly no damsel in distress needing saving by a man. She was a predator in Prada looking for penetration by one cock only - Troy's. Alex did not know whether to believe Debbie. Just as she was about to cross-examine her Mindy butted in.

"Well I think you look amazing." Alex could have punched Mindy broke her jaw to end Mindy's talking.

"Oh thank you sweetheart." Rubbing Mindy's back as if she was old relative who manged to eat her soup without spilling a drop. "It's so nice to have a reason to get dressed up for once isn't it? Love your fringe." Mindy was blind to the real reason Debbie was dressed up like a porno-clad Jessica Rabbit, but, she was first person ever to give a compliment to her fringe, she was team Debbie on that only. Debbie turned to speak to the panting male on her right, leaving her blonde hair to face Alex. Her little compliments to the redhead gained her brownie points. Debbie hoped that the dose of sleeping tablets she had crushed into Jean's tea did not kill her.

The arrival of platters of miniature starters, including king prawns wearing veil foundation of garlic and ginger gave excitement to the mouth, miniature chunky meatballs dusted with chillies, drenched in lemon juice promised an hot explosion for the palate to moan in delight, mouth-wateringly slices of crispy chicken wrapped lovingly with thin chorizo soaked in sour cream silenced the table. The silence spoke louder than any praising words. The taste explosions numbed tongues, with everyone agreeing that they were all worthy of Michelin stars. Debbie worked a meerkat look, scanning the whole restaurant for a glimpse of Troy. Alex was nothing but rude to her, cutting her conversations short and not once engaging her within the group, fuelling her plan for the revenge fuck, she looked sensational though, Debbie had to give her that. Alex premonition while doing her makeup she was coming, wore her couture armour ready for battle? If this was a Disney film, Debbie would be the wicked witch that even Hercules and Hades would fear. Debbie was going to use champagne, not an apple, to put to sleep her target.

"Just popping to the bar." Leaving her seat, her round arse seduced everyone hypnotising them all as she sashayed side to side towards the bar in her 'come fuck me' heels.

"She's lovely, isn't she?" The crab claw filled with garlic crab pate and peppered olive oil sprayed her lap as it was demolished by her molars, Mindy spoke, didn't care if her mouth was full, the food was delicious whole table forgot their manners chatted like macaws at a fruit tree over how good the food was.

"She's bad news is that one. But if it's true that Jean gave her the ticket for helping her out then she can't be all bad." Suspicious saturated her voice like the pork medallion bathed in peppercorn. It was an hour after her first text to Jean and she had still not replied. Alex felt something kicking in her gut - first she prayed it was not food poisoning, and second prayed that it wasn't an early sign of pregnancy, nope just good old fashion gut feeling.

"Maybe you're just a bit tense with it being Troy's big night, and worrying a little about Jean? Debbie said she's fine at home in bed and sent her here, knowing it was important that Troy had support. So, relax, and give the girl a little bit of attention and enjoy our civilised evening." Mindy had noticed how frosty Alex had been towards Debbie - even the Arctic Sea didn't give living mammals this type of cold shoulder.

"Yes, maybe you're right." She was right. Since New York she had been running around all over Mayfair today to get ready and hoping that Troy was ok. Maybe she should thaw a little and at least engage with Debbie, shock her, and maybe actually like the girl.

"Here ya go ladies, a little glass of champers for us all and a cheeky tequila or two." She sang the tequila part. Maybe Debbie wasn't all bad, Alex wondered, taking the glass of champers and generously filled tequila shot glasses. Tequila forever reminded her of her and Mindy's first visit to Magaluf, which they nicknamed 'Shag A Muff', first and last time Alex kissed a female. If only drinks could talk, the last bubble dissolving from the little added extra in Alex's drink going unnoticed would have screamed to warn Alex not to accept a drink off Debbie. Debbie watched in sheer glee as her plan of destroying Alex with the first sip that Alex took, it was the second weapon in her plan.

*

The starter's plate was a licking success, but the chef told them not to get carried away. There were two courses still, and plenty of room for 'critically chopping off their fucking nuts'. Troy started to prep his salad garnish as one of the waiters came in. His bushy beard made his young face look too small for his thin body.

"Some cracking birds on my table dude." His northern accent was bold and blunt as his statement. The waiter took a few cheeky swigs of the red wine at Troy's counter used for cooking the sauce, and Troy laughed.

"There's this blonde bird, dude, tits trying to climb on her head" another swig. "Redhead with amazing skin" another swig disappeared from the bottle "and some sexy scouse bird pouring champers down their necks like it's an Olympic sport. Fucking gorgeous, all three of them." Last swig longer than the other two, celebration landed the best table out of the twelve, few male waiters high fived him on his way in the kitchen. Troy took the bottle back form the young waiter. The waiter was at that age where sexual, beautiful women were impressionable on him. He took another cheeky swig "get off and get this out" Troy flicked his checked tea towel t him that rested like a parrot on his shoulder. So, Alex was here, Troy smiled. He knew Alex would cause a stir - she always did with her beauty bold and her aura bright. His slicing of his avocado was accompanied by a cheerful whistle to keep him sane. His confidence was boosted by his fiancée and friends' show of support - only *why had Jean dyed her hair blonde?* he wondered.

*

Another champagne bottle arrived - it was the fourth to visit the table, with three tequilas following like rats to the Pied Piper. Alex had relaxed enough to enjoy Debbie's self-deprecating banter, enjoying her drinking a little too much, Mindy noted. Alex started to get a little loud, a little drunk to the point where everyone knew she was in the building. Mindy gathered that it was sleep-debt related and thought no more, but introduced a glass of water into Alex and Debbie's binge drinking. Debbie was yet to drop a hair out of place, knocking the shots back the way a bouncer does with an underage mini-skirt-wearing wannabe. Nobody got drunk on water even if turned to wine; Debbie smirked with her watery secret. Mindy hoped that Alex was going to be in a fit state to taste the mains.

Mindy was shocked as the warm air tried to slap her back to normal. She had never been thrown out of a place since the age of twenty-five, but here she was, sitting on a kerb, rubbing Alex's back as she vomited up champagne and tequila, watching crab meat floating down the small river of sick.

"Hope she's going to be ok, Mindy?" Debbie kept Alex's beautiful hair from falling into her face.

"Never in my life have I seen her this drunk." Mindy pleaded as if to a judge about to sentence Alex down for her state of drink. Alex held her drink like most northern women, held it as if she was a cactus, but now she was creating a mini flood of fine champagne hitting the stony banks of the grey kerb.

"Do you want me to take her home?" Debbie offered.

"No, thank you Debbie. I will take her home and get back for when Troy finishes." Mindy knew it was nigh impossible to get to Alex's riverside apartment, clean her up, put her to bed, and get back within the hour - even if she had been blessed with the power of transportation. This was London - even the sun rising was delayed.

"I can wait for Troy - explain what's happened, if you want?" Mindy too concerned with rubbing Alex's back failed to register the speed Debbie replied

Mindy rubbed Alex's back as she vomited again, listening to Debbie's generous offer. It made sense - Debbie was a .work colleague, and Troy needed at least somebody to applaud him.

"You sure?" Mindy hoped.

When does a bitch need to be sure? Debbie should have said, but instead she said: "Perfectly sure. It's the least I can do - I feel terrible for introducing the tequila." She held her hand to her blow-up chest adding the fake effect of concern and worry. This was too damn easy.

"Alex needs no encouragement for a drink," Mindy said with the tone of a disappointed mother.

"What does Troy look like, by the way?" Debbie knew what he looked like. The image of him naked showed no signs of vacating her troubled mind, and it was the reason her dildo had drilled her to the dozen before she had left home tonight. Mindy gathered she didn't.

"Tall, stocky, bald. Probably dressed in chef whites," she said, failing to add hunky, possibly angry, let down and needing to de-stress from the stress of the cooking, and maybe wanting to drown his sorrows about his fiancée getting kicked out before his award winning main.

"Ok, got it. Taxi!" Debbie came to the rescue, pulling a taxi with the wave of her hand and the age-old flash of the legs, helping Mindy to drag a drunken, legless Alex into the cab.

"Thank you, Debbie. See you soon." Mindy landed a kiss on her cheek, ignoring the taste of cheap make-up. Debbie watched the cab drive off into the cool night.

Debbie smirked, *stupid bitches*. She lit up a cigarette in satisfaction, which she would also do after she fucked Troy. She headed back inside the pop-up for her tasty reward, chuffed that her plan of drugging Alex had worked. Now for her third weapon of attack - herself. After all, revenge was a bitch.

New York

The sudden death of Ruddick St. David had sent shockwaves rippling through the land of the rich and film famous. His heart attack brought on by a cocktail of cocaine, Viagra, and rampant sex with nympho twin hookers had brought sympathy to his long-suffering wife, Suzie, who was now rich beyond her wildest, gold-digging dreams from the tragic death. It also got a few cheers from envious males toasting, *what a way to go.*

Maria sat at the small table in the trailer on the set of Chad's new movie with a slice of wholegrain toast smothered with avocado and a herbal tea to keep her company. The soft chewing fifteen times before swallowing trimmed her imaginary double chin. Matching gold gladiator bangles covered the healing wounds caused by Ruddick St. David's rape all week. Chad had asked on her arrival back to the hotel where she had been. His tears had shocked her - real, exclusive emotion had poured from his eyes. The old Maria would have fell into his strong arms and forgiven him, but not this new Maria. Forgiveness was for the weak, she muttered as a mantra every morning. Maria wanted revenge and revenge she would get; the pocket calendar she carried in her back each day crossed off and judgement day would be a month after their wedding. If Chad wanted to jump a level into global stardom, he knew a marriage would generate press publicly around the world. Maria just needed to slowly bide her time - there would certainly be a ring on her finger soon.

Her beautifully constructed Birkin bag took up a seat like a precious first-born child - a gift from Chad to cover his guilt. Maria was unaware of this and thought it was simply a token of his loyal love for her.She read all the obituaries and stories from the film world for the deceased film director feeling extremely calm, twirling a strand of her crow-black glossy hair. Her grandma's words kept on repeating in her head; Maria needed to break away from needing a man in her life, stand on her own and be worshipped more than for making a dress a sell-out. Maria decided to help women who needed her help. It was a hooker who had helped her fuck revenge on the film director. She would work with women trapped in the sex slave industry and bring justice to those running the lucrative trade, and was already looking at premises to set up a safe house in New York.

Maria was a woman on a mission and nobody - certainly no man - was to stand in her way. Maria sipped her hot herbal tea, cupping its warmth and agreeing on her plan. While Maria sipped her tea reading on, her partner in crime boarded a rusty Greyhound heading to the Big Apple.

*

Normally immaculate, the grand bedroom looked as if it had let a hurricane in - not fresh air from the open balcony doors. Bedsheets were balled up and tossed to the floor, discarded like rubbish. Drawers were burglar-rummaged through, and one was smashed in pieces leaving dangerous sharp wood. Designer clothes lay dead all over the floor. The military-organised dressing table resembled a mudslide of careless organisation, as exotic and rare rings and jewels, with no regard for their beauty or worth, laid like dead victims of a rebel attack. Helena had fled in fear. The energy in her escape gave her creative inspiration for her explosive whistle-blowing book on the rich slut of a bitch.

"Where the fuck is my ring?" This simple question started innocently, but now it rose, churning anger and worry in Saffron. Saffron ripped the whole apartment apart in fury, fuelled by the panic of looking for the ring that morning. Her old fingers ached and the arthritis crippled her joints, trying to slow her down before she had a heart attack - but nothing stopped her.

Busy attending interviews due to the death of Ruddick St. David, it had been about half a dozen days since she had last worn the ring and now it was gone, vanished. Poor Helena had taken the brute of Saffron's false accusations and had fled in tears after Saffron smashed up a mirror and shattered vases on all four of the walls. Nobody, apart from her and Helena - who was currently writing an explosive chapter to her secret manuscript in the third bathroom - had been in the penthouse suite since the Gala. It hit her just as she was about to rip the lynx fur carpet up. Someone else had been here, and that someone was Chad Rise.

Camden Town

The aroma of the place, unfamiliar, hit him hard, pushing him back on his heels wanting him not to enter, or was that the drink effecting his balance? Never had he liked cinnamon - he crinkled his nose in disgust. The spicy smell singed his senses as if trying to get him to come back to them. The strangest part was that he never normally climbed stairs, feeling one of his shoes slip off, tumbling down to the hall. Was it trying to coax him down to get fresh and realise what was going on, and let him escape? Troy was a little too pissed to care.

Tequila chasers and champagne had gotten him in a state quickly, and let down by Alex he chased each one of his shots, her absent as the buyer of the next round. His legs felt heavy and his mind was careless like a newborn. *Alex could go fuck herself, selfish bitch,* he toasted in his drunken state. He was vulnerable to the persuasion of a celebratory drink with the staff, and reminding him that customers had all cheered his success made Troy forget that Alex had been drunkenly escorted home by Mindy. Debbie was the only one to stay to cheer him up, and she had told Troy that Alex and Mindy had told her to stay so that he was not alone. He had stupidly decided that Debbie was better than no company at all. Looking like a knockout in her tight, dick-teasing dress, the bearded waiter had begged to join Troy's company.

He was drunk quickly for his build. He was a lightweight when it came to drinking, Alex was forever teasing. People floated out into the evening as the pop-up closed its doors to the successful night, though most guests that had eaten Michelin star-worthy food detoured to a late-night kebab shop - out of tradition, not hunger. Sadly, Troy was on the menu for one guest.

The fresh air of the night had knocked him. Debbie had kindly offered to get him home, taking his arm. His built bicep was foreplay to her, and she held back from pouncing on him in the taxi. *Where was Alex?* he asked himself as he got out of the taxi - but this was not his beautiful home he shared. *Where was this strange place and why was he still with Debbie?* These questions stumbled and bumped inside his dizzy head.

This was so easy, Debbie thought, tossing Troy onto her small sofa. His muscular bulk filled the whole couch, and his one shoeless foot sunk into her thick shag pile. He was smashed. She thought he would be able to hold his drink better than this, being built like small house. The thought of being a borderline rapist, taking advantage of this drunken man ran across her mind, too fast to register her wrongdoing. Her revengeful state raced after, it threatening harm on its return with a knife.

"The room is spinning, make it stop," Troy laughed, rubbing his thick fingers on his eyes. This failed to stop the spinning, his head washed with drinks and dragged down in his anger for Alex, into him needing her to look after him in his drunken state, and it turned to needing her here. "Maybe this may help." He felt the cold can press in his hands.

"Cheers. Such a star, Deb." His hiccup cut short her name, guillotining him to be awake or fall asleep to kill his chance of a Judas erection. Debbie flared with the short name; she had been christened by a ruthless man who had introduced her to the bad side of what men were capable of, reinforcing her learning that the word 'no' sometimes failed to stop action called her Deb against her teenager pleas. "You look very pretty, Debbie. By the way, red suits ya." The compliment came purely innocently. Troy was forever complimenting anyone where it was due; the cold larger cleansed his dry throat, *'where's Alex'* something internal fired up but was extinguished by another swig of cold cheap larger.

"Thank you." She knew she looked a knockout - the bearded waiter had told her as she sucked him off in the toilets, his spunk bitter, but not enough to hit the back of her throat, showing his immaturity. It was the perfect starter before the main that she was to devour tonight. Debbie took the compliment as a hint that Troy was eager to engage. "What about now?" She peeled out of the red dress with the ease of a gorilla peeling a banana, exposing just a lacy thong and her big tits. Her nipples deep pink were stud-hard demanding attention, and attention they got.

"Whoa Debbie! You didn't need to do that." Troy sobered up a little with Debbie revealing her birthday suit minus the chorus of happy birthday or any sign of a cake; he could murder some cake, his belly rumbling. Troy smelled her fragrance becoming stronger as she came closer but felt paralysed to move, unable to function to leave her place, did she wear chloroform? His mind, soaking in booze bullied him in to thinking it was all innocent - that this was her home, maybe she was just changing for a shower. This excuse sank.

He felt his Levi's start abandoning his legs, the coldness of the flat slapping at his rugby-built thighs, wakey wakey they seem to say. He tried to grab them and pull them back up, but weakened by tiredness and drugged by drink, Debbie pulled them free. His cock refused to harden beneath his tight briefs, as if it was in no rush to betray Alex by allowing an erection for Debbie to get her way straight away. The bitch wanted it - she would have to work for it.

"Nice bulge," Debbie purred at the mountain of flesh under his black tight Calvin's waiting. Tight brown tiny curly hairs ran from the rim of the pants all down his legs, warning the rest of the body about the predator prowling the plains of his body. The thick band lying flat against his toned midriff created no barrier to stop her, she was unstoppable. She stroked his legs and the muscles under her unwelcomed touch made her inhale slowly; they were so muscular and hard, and she couldn't wait for them to be banging against her arse as he fucked her doggy-style. She unbuttoned his faded denim shirt that Alex had forced him to buy on a trip to Bicester Village, saying that it gave him a sexy mechanic look. His raised chest appeared, instantly turning Debbie on. Pins and needles attacked her body, and anticipation became foreplay. His nipples were studded on perfectly worked-out pecs, his chest smooth and free of hair. She slid a willing finger into herself. She got off on men's chests - she was a massive fan of prawns (men with great bodies, pity about the head). She felt herself relaxing as each thrust from her index finger, familiar at this exercise, touched her soft and sensitive personal skin readying it, for the invasion of his dick. The supporting act before the main event built her whole body up, until his cock, flaccid and faint now, would be taking over the place of her finger, warming up inside her engaging her willing clit for once he was hard.

"Debbie, please don't." It came out weak, with no weight to push her off. Playing with one of his nipples - a weakness - the massaging effect was relaxing. She felt it, teasing his nipple now with her wet tongue. Debbie wished that all the men she fucked possessed a body like this. Each muscle of his was individual, raised and hard, running her tongue down his sand dune inspired abs before returning to his nipple. He reminded her of a Roman gladiator. She kept her finger working deep in herself, ignoring the ache, ache in her finger and the ache in her vagina if her clitoris lips process the ability to speak, not lubricate they scream 'fucking give me that dick'. The lacy material of her knickers rubbed on her hand, encouraging her to go further, peer pressure for her to dig deeper than normal. She came to the rim of the iconic brand of underwear, and stopped.

She was anticipating, nervous about what lay beneath his briefs with the fear of jumping into the sea of the unknown. Her callous heart raced. She lowered to his stomach and settled a thin white line on it: "Do you mind?" Before he had a chance to voice his disapproval of drug use, he heard a satisfying sniff. She was paranoid that Troy was doomed with a small cock - maybe it was too good to be true. The best-looking men forever had let-down cocks in her experience. Debbie rubbed her hand over his briefs smiling, knowing there was no danger of a baby dick on this hunk. It failed to swell and grow, but Debbie would take pleasure and time in making it hard and fill her mouth, knowing she also had some allied Viagra left if all else failed in the war of an erection.

"You deserve this Troy for all your hard work tonight. Alex let you down, disrespected you and showed she didn't care. Just call this a little payback to even it out." She felt herself wet, her sexual desire dripping down her finger that was buried inside her clit. Stroking his chest with her spare hand, the ends of her hair tickled his neck and face. Using Alex's disrespect to her advantage, she preyed on Troy's upset with his fiancée. Manipulating his drunken mind into getting payback on Alex, she felt that the best way to wreak revenge on a loved one was by having sex with someone else. Debbie lowered into Troy's ear and whispered *'she will never know'*. So close, she smelled divine and tasty, and Troy debated the carnal idea, just.

She decided she would make his cock hard - not his life. This would be a one-off, and she would be taking it no further than just sitting across from Alex knowing that her beloved fiancé had fucked her enough to satisfy her thirst for revenge. She wanted Troy to break her bed, and for him to break Alex's heart when she smelled her perfume on his body and the marks that she had been here on his board back.

Slowly her thirsty tongue glossed across her eager lips, lubricating them as she clipped a finger under the popular brand of men's underwear to pull them down and reveal the cock she dreamt about, longed for, craved going into her mouth. It flopped out fat and flaccid, with trimmed pubes that added length. She was shocked to see a Prince Albert piercing, like a kind of flag in a mountain, Alex claiming this dick for her? Either the thick piercing weighed down his cock, or it was the dreaded brewer's drop.

Debbie was a persistent, ruthless woman even in her days of competitive cross-country - she kept going until she finished. Running ten miles in rain soaked fields without stopping, getting this girth-generous cock hard would be nothing but a quick sprint in comparison. If it took all night to get it hard and to swallow his spunk, so be it. She was off tomorrow anyway.

"Ready?" leaning forward, her tits bounced an inch with delightful pleasure. She lowered her head, her box-yellow hair falling and acting like a curtain on a VIP sex booth. Her mouth opened, ravening wide as a cuckoo chick, blowing hot air onto his cock like the adoptive feeder. Each second passed her mouth lower down about to put his limp cock into her hungry mouth, he felt her hot breath warm on the tip of his dick, suddenly she let out a frightful scream of sheer pain - her hair extensions pulled at her scalp was the reason. Sharp shock of the attack a result of her own stupidity for not locking the front door, sent pain throughout her semi-naked body, before Troy's cock could feed its first inch into her hungry mouth, her adulterated head happily hit the hard floor with a sickening crack.

New York

New York was chaotic, tall and terrified Sally with the excitement of the unknown. It was bustling with a speed you only saw in Los Angeles on a treadmill. It was chilly too, and claustrophobic. She was missing L.A already. She was here to teach Chad Rise a hard lesson, and once taught, she would be back on the exhausted Greyhound out of here and back to L.A, Pepe and sucking dick.

Dressed in camel beige skinny jeans, a pale pink cotton jumper, leather bomber and heeled trainers, she looked slightly fashionable - just not warm. Hurrying along towards a coffee shop with her collar up and head down, one pap mistook her for Kate Hudson and snapped away as she was real pretty. On the refugee crowded coach, ideas had wildly hijacked her head on how to wreak revenge on Chad Rise, keeping her company, ranging from shooting him flat in the face on one of his premieres, to even getting pregnant and screwing the coward for child maintenance. Her father may have been dead, but his fierceness lived in her; as a gangster's daughter, fearless was her middle name - well, it was really Margaret.

The gingerbread latté warmed her hands up, dissolving the nagging, cold tingle that the chill created. She found a quiet corner in the coffee shop free from laptops and smartphones and people, the perfect seating to people watch in the city that never slept. Countless times New York had played host to many films that she had watched over the years, but she had never been - not even with her father, probably afraid of the Mafia, she flirted with. People in New York fled past the window with the speed of a tennis ball hit by Venus or Serena; she was forever getting the two mixed up as to who was the champion hitter.

She relaxed a little, and gradually New York bit her with an invisible, contagious infection that spread through her veins racing with her blood. The symptoms made the infected ask what she was really doing with her life. Where was her life going? Where did she want her life to go? What was her life doing for her right now, in this moment? She could do anything, so why was she parting her legs for fifty bucks, taking part in seedy threesomes in hotel rooms eating up much of her life? It never left job satisfaction, it did not make her happy, and she never got invited to office Christmas parties - only the alleys where the bars lived.

New York teased her with the possibility that she could be anything she wanted to be. Maybe she could be an au pair, a club singer, or a wife to some hotshot lawyer rushing home to be with her and hopefully their babies. Babies were something that Sally lingered for. Yes, even hookers harboured the same dreams that fans of monogamous 'lights off' sex did. She had gone bareback plenty of times hoping to catch an unexpected pregnancy, setting her menstrual calendar to higher the chance of conceiving. In darker days she had purposely set out with the risk to fuck as many men as she could, ignoring the discomfort of walking the next day, and double penetration just to land that one sperm with the bulldozer strength to crack her stone-hard eggs and give life to her temple-ruined womb.

They must be dead, or not live there anymore - not a scare, not a bone-idle, lazy missed period to jump on with promise, or a negative, piss-soaked pregnancy test in the waste bin in the bathroom. She wondered why everyone tested in the bathroom, it was too common and the germs oh lord. Sally would test somewhere fabulous like the Taj Mahal. Motherhood was just not meant to be, her baby-delivering stork shot dead just like her father.

Sally added more sugar to her hot beverage to sweeten her sad mind away from the disappointment. Allowing her mind to wander to a place of no solid interest, the blast of cold air hit her on the turning of the door as if someone threw a snowball in her face. The culprit of the open door strolled in with the most vibrant white fur coat ever. Black spaceships covered her whole face disguised as sunglasses, and hair as black as tarmac was pulled up into a ponytail. Sally knew this woman was immensely beautiful and rich too, checking out her Louboutins and Burberry bag. Sally was in awe - this was the type of woman Sally longed to be. A dog with a golden mane sleek and straight sat beside her designer feet at the counter being well behaved, and then it looked over in Sally's direction.

Suddenly the dog broke free from the glamourous woman, wagging its tail and coming over to greet Sally whose immense strokes had the dog rolling on its back. Its soft fur felt alive between her fingers. "Hey there" Sally lost her hands into the fur of the dog, so soft felt like baby hair

"I'm so sorry. She's a bloody nuisance today, must be on her menstrual." Stern tone aimed at the dog from the ravishing woman who took the vacant seat, placing down a pack of chocolate cookies and a hot chocolate crowned with whipped cream wearing tiny marshmallows like pink diamonds. Leaving the sunglasses on, she was smiling a smile as wide as Sally's legs had been open that night with Chad Rise.

"She's ok." It had been a while since Sally had received any affection or attention from a living creature not paying a fee. She was enjoying it; so what if it was a dog?

"Roxy, leave the poor lady alone" pulling on the pink collar and dragging Roxy back. Maria relaxed a little with the blonde stranger. She was very pretty and athletic-looking, Cameron Diaz style, beneath her unsuitable clothes for the New York chill.

"How's your day going?" Maria asked genuine. She had not spoken to a real person all morning, just phones and emails. Chad had pissed her off with his silent treatment for her refusing him sex - the mood was not there this morning, plus there was no point, since her risk of pregnancy was extremely low.

"I've just arrived to be honest from L.A. I'm a New York virgin." The last time Sally had used the word 'virgin' in a sentence was when she was thirteen - she had told her father she had bagged the role of Jesus's mother, the Virgin Mary, in the school nativity. Her father had stayed up all weekend to stitch together a blue outfit made from a tablecloth that gained the biggest cheer at the play. The memory made her smile.

"Oh wow you are going to love New York if you can handle the noise, traffic, and being hit on by every living male." Protested Mariam Sally laughed knowing eyes rolled behind the giant shades; she liked this woman. "Roxy, stop sniffing. God, I think this dog was a coke head in a former life," pulling Roxy allowing Sally's crotch some freedom form the nosy nose of the pedigree. Sally laughed hard. Again, it had been a while since she had laughed a belly-rumbling laugh made from genuine laughter. Maria noticed the heavy foundation on the side of her face creased into the folds of recently charred skin. "What are you going to do in New York? Is the trip pleasure or business?" This was asked by airport security each time she landed at JFK, mostly by males whom she knew their cocks would harden when she pressed her perfect lips to rest a cock on tight together, leaning in and purring *'pleasure'*.

Business - to get revenge on a man - and pleasure when I do - Sally did not know the woman well enough to share this information. "Honestly, not a clue. Maybe find a job, a little place to live." New York was taking another resident rent to live here in the Big Apple. Sally did not register the fact that she had said this.

"What work are you looking for?" Maria dipped a cookie into her hot chocolate waiting for an answer. Sally decided that blurting out 'sex worker' - as if her mouth itself was a penis spunking - might be a bit too early in the morning for, woman seem have enough cream on her hot chocolate for anymore. She took inspiration from Roxy, burning her glassy eyes into Maria in the hope that she would feed her a bit of her cookie.

"I used to be a dog walker in L.A." Lying was easy to Sally - she had had plenty of practise lying. She remembered lying to pretend she was a schoolgirl to a bulky, stressed out policeman she had let fuck her in a school skirt at his flat - borderline paedo, he had flirted with the fantasy, and Sally in a uniform was the closest thing to reality. Sally was glad she had turned him in.

"You're hired," Maria said. *Who the fuck is she talking to*? Sally looked behind her and only the cream wall stared back at her with a black and white picture of Milan.

"Beg your pardon?"

"You're hired. I need a dog walker. You walk dogs - simple." Fuck, New York really was fast. She had a job in time before her latte was half-empty. If all men Sally serviced cummed as fast as New York worked, Sally would have a massive turnover, tripling the clients she fucked and becoming a millionaire in at least five hundred wanks.

"My pleasure" she took off her designer glasses and held out her manicured hand, generous rock of diamond entombed in an engagement ring dominated the whole hand. Sally recognised the features faintly. If the lady had been wearing her usual full coat of make-up, her famous face would have clicked into place.

Maria felt that this woman could help her with more than just making sure Roxy got her twice-daily recommended walks. This woman's eyes poured that she had witnessed things that most women only read about while waiting for their salon bought blow-dries to finish. She was fearless and a survivor; Maria liked this. She wanted another strong woman in her boring life. She would be Chad-proof, too. Chad would never fuck a woman with bitten nails, so the dog walker sporting a crispy bacon scar to side of her face would be immune to his sexual advances, lucky bitch. As a perfectionist, no flaws were allowed in his women.

"Sally Cockling." It was ironic for a street whore to have 'cock' in her surname as well as her pussy. Sally had dropped 'Margaret' from the day her spelling had received a gold award in grade school.

"Maria Dieppe." Sally clamped her blotched veneers hard on her tongue to stop herself from screaming: *'Maria Dieppe? Maria fucking 'I am Chad Rise's fiancée' Dieppe'*

God, New York certainly looked promising. Sally smiled, sipping her warm latte; the sugar gave sweetness to her budding plans. This revenge business was going to be as easy as walking a pedigree dog in the park.

*

The letter was crisp. It was unusual for fan mail to be free from lipstick marks, pubes and skimpy knickers, but whoever had sent this letter wanted it opened and read with respect. Normally Henry Dooley allowed Patricia, his PA, to open them. Patricia read at a book club in her spare time and was addicted to reading, but today she was at the vets with her cat. On the off chance, Henry had bumped into the postman who was shell-shocked at the star as he passed this single envelope on. Henry always felt like a fool when the public became star struck; it never lost its nauseous feeling, and he made a note to donate something to charity to balance out the karma. The envelope stamp mark showed English heritage and class, and despite being thin it felt expensive. Something deeper told him that it was not the usual fan mail, or an invitation to a charity fundraiser, or a 'thank you' letter.

He took a seat in his battered Chesterfield, leather faded on the arms - the first of only two items from his marital house, the second being his wife's urn. He pulled out his reading glasses that had been loyal to his sight for forty years, sat back, and turned the envelope around to open. His old fingers opened the envelope to reveal a simple folded letter. Unfolding it, he scanned the beautiful italic words quickly. Suddenly the letter shook in his hands, trembling with the realisation of the words hitting home.

Was it a sick joke? Was it a wind-up from an envious actor, or a bitter ex-girlfriend wanting to make quick money? Maybe it was a stalker playing mind games to lure him into a hopeless situation and slit his throat.

Maybe it was a mistaken address. Was there another Henry Dooley meant to receive this confession? Did the press know of this, about to run it publicly, damaging his perfect, untarnished career? The truth punched his heart for being stupid. In his heart he knew deep down what the letter revealed was all so true, and something call joy started to seep into his soul.

The hangover hit her hard with no warning that it was coming for her. It crashed into her slender body with the force of a car bonneting, avalanching her whole body to surrender any mobility to the soft bed and the darkness of the room suffocating her. Was it killing her? Her kidneys had been rugby kicked due to the irresponsibility of her drinking too much, working them overtime like some illegal immigrant who has left one hell only to enter the hell of underpaid work, normally like a kitchen porter. Dehydration made her skin feel sluggish Alex feared death only way to cure this hangover.

The faint taste of sick minus spicy kebab meat showed that she had been too pissed to even eat a kebab - it made her breath dangerous to anyone unlucky enough to smell it. Taking a few muddled moments to gather her head, she could feel it splitting in two, each part on opposite sides of the spacious room playing a tug of war on her low energy.

Dehydration choked her brain, dryness coated her tongue, and the empty space in the bed yet to be filled with children told her that something was seriously wrong. Where was Troy? Alex had last had a hangover of this paralysing proportion when she had been on a hen do a decade ago, drinking straight rum, giving the impression that she had been born and bred in Jamaica - not from Kenny in Liverpool.

Alex handled hangovers very well, just as she did with confrontation, cross-fit training and knitting patterns. Her indication of a hangover was normally a minor craving for anything greasy, and feeling lacklustre until she showered. This hangover was different. This hangover felt like a warning she was getting older, and that she was not Kate Moss who could appear on Vogue hungover and looking angelic after a night on the tiles. It was a warning that someone had planned for her to be this destroyed, maybe drink-raped for someone to take advantage of. But who? Alex was fucking ruined.

Someone had undressed her as she was in only her bra, knickers, and stripy socks - Alex hated cold feet in bed. No ache of a sexual encounter did her fit body feel, which was solid proof that Troy hadn't stayed in their bed last night. The bedroom was black, soundless of male snoring as an indication that her bed was empty of her fiancé. Running her hand over to his side feeling his side cold backed this up., sent her hand back to her side with worry. Had he been ashamed with what he saw, maybe? Worse, what did he know? The last thing Alex remembered was having tequila with Mindy and Debbie, then a smartly dressed man coming over, fresh air slapping her, and then waking up this morning.

Why can I not remember anything? Never do I lose control. The uncomfortable question was followed by no answers, making Alex get out of the comfy bed. She needed a drink - the good old water kind - walking off the nausea of the feeling that something bad had happened may help, reaching the kitchen, it didn't. Where was Troy? Then it hit her as if a piano had fallen on her head from her neighbour's upstairs ready to play a melody of doom. She gripped the wooden breakfast table her and Troy found in a skip down the canal walk restored over a weekend of sandpaper, vanish and Chinese takeaway. She had no recollection of seeing Troy last night or of tasting his main course.

Did he win? Had he seen her escorted out? In his hour of glory she had let him down in her absence, became Judas to his Jesus gift of feeding the five thousand (well fifty) with King Prawns. Dense guilt choked her heart, kicked her eyes hard to form tears.

More worryingly, had he come home? The lack of evidence crushed her, her fear rising. There were no shoes laid obediently by the front door to lay to rest the worry walking up from her heart towards the summit of her brain. No 'Good Morning, Handsome' cup in the sink from his morning coffee waiting to be cleaned as clarity that he had returned home. Alex had received no tea and toast in bed, a tradition that Troy had delivered every day without fail if off work - it normally led to a fast fuck. Sickness swirled inside her empty stomach and it wasn't due to the epic volume of tequila sinking in her organs, drowning her self-doubt. She knew the gospel truth was that something serious had kept Troy from coming home; her female intuition joined her gluten free gut instinct preached, bravely knocking on the front door to her heart telling it that the something serious, was female.

Concentrating on trying to fill the water filter jug up, it was impossible due to Alex running a thousand ideas through her head - the ideas were sluggish and slow treading across her mind filled with sand. Prolonging the sadness, she was so angry that he had not come home to her. Alex felt the sip of water was nothing but air, it failing to regenerate her dry mouth, punishment. It failed to rehydrate her, so she tossed the remaining water into a nearby palm tree, ignoring the advice that you should try to mimic the rainfall of a tropical habitat, not a monsoon. The plush living room curtains were drawn perfectly, and not a blade of light cut in, she didn't deserved the glorious day she told herself. So, someone must have closed them, but whom?

Alex was not a drunk who possessed the ability to do normal things while trashed coming in from a night out. Once she had managed to drink the two pints of water recommended to ease hangovers in the morning, accidently spilled them in her bed and woke up to the horror of thinking she was back to her bed-wetting drenched nights, her inner six-year-old coming back. She walked over, opening the curtains, and glorious bright light washed the completely open living area in a glow. Blinding her it lifted her flat spirits a little - everything always seemed better in the light. It gave hope, the day was losing to the night with each second passing. This day would end, and so would the hangover - that was the only joy so far in her bleak morning. The breath-taking view of London showed her success as she sat on the small grey leather tub chair facing out. Bringing her knees up to her chest, she hugged her knees in comfort. The murky Thames flowed quietly past, and homebred seagulls glided, cutting in with their white colour to make it look like Alex was looking down through the clouds.

Being an independent woman like Beyoncé, Madonna, and even Rose West, Alex rarely felt insecure, frail or needy for a man. But Troy was nowhere to be found or to answer, trying his mobile four times. Being switched off was never a good sign or a healthy one for a paranoid, hungry, hungover mind. A plausible excuse that his battery had died stood behind a queue of thoughts that he was dead, had been mugged, had ticked it in for crack (despite Troy's strict hate for drugs - but Alex was now in a state of dramatic delirium), or had lost it as he walked the streets of London in the night to keep himself away from his home and her. The *'her'* part hurt the most.

Of all the nights to slaughter her soul with tequila and champagne, why had she done it during Troy's big break? Could she not have waited another four weeks for her niece's christening to go all George Best for the night? All his hard work over the past weeks, and she wasn't even fit to celebrate with him. The shame soaked over her the way that the sauce did on the chunky steaks last night, she guessed. Mindy and Debbie must have felt right embarrassed. Well, it was all Debbie's fault for ordering tequila with the gusto that Angelina did with adopting rainbow children. *Debbie?* Sick started to rise from the pit of her stomach with volcanic burn and speed, with the flashback to Debbie making love to the picture of her and Troy with her feline eyes, hungry for sex. Could she? Would she? Was she the something that was keeping him away?

Sick seeped into her mouth with the question surfing: *Did she? Did he?* She raced to the kitchen sink, borking frothy bile rained on few dishes. Fresh air, she needed fresh air as her lungs felt constricted. She needed to jog off the hangover, air out the ridiculous scenes that Troy was in, or call her mum, she borked again. Mums are useful with wisdom, like: *'Oh I remember your Dad going missing. Bless, it was in his early stages of Alzheimer's'*. Momma Carol was a massive fan of misery magazines with headlines like *'I killed my husband for a new house'*, or *'my toy boy waiter took my heart, house and my little dog too'*. Constantly consuming crappy daytime TV, she would ring the producers and next thing you know, Alex would be on stage with the title *'My daughter's drink problem made her fiancé leave her for the receptionist - a temp, not even full time'*, with roots to her shoulders, uneven teeth and wearing a Kappa tracksuit for effect, with her mum posting pictures of their complimentary hotel on Facebook with five star rating of a Barbados hotel smile.

She jumped up and raced to her bedroom; jogging was the safest, sanest option - just in case she was to go on Jeremy Kyle, she at least wanted to look fit in her Kappa trackie. Alex was ready to go in under a minute. It was a killer to sum up the energy to move, but she felt she was safer to be out among people than sitting with self-pity, town-crying about her drunken antics, paranoid and patting her back with the insane idea that Troy had fucked Debbie now living happily ever after. She opened the front door and screamed with ultimate shock.

The thunderous scream woke up the human lump outside the front door, working a new fashion of human doormats - either that or the homeless of London had gone up-market, preferring hallways in Zone One to alleyways and subways. He looked up, his eyes bloodshot, whiskey morning breath, and his handsome looks pale and lacking a decent sleep. Dried sick stained his chin and denim shirt, and *'2 heavy 4 me 2 pull in, heart Moo* x' was scrawled across his forehead acting like a trashy neon bar sign in bright pink lipstick.

Alex fell to her knees, devouring an extremely hungover - confused as to why he was lying outside his front door - Troy in kisses of sheer joy, pulling him in from the corridor. The negative mood of the morning left her faster than head lice when Momma Carol brought out the comb of torture every Sunday back in the day.

*

"What happened to your hand, Mindy?" Maud was a stickler for gossip, but showed a rare, caring side, and was also in a cheery mood every second eclipse. *Had she run over a child this morning to account for her good mood?* Before allowing Mindy to explain or lie, she butted in. "You can wear my copper bracelet if you want. Works wonders on my arthritis." Maud was the only sufferer of arthritis to wear an actual copper band like those found on construction sites, rather than the pretty ones that you buy in those catalogues posted through your letterbox by someone with more determination for a sale than a Jehovah's Witness for an answer. She put down her cream cake, struggling to detach the band from her chunky wrist, her skin red raw with the struggle, choking the blood flow in her wrist. Touched by the show of rare caring, Mindy opened her face with a smile and placed her hand on Maud's, noticing how slim and feminine her hand looked against Maud's chunky, transgender-looking hand. "It's nothing, Maud. E.T caught me with his claws this morning. Just wanted to cover it today, but thank you anyway."

Leaving the yellow roses in the vase, the bunch hid her lying face as she went to her little studio to start work. The dead waited for no one. "What's up with Mindy's hand, Maud?" Annie the sloth cleaner appeared. The thickness of her glasses failed to help with her blindness, which was the main reason she missed the dust around the place. Her hair was mousy brown, lank and she had one front tooth missing, but she was one of the best scrubbers in the city - her CV and police caution referenced. "Something about it being Remembrance Day for Michael Jackson, so fans wear a glove, or something like that," lying chuckling with joy. Annie was gullible gave the look of *sad bitch*, and went off to put Henry - the best sucker she worked with - back in the cupboard.

Mindy had never really been a fighter. If she ever got caught in a house fire she doubted she would fight to get out, or wake from a coma. Normally she would rather walk away or attack with a smart remark, but last night, she had reverted to the time she had punched Molly Simpson square in the face in the school yard. Poppy did not encourage violence but always said '*as long as you hit them back*'. Mindy had never ever used the Stanley knife her mother had given her as a sixteenth birthday present or the knuckle duster she found under the pillow left by the tooth fairy.

She had arrived at her poxy flat just in time to stop Troy committing the biggest mistake ever, and to be honest, from becoming a victim of male rape. Her hand had been taken over by something possessed by violence, and it had reached out before Mindy could conjure up the act. She had walked in on Debbie in her heels and on her knees, about to put Troy's knob into her mouth. Debbie had screamed when Mindy's hand entangled itself in her dry hair and yanked her head back with sharp force cracking it on the floor. Debbie screamed again when Mindy had thrown a punch so hard that it sent her over the small wooden table, crashing to the floor in a topless heap, her own tits slapping her hard in the face for stupidly taking advantage of Troy as she landed.

She was just so glad that the bearded waiter had given Mindy Debbie's address when Mindy returned to collect an absent Troy. Mindy was not a woman whose cock-sucking went into double figures, but she knew that this situation was wrong. To save blushes for Troy and to show loyalty to her friend, she had tucked baby Troy away into his underwear using a pair of tongs and with her eyes closed. Debbie had regained her feet and stood - half crying, half screaming - with her tits still on show, her envious body bruised, screaming about how men had ruined her life and questioning why Alex should be so smug and happy. Mindy had simply told her that to be happy she had to stop causing unhappiness to other people, giving Debbie a hug as she shook sobbing in just her heels and underwear, looking divine.

Mindy, back to being the pacifist, dragged a comatose Troy down the stairs and into a taxi. Why serial killers went through the hassle of dragging their victims, she would never know. Her back ached, her shoulders fell out of joint on more than one occasion, and sided with her to give up. With all her energy gone, she had left him safe outside his front door after knocking for an hour to try and wake Alex up. She had left a note on his forehead in lipstick.

Troy was not the only man to be getting her attention. Chad Rise - since their brief meeting outside Simone's apartment - had lingered a little too long like a bittersweet memory of an ex. She had googled him a few times and had actually subscribed to an online American gossip site; he certainly was something to write about.

Ruddick St. David's sudden death exposé had linked him in various articles. He was extremely good-looking in a Ken doll look, but more of a rogue Ken, as if your jealous baby sister had taken a marker and drawn stubble on the doll in an early sign of being a feminist. His fiancée crowned this too; Maria Dieppe, the stunning, curvy Mexican bombshell was draped on his shaped arm in most photographs, with a golden Labrador by his side in other photographs showing his caring compassion for animals.

Chad Rise pushed thoughts of Joe-Ryan out too. She had not spoken to him since yesterday morning, leaving him with his Gran at the hospital. Why was Chad Rise photobombing her and Joe-Ryan's day? It was all to do with the way he had looked at her, as if she was a runaway child that had returned twenty years later, the family gobsmacked that she was back and freaked out by how she had changed. Mindy knew she was pretty, but she was no Maria Dieppe - or the golden dog - so she crossed the thought that he might fancy her off the list in her head. Maybe she reminded him of a relative, or had mistaken her for an actress? She had once been told that she looked like a younger, fatter Julianne Moore, which was a break from the more common remark of *'you look like Henry Dooley'*. Endless possibilities twisted her beautiful face into angst, wondering why he had looked at her the way he had. His piercing blue eyes had been pebble dashed all over her face, she remembered, but why?

Mindy collected herself to prep for her client. She texted Alex to hope she had found Troy at the front door like a human foot mat, praying that Troy had no memory of the night. Debbie was such a conniving cunt, after Alex bringing her into their company - and this is how the whore repaid her? Mindy was shocked by how some women went out of their way to hurt another. She battled with the idea of confessing to Alex, with whether it was the right thing to do to be honest, or keep quiet and not create further upset and drama. What good would it do for Alex to know that Troy was about to receive a BJ from a single white fe-fuck-male? Technically Troy was unaware; his cock stayed loyal to Alex by not hardening. She had felt it soft through the tongs, and its girth too - she had thought Alex was lying when she explained in the early days how big it was and she may need a wheelchair.

No good would come from it, so she would keep it to herself along with the time she had caught chlamydia. She would simply tell Alex a tiny white lie that she found Troy drunk and slumped back at the pop-up - sometimes a secret kept does more good than harm.

Last night brought back the harsh memory of seeing 'Him' in the position of sexual satisfaction from being serviced by two young girls. The way that Alex charged in like a defending lioness for her friend's upset fuelled part of Mindy's attack on Debbie last night. Saving Alex from heartbreak, from nights of sharing a bottle of wine with self-doubt, knowing that Alex would be popping the champagne with positivity, she didn't do wine. Glad to be rid of a cheat from her life sharing a kebab with worthlessness was spared by Mindy's great timing. How being at the right time at the right place could save a life from being altered, fracturing the future for the person, was amazing. If Mindy had just walked around the supermarket one more time, or had taken up the offer of another cup of tea in the café that fateful afternoon, would she have gotten home just after 'Him' had finished fucking the life out of them? Mindy spared the years of heartache, left out on his sordid secret. Would her life have benefited from being in the dark? It had taken at least a year to get over 'Him'. Every time she heard a man's voice she twisted her neck with whiplash speed to see if it was him. Every time someone mentioned United he scored a goal in her memory, opening up her healing scars to bleed again. Smelling *Cool Waters* was enough to bring tears to her eyes. The day she found a photograph of 'Him' and her riding a camel in Turkey, Alex fought hard to get it out of her hands, ignoring Mindy's woeful cries as she tore the memory of happier times up.

Each passing day she plastered over the betrayal thinly, extinguishing the fire dying to burn her trust in love forever inside. Day by day, the old Mindy returned. He had ruined the relationship - she treated it like a death and she moved on with time, her best friend. Time didn't rush her or try pouring her a vodka, or set her up on a date with Johnathan from Lewisham, a banker, who after Mindy's political rant on all things wrong with men and her medieval punishment bill that she would instate if she was in power to punish cheating bastards, confessed that he was going to transgender into a woman - plus, he didn't want his balls dipped in a melting pot of tarmac. Inspired by Mindy, he felt brave enough to pour out his heart and adored Mindy for the package of make-up she had sent him the following day.

Time simply kept in the background watching her, only highlighting that it was there when light turned to dark and back to light again. That was it at that moment. Her hurt was the dark, but surely in her future the light would come again. It never rushed, dazing her, forced her to run when Mindy could barely get out the bed. It was steady, consistent, and stopped at nothing. It brought days of celebration: weddings, communions, friends' landmark birthdays and promotions, for her to see that good existed in the world. It turned the days into weeks, and morphed the weeks into months, until one day it delivered the year anniversary - Mindy's first day since that she hadn't cried.

Mindy took great comfort in time, and used the time to heal. 'Him' was now a distant chapter in her bible-fat book called life, and it was the thinnest chapter of her thirty plus years on earth. The power to cripple her with upset was no longer the powerful spell it used to be.

She imagined Chad Rise to be a doting boyfriend. Maria always seemed to smile in the pictures, and Chad Rise was quite friendly in the interviews she had seen on YouTube. He was humble when he won an award and a gracious loser if he hadn't. The only thing Chad Rise shared with her cheating, cock-wandering ex Edward was that crooked little finger, and this had been the biggest culprit in introducing 'Him' back into her head. *Imagine if 'Him' was Chad Rise, as if he had transformed himself into the TV star?* Mindy joked with herself as she whistled along to Stevie. If Michael with the deep gash to his temple lying on her trolley to have his make-up done - the deadly gash a gift from a fed-up, broken wife - could speak, he would remind Mindy that 'stranger things have happened'.

The Blouse Brigade, New York

Rare caviar, that had been sourced from some secret location or some shit, failed to excite her taste buds that were immune from years of eating the delicate dish - it tasted dull. The conversation was merely background noise like the benefit of a radio playing in the room of a coma patient for comfort, yet even the coma patient would jump out of the bed to stop this dull conversation. Conversation failed to stop Saffron from racing to places the ring could be inside her head like a Generation Game conveyor belt. The last place Saffron wanted to be on a wet afternoon was lunching with the boring Blouse Brigade; a stay at Guantanamo Bay more relaxing as a spa than lunch with these unenthusiastic ladies.

She didn't know whether it had been misplaced during the hectic week of the Golden Gala, or if it was the first stages of Alzheimer's kicking in. Either way, the precious ring was gone like Clinton from the White House, its secret place empty, stolen - but by whom? Helena was forever emptying her ghastly beige canvas bag on the way out, being stripped to her frumpy underwear on questioning. Reggie was a street chancer; his alibi was that he was rarely ever at Saffron's place alone, as they would normally rendezvous at hotels. He had not returned her calls since the Gala for her to question him. This pissed her off immensely - or was it jealousy? She was receiving the silent treatment from him. Had he seen her flirting with Chad, leaving with his limo in tow?

Maybe Mabel? But no, Saffron remembered wearing the ring the afternoon that the wonderful news of Mabel's death had come through. Or had she left it there when she had visited with Lucas?

Chad Rise? Now this was the name putting its hands up in her line up of suspects, as she had been absent the morning after the Gala. Helena had confirmed that she had been in the bedroom most of the time when Chad was there. Had Helena fucked him? Saffron scowled with her narrowing old eyes. She was annoyed that jealousy was riddling her aging body as if her aging body didn't have enough aliments to battle, creaking bones, loose skin, and grey hairs. No man had ever made her jealous, but Chad had gotten under her skin like a

Voodoo needle. He was immensely passionate in the bedroom department; his dick touched parts of Saffron that an internal by her private doctor had failed to. She had considered making it a regular, seeing that Reggie had vanished.

"You ok there Missy, in the land of cuckoo?" Doris broke Saffron's distant detective thinking, and brought her back to the dreaded weekly lunch with her husky, broad American accent. Doris held two achievements in her successful life high. One, she was a woman who had made it successfully without flashing her tits or bones, and second, she was American. Doris noticed Saffron's glass flute was full; not a sip sacrificed to quench the bitch's thirst. It was a clear, solid indication that distraction ran riot about something - unless the bitch was detoxing. Saffron stared at Doris with the venom of Medusa, the motorway lines created by age filled in with cheap make-up seemed alive. Doris chewed a meaty rib with the hunger of a hyena, too engrossed to notice Saffron's disgusted look. It took all of her willpower not to beat her face with the ceramic plate and kill the Fat Queen of Food.

The Blouse Brigade was the most exclusive and longest-serving members club in New York. Members were the richest wives and ex-wives of the city. It would be easier to turn a chicken back into an egg than to join this club. Anyone powerful and rich enough lunched together, keep your friends close and your rich enemies' closer, silent motto of the brigade. The perks of the club were never-ending scoops on the goings-on in New York, in the company of other influential, rich, gossip-eating women with regal style, reputation and honour. Members started off in double figures, more secretive than the Mafia. The Mafia were rumoured to fear the combined power of the dozen or so menopausal millionaire broads. Scrutinising members better than the Academy board, bonus for The Blouse Brigade allowed diversity and even had a black transgender. It was a massive charity fundraiser if The Blouse Brigade got behind any worthy cause - the city noted that any change would be done before dessert arrived. Men may think that they rule the world, but women certainly owned it.

The club had been running for six decades and always met at La'Roux every week on a Wednesday without fail. It had survived poor health, illness, murder, prison and sudden death, Mia May-Luis exiled and deported, and since Mabel had died and Delia Von-Grouse's death, it now consisted of three surviving members: Saffron, Doris and Grace.

Doris had been a cooking legend back in the seventies and eighties. Brassy, loud and very opinionated in conversation, she was also chubby even for American standards. Her cookbooks sold millions. Her cookery programmes aired around the globe and paved the way for many families to enjoy food with generous portions of nutrition. She tackled third world famine with a dozen ways to cook rice. It was good, hearty American food - she cooked none of this 'fancy shit'. Doris' downfall deflating her popularity was her rising weight. In the era where nothing felt as good as skinny and carbs topped a poll of the most evil thing on the planet, those trends started to gain popularity. Soldiers of skinny bitches campaigned to kill off the carbs. Doris worked a chunky look and had inspired a few fat jokes; her weight was her biggest casualty. She was their main target.

The obese became the new race of people to hate, castrated in the media. Brainwashed women started to turn away from her carb-swimming stews, cheesy fat pastas dishes, belly-bloating BBQ food, and creamy calorie-busting baking. Exercise took over quality time with friends and family around the dinner table, and supermodels shrinking with each flash of the camera on the catwalk became like her Daleks. Social media sent out armies of skinny minnies, and reality TV stars ganged up and toppled doctors and nurses for the young to idolise, becoming thin inspiration.

Doris refused to slim. She refused to cook healthier foods. *'Who the fuck gets joy from a salad? If you wanna feel a rib, make it a BBQ rib in your mouth'* she had quoted on daytime television. Slowly her name dropped down the book charts, her cookery shows were dropped in the bin from national television to online channels dedicated to cult classics, until her career dried up as quickly as a pan of water on the stove.

Doris didn't care. She was minted as an established icon, and she was an advocate of good American food. She gathered interest at conventions and became a plus-size inspiration alongside Oprah and Kirsty Allen. She reinvented herself as a fierce food critic of the New

York food scene, writing an article called *Feed the Fatty*. Hugely popular, her blog *Humour against Hummus* topped the top three most read blogs each week; her weight finally became her unique selling point in a world obsessed with self-image.

Today's blouse was a silk Missoni with a stencil of macaws all over it. It was loud, slightly tight around her huge bust, but showed off her real pearl necklace wonderfully. Her orange dyed wigs hid her balding from acute alopecia underneath, and her plum purple nail varnish was immaculately painted on. If Doris did not have her nails painted, it might indicate that all was not well. Her make-up was as heavy as her BMI and as colourful as her sugar soaked trifles.

"You don't seem to be yourself Saffy?" Saffron hated the name Saffy, and she hated Doris. Doris deep-throated another meaty rib, the bone sliding out bare of any meat as she knew she had scored a point with the 'Saffy'. She licked her fat lips free with satisfaction and BBQ sauce.

"It's just the shock of poor Ruddick St. David dying. Can you believe that his obesity maybe the real reason?" she lied, to equal the score to one-all with fat Doris. The women may have been in the same club, but there was no rule that said you had to like each other. She didn't give a fuck about the rude, sexist pig but the coverage had dropped her name and a collection of glamorous pictures all week. She raised a small toast to his departure.

"So sad, isn't it?" Grace La Wren pipped in from her place at the table; they had held it for years, it could seat ten. Grace was the opposite of Doris. She was extremely thin, skeletal, and so fragile that you feared to sneeze in case you snapped her in two and got done for murder. She wore vintage Chanel as her flesh. Her hair was snow white, long and dense as if it was a waterfall frozen by a fierce winter, touching her enviable waist, it shrinking her head like Beetlejuice - it had been stroked by a toyboy in every country.

She was a vision of preserved beauty, tiny like Prince. Nobody really knew Grace's real age; she had stopped at seventy and that was at least a decade ago, and her skin was pebble-smooth. The only line to be on her forehead was her dense fringe line. She was a world-renowned old school jazz singer, her voice having been heard all over the airwaves from the war straight up until the previous year on the controversial track of a rapper who claimed to be Jesus but spat words out like Hitler. Her harsh attack of throat cancer had taken her heavenly octave-high voice to the bottom of the soles of her feet. The world didn't know about this dramatic voice change in the miniature songbird. Her voice couldn't even be sold as a Halloween sound effect, so Grace became a recluse in the music world, lived off the royalties enough for five life times over, and had rumours spread of a Vegas return. Why Grace came to these boring lunches, Saffron wondered. She never ever placed anything into her mouth other than the champagne.

"Yes, extremely," Saffron muttered.

"Extremely," Doris agreed, giving a chicken wing a blowjob.

"Extremely," Grace whispered. For a singer/songwriter she was low on words, and her volume of speaking was a whisper even when shouting. Today's lunch agenda made Saffron slightly nervous, and the reason sat facing her in an opal ceramic picture frame draped with rosary beads made of rubies, emeralds and sapphires. The crucifix stopped on the woman's forehead in the picture like a bhindi. Mabel's remembrance lunch was today. It was a long-serving tradition in the private club, and at least one every year was held as a dinner of celebration in honour of the deceased member. Saffron looked forward to hers just so that she knew these ghastly lunches were over. *Be careful what you wish for* came as a side with her succulent roast beef.

The deceased member was always placed in the same frame blessed by every Pope to release a dove from the Vatican. The V&A museum in London prayed that the remaining three died in one go just to get their historic mitts on it. Mabel seemed to be having a wonderful time, her bright smile wide, perfect make-up, and staring hard, penetrating through Saffron, knocking on the steel door to the secret that Saffron hid inside; not once did it falter. The door was heavily built on Saffron's secret to stay put for now, so Mabel failed to gain access to the secret in the dusty room of her conscience, but screamed through the letterbox before she left: '*revenge is a bitch*'. Mabel may not have been here in person, but as usual she dominated the stale conversation and table due to her funeral plans, which were completely unknown.

"Any news on where the broad is getting buried? I heard Vegas." A couple of fries rode by with melted cheese and pulled pork, committing suicide by jumping into the dark hole known as Doris's mouth as she spoke.

"Sorry, I don't know," Saffron hissed, fuelled more by the fact that she was in the dark about her own sister's burial arrangements, which wouldn't sit well with the gossip mongers already making up conspiracies. A waiter appeared, gangly, tall and extremely skinny. A coke habit was the real reason for this, and the fact that the boss refused free food for his staff. Another out of work actor the backbone of New York, if he never won the Emmy he daydreamed of, serving these women was a fabulous consolation, and Mai could not wait to call his mother back in Thailand, praying that her weak heart wouldn't stop with the joy.

"More champagne?" Stuttering over his question, an anxious sweat swung like Tarzan from his long fringe crashing into his eyes. Despite having a combined age that would have had them read the Bible at book club, they still possessed an intimidating power over men. Donald Trump was terrified to be in the same room as Doris. Not one woman acknowledged him. The back of Saffron's hand greeted him with her ruby ring threatening to take out his eye. Security acting the expensive ring rudely told him firmly to leave, and he left in the escalating silence vowing to quit after this shift.

"I will go first with the toast, shall I?" Doris answered her own question, placing a juicy meatball slobbering with Bolognese sauce into her mouth like a mint imperial.

"I'm so going to miss the crazy broad. That laugh, those tales, and that amazing dress sense," she said, speaking in her deep drawl with a bare rib bone inches from her mouth like it was a microphone. Saffron slowly took a sip of her Bollinger with the menace that a lion does at a water bank.

Grace whispered, "So true," clicking her stick insect fingers for her PA to wipe her single tear away - that tiny amount of moisture leaving her face made it shrivel up more. Grace employed someone for every aspect of her life. No one had the job of wiping her arse because she did not eat, so she did not shit.

"She could tell a good story, could that one. Never a dull moment, never an ugly man on her arm and certainly not a dull outfit." The smacking of the ribs annoyed Saffron. She shovelled caviar into her mouth to weigh her tongue down, placing her plate over her steak knife. Doris rested her green eyes on her with the 'dull outfit' comment. Saffron had gotten rid of Delia Von-Grouse with a push; Doris was next on her hit list, with food poisoning.

"Even with all that bullocks about that bloody racehorse!" Doris rolled her eyes threw bare bone on the plate, laying there glistening with saliva of Doris mouth, gave Saffron severe flashback finding the horse dead, burning it and the collapsed scaffolding of bones in a heap, she felt her body heat up, took napkin dabbed her face. "She kept herself dressed with dignity and beauty throughout." Another rib rode into the tunnel of doom known as Doris's mouth she ignored Saffron dabbing at her face too late for tears now she wanted to say. "Her loyalty to friends and charity was indestructible; it was inspiration of the highest." Doris glared at Saffron and tore the meat from the rib like a cannibal, not once lifting her gaze.

Doris never had liked Saffron since their first meeting in the seventies at a brunch in Beverley Hills for Jane Fonda. Saffron had worn a dress with more cut out pieces than a butcher's pig. Men were draped around her like furless fox shawls, and Saffron never once complimented another woman in the room, including Farah Fawcett. The campaign against her dislike for the whore was from multiple marriages, to her penchant for toy boys, to her ill treatment of Mabel - her best friend. *'Nothing but a crusty old cougar in borrowed couture,'* Doris had once told Mabel's common tears over lunch one day. Taking out the garlic baguette in two bites, Doris gave the impression that she wished it was Saffron snapping in two.

"It inspired me to write 'My Heart Rode Out on a Horse'," Grace piped up. Grace twirled a tiny glass bead on her plain blouse. It was a pity it was not a volume button, as her guests struggled to hear what she had said. The number one smash had knocked Celine's wet attempt into the ocean as the biggest selling soundtrack, and millions flooded her bank account faster than said water on a certain ship.

Silence fell between the three women of individual power. The silence was not due to an uncomfortable lack of gossip or the death of their dinner companion, but it was due to Saffron not putting her good piece in for Mabel, her sister. Grace gave a little nudge in the shape of a thin cough; it nearly killed her off.

"Oh, um..." caught off guard; this was unusual for Saffron she stuttered. This woman could give a winning speech in front of America at any political rally. She had married some of the most sought-after men in Hollywood, so public speaking and attention was like oxygen to her - so why did she seem stunned in giving a sentence for her sister? She could say plenty about her sister. She could talk about how growing up the first emotion she had felt towards her sister was not love, but jealousy. She had been insanely jealous of her popularity, her blonde bombshell beauty, and the personality that charmed anyone on her first word. She could talk about how Mabel had saved Saffron from a starving coyote once with just her skipping rope, fearless against the wild animal and risking herself to save her. The way she had whipped that coyote had inspired Saffron to indulge in a bit of S&M with an oil tycoon.

The gift was that Mabel saw the best in any situation and was never judgemental, and her flare for fashion and good times infectious. She had a charitable heart the size of space twice over, with religion-worthy devotion to any cause needing her strength and power. She was a modern-day Superwoman wearing fur instead of a cape, and a few police cautions rather than enemies. The devoted nursing to their parents in ill health she had done so that Saffron could attend failed auditions in the city, and she had held off from starting a family to make sure that Saffron was looked after. If Saffron wanted to dig deeper and shock Doris and Grace, burying them in an early death with a killer confession as a spade, killing the two old birds with one stone so that she would never have to sit at this darn blasted table again, she could tell them about how Mabel had stayed loyal despite Saffron sleeping with her husband, and about framing Mabel for Ballet Foot's disappearance. God damn, she needed to find that bastard ring. Draining the champagne in one and leaving Grace and Doris waiting, she hoped that they had patience as she clicked over Mai the waiter.

Sally loved her new job. In two days she had not craved a drink or a dick. She had not wanted a sip of alcohol to wash away the feelings of despair and the feeling of being unwanted, passing her lips. Roxy needed her even for her own selfishness, and Sally needed that to beat any straight vodka. She was yet to meet Chad Rise who was busy filming for the new film and was away for the moment, so she mainly met Maria in the plush hotel lobby, forever looking beautiful - Maria this was, grand surroundings of the hotel mere back and white backdrop. It thrilled her, being inside the building where the target of her revenge lived, unaware that his days were numbered on each morning coffee she drank; her free stamps heading towards a free coffee kept tally. Sally liked Maria too much to slash her throat as revenge on Chad, but meeting up with a dodgy guy for a gun made her feel dangerous, Bond style. Ignoring the fact her eye to hand coordination was awful, amount of time she put a penis in her eye instead of her mouth, shooting a bullet anyone's guess where it would end.

Sally felt when in the park that she was at her most relaxed and happy she been since a child, when the big bad world was just sometimes you painted as stripe of blue on picture. This big open space drowned her dark thoughts. Mother Nature showed that beauty came in various sizes from a tiny acorn crushing under people's shoes, to giant trees standing strong, standing against the testing, changing times of New York. The trees kept on growing towards the sky no matter what came their way; in rain or shine they grew, and so would Sally. The best benefit was that it was nice to walk past a male simply smiling as a hello, not to hint that they wanted their cock sucking. She knew the power of parting her legs for a trick, but she preferred the power of not having to.

Fresh air cleaned out her lungs, flung them over a washing line and beat away the dust and mould. She felt like she had developed a slight cough - different to L.A touching her skin, it was as if Mother Nature was breathing directly on to her skin, giving cpr unpolluted by the flakiness of L.A, as if the oxygen was not a fan of plastic surgery. The fact that people actually ate in New York showed in the slight weight gain that Sally had tried to hide under a Wicked t-shirt that she had bought after seeing the award-winning show with Maria.

The park was beautiful and possessed the power of time elapsing. Her normal hour walk would last five hours, lapping the park and each time finding something new and beautiful to appear. Once, Maria had to send out security to find her.

She caught a majestic swan floating across the still lake effortlessly like a white ghost as fog shimmered on the morning lake. A giant fish came to gasp at the surface as if they themselves were in love with the trees around. A leaf was leaving its winter branch to begin an affair as a new leaf, to grow in film-like slow-motion, giving you a chance to see the elegant fall to the ground complementing a feather from an angel. Squirrels were racing around for nuts around the brown leaf-littered ground, as birds chatted above using a spider's unique webs linked across the iron rails like broadband. Each bench pledged devotion to people gone but not forgotten, and the bench that she was on reunited Edna and Barney.

New York gave an insight into the beauty that Mother Nature created every day despite its speed and noise. L.A felt like a lifetime away. New York was nowhere near as warm, and the last time Sally had seen her bare legs was that morning coming out the shower. Maria had paid generously to secure a nice room for her with a lovely view. Everything was high in New York, as if New York held you high and it pumped your self-respect high, making the impossible closer to reality than you first thought. It wanted its people to be as tall as the skyscrapers, wearing clouds as hats. Sally had started to see life outside of dropping her knickers and servicing men as if she was a human garage for the male MOT. She had started to see life as living; she wanted to live, love, laugh and leave when her time came.

Roxy was perfect on the lead - if she had been a real woman, she would be a pillar of etiquette. She had great dog social skills, and everyone commented on her lovely disposition. Sally vowed that she would be a bit more like Roxy - apart from the licking herself clean, Sally had tried once for a punter, but Sally was not flexible enough and gave herself cramp in her neck and back, begrudged hundred fifty dollars went on a massage not new shoes. Another thing that was breaking into Sally's roof of depression, allowing light to penetrate give much needed energy for positivity to grow, pushing the revenge for Chad Rise to be her second thought once she awoke in the morning, was that her first thought was about Maria, but why?

*

"You sure this ain't going to tip your Mother over the edge?" The whisper echoed in the small chapel for everyone to hear. Never religious or kind to other people's emotions, Maud's vision of respectful attire for funeral wear was showcasing more flesh than the crucifix of Jesus on the wall in his loin cloth - it was funeral cheap instead of chic, in her orange bodycon dress. Carrying on, she said, "I mean, it must be hard for her - she could be next."

It took all of Mindy's restraint, and deep breath of blue whale proportion not to butt the fat bitch, tip out the deceased from the coffin, and bury Maud alive. "You want me to hit her with my shoe?" Alex whispered, being respectful of where they were.

"You not got anything heavier?" Mindy squeezed her toned arm as a 'thank you' gesture for the offer, knowing that a statue of the great Virgin Mary with her hands in prayer would be praying to be the object chosen to beat Maud to a messy pulp. Resting her head onto Alex's shoulders, her hair smelled of strawberries and cream; it was comforting and soft, like she had never washed the conditioner out, calmed Mindy instantly.

The tiny chapel hid away behind the row of shops in central London as if religion shy to preach today became the last resting place of Mabel. Today, covered in white lilies, it gave the impression that it had snowed overnight and looked heavenly and pure. Candles in their hundreds gently flickered in height all around - you'd be burnt alive if your dress caught fire, cooked to a crisp. Mindy was tempted to nudge Maud closer to a five-foot candle that was acting as a lamppost. The huge closed coffin dominated the space as the small, extremely small gathering sniffled at the great loss. Mabel's funeral had come around. It was to be a reflection on her colourful life - someone must have missed out the actual living part, colour blind and forgetting to entrust the world with the time and date of her funeral.

The only guests were Mindy, Alex and Maud, who insisted on representing the parlour, two aging men in suits that were flamboyant enough to make you think that they had mistaken the quiet funeral for a David Bowie convention, and Poppy, who had demanded that she came and had told Mindy off for not telling her personally about her good friend's death. There was no Saffron present - Mindy was slightly glad, or paparazzi - Maud was fuming. There was not even Elton John at a piano, holding back his tears while playing a song; Alex was gutted. It was humble, subtle and finally over, seeing the only one request that Mabel had instructed was indicating that it was time to leave with the first opening bar of the song. Maybe coffin carriers in the buff would catch on. The muscular backs paired with the waxed, bare, tight butts of the carriers leading them out to the tune of the Britney classic '*Oops I Did It Again*' brightened up the sad day.

"I mean, bloody tuna sandwiches and cheese and crackers?" The disappointment expressed at the poorly nutritional buffet was in word and not mouth, watching Maud as she attempted a world record for how many crackers she could fit in her mouth. The glamour of the wake being held could not make up for the upset that Maud was feeling over the lack of pastries. Crumbs rained down like ashes from Pompeii into her chunky cleavage, lost forever and buried under a tonne of fleshy weight.

Mindy sighed and raised the champagne to her mouth. Even the butlers in the buff/coffin carriers failed to add any cheeky cheer to her mood with their smooth arse cheeks on show now. She found it so confusing as to why the funeral was so low key. Why was nobody apart from Ziggy Stardust One and Two allowed to the cremation, and no one else? The wake was held in the grand tearoom of The Ritz, and played host to many mourners jam-packed in every colour imaginable and every stage of celebrity. It was a huge contrast from the service, and Mindy was stalked by questions of how it went, etc.

Poppy worked the room well. She chatted to everyone, as if her illness had taken pity on her and showed its caring side, allowing her one day free to remember and recall wild adventures with Mabel's friends - to soak in stories of her dear good friend, and have a glimpse of happiness in her late life for just one day. Mindy did not want to interfere in her mother's rare day of remembrance; it made her smile just to be able to watch her animated mother being normal - not that she was not normal, but Mindy knew what she meant.

Poppy's funeral wear certainly wasn't normal in the traditional black - she was wearing orange and yellow splattered all over a maxi dress, with a sunflower appearing here and there. Another thing that was puzzling Mindy - apart from why Mabel had chosen a cheap arse buffet and half-naked men serving champagne - was the question of what was she supposed to do with the ring now? It was in the safest place that she could think of where no one would look. Alex had said that nobody in his or her right mind would dare attempt to look there, as she pulled a ginger hair from Mindy's chic jumper. She could not sell it on, nor pass it down to any of Mabel's children - her being childless the reason. So, what was she to do with a ring made of history? Maybe take it to Cash Converters, she joked. Did she want the stress of going to the police sounding like a lunatic, and then dealing with a court case?

"What's up, Moo?" Sliding up on cue to her friend, Alex was dressed in an amazing fitted Lanvin dress distracting the poor butlers in the buff. They were in danger of becoming butlers with a boner, seeing the sexy Megan Fox lookalike working curves better than the charm they laid on. Mindy snapped out of her idea of holding a raffle in Poppy's care home to rid her from the ring. Sadly, the ring was drawing trouble, letting off an invisible scent into the air to reveal its location to the Queen Bee - an old hand at murder - flying over here on her private jet, wanting the ring back and Mindy ruined.

"Just confused, Ape. All that way for a ring. Now what?" She shuddered, remembering spending that night under the bed of bonking. She was yet to try out any of the moves she had heard. Joe-Ryan had not been at the manor this morning when she had picked Poppy up. No one had seen him for a few days, and this kicked at her heart. *Where was he?* Their date was yet to get an official day. A thousand negative reasons for this raced to trample her mind like people at a Christmas Sale. But, today was about Mabel being laid to rest, and being out with Poppy. She closed the door on her trampling thoughts before they got inside, hearing them kick. "I mean, if you want people at your funeral then you should make the effort with them in life - and she sure did." The quiet service was playing on her mind.

Leaving the manor with Poppy was a wish that she forever dreamt about, as if she was saving her mum and brightening up the darkness of the cloud of confusion floating inside. Tonight, it would rip Mindy apart like a tug of war taking her back to the manor; one side would be pulling to keep Poppy at the home, and the other side would be pulling her towards sadness for leaving her. Luckily, Alex offered to accompany Mindy, knowing that she would need Alex to turn into cold-hearted lawyer-mode and drag Mindy like a dead corpse during the plague away from the manor.

"Maybe the fact that Saffron no longer has the ring is enough for Mabel. Mabel's ring is back where it belongs out of harm's reach." Her tuna sandwich became extinct with one bite. "I mean, maybe Mabel thought that the ring being out of Saffron's hands was all that she wanted - the fact that the power to expose Saffron was so easy to get? Her living in fear is just as rewarding as physical revenge," Alex offered her take on the loose end of the whole saga, sipping her cranberry juice. She had vowed not to drink to Troy to prove that she didn't have a drinking problem, and she would definitely not have a water infection with the amount of cranberry she had drank during the morning. She had felt awful when Troy had started to cry, talking about coming out to his applause to see that she was not there. The guilt punched Alex hard, but she was a woman who found men crying to be quite a turn-on and ended up jumping on Troy. Maybe having a baby was not a bad thing, she thought, lying in his strong, familiar arms afterwards, blinded by bliss. She hoped that returning home sober would soften the silent treatment he was giving her, not knowing that the silent treatment was due more to him being horrified that he had put himself into a position of near relationship destruction, where his penis had been about to disappear into another woman and not his fiancée.

Mindy was relieved that Alex and Troy were ok. What good would it do for Troy, and certainly Debbie, if Alex found out the truth? Mindy didn't want to lie, but she also didn't want to hurt them - so for now, she would keep schtum until she at least could speak to

Troy. Or, maybe wait until Debbie died to save the bimbo from a brutal beating from Alex.

"Yeah Ape maybe." She was downhearted that Mabel was not alive to collect the ring, but also lightly relieved that there would be no more surprises from Mabel. Mindy was on the lookout for anyone looking like Mabel in disguise, and was glad that her six-inch heels propelled her high enough to scan the crowded room. The three Mabel drag queens were out of the question; one was eight-foot-tall, one was black, and the last one was a midget. Her dreams of the Mafia bursting in to her bedroom and beating her up with horse heads dripping in blood soaked the pillow with sweat each morning when she woke. She was paranoid so much so that she put E.T in the bedroom of a night just for safety.

Mindy caught a frantic hand waving from over by the piano. Poppy called out over the colourful crowd in her best Queen's English, "Mindy, darling, come over here. One must come!" Poppy's orange tie-dyed maxi dress accessorised with a bowler hat were sadly not victims of her waning mind - she had chosen this outfit with her own sane mind, the entire group of nurses said on catching Mindy's concerned look that morning.

"Excuse me, Ape. Madam Madness is calling me." Alex gave a giggle and sloped off to chat to Boy George and warn him of the dangers of radiators and butlers in the buff if temptation won, fingering her shiny business card.

"Mindy, darling, come hurry! I want you to meet someone," Poppy called before Mindy reached her. Mindy dodged and weaved among the colourfully dressed crowd, descending towards her mother and the mystery guest she must meet. On her way she managed to grab a refill of champagne from a butler in the buff who may have been a puff, seeing him gently squeeze the crotch of an award-winning male poet. Mindy reached her mother slightly breathless; cardio never had been her strong point. Poppy stood to one side to introduce her mystery guest.

"Mindy, I would love you to meet Chad Rise." Mindy froze as Chad Rise smiled his Hollywood hunk smile. Her legs weakened as he reached out his hand with the crooked finger.

*

"I love your necklace. It's so jazzy." The word 'jazzy' made the owner shiver inside at the offending vulgar word. She doubted that anything worth fifty thousand dollars could be described as 'jazzy'.

"Thank you. I just adore your..." scanning the podgy woman on the desk in the funeral parlour, displaying her chubby top half, to pick out a false compliment. A dark circle that she was presuming was her nipple poked through her thin blouse - not with sexual friction, but with the strain of wanting to breathe. The bottom of her was hidden by a desk, like the dirty, tangled roots beneath a tree. There was nothing on this human that she adored, not even the fact that she was publicly confident enough to squeeze into a blouse three sizes too small for her. "...Eye make-up. So..." Over the top? Smudged? A little too young for her? There were many words that came to mind, looking at the eyeshadow that looked like RuPaul had applied pissed with his eyes closed. She swallowed, "...vibrant."

"Thank you. It's a new look I'm working." Maud fluttered her eyelids with the grace of an epileptic in a strobe light convention as a lump of blue eyeshadow bombed onto the reception saving the woman's brains playing scrabble to find a suitable word. She loved the woman's American accent, coming in and asking for directions to the Tube.

"You work here alone, do you?"

"No, no." Maud opened another packet of plain biscuits and offered one to the woman, who declined with a wave of her gloved hand. "I'm the first port of call, which is quite important you see." A digestive muffled her words, but Maud multitasked and carried on talking. "But I'm from the school of minimum wage, so, minimum work." She laughed at her own joke as the American lady smiled. The dead fox around her neck snarled.

"I thought you would have done the make-up, maybe, seeing how erratic and fabulous yours is." Flattery gets you everywhere.

"Oh thanks" Maud blushed under her three layers of purple blusher. "But no, sadly I'm not. Even though Eric - that's our cross-dressing, bird watching boss - says I have a gift." Another biscuit toasted her cuckoo chick wide mouth, disappearing completely. "But we have Mindy." Sulking, Maud spoke as if the word 'Mindy' was an illness to be ashamed to have. This was the foot in the door of information for the guest.

"Mindy? Such an old name is she very old?" Taking part in the biscuit sharing showing something in common with her informer, acting as a lure. The fucking British and their biscuits she didn't get it, even having tea with the Queen of England a china plate of biscuit ufo landed on the table.

"No, she's like thirty or something. But I blame her mother - Poppy, that's her name. She must have had Alzheimer's when she gave birth. Should have seen the state of her dress yesterday at the funeral," Maud laughed.

"Alzheimer's, poor woman. Does she live local, the mother?" snapping the cheap biscuit in half, the crumbs irritating her as much as this fat woman was. "No, she lives in a care home manor in Hertfordshire somewhere. I remember seeing it on Country File."

"Country File?" she asked puzzled, thinking that such a name must have meant a criminal file on the whole country.

"It's like a farming lifestyle magazine. Bit shit, but if ya Sky Plus is off it's the only decent thing on of a Sunday." The loneliness of her life screamed out in that sad sentence alone. Maud felt her heart drop into her arse, adding another few pounds of unwanted fat. Even the ginger biscuit failed to pick her up. "We attended that Mad Mabel's funeral. Quiet affair, the old woman mustn't have been liked." Funeral mention rick shaded of her extinct emotions, didn't give a hot fuck the world gossiped why she weren't invited. That was enough information that the guest needed.

"Well, thank you very much Mary." Her eyesight was leaving her as she aged, and she refused to wear glasses.

"It's Maud." Nevertheless, the expensively dressed American woman was already gone. Chanel No.05 lingered, warning that this lady was here for revenge - not a fucking biscuit.

Mindy had wanted to write a book ever since her first complete sentence in its cute, alcoholic-looking state of shaky and slanted writing in infancy. She harboured a living desire to write a book, and today's coffee meet in the plush Knightsbridge area could easily be the opening scene for a romantic novel.

"Skinny latte with one shot extra and no chocolate sprinkles for you." He was extremely handsome. Mindy blushed due to the stares from the other women in the coffee shop; he would be perfect for the male lead in her unwritten romantic novel. His soft American voice gave Mindy the kinky thought of what it might be like hearing him whisper sweet nothings into her ear. *Stop it, Mindy!*

"Thank you, Chad." It was hard to make eye contact with him. His eyes simply pierced into yours, searching for your weakness, desires and dreams, reading them, pulling them to the surface like a blackhead remover tool on a pimple for all to see the dirt. Working with the dead for so long, Mindy had been diluted a little of her people skills. She had been undateable for the past three years, so finding eye contact with a man was like foreplay. A few of the yummy mummies moved a little closer; one applied make-up into the reflection of a teaspoon, ignoring her child in the pram licking a butter knife. She would pass him off as her nephew - not her first born - if Chad spoke to her. All women wanted in on this hot piece of male perfection, and one desperate housewife wondered if it would be possible to slip rohypnol into his coffee. Knowing his face from somewhere but having children and a sleep debt that was years old made watching grown up television impossible for her to be able to picture his face in the hit American soap that he had once starred in - yet this mum could name all of the Teletubbies in three languages.

Brightening up their groundhog morning of child-rearing, this hunk beat any Heat feature of *Torso of the Week*. A few babies were cooing and finding their musical voices, bringing a light soundtrack. Maybe it was a sign that Chad could be the father of her babies, Mindy wondered. She crossed her legs before her eager womb jumped out pounced on him.

How was Chad Rise the American TV star, having coffee with her, she asked herself every second as he stood in the queue. Yesterday at the wake they had got gabbing away. Chad spoke with the gentleness of a priest and a firm interest, like he knew her inside out. He was knowledgeable about her mortuary career and how interesting it must be, making Mindy feel privileged to be in his charming company. She thought about how sweet he had been to Poppy, telling anyone who would listen that he was her boyfriend, and then Poppy declaring to all during her toast that she wanted to toast to Mindy and her new boyfriend, Chad. The rapturous cheer had been deafening; Mindy had put it down to her mother having an episode, but Poppy defended that she was perfectly fine wearing her bra on her head.

It was as if Chad had known her all his life. It was as if there was a secret autobiography on her life that he had read before he had met her. She had this strange sensation that they had met in a previous lifetime. Being the centre of attention of all the envious females in the coffee shop flustered her, and made her instinctively unhook her earrings in case of any brawls that could leave her with dangling earlobes like a tribal warrior. Mindy was never the centre of attention with men, Mindy joked all her friends looked like Victoria Secret models and Mindy more of a Victoria sponge - Alex always centre of attention with men, and even Poppy, but men chasing Poppy were generally men of the law. Common sense along with her normally good judgement of 'bastard men radar' was diluted dangerously low by his sincere flood of intense interest. Chad reached for the plate of biscuits and she noticed his crooked finger again. It poked at the faint memory of her cheating ex, 'Him'. 'Him' had always complained about how he hated his little finger and called it his gay finger, as it was bent. It always made folk laugh, but Mindy scolded him - she hated any degradation of people due to their sexual preferences, colour of skin or religion. 'Him' complained that it ruined his confidence and made him feel insecure, but obviously not that insecure to be able to have a threesome, she now told herself. However, Chad Rise never mentioned whether he was comfortable with his digit deformity. You would think that with being a star that he would have huge hang-ups over the finger, and surely he could afford the best corrective surgery? Did the gorgeous Maria ever mention it? Damn, if you could chop your dick off and turn it into a vagina, to straighten a finger would be easy; Mindy asked the universe of her mind.

"Thank you for meeting me today, Mindy. I just wanted to meet you for a little 'thank you' coffee for keeping me company yesterday at the funeral, and keeping my mind off Maria leaving me" flashing his bought smile and gently laying his heavenly blue eyes on her face. His accent was soft, yet strong. Its power worked, wilting her from a confident woman to a schoolgirl crushing on him. His ageless eyes fought to be the winner as his main attraction, yet his smooth skin - with a little help from Botox - ached to be stroked. Mindy had worked on skin all her life and she was forever pointing out work on celebs who claimed that they hadn't gone under the knife to a delighted Alex. His strokeable, square jaw allowed stubble to grow structured around his board lips. He licked them gently; Mindy was jealous of his tongue and wanted to rip it out of his mouth stamp on it. *'Mindy, get a grip!'* the sensible part of her spoke before the idea egged her on. She noticed his wet lips part. *Was he about to ask her on a date? Kiss her?* The idea of the latter made her squeak, but luckily it came out as a squeaky sneeze.

"Bless you," he spoke in his soft tones.

You can do more than bless me.

Mindy, stop it!

A strong nose took your vision towards his beautiful eyes like a staircase, and they were levelling with her own eyes - not her generous chest, which was a rarity for men. It was the soft stroke of his hand on hers that made her want to sleep with him, plus the year long absence of feeling the touch of a man on her born-again virginal skin, if she asthma sufferer she die of a dust attack because dormant activity of her vagina. She enjoyed the thought of feeling a man inside her with his penis - not a rubber impersonator or a smear swab, but a live, hard penis penetrating places that had been dormant and untouched for years, breaking the dam that was holding back the warm lushness since she had flooded herself with 'Him'. She cheekily imagined his knob to be a thick piece, girth and length generous enough to fulfil an aching yearn - unless it was bent like his finger, in which case she would have to get into yoga positions to be able to sit on it. The afternoon sun blessed this idea as it shone brightly into the window seat like a spotlight focusing on the two. The weather forecast might protest that it was blinding Mindy's judgement of the situation.

"So, once again, thank you for meeting me. It's been an enjoyable morning." Lowering his eyes, he sipped his latté and not once did his stare on her drop.

"Completely fine, the pleasure was all mine." She smiled, ignoring how desperate the *'pleasure was all mine'* bit came out. Pleasure was all that she had on her mind, and her knickers on the floor giving her away for pleasure mopping up wetness from her sexy thoughts. God, he was beautiful. His lips thick and perfect baby new pink, ladies spend fortunes on cosmetic to achieve, and the way his tongue licked his lip free of foam had Mindy worked up. Was the universe trying to tell Mindy something, first meeting him in New York and then yesterday at the wake? He had even managed to keep thoughts of Joe-Ryan behind a locked door, for the moment. The only thing stopping Mindy from digressing further despite Joe-Ryan being locked out by Chad was that he was refusing to give up knocking for her attention and his kiss. Mindy needed to break the erotic thoughts being dragged out willingly by Chad Rise stroking her hand. "Do you mind if I ask you a question?"

"Ask away, Moo." The relaxation of him being in a comfortable state allowed her nickname to slip out - and nearly his secret.

"Moo? That's my nickname." Mindy failed to recall telling him this information, deaf to the alarm bells ringing that were being rang by the entirety of women in the coffee shop, all in on his deadly plan.

"Yeah, it's a word we used over on the west coast for females - like black women call each other heifers." The lie covered him up leaving no crack in his identity, flawless. His acting skills proved useful in the spontaneous reply, impeccable.

"What happened to your little finger?" Her lips drowned in the milky latte as she waited for an answer. *I bet his lips would feel this warm against mine. Stop it!*

"This?" he said, holding the crooked finger up as if he was proud to show it off, like an Oscar before he was about to give a speech of wet, arse-kissing thanks to all but the fans who paid to see the film. Treading carefully, he knew his normal reply of it being gay would certainly blow his cover wide open like a shot gun wound, making it accessible for her to see the real him.

"I wish it was something as dramatic as a shark bite or from a horrific seventeen car pileup accident, but it's simply a deformity from being in the womb of a crack head." Dropping the 'defenceless in the womb' act worked every time. Lying that the cause was neglect by his own mother always gave him the outcome that he forever got from women.

"That's so sad." Mindy returned the soothing stroke of hand on hand, touching said deformity as if she was cradling a skeletal orphan on an AIDs clinic visit. She felt strangely protective towards him. If any of the bored, horny housewives in this coffee shop decided to approach, Mindy would snarl like a pedigree winner dog protecting her money making litter. Chad simply smiled; he knew this bright morning that he would gain access to Mindy's home with this genius lie. His dashing veneers held the prisoner truth behind that was trying to jump off his tongue to warn her.

Women were so pathetic with a sob story, and if another woman was the villain, they drenched the man in sympathy - especially if that villain was a mother. Women were forever hampering on about supporting each other, yet they were the first in for the killing if a woman did wrong. *Yep, women are the weaker sex.* Sipping his latte hid his killer smirk, as he readied himself for his trap.

"So, will you allow me to take you out for dinner tonight, it being my last night and all in London?" Chad gave her a pleading look as if she was the only woman in the coffee shop. She blushed, burning the colour of her red roots. Being in London brought back memories, but he refrained from driving down any memory lane. He was here to do a job, and a well-connected job at that if he pulled it off. Getting Mindy on his side was the next step in his plan of revenge on behalf of someone who could give him the career he dreamed off. Now, it was time for the bait to bite. "I mean, I would cook for you but the hotel I'm in doesn't have a kitchen in the room," he said, laughing at the poverty of it - his hotel was The Dorchester. Sadly, if Mindy had studied acting instead of fine art she would have known that this was a stage laugh.

"Use my kitchen." Bingo, she was hooked.

Chad simply lay back smiling, allowing the warm liquid into his mouth to send celebration to his body sending a swift text that read *"I'm in."*

"Me too," the number replied.

*

The evening air was decidedly cool as sedative dusk settled around, fell unnoticed for the people of London. The power of darkness came in like a relaxing tide against the hard rocks, washing away the high noise of the bright day. Traffic noise gently hummed, day birds flew home to roost, and skeletal public transport services took on the night shift. Sparse streetlights flicked on to lend light to the gang wars between the local gang of street cats, sharpening theirs claws ready to duel with the invading city foxes for territory, UFC style. Most people were drawing the curtains to settle down to a calm evening, but Joe-Ryan was ripping his black hair out in clumps.

"Don't need ya to fucking help me bathe, Aoife. I'm a fucking angina victim, not a bloody invalid!"

"Mammy, you heard the doctor. You need rest! So, you sleep in the bath and I'll wash ya down."

"I am not a fucking car, Aoife. Piss off, will ya! Go wash yourself. Will rest when I'm fucking dead which may be in this bath with any fucking luck."

Hearing the bath taps running, this conflicting conversation played out in his flat as Granny C and his mother battled for dominant female, one offering help to bathe while the other one rejected it, vocally playing out each night since three nights ago.

It had been three days since Granny C had collapsed with a sudden angina attack on the pavement of Oxford Street. It had delayed their flight home with the doctor's orders to rest, and they decided to rest at his small, one bedroom flat. Refusing flatly to take his big-hearted, expensive offer of a hotel room, he was shocked that Aoife hadn't offered to stay alone at a hotel, hearing her dating site alert of a dozen messages or so potential men to keep one side of the bed warm. Aoife insisted that the site was 'quite shit for dating, but good for sex', and he cut her short before she drew the similarity to fruit picking/playing bingo, or how she was a whale in the ocean looking for fish to eat.

His mother insisted on helping her mother with any task. Granny C went ally cat mad, spraying his deodorant in Aoife's eyes when she had tried to wipe her arse for her. Guilt had probably spawned this recreated soul of Florence Nightingale, replacing the usual Myra Hindley disposition in his mother at the moment. Or, it could be the fact that boredom badgered her. He adored his Granny C and his mother, but his adoration was a lot stronger when they were in Ireland and mute - not clashing as if Venus had decided to take on Thatcher. He sipped his can of warm Guinness and watched a repeat of Top Gear; the driving took his distraction nowhere and left him in the layby.

"Ow you eejit! That's my ear you're rubbing like a fucking dog."

"Shut up Mammy, or I'll see if you can hold your breath for as long as a fucking fish!" Aoife slowly dropping the Flo' act. Patience was not high on Aoife's list of human qualities, but murder was looking good.

Joe-Ryan exhaled in a long huff. He was cracking up; he had wisely thought that taking a few days off work would help the situation, but it did nothing but worsen it. He had been sent out to fetch this and that, and forced to make numerous cups of strong tea. He would curse the kettle each time he had to flick it on. Sleeping on his two-seater couch that cut a foot off his frame left him with a constant ache that chipped at his neck. If he had to watch one more afternoon relationship TV programme where a woman with less teeth than a baby, with one eye looking at camera six while another looked for cobwebs on the ceiling, and long tits sitting at her feet like shopping bags, yet had three men fighting over her like she was Godiva, he was going to do himself in.

"Jesus Christ woman! Don't ever become a carer. Fucking Shipman would use you as his idol."

Joe-Ryan could cry in cooking frustration. He needed out for some fresh air, quiet and distance to calm down over his battling relatives. He was relieved to be going back to work tomorrow, and that was his 'get out of jail free' card. Work was open twenty-four hours, so it would be ideal for a few hours to de-stress.

"Joe-Ryan, was that you?" his mother called on hearing the front door slam, ignoring the small lake of water leaking through to the downstairs flat's kitchen.

*

The last time that Mindy had had a man in her kitchen was when her boiler broke last year pissing water all over her new slate grey floor like a fountain. The year before that was a petty burglar, and the year before that was an inflatable man for Sheila's pre-hen drinks. Now, there was a man in her kitchen - one that had been invited and was happy to stay. He was chopping vegetables and throwing them into a pan with no coordination as a child does with their Lego blocks into a toy box, but the smell was divine. The presence of a man in her lovely home oozed a warm and welcoming feeling, and it felt right and overdue.

Chad Rise had decided to cook her a slap-up meal in the comfort of her home; being inside played out his plan safer. Mindy relaxed on the soft couch with a glass of prosecco bubbles galore, fizzing away as a strawberry deep-sea dived to the bottom. She enjoyed being looked after. It had been a long time, failing to remember the last. Chad Rise was a whizz in the kitchen. He didn't even need to ask Mindy where things were; it was like he had x-ray vision and could see where everything was. Either that or he had been here before, Mindy joked. E.T failed to show grace towards the celebrity visitor and gave a burning hiss of dissatisfaction. Alex never got a hiss.

E.T sloped off outside into the garden as Mindy apologised, not noticing Chad closing the door locking her beloved cat out. Thankfully for Chad, E.T had not mastered the art of speaking and was safe with his secret past - the real reason for him being in Mindy's cute kitchen, cats have six senses and all of ET's worked fine. Chad got underway with his cooking. It felt surreal, as if his life had gone full loop in this kitchen. It unnerved him, and the reaction from the cat had given him a slight cold sweat. Chad Rise had to keep his cool for just another hour; it would be worth the award.

Joe-Ryan loved the peaceful state that the majestic manor forever existed in, as if time never moved on, days never aged to night and no resident's seemed to die come to think of it. Despite the age of the residents and their illnesses it was calm chaos, he found, sitting in the grand lounge relaxing, peace rushed at him like a dog hard for its owner returning. The best bit was that there was no noise from Granny C or his wayward mother tormenting his ears, piñata his normally peaceful home with explicit caring not bats. The lights dimmed created a twilight state of light, relaxation, moths felt to drowsy to flock, only one resident sleeping in the armchair by the open fire with not even a snore. Unbeknown to him, poor Alf had passed away.

Joe-Ryan sat with only his thoughts for company with the gentle crackling of the orange fire in the background silhouette reds, yellows and ambers danced on a wooden stage of a fireplace. The red and orange long flames waved reminding him of Mindy, beautiful Mindy. Mindy was the type of woman you wanted to marry after all of the fooling around with floozy flings and humping away with hoes. Mindy could be the one to instantly banish any behaviour as such away into your past. The thing was, he didn't have the confidence to ask Mindy out for a date - a proper one, not a plastic cup filled with lukewarm tea in a hospital canteen as bright as most of the doctors. Mindy had asked him, but they had never gotten around to arranging a date as Joe-Ryan choked on a shortbread in disbelief that she wanted to date him, dam shortbread. Then his mother had come screaming into the canteen with a worried rush that got Joe-Ryan and Mindy to their feet within a heartbeat second, with Aoife shouting *'she's alive!'* as if Granny C had been pronounced dead on arrival now Frankenstein.

Granny C raved that it was not her iron levels, but a premonition so strong that it had floored her. Obviously, Aoife told Joe-Ryan to ignore his Granny C and said that she was talking doolally from the bump to her head and had he seen his Granny C's purse, rooting under pillows, the hospital bed. Yet she constantly repeated that the premonition was about the biggest power of all: love. But love for whom? His Granny C had been walking down Oxford Street, the most popular shopping street in the world. Anyone could have hit her with the power of fortune. Maybe it had been a lone pigeon, terrorist or celebrity, he humoured her.

He sat, just himself and his thoughts, until a sweet voice interrupted. "Can I sit?" said a soft voice, warm like honey with a dash of spice.

"Of course, please," pointing to an armchair and watching the woman take a seat, her dressing gown loud with bright flowers patterned all over and with the thickness of a polar bear; two odd slippers lost none of their comfort on her feet.

"What's troubling you?" Her face made old by age, but not by the stress of life. Her eyes were bright and wise, and her smile engaging, warm, and familiar - even as if he had seen this smile in a younger version of herself. Her question of genuine concern acted like a pulley and pulled out what was troubling him.

"It's a girl." Such a cliché.

"Why does that not surprise me?" taking a sip of a cup of refreshing herbal tea that she had brought with her, knowing her extensive wisdom taught by life would be helpful to this young, beautiful chap.

"I think I love her." He blushed, glad that the dimness of the room hid it. Love, knew Mindy for a month at that, but Joe-Ryan knew it was more than lust, infatuation, was the fire release monoxide fucking his senses up? Smile pinned it up like a banner across his face, love.

"Have you told her?" the old woman asked, smiling.

"No, she's out of my league." The realisation of this rugby tackled his heart and floored it - the reason why there was no official date set. The reason hit hard; she was out of his league, and she had simply asked out of politeness, *you fool* his ruthless insecurity told him ripping the love banner from his smile into pieces throwing it with no grace he imagined people throwing confetti at their wedding into his handsome face.

"Nobody is out of anyone's league. Love is a conqueror. There are no boundaries it can't break. No race that it can't bring together, no colour does it see. It doesn't judge - it allows whores to marry. Love only sees love. It can't be tortured to weaken; it can't be told what to do. You simply *love*. Bring back chivalry and go win your woman. For life without love is, well..." The sip of the tea gave her a break. Joe-Ryan stared, waiting for the woman to reveal the big secret of love.

"What you looking at?" she asked, confused as to why this extremely beautiful man was staring at her like she had two heads.

"Oh, I am sorry. Just waiting for you to..."

"Don't be waiting for me to tell ya, sunshine. I've got fucking dementia - you've got no time to wait at all!" With that one sentence, Joe-Ryan rushed out, speed blew the warming fire out. Poppy sipped her herbal tea, thinking that the young man would be ideal for that Mindy who visited.

New York

Maria sat on the posh balcony of the plush hotel with a glass of champagne and bowl of ripe strawberries. Only the vivid stars above twinkled, shining serenely mimicking paparazzi flashes - or drone lights flying, Maria mused. Maria was dressed casually, off guard from the paps who ruthlessly tried to have her papped looking rough. She was always chic and perfect, and it would only digress rumours of a troubled romance with any unflattering photographs. To dress down gave her pleasure, like a glass of cold wine to a mother whose insomniac kids are finally asleep.

Maria had enjoyed Sally's company in the week or two of employing her to walk Roxy. She had grown to like the woman. She was fun, feisty and a great storyteller. Her hilarious disasters at dating made her sides split, and she told Sally that writing a sitcom about her experiences would be a big seller. Chad was away working on location in London for a few days, and it was nice to have company - female company - tonight. Strangely, she hadn't thought of him once this evening.

"So how do you like New York?" filling up Sally's half empty flute dropping a strawberry in. She noticed that Sally's skin was fresh with a new glow, but the scar red and dominant still. A goose grey flannel blanket wrapped around her more for comfort than warmth made Sally appear cute and vulnerable to Maria.

"It's so different to L.A. The speed, the people, and wow, the buildings - so beautiful. And Central Park...oh my gosh, so wonderful, being looking for a dogging group just for another reason to go." Tasting sparkling wetness excited her taste buds, and beat salty spunk any day sipping the fresh champagne, both Sally and Maria laughed.

"Do you mind if I ask you something, please, Sally?" Maria rarely delved into people's lives too much; she hated being nosy, strawberry sacrifice its juicy ripeness to her mouth. She herself experienced ruthlessness from the media wanting to know all about her, but she was intrigued at how such a sweet woman had acquired such a nasty burn to her face. It was so tender that it looked recent, and she wanted to know who had hurt Sally.

Sally had blossomed of late, as if the spring sun flourished life not only in the park, but also in Sally. Her blonde hair was glossier, her skin was brighter, and her eyes - that always caught Maria's - seemed to have shed a little darkness and gained a glimpse of the light. A little weight gave comfort to her frame rather than a coke habit.

"Of course you can, Boss." They both laughed with Sally's nickname for Maria. Maria was breath-taking; her thick hair casually tossed up into a scrunchie, and her skin was free to breathe from suffocating make-up. Maria was beautiful - simple. How Chad could fuck behind her back was madness. The image of Maria naked flushed Sally, who had to hide in her wine glass pretending to fish for her drunk strawberry at the bottom.

"What happened to your face?" Instantly the atmosphere became stiff and uncomfortable like waiting for the DNA result of your real father on a chat show, camera six zoomed in on your face for your reaction. Sally was taken aback with the question and forgot her daydream of Maria converting into her birthday suit calling for her to join. She was now reminded of the real reason she was in New York, revenge. "Sorry, Sally. I didn't mean to make you feel uncomfortable."

"No, it's fine. It's a reminder not to get involved with a man who likes to smoke in bed." *Moreover, rimmed, sucked off and fucked with a stiletto heel.* Sally wanted to keep her job, so she decided to keep quiet on confessing that she had fucked the boss's fiancé, the drunken strawberry finally hooked mashed by her molars easily Chad's brain if Sally went ahead with her idea of a hammer attack .

"That's sad." Maria fell quiet.

"It could be worse." Sally knew it could be worse - she could be dead from the blaze.

"Yeah, you could get raped on your engagement night as your fiancé watched." Maria's black secret slipped out with straightforward ease better than a new born from the womb of a mother of eight who needed the child out before the weekend to claim welfare for the Monday. Suddenly it dawned on her that she had finally confessed to the sordid night; her pretty hand flew to her mouth in shock, slapping her for her stupidity and tasting a hint of blood with the hit. "Ignore me, it's the champagne." The weak laugh fooled nobody - certainly not an ex-hooker who had been the base for many a man's beatings and dirty use. She watched Maria trying to discreetly dab the blood with a napkin.

"Maria, that is awful." Her arms were on her shoulders in a flash, her words high and stunned. "Have you spoken to anyone about this?" Sally's voice was tender and light as if the confession was sleeping and she did not want to wake it again.

"Who is going to believe me? I mean, who gets raped in the same room as their future husband while he is watching? Doesn't sound concrete, does it?" The tears were at her eyes already.

"Listen! Listen to me." Sally took the tone of a woman who talked sense and experience, cupping Maria's wet face in her hands. "If any man forces you to participate in a sexual act against your will then it is rape." She wiped away Maria's cold tears and leant in closer. "And if Chad sat and watched for some sexual fucking kink, he's just as guilty. You understand?" she spoke slow, as if Maria was foreign. Sally knew that she should confess there and then - it was the ideal moment - but Sally decided to try using this to her advantage. The hooker had not left her completely, yet. "You need to tell the police and get that bastard done for it - both of them." Sally wanted Chad to be ruined and this would be it, she thought, sipping her champagne to douse the rising anger.

"I can't report it, it's been too long now and the media will make me out to be a jealous bitch." The reality of it made her cry aloud, stars dimmed in mourning respect.

"Fuck the media!" Sally blasted. "You're fucking Maria Dieppe, one of the most famous and beautiful women in the world!" Tears filled her eyes. Sally had never had to deal with gossip sites attacking you, abusing your looks, waging war on your weight, and ruining your relationships all for column inches. It was exhausting being in the public eye. Internet trolls talking disgusting things about you, and having comediennes using you as the foundation of their jokes. Sometimes it was a hell of a lot easier just to be quiet in the world of celebrity. Sally had once received a threating text, but to be fair, the landlord was at the end of his tether with her late rent. So, she was immune to media mauling.

"It's not as easy as that. I have no strength to go it alone." She looked up - fucking gorgeous - with wet eyes raining mascara down her face.

"You're far from alone. You've got me." The squeeze of her hand told her this woman meant every word. Maria hesitated; she longed to put her lips on Sally's. Lately the feelings she felt towards Sally had transitioned from professional to wanting to be personal. Maria was a woman who could appreciate another woman's beauty, compliment a dress or praise a hot body, but that's as far as it went - never sexual. The arrival of Sally changed that.

Maria found herself replacing Chad in dreams of her future with the lead role played by Sally. Was she so sick of men hurting her that her brain was forcing her to walk over and bat for the other team, free from the dangers of men? On one occasion while she bathed, she wondered how Sally would feel to touch and taste, the soap suds smooth across her wet skin as if this was a taster of Sally's graceful touch. The smell of white lilies candles burning around her, refreshing and calm, she imagined as Sally's scent, arousing herself so much that she gave herself the best orgasm ever using her fingers to penetrate her. She had slept like a baby that night. The idea gave way to possibility and a sense of raw reality.

"There's something else we can do." Sally lowered her blonde head cutting out any listening ears, knowing that Roxy asleep at her feet wasn't an issue.

"What?" She was disappointed not to kiss Sally. Her urges for Sally were growing rapidly and fast, just like a fashion trend at fashion week.

"Revenge" Sally raised her glass, feeling disappointed not to have kissed Maria. Of late, something was building up each day towards Maria and Sally knew what it was. She had experienced it with her father, and that feeling was love.

"Revenge is a bitch." Maria's glass clicked against hers both girls popped a strawberry the sweetness matched the sweetness they felt, and the ever watchful stars sparkled a little bit brighter.

Roxy woke up, gave a shake to wake her golden fur and barked with the cheering noise, giving the revengeful ladies some much needed inspiration.

London

He made sure the front door was unlatched if the plan was to work better, and he needed to hurry up and get Mindy to the bedroom. Dinner eaten in a jovial mood, he enjoyed her banter as always. Maria lacked banter. She never used to, but since the night of their engagement things had swiftly changed, and she became a little withdrawn, sensitive to sex, forever rushing off to the bathroom once finished instead of embracing, wrapped in each other's arms. With Mindy tonight had brought up sweet memories of his old life, before all the magical surgery and modelling clay style reconstruction to give him his luxury Hollywood life. Could he reverse it all?

He knew he treated Maria badly, but his ravishing hunger to succeed and become the world superstar he knew he could be took the driver's seat on his road to success, ignoring anyone he ran over and left as roadkill. Chad never used to be so callous towards women; he certainly couldn't blame his own mother, who had showered him with so much love and affection his bones got a cold. His summer holidays had always been a joy, remembering that he had been allowed as much ice cream as his little stomach could handle. He was allowed to watch films until he heard owls, and spent many days at the beach until the tide chased them off.

Maybe he should visit them?

He knew they were still alive, but he knew they were mourning his death - well, his old life. A sick idea tempted him to spring his surprise on them, but it would definitely kill them off. His dad's heart had always been fragile.

Greed and power were the reasons for his negative attitude towards women and life. The question of why women stalked him with their insecurities or were clingy, as if his heart was a cliff face and they were hanging on for dear life, pissed him off. Moaning replaced oral, frumpiness replaced fun, and staying in replaced shagging like teenagers. He took another beer from the fridge and sat on the couch waiting for Mindy to change. All women were good for was fucking and cleaning. He was impressed with his idea of spilling some ice cream on her top, forcing her to change and hoping that the vast amount of wine he had given her would encourage her to put something a little sexier on, wine courage working in his favour. He knew that Mindy fancied him, yet he also knew that Mindy was not a woman who opened her legs fast. Imagining fucking her, he wondered if it would feel the same. Would his dick fit as it did? He wondered if she had changed in the sack. He needed to rain, no torrential rain the Chad charm on soon create a flood, drown her, her to beg him to save her, help her breath, seeing as his partner in crime would be arriving within the hour checking his watch.

"Sorry if I took too long." Mindy came in little unbalanced on her bare feet, her focus uneasy, she swayed. God, she was drunk. Mindy was fortunately a woman who preferred comfort to crotchless knickers. Fleecy pyjamas gave Chad the impression it would be easier to undress a homophobic cage fighter for sex than Mindy in this get up.

"No, you were not too long," he lied. The evidence of three empty cans of lager on the kitchen table told of the true time he had waited. Mindy came closer and sat next to Chad, bumping into him as her balance was affected by drink, making her look cute and clumsy. He smelled so sweet - a familiar scent too, she closed her eyes the smell sketched an image of a life where Mindy and Chad lived happily ever after using Mindy's daydream of a life with a partner as a life model. Chad was impatient. His plan had started well - swoon, wine and dine, get her in the bedroom, fuck her stupid, then leave with what he came for. Due to Mindy dressing like she was about to watch a Netflix marathon with an overweight husband of twenty years and not a Hollywood star, he would have to be a little more forceful and upfront, easy.

"You should put something a little sexier on," he said stroking her earlobe, knowing that she loved it. Feeling her lean in at the soothing stroke of his fingers collapsing to his touch, it was working "something easier to slip out of" he added.

His soft, killer lips brushed against her neck as he whispered. Mindy did not know if she was wet with lust, or if she had accidentally let a bit of piss out due to being drunk and having a weak bladder but on that touch of his lips something broke. Her head started to descend towards his strong shoulder, and he gently kissed her warm cheeks. Suddenly, Mindy felt his lips on hers, and my God, they were some lips. Full and warm, they pressed against hers, giving life like defibrillators. She pushed her lips onto his - familiar, too. Why was this man so familiar but so different at the same time? She thought she was deluded by wine, but sometimes drunk-thinking makes the sanest sense. Could it be? No, it couldn't...Shit like that only happens in movies. She imagined just for fun that it was Edward but in a whole new body, kinda like Mrs Doubtfire. She chuckled with her drunken thought. "What's so funny?" he pulled inch away his breath warm on her lips. "Nothing" her eyes didn't even open, her eyelids didn't want light to be part of what she was thinking, she lingered from the long missed touch of man.

His kiss travelled through her body, waking her sleeping soul the way summer sun melts the frosty ground allowing summer to grow from the ground. Allowed life to grow and inside Mindy was growing, growing with lust, growing with confidence Chad and she could have something meaningful, too drunk on lust she didn't see growing towards her, danger. Retaliating, she clasped her hand around to push him closer and Chad knew he was in.

"Let's go to the bedroom," he said leading her towards her bedroom - he still knew where it was - glancing back to see E.T hissing at the kitchen window, his spit furiously splashing the pane at what was about to happen to his lovely owner. Chad's smirk was bone-chilling.

The silent treatment would make even the hardest of criminals confess. No matter what Alex did, cooked, bought, wore or booked, Troy barely engaged in conversation. He had been refusing any invitation for sex, settled for a weak wank. Surely he was not that mad at her for being escorted out? To be honest, Alex had every intention of staying at the restaurant - drunk or not - but management had made her leave. She was fed up to death of being made to feel like she was the worst human ever for enjoying an evening with friends for his culinary talent. She stretched out her desirable legs on the couch so that her feet ended up in Troy's lap, where normally he would rub her petite feet with his big strong hands to relax her, and they would travel up her legs until they hit the Lourdes of her body, her vagina and anything limp or small, swelled and grew came alive they ended up both naked and shagging on the couch, Alex put the couch professional cleaned before morning after pill. Instead, he abruptly lifted her petite feet up as if they were putrid and foul, got up and walked over towards the fridge as if her feet were objects of disgust. Alex had had enough. She was a Scorpio; she wore her mouth on her sleeve.

"For fucks sake Troy I cannot apologise any more than I have. So, this silent treatment is too much for me, so I'm going to go to-" she stopped, not for dramatics, but because she couldn't believe that she was going to say this, could kick herself for not picking up bottle vodka, stiff drink was needed for this rare revelation, desperate times and all. Taking a deep breath, she said: "-Carol's tonight." Never in all of their relationship had she threatened to go to her mum's in Southport. Alex rather go to Syria in a bikini made from the American flag than go back to her mum's. Troy span around hearing bones crack on the threat of her leaving, never had the idea of her leaving ever polluted the air felt wrong didn't sit well with the lush interiors of the apartment. The sentence stalled his heart, slammed on his emotion he felt them crashing out of his chest. Alex fretted that maybe he was going to help pack her bag with his exorcist spinning around, due to excitement, the promise of her leaving; she prayed it was to stop her. She loved her mother, but spending the night in a single bed still decorated by seven year old pony mad Alex, seven semi-stray cats and portraits of the last four popes watching her sleep, she prayed he asked her not too His face was white, and he knew that if he didn't tell her, he would lose her.

"Alex, I need to tell you something." Taking a deep breath, he told her the real reason why he had been acting so distant - from behind the fridge door, just for safety.

*

The door simply opened as planned; she went in easier than a hot knife through butter. The home was extremely beautifully decorated, and it felt homely and loved. The sad fact that her own extravagant home lacked love failed to chip away at her dead heart. Saffron was not here to pick up interior design tips - she was here for her ring, and the ring was in this fucking house somewhere. After seeing Chad about the ring, he mentioned the redhead he had bumped into on the landing. Saffron knew that the redhead had connections to Maud, and that she had the ring - somewhere in this fucking house. Seeing the living room empty, she gathered that Chad had managed to take Mindy off to the bedroom to fuck. She felt a faint pang of jealousy stab her, but she brushed it aside as a water infection and went into the kitchen.

Where the fuck was the ring? The place was spotless; everything had a place, apart from four bottles of empty wine and lager cans holding a private party in the kitchen. Drying plates watched from the draining board like children did from upstairs at a parent's house party. Even the cat basket was free from a single hair. Saffron liked cats, but she was yet to meet E.T who would change all that. Passing the bed of the killer three legged cat, she failed to check the cat bed.

Saffron started to look in drawers and cupboards anywhere and everywhere. She looked under cushions and in cupboards. The bitch must have suffered from OCD - everything was placed with military precision. Moving silently with experience, she left no mess or anything out of place. Certainly not with Delia; the city pigeons had seen to that. The fear that the ring was in the wrong hands kept her awake, draining her limited waking energy. She could physically feel herself dying, and she needed to find it to keep safe her secret. Saffron had fended off her plenty of enemies in her life - and even killed a few times too - so this thieving broad was no match. She had been powerful and rich back in the day. Murder was easy; once you had murdered it was like riding a bike, you never forgot. The missing ring was killing her with stressful worry. If it was to fall into the hands of the law, as a powerful woman she would be a dynamite catch for the police to arrest and jail. Saffron adored luxury, so sharing a bunk bed with a cellmate sobbing about leaving her children for a gram of crack was not how she planned to live out her last years. Unfortunately for Saffron, she was about to meet her match as he came in through the front door behind her.

*

The fumbling down on the bed made Mindy giggle. She could feel that she was in the bedroom her thick grey throw seemed to hug her more than normal, feeling sexy and lustful and merry, but she was not completely paralysed by the wine to know Chad Rise was being a little forceful.

"Let's kiss a bit more," she said, pulling her neck off the bed to kiss his luscious lips again. She made contact with them, but this time they were stern and harsh like she had touched the thorn and not the rose bud. She felt him muttering something about *fucking knots* and he was pulling a little too hard on her bottoms, clinging hard to her hips refusing to pull down. He was naked already, and she felt the heat from his hard-on pushing on top of her pants. One hand held both of her hands above her head while her body felt completely heavy and immobile, froze by something one glass of wine to many to realise it was fright. Mindy was confused. She wiggled, trying to halt the rough action of pulling her pants down - but the wiggle was stronger in her mind than in practice, and let her down. Chad started to kiss her neck extremely roughly, and the activity of it made trying to dodge them hurt her neck from the twisting side to side like a window wiper wanting to wipe away the hard kisses raining down from Storm Chad.

"You want this, don't you Moo?" he spat, his once immaculate hair now straggly seemed to want to strangle her, his eye turning bloodshot as his anger panted. Mindy's mouth was too dry to answer from the combination of wine and her fear that she was about to be raped. Word no vanished from her tongue, abandon her intellectual vocabulary moment she have needed it more than ever. *Where are you cunt?* Inner voice bawled, her absolute panic deafened any reply. She would never ever take the word No for granted ever again if she survived. Chad was a man possessed. Tearing her pyjama top in two halves, her bare breast was exposed, free for his taking. He roughly grabbed it massaging it hard as if he was trying to find a lump. Suddenly it clicked. Chad Rise was not the Chad Rise he now was with his Hollywood smile and film star looks. Something inside Mindy, beneath her wonderful heart, inside her kind soul, knew she had met Chad Rise before he was Chad Rise; it was 'Him', Edward.

"You like that, yeah?" asking her the question and taking it upon himself to reply on her behalf. Mindy couldn't believe this, how 'Him' had managed to become this star that ladies lust after. Would they be lusting after him now seeing how animal he was? Mindy couldn't think of a species that committed rape. Turning her face, there it was next to her head, the biggest clue after the warning sign in America, the story of abuse from his mother - who Mindy knew as an adorable and loving mother-in-law to be at the time. The bastard crooked little finger. *You stupid bitch,* it roared. *Mindy scream do something* fear took her voice away - no rapist liked a vocal victim, did they, her fear sided with Chad with its gagging of Mindy. Mindy fixated on the little crooked finger. All she could think was that he was about to ruin her life all over again as he grabbed her face and turned it towards him.

Mindy's tears formed a barrier from her sight in an instant to protect her from witnessing the evil look on his face. Chad was going to fuck her whether she liked it or not, and there was nothing she could do, feeling her helplessly tried to get out of his grip, she would weaken, he would wait, they all weakened in the end, experience reminded him, patted praise on his back for his patience. She was powerless. She wanted it; he knew that she did, just maybe not at this time. He was a man possessed. His rough rubbing of her tit left it red with tracks of where his wandering hands had been against the white of her fighting skin, deep and red he imagined them to act like cave drawings for future men to who slept with her to read, indication he was here first, this image made him delivered his mouth to her nipple. Her nipple red raw, his teeth marks dented in sending pain warning for the rest of her helpless body it was not over yet. His spare hand was sadly winning the battle of pulling her pants down, seeing the band of her sport knickers appearing, terrified. It would not be long until penetration; his hard dick was eager to protest, pumping hard into her, his purple tip wet as a lion's mouth at the fresh kill of a carcass wanting to deposit his signature foul semen, his two condom rule didn't even enter his criminal head.

"Please stop." She manged, though it was weak in sound, it was strong in meaning any form of the word 'no'. Even a simple shake of the head or a cry should have been enough but it went ignored, hearing him breathing rapidly, his hot breath encouraged by drink slapped her hard, hitting her telling her to shut the fuck up. His dick punching at the barrier her knickers had created in a last attempt to keep him out, the pants started to lose."Please, no, please don't do this." She cried. She never noticed the darkness of the room until now. All her beautiful furniture turning away, how could they witness her being raped? Her fur throw tried to wrap her up created a cocoon of protecting, add a barrier for Chad to get throw in hope he gave up but it failed, proof was the cold air on her bare legs. The solid darkness and protecting tears least promised together they wouldn't allow Mindy to see pictures of loved ones watching in on the horror from frames of love, memories, loyal they kept her blind, least they could do.Chad was immune to the word 'no' from women in this situation, deaf to their defending pleas - just like Claudia had struggled as he strangled the bitch dead in the cubicle of the bar, feeling thankful to have his Rolex returned. Women always said 'no' just before, but after the act they just stayed silent once they carried on with their boring lives. Chad could see the end soon, the pants slipping lower as their grip was lost on her hips, ginger pubes peeked over the elastic band to see if this nightmare was really happening, more came into view to see, indecent giveaway the bottoms were getting lower, losing, sickening fact they were coming off. No woman ever said 'no' to Chad, but karma and faith both knew a woman who would.

The noise from the room off to the kitchen indicated that Chad was having his wicked way with Mindy, who was either mute during sex, or asleep, or was kinkily gagged and making no noise. Saffron knew that Chad was a great fuck; he made her scream and cum in minutes.

The noise was a perfect blanket to mute the noise of the intruder as she rummaged through searching for the ring, but also perfect to mask the footsteps of the killer finally behind Saffron.

*

Joe-Ryan entered the posh street that was very different from his council-bought flat; it intimidated him more than any muscle head in the gym. God, Mindy was successful, seeing the slim house all polished and in neutral colours, the street lights lit, gave a glow against the brick of the houses in the darkling evening. The fact that these houses worked driveways showed their expensiveness. Tall trees in a symmetrical face off ran the whole length of the tidy street. An image of living here with Mindy and a few kids tugged at his heart. Karma prayed that he would hurry up and get to Mindy's front door before it was too late and her life changed for the worse, and her trust in men was smashed forever.

He slowly walked on. The idea of asking Mindy out for a drink, was diluting with each step, darkening with the evening the reality that she may laugh and say 'no', pitying his old school approach jumped in front of him stalled his footsteps until he stopped.

What the hell are you doing, man? his self-doubt spoke to him.

She's out of your league. I mean, look where she lives! You think she's going to want to shack up with a gypo like you? His lack of confidence chipped in, too. They were right - what could he offer her? A decent garden, probably pie and chips down at the local once a week. He sat on the wall and sighed loudly, rubbing his hands over his face in disbelief at what he thought was a genuinely good idea.

Silence stayed with him. He was only at least five doors away from her house; the saying '*so close, yet so far*' rang true if trees could talk *they shout hurry the fuck up*. He checked the time on his watch and realised that if he turned back now he could catch the last train home even grab few cans to drown his sorrows from Auntie Ali's Express Mini market.

He rose to his feet as a car pulled up on the driveway with an elderly couple in the front. The old lady - he assumed the wife - got out of the car and smiled a good evening to him. It allowed the song from the radio to filter into the street, and the words *'all you need is love'* grabbed Joe-Ryan by the shoulders and shook some sense into him. Joe-Ryan smiled; it was a sign from God. In that moment, it was now or never. Grabbing the old woman, he kissed her on the cheek and said, "Thank you!" He walked on towards Mindy's home. All you need is love, and that's what he could offer her in a wheel barrowful.

"What was that about, Mavis?" George saw the handsome chap kissing his faithful wife on the cheeks. Mavis was in shock, but touched by the kind gesture.

"Oh you know, George. Revenge is a bitch." With that simple sentence, she knew that all of George's affairs and secret love child would be crushed by that youthful kiss.

*

The taxi screeched into the road. The taxi man was delighted with the fare from the river to Notting Hill certainly take the weekend off based on this pricey fare alone. The beauty in the back of the car beat his normal boring rides of drunks and tourists. Ok, she was a bit rude knocking back any of his invitations to chat, but she was the ideal excuse to stalk his interior mirror.

"Here we are. That will be eighty-three pounds please," smiling his best 'I hope you leave a tip' smile. Alex flung a two fifty notes at him and ran out of the taxi in a flash, not even closing the door behind her. Alex knew that Mindy had been holding back the fact that she had found Troy in a situation where his penis was being held hostage by that slut Debbie, and knew all about the heartache of what infidelity caused to the soul of a woman. Alex needed to let Mindy know that she knew about it all and to thank her best friend for it, but Alex needed to hurry up before her best friend became woman unrecognisable and hated men forever.

*

The cool air from the open window blew on her exposed vagina as if it was soothing her for the burning pain about to come, sadly indicating that her cotton pants had lost the battle. The dense heat of his breath burned her face as stinging tears made her skin raw as they ran down in speed.

"You're going to enjoy this," he promised. His evil smirk was heavy with delight and triumph; her body dead with disgust didn't respond *pretend to be dead* her numb body said, but she knew Chad fuck a dead body. How had she let this happen? How had she become a victim of rape in her own bed - a place so personal in her home, now violated by a crime that no woman should ever suffer?

Are you really that sad and lonely that you invited a rapist into your bed? It serves you right, you pathetic bitch. Her inner voice tried to make her take the blame always did like a jealous rival; it was her body's way of trying to cope with what was happening.

All because he's a famous guy. At least it will be a story to tell that you were raped by Chad Rise. If he had not been not pressing down on her crushing her lungs she would have laughed with sheer disbelief.

Mindy, this is not your fault. Fight back! Her self-respect teamed up with self-worth, but it was too late. Mindy had given up the fight, accepted what was to come, and hoped and prayed hard he delivered the punishment fast.

The bed normally offered comfort from a long day - her beautiful bed she had been inspired to buy when in New York. The bed had nursed her many times when she was ill, had held slumber parties with Alex, and Sabrina when she had been younger and not so scissor-happy. All she could think now was how much the bed was a bastard to be allowing this. She would do anything to distract herself from what was happening.

Why did I have to drink all that wine? The sensible part of Mindy managed to push through the hordes of emotions fleeing her under-attack body. Why my kitchen and not a restaurant. *Too late now sweetheart* she felt Chad soul whisper into her ear.

Since when was it a crime to enjoy a wine in your own home? Frightened mind screamed.

You have done nothing wrong, her conscience shouted. Her half naked body shut down. Hoping to numb the life-scarring pain, her deleted mind raced trying to find anything to distract her, take her to a safe place before all this had happened.

Everyone she loved passed through her head in a sign of respect - her dear mother, Alex and Troy, Eric, and even Maud. How would this indecent incident affect him or her? Rape was like an atom bomb, spreading destruction outwards in crippling waves of devastation to all that were close. Again, Mindy was worrying about others before herself at a time in her life for once when she selfishly needed to think about herself.

Growing up fatherless, she failed to register appropriate male behaviour. Was it Poppy's fault? Or her father's, for not being in her life? Mindy ran a thousand questions through her head - anything to not register the true horror that she was experiencing at the hands of this handsome, cruel monster.

Mindy closed her eyes, the salty tears filling in the pools. An aching pain ripped through her head - it was her head's way of killing bad thoughts. She felt his longing to pierce her, just to know it was ending. All she hoped to God was that when he finished he did not kiss her. To feel his vile lips touching hers after his act of rape would kill her. It would tarnish her lips; she would never be able to kiss her mother on the cheek again with lips violated by a rapist, the cowardly fucking bastard, volcanic anger rose with furiousness speed, tried to flared up but doused out by tears it was too late to get angry. She would never know what it was like to live after this. Feeling the gap dissolving between them as he lowered himself towards her, she knew now and then that the life she once knew would be gone. She prayed that if God had mercy on her gentle soul, if he looked back on all of the good that Mindy had done in her life, and then Mindy herself would develop Alzheimer's like Poppy to be able to forget this awful, life destroying night.

His lips tried to touch hers; smelling strong lager burning a warning on her lips, she gagged to be sick and turned for the sickening kiss to land roughly on her cheek. She knew that trying to kiss her was a sick signal that he was about to enter her. She tightened every muscle that she had in her body. He was literally an inch from penetration, and his tip brushed against her pubic hair. *Not long now, Mindy*, she told herself. She would try to scream at least, but his hand got to her mouth before she could, and she knew that this was the end. She took a huge breath - her last before she was to be a rape victim statistic - then the breath to be released would be the first breath of a life of self-torture and indescribable upset. "Goodbye old Mindy, thank you and I love you" she tenderly whispered in the darkness of the room and the darkness of her old life.

The brutal weight disappeared with sudden ease pulled by the threatening words jumping on him "Get the fuck off her! "Hearing a heated tussle and hearing things smashed and toppling over in her bedroom as if hurricane had got inside, she wondered what was happening. Yet she still clasped her eyes shut tight, just in case it was a dream and Chad was still about to rape her.

"Mindy, it's me you're safe, you're ok." The voice belonged to Alex. She wondered again if her mind was playing tricks on her to coax her into a false sense of security. Maybe it was her mind's mechanism to cope with the brutal attack. Chad Rise was an actor - was he mimicking her best friend's voice as another weapon in his assault? "Please, Moo. Open your eyes - you're safe now. It's me, Ape."

Mindy weakly answered, "You're lying, stop it." Her heart-breaking cry was hard to distinguish between joy and fear. To see Mindy so afraid tore Alex's heart in two, and the tears rolled down her own face for her best friend so hot that they stung into her soft skin. Mindy was paralysed; her mind had put her into a realm of fantasy where it was safer to keep her eyes closed and wait for the piercing hot pain to burn her body - yet it was not coming.

"Please, Moo! Open your eyes, it's me." Alex gently kissed her tight face as if she landed Sleeping Beauty the kiss to wake her. Mindy smelled the famous perfume on her friend. Slowly, the restricted skin around her eyes relaxed. Her perfectly groomed eyebrows lifted and stretched out their ache, and tears rained down painstakingly revealing her beautiful eyes to a tear-stained Alex.

"Alex!" Mindy sprang up and threw her arms around her best friend, her saviour - the woman who had saved her from spiralling into depression and losing her faith in love, and attempting an overdose. The two friends held on tight without an ounce of air between them. Suddenly Saffron burst into the bedroom raging like a banshee, her nose dripping from the slap Alex had delivered knocking her away from the bedroom door.

"Where the fuck is my ring? You little peasant whore" Throwing a glass lamp over towards the wall behind them in a furious flare, shattered glass rained down sharp shards on them as if Zeus threw lightning bolts. She launched towards Mindy who screamed, terrified. Alex jumped up and sent another mighty slap to Saffron's face sending the bitch backwards into the grand dressing table behind her; she hit it and fell with sheer force. Hearing a crack in her hip she crumbled to the floor, defeated. Or was she? If Saffron had not been in such a rage, she would have found the glamorous dressing table that she had been looking for - for six decades - right behind her.

She jumped up, ignoring the searing pain in her hip raging angrily, warning her old body not to stop her, it obey allowed her movement. This time, a dressed Chad burst back into the bedroom with a cut on his handsome cheek waving a big knife manically. A wildness in his eyes turned his ice blue eyes black, blinding him of any sense, a look so evil only death would bring back sight. Glad of reinforcements, Saffron's smile reeked of evil as it spread across her face with a sinister idea; if murder was the only way then so be it, knowing Chad would be the one serving the time if caught. Both Alex and Mindy froze. Chad stood there, his eyes wolf hungry. Who would he slice up first - the sexy brunette? He owed the bitch Alex a wound or two remembering the cracked ribs she had given him as a departing gift that afternoon. Or, sad dim Mindy? Saffron stood by his side empowered by his manic waving of the knife. They knew it; this was their time to die, holding each other. This was it. It was the ending of their lives. No more heroes' coming to save them.

"Mindy thank you for being my best friend ever," Alex whispered hugging her best pal for past twenty five years. The laughs, the holiday's, the fun, drunken drama all waved from her memory on the bus leaving her mind. Aging together in a nursing home a garden full of wonderful rose while drinking wine in the afternoon heckling the young and how they waste it, recalling tales of their own youth to nurses, Alex shed a tear.

Mindy was so choked with raw emotion that she could only stuttered, "You too Ape."

"Hand over the ring you fucking sluts, or I'll chop the both of you up" swinging the large knife at them and missing Alex by life-changing inches. Alex rose ignoring the dangerousness of the deadly situation, but Mindy pulled her back. They needed a miracle, and before Mindy had even finished her prayer, out of nowhere a ginger blur flew past Chad's head and attached itself to Saffron's face like a ginger oxygen mask. Saffron screamed in high pain, trying to pull the crazy cat from her face as it hissed. It clamped its razor-sharp teeth into her face, drawing blood. She fumbled backwards, and in a second, she disappeared out of the open window. E.T had finally got his prize prey.

This distracted Chad Rise for enough time for him to take a cold spot on hit on his head from a terracotta stone flowerpot. It crumbled as he fell to the floor with a deadly thud, as compost became ashes on his beautiful face and few tulips hit his body thrown in mourner style. As he fell he gave light to Joe-Ryan, who looked a little battered with his top torn slightly and a cut bleeding from his chin.

"You ok, girls? Sorry about throwing your cat, not really the friendliest of cats is it," he said, running his hands through his sleek black hair, his apology cute and lifesaving. E.T returned meowed from the snow white glossed window ledge licking his only front ginger paw with a 'job well done' kind of lick: no one was terrorising Alex apart from him, he really said. All Alex and Mindy could do was release a mongrel breed of hysteric cries of joy and blessed laughter at Joe-Ryan and E.T, their life saving, restoring faith heroes.

Two Months Later

Maria relished the glowing attention the recent million-pound wedding to Chad Rise had brought, whose new film a global box office smash, ranked him with a few million pound and world fame. She had grown like a sunflower in all the glorious attention, big, bold and demanding attention for its beauty. His already out of control ego was singing from the roofs of Tinstletown, all the magazines ran his antics each week in the issues, Chad nothing but a show off prick, but a show off prick in demand and a money maker of film. The glamorous wedding jam-packed with the Hollywood elite was covered in all of the major magazines, Lush did the dress, superstar R&B queen did the entertainment, and Testino did the pics, no one ate at celebrity weddings. They had been showered in a monsoon of media attention, enough to make them both worldwide famous a week later still. Her wedding dress was one of the most beautiful dresses ever made, propelling Maria into high fashion thanks to wedding dressmaker supreme Cassie Lush.

Maria kept one more belated honeymoon surprise for Chad, her husband for now. A surprise that he would never ever forget - nor the thirty million viewers from around the globe, hence her wearing her bondage style underwear set. Her curves restricted underneath seemed alive to get out, she oozed sex, made Chad's dick hard instantly, pre cum popped like champagne foam on her disrobing in their hotel room. He was glad that Maria was back to her sexy, confident self, like a wildcat under the sheets, and this afternoon he knew he was in for an erotic treat on his throbbing erection. He couldn't wait to be handcuffed to the bed, blindfolded and naked.

In character as the horny bored wife, he the handy man turned up to fix the plumbing and hers. Maria calmly handcuffed Chad and blindfolded him using his silk wedding tie, yet made sure that the blindfold hid none of his recognisable face, his square jaw dusted with stubble, instantly recognizable. She gagged him and handcuffed him to the big bed, naked, his body cut and ripped more than ever vibrated with anticipation for the sex. His new lion tattoo on his chest roared with excitement as his chest rose up and down, impatiently waiting for the foreplay to begin, the feast of the fucking.

"Come on Maria, I'm ready to blow," Chad called from the bed, his patience even shorter since they married, playing the part of kinky handy man Oscar worthy. His love of role-play made him stiff that his dick ached, and his erect cock was wet as if dribbling as whipped cream gave more height to his cock whipped around the base. It looked like clouds squirted around his thick base like Mount Olympus. He did have such a generous cock, and she was tempted to sit on it one more time for old time's sake - but, Maria resisted temptation. Temptation was a weakness, and Maria was no longer weak.

When Maria had mentioned one night over a steak dinner about the possibility of them making a sex tape, Chad was over the moon. Nearly choking on his steak cooked how he liked his blowjobs, well done. The gracious kiss he landed on her lips was more genuine than the kiss on their wedding day; sad reality left her with a cold sore, that painful weeping sore kill matched her heart. This confirmed her racy plan was solid. Knowing that once it was 'accidently hacked and leaked' - in others words, after he had sold it to a private investor - it would send his career even higher, Kim K style, but sadly not Maria's, thank fuck, she gloated. The camcorder was hooked up in the corner hidden like a spider gently behind a dream-catcher that Sally had made her in the little art classes she was attending down Brooklyn. Maria used it as a perfect cover up. She was looking forward to Sally giving birth; luckily it was not Chad's, and Sally said that there were not enough raffle tickets in L.A to find the real father. Sally had explained all about the scar, Chad's love of hookers, and coming to New York for revenge. Maria had been shocked, yet it did not stop Maria from marrying him - after all, she needed him for their big revenge.

Maria was ready. She switched on the tiny camera and it blinked red, letting her know that it was ready to film the most shocking sex tape in the history of celebrity and sex tapes to be streamed live. She went over towards the bedroom door making sure she was out of view and opened the door.

"Come in, girl," she whispered so low level of mime. All good sex tapes benefitted from a third, didn't they? The blonde was so eager to please she literally ran towards Chad in a blur and jumped on the bed in excitement. She started licking his balls and cock free of the whipped cream Maria lay on the base of his dick with the relief of a dieter hitting her target weight. She was not at all camera shy.

Chad Rise moaned with excessive delight. The vigorous, wet tongue was lapping at his heavy balls and dick speed of humming bird's wing, levitating his groin up and down, wanting to vanish the distance between the tongue and his cock meeting; it was heaven. Maria's smile was so wide that it cut her dimples up, reaching her temples. It took all her strength not to laugh. This was what being a wife was all about, making a husband happy. His ecstatic groans made her want to be sick. She tiptoed out of the bedroom in her six inch spike heels closing the hotel door behind her on her life of misery and her cheating cunt of a husband.

Chad Rise's harmful rule over her came to an abrupt end as he arched his broad back in sexual pleasure, giving himself to the God of sex as a human sacrifice. This revenge was killing dead any hot film career path he was on, as each second passed in shock it excessively burnt his lavish life to the ground never to 'Rise' again.

Maria had committed the ultimate revenge. She did this for the entirety of women he had ever hurt in his life, knowing that her multi-million-pound divorce settlement would get Sally her face back and she could afford the best plastic surgeons in Beverley Hills. Hearing Chad moaning in a sexual state of erotic delirium, fulfilling a lewd fantasy, he was blind to the disgusting reality. She wrapped her gorilla fur around her and walked away from the life of being a battered wife, muttering her mantra: *'revenge is a bitch'*.

"That's it baby lick those balls clean the way daddy likes it. You little sexy slut of mine" Just like an obedient blonde bitch who adored licking and adored Chad Rise more, her tongue raced all over his hard dick, Roxy his golden Labrador did just that in front of twenty million - and counting - shocked and disgusted viewers. Revenge, for Maria, was a bitch called Roxy.

Mabel's flat sold, and the hefty profits after the bidding war were split over a few charitable causes in New York; Super Soup the soup kitchen was given a million dollars. Saffron was here after a hidden break to dodge rumours of a face-lift and a rehab spell, hiding to heal her facial injuries from that fucking cat. Collecting a few of Mabel's belongings, she had come mainly for her jewellery and art collection worth thousands - this visit was completely selfish. The incident at Mindy's home was haunting Saffron to the point where she had hired a hit man to kill the bitch and bring her that ginger cat to boil alive, than she would eat it with pleasure.

This afternoon she was meeting said hit man to show him a picture of the target and give him the address. This taste of revenge had put a spring in her old step, dusted off skills form her young years. She declined to invite Lucas to visit this time; the faggot had recently got married to his boyfriend, and was honeymooning in Scotland of all fucking places. Saffron disagreed with same sex marriage - it was sickening and wrong, and an utter sin in her eyes for gay people to marry. However, she sent a nice vase to show good face though, knowing that Lucas would brag about it on social media.

The flat was eerily quiet and shadowed by closed curtains, and empty. The squatter's right dust was starting to thicken due to the neglect of life, coating all the rich possessions with a thin layer, trying to protect it all from Saffron. She passed on, hobbling around hating all of the bad taste of the décor, but hating more how the walking aid aged her. Pain sucked youth from her face-lifted face leaving a mask of chronic pain. Many designers did not want their flowing frocks on a cripple, so she had slipped from the fashion circles and was having to dress in last season's styles for now. The reminder of falling out of a window while a man-eating cat was strapped to her face was the furnace of hot anger in her sore body; she could literally feel the heat vaporising from her body as she touched her back, forgetting about the heat patch that Helena had applied.

She walked over in pain towards the giant portrait of Mabel that had been famously painted by a huge artist famous for his late night graffiti attacks to help the poverty-stricken community. Standing beneath, she looked up at the huge picture and looked hard into her dead sister's eyes; they still shone.

"You always were a stupid bitch. You honestly think I won't find that ring?" scolded at the painting. "Well, poor little Mindy will be in for a shock soon. Overwhelmed by grief she will simply hand over the ring before she is shot dead. No wonder your poor husband died of a heart attack, just to get away from you," she snarled venomously, followed up by a cracking laugh. Saffron decided that she would play little deadly games with Mindy before she was killed. So, Poppy was on her list to die too after a brief little visit to the manor home. A little suffocating would make it painless for Poppy, but extremely painful for Mindy. The handsome dark Irish man is next, shame Saffron wondered whether to fuck him first, last time she had Irish was in a liqueur and that slut Alex, and well Mindy would be forced to watch her bleed to death till the last drop of blood left her throat.

Saffron looked up once more and was again greeted with the huge, famous smile of Mabel, as if her stupid little sister wasn't listening to her threats. Saffron spat onto the grand painting with venom, yet Mabel's smile never faded even with the disgusting act. The spit slid down her beautiful face like a tear - was Mabel crying? Maybe she was shedding a tear for her old, evil sister or was it with joy, finally free. Saffron smiled. She had to get moving; she was meeting the hit man in less than an hour and she planned on fucking him too. In her head she was still desirable, ignoring the fact that there had been no returned calls from Reggie and the hitman was happily married. At the moment her hip hurt when she pissed, so accommodating a dick, ouch. Reggie seemed to have disappeared without a trace, annoyed Saffron when men disappeared on their own accord and not her instruction. Saffron whacked the portrait hard with the metal crutch; it had its uses.

"Goodbye." She turned to leave, but she felt a huge cloud of dark appear over her. Turning to see the cause of the darkening shadow in the home, she screamed with fright and a cry for mercy as Mabel's three-foot smile came towards her in slow motion. The portrait came away from the wall and all thirty stone of canvas, oil paints and real oak frame crushed screaming Saffron to death in an instant. Her single crutch peeking out like the ruby slippers in Wizard of Oz after the noise and dust settled, laid peacefully. Peace had been restored to the home; finally, the wicked witch was dead.

*

Three hours had passed and Saffron had failed to show up. The hit man sitting at the private members club in uptown New York cracked his knuckles impatiently, knowing that the time delay was a sure hint that his plan had worked. He picked up his large scotch and took a pleasurable sip, swirling the remainder in the bottom of his glass like a whirlwind of celebration. Distracted from his lonely company by a sudden whispering in the club, he raised his thick glass in a toast towards a good friend - a global superstar who had helped his dying son live a life long wish, Simone Delvin.

Looking fucking fabulous as always, Simone was glad that he had given her the tip off about Saffron's deadly deed. As long as Simone Delvin was on the planet, no one was going to harm kind Mindy.

A few dusty screws rolled around in her Hermes bag. Their days of holding a thirty-stone picture up were gone, able to retire in the luxury of this bag. They reminded her to happily promote Helena's new book *What the Scrubber Saw*, all about the dead bitch.

London

Debbie loved nothing better than the erotic sex-filled glances from the hot males in the gym. The workout heat from their lust became a heat wave rippling in her path; she was a snake, and snakes needed heat to live.

She faced jealous, envious stares from every woman - both fabulously fit and fucking fat - as she crossed the main weights studio towards the studio where the fitness classes were held, confident walk of predator across the Plaines. Failing to attack her with negativity, the snarls and glares bounced off her Lycra armour. Debbie was Venus with the attitude of Medusa and a sex drive higher than Lovejoy, feeding off both reactions from the sexes like photosynthesis to her fuckable, temple-worshipped body. Most visitors were male, and she needed their attention to feel alive. Attention had been sparse when she was younger, but now she controlled it, drenching herself in it as if it was golden shower, and she made sure she never went without attention again.

The sweaty aura of muscles being ripped and re-grown bigger, better and stronger, and bodies losing fat was a turn-on scent for her. She loved collaborating with the big bass beats of club music, creating ecstasy inside. Nothing beat a workout on her body and a workout on a cock, she thought to herself as she caught Brad's eye - he was one of the personal trainers who was deadlifting in the free weights, and a firm favourite of hers to bed. His cum always tasted of coconut, and that would be her cool down; she winked, he winked back rearrange his crotch. Debbie possessed the body to promote the gym gear that she wore, once featured on a glossy gym flyer for new members, and she was proof that hard work paid off. She was inspirational, if truth be told, but that is where the inspiration stopped.

She was off to a kettle bell class for an hour where you swung a bell of weight around to tone, strengthen and work up a hot sweat. Entering the bright studio and noticing she was late, all other members stared she loved the fact that she was disturbing the class and that all had to stop for her, eyes all on her, she got off on it. She positioned herself in the front as normal with the huge wall mirror; she knew that she was visible on the outside and that male members would be gathered and watching her like she was a killer whale at SeaWorld. She gave the reflection of what the red blooded males wanted to see, and she was happy. Tying up her blonde peroxide locks that were fresh from a retouch, the tightness pulled back about three years off her face. Her Botox was due that week.

An added bonus was knowing that Gordon, the hot, muscular Asian fire-fighter with one ball, was taking the space behind her. His sweat was nothing to do with the weight if the kettle bell, but brought on by his randy thoughts about what he would like to do to her pert arse with his surprisingly big dick.

She had made the effort today. She was wearing a tight crop top in danger red teamed with leopard print second-skin leggings, that when she bent over left little to the imagination. Being commando today, they showcased her accommodating clit, slight darkening damp patched show she was wet already to Gordon who would definitely fuck her, catching a glimpse through her exhibitionist sheer material. The failed night with Troy had hurt her pride a tad, but it just made her realise that on her next attempt she would need to lock the front door.

Another woman joined the class who Debbie had not seen before, cutting her from thinking of her next plan of bedding Troy and getting revenge on Mindy. Debbie was fixated on bedding him. It consumed her every waking hour, and she had watched *Single White Female* seven times that week she became an understudy. She understood the deranged pleasures that stalkers got; she was addicted to the idea of getting Troy. Debbie was a woman who got her man one way or another. She was a big game hunter, and Troy was the beast that she wanted to mount.

Debbie sought out any new woman in the gym like an Alpha wolf did with a trespasser in its territory, to see if they were competition to her crown or if they were comical - comical meant that they did not stand a chance, and this woman was pure comedy gold. Dressed in battered joggers and a neon hoodie with scruffy trainers looking like they smoked, her short, dry black bob was tatty and greasy but her face seemed familiar behind her thick glasses and braces. Debbie was too interested in her vain reflection to pay that little bit more attention that she needed to know that this woman was bringing revenge and dramatic results to her promiscuous life.

Some women excel at cooking like Nigella, never to break into a sweat, a curse word, nor cut a finger on an open tin of tuna. Others' child-rearing skills made it look like a breeze as they tackled politics in war-torn countries whilst wearing Versace and keeping their Hollywood hunk from thinking about their beautiful ex with great hair. Some women were so talented that they out-sold any Vegas concert with their octave notes killing any diva in the bath that came close to their crown. Other women got away with murder - made a career from murder, even - and this woman had spent all her career working for dangerous people. Therefore, she had picked up a few helpful tips in her time and enough deadly information to get away with murder if she really wanted too.

The workout music came on in big beats and fast techno vocals deafened the studio. Dane, the Swedish hunky instructor, started to show the fitness class the move with the kettle bell. "Lift it up and swing through your legs. Knees bent, and thrust!" His abundant thighs raised his Speedo short-shorts...another set to have banged against Debbie. Debbie was thrusting like she was trying to get her fanny to spit a tampon out with more power than what Dane should have used when pushing his cock in her. Unfortunately, the baggy woman stood in front of Gordon, Gordon sulked walking to the back.

The baggy woman swung with uncoordinated balance as a novice to the class would do. Every time Debbie bent over, the shading of her pubes fuelled her plan of revenge even more.

"Ten more left!" The instructor, who was yet to perform the moves himself, dabbed his forehead with a towel. The baggy lady found the rhythm, and after counting steadily to three, she let go of the twelve kilo kettle bell sending it with sheer force towards her intended target. Hitting the bullseye, she watched it hit Debbie right in the back of her tarty blonde head. The heavyweight force sent Debbie screaming and flying forward towards the shiny mirrors with such power that her pretty reflection smashed the mirrors - not due to being her ugly, Debbie was far from ugly even baggy lady agreed on this, but her artificial beautiful face went straight through, the mirrors shredding it to pieces with the ease of a lawnmower on grass.

The whole class screamed in horror as blood sprayed Dane's shocked face; Debbie's head acted like the tyre of a car going through a puddle. All were running in all directions apart from Debbie's, and chaos erupted as Debbie lay bleeding to death. Thick red blood poured into her blonde hair thick like conditioner, dying it red. Surrounded by smashed mirrors she looked at peace; she was extremely beautiful, like an Angel crashed through the windscreen of an airplane in a fatal collision. No one rushed to her aid - not even Gordon who was a fire-fighter and highly trained in first aid. Was it shock? Was it on purpose? Nobody really liked Debbie, and in her time of need, no one came. In her past plenty of men had come, but only inside her. Was this karma?

Remaining calm amongst the panic, the baggy lady left the exercise class without losing her breath or building a sweat. "Revenge is a bitch," she said, dumping her polystyrene wig that she had worn once as Thelma from Scooby Doo to an office fancy dress party into a bin, going unnoticed. The staff were fixated in horror at the wall where the mirrors used to be; not one of them remembered her when later questioned. Satisfied that the class had helped her lose some weight, she lost the weight on her shoulders of Debbie trying to seduce and fuck her fiancé. Alex was one woman who simply would kill for love. After all, revenge is a bitch with a kettle bell.

Mindy's Home

E.T curled up in the familiar lap as he had done for the past month. It was secure and homely, even if the lap was new to his home. Forgetting his attack on Saffron where he had taken her clean out, he had enjoyed the huge, fresh piece of salmon that Mindy had bought him; it was a reward from heaven, and he was a happy cat. The sun was trapped in the garden, and none of the guests were in any rush to leave.

"Isn't this weather so lovely?" said Poppy, wearing swimming goggles. They were not ideal for protecting her eyesight from the harmful sunrays, but they worked with her Sally Bowles bowler hat. "Reminds me of when I was stranded in the Sahara with only a can of coke and Viennetta to survive." She held her smooth hand to her face, through the goggles saw her perfect nails painted in neon orange.

"Wouldn't a Viennetta melt in the desert?" Joe-Ryan really didn't want to draw attention to the obvious, but he was intrigued. He remembered having the posh dessert made of ice cream at a wedding. Poppy looked at him as if she had lost her mind. She surrendered over her other hand to be painted, this time into a purple plum shade. She let the question drift off into the clouds and took a sip of her homemade cloudy lemonade to cool herself from the heat.

"Thinks I've lost me bloody mind," throwing her enlarged eyes towards the culprit, who was avoiding her stern look. He stroked the temperamental killer cat trying not to laugh.

"What have I missed?" Alex arrived fashionably late dressed in a superb monochrome jumpsuit and gold sandals that she had picked up in Dubai the week before. In her hand she carried a generous magnum of champagne for the celebration in the garden this afternoon - she was none the wiser what the celebration was actually for, not the champagne. Troy followed close behind dressed in a white vest that was refusing to rip due to loving being close to his recently Dubai sun-kissed rippling body; his veins flowed to the surface of his skin trying to cool down in the heat. A little weight loss streamlined his muscles from running around in the kitchen of his new small bistro - it was the ideal cardio, and he looked immaculate for it. Shaking Joe-Ryan's hand and accidentally crushing it in the shake, he was hoping that E.T didn't take his finger off. Troy kept an eye on the lunatic cat.

Alex planted a loving, long overdue kiss on Poppy's face, ignoring the goggles but loving the African inspired kaftan. Alex looked at Mindy painting her mother's nails, throwing a smirk of her red lips with a look like *it's about to kick off in here.* "I'm so hungry," Alex moaned, rubbing her belly.

"There are nuts in the fridge. The BBQ will start up soon, that should tide you over," Mindy offered.

"Fucking nuts? I'm sure if Jesus can rise from the dead after three days, I can hold out for half an hour." The hormones were making Alex a sailor-swearing carnivore. She needed meat - maybe she was growing a vampire in her womb.

Eric and Maud greeted the back garden, cutting Mindy off from telling Alex why Poppy was annoyed. "I love the glasses, Poppy very erm unique" Maud came over two stone lighter with the new diet working wonders for her, and dating Eric being a valid reason for her to get fit and healthy, she wanted to live longer than his ex-wife out do her, green-eyed insecurity not completely gone. She was a success story from *Single2Mingle,* and her counselling sessions had worked wonders on her past and cut attitude, hence the invite. She had realised that her parents' death was inevitable, and she had no control over it since it was a faulty electrical wire that sparked the killer flames. "What's up with your gob?" Maud had failed to lose her mouth completely in her dramatic weight loss.

"He thinks I've lost me fucking marbles!" she said, pointing with one orange talon towards Joe-Ryan, who now felt like he was an old woman bully as all eyes from the party were staring hard at him. He shrunk a little.

"I only asked wouldn't Viennetta melt in the desert?" His whimper was cute. Mindy was laughing.

"Fucking hell the place is like a fucking show home! Trust our Joe-Ryan to hook up with a bloody Stepford wife. Aoife, you got to raise your game. That bloody caravan's got more mould than a block of blue cheese." Granny C appeared, while Aoife followed behind. Joe-Ryan could kiss them both for diverting the attention from him.

"Oh Mindy, do my nails too." Any chance of a beauty freebie got Aoife wet, as she ran out to Mindy picking a trashy Barbie pink colour.

"What's up Poppy?" Granny C ignored Poppy's fancy dress, just as Poppy ignored her thick cardigan.

"Your grandson thinks I've lost the plot."

"Oh aye, that's only on a Monday" Granny C gently mocked, kissing each of Poppy's soft cheeks and turning to the offending grandson. "Lay off my mate you fucking eejit, or I'll bury you alive like I did with an ex-boyfriend." Knowing it was true, Joe-Ryan wished he hadn't mentioned it now.

"Look after me please, old boy," he whispered into E.T's ginger ear as he purred from the warmth of the sun and the warmth of the stroke.

That's strange...Why would Mindy hire a Cher lookalike? Alex asked nobody but the inside of her head, seeing Cher - but minus at least two foot of height - coming into the garden. "Sorry I'm bloody late, that tube is a nightmare!" The tone of a dizzy teenager gave the identity away.

"Sabrina, you look wonderful!" Poppy declared to the entire garden of guests who were all wondering why a mini Cher was here - or maybe a transitioning male, since Sabrina worked quite masculine features. The fishnet tights and fading black leotard had gathered stares on the tube, while the big, curly black wig gave the impression that she was a drag queen. Yet Sabrina's beak nose - something that the poor girl stalked discount sights for rhinoplasty and Mayfair clubs for a sugar daddy to fund it - broke the image.

"Why are you dressed as Cher?" Mindy asked her gentle goddaughter.

"I've decided to become an actress, haven't I?" Proud she spoke. "Bagged a small role in an amateur Cher musical down in Hackney so I'm a meth actress, prepare for the role all the greats do it." Smiled wide, impression a practise run for winning an Oscar? Mindy knew that Sabrina meant method actor since it was all the rage to live as your character twenty-four seven, but looking at Sabrina's get up, she also thought that she could be on the city's candy of crack of crystal meth, hence the mix up.

"What happened to being a vet?" Mindy asked.

"Don't like animals." Noticing ET curled up; Sabrina kept her glass handy for the temperamental, human terrorism cat.

"Midwife" Troy questioned.

"God no, the thought of my own fanny makes me sick, so someone else's pushing out a baby? Putting her hand on her mouth blew out her cheeks.

"Fashion designer" Alex wondered, her glass hide her smile. "Have you seen the price of fabric to dress anyone bigger than a size six?" Sabrina huffed.

"Nun" Poppy quizzed doing the sign of the cross.

"Don't think I can commit to one man."

"Hairdresser" Eric was intrigued; everyone looked at Mindy's fringe, Eric shrugged his board shoulders in defeat.

"Jihadi Bride?" Joe-Ryan failed to see the truth in all of the previous job roles that Sabrina had decided on as career paths, thinking it was a running joke. Everyone looked at him with a look that said terrorism was neither funny nor clever, and Aoife threw a scolding tut to show that being his mother, she was certainly not impressed. Joe-Ryan gave up.

"I don't like spaceships," she said with an innocent, youthful ignorance to anything that wasn't related to celebrity, confusing the deadly bride with sabre swords for something else. Everyone burst out laughing, not able to see Sabrina's look of confusion under her three internet tutorials on drag make-up. Mindy planted a kiss on her goddaughter's heavily made-up face, watching as she went off to introduce herself to the garden. Since Sabrina's mother had passed away ten years ago, Sabrina was the closest thing she had to a daughter, love just as solid.

Two chairs were left vacant of their guests before the party could start, and the sun stalled above creating a heat of pure bliss and worship, all offering their skin to be scorched on the BBQ of the sun. Mindy carried on painting Aoife's nails as she gabbed to Granny C about how she was enjoying London. Aoife and Maud discussed men, while Eric delighted Troy with praise about how amazing his restaurant food was, and Troy returned the compliment by asking how his trip to the Puffin Island had gone over by the BBQ. Joe-Ryan handed out alcoholic cold drinks to all. Alex stuck to red wine; she might have been pregnant, but a glass a day was good for her heart she told Troy's annoying mother last Sunday, swigging straight from the bottle to her disgust.

Could life get any better than this, Mindy thought, stopping to look at the company in her colourful garden. All of the pots that were bare before gave birth to style and carnival colours, bringing an idyllic backdrop to the party. The sun was shining high and clear skies as blue as Alex's pregnancy test canopied above. Her mother was finally home - well, next door with Aoife looking after her, who discovered that she actually enjoyed caring and was training to become a carer, Poppy as her guinea pig. A strange occurrence had been happening of late concerning her mother; her memory was still failing, but she seemed to be getting glimpses of Poppy's present memory, too. There had been no major episodes, only minor blips lasting no longer than a few seconds of the puzzling pause that a goldfish suffers. The sun glowed on her face, its warmth reassuring her that things were going to be good from now. A cool breeze perfumed the garden with a scent of the expensive, and Mindy opened her eyes.

"Simone! About bloody time!" Poppy cheered, greeting her with a warm kiss, embracing a loving hug around the famous bitch. Simone smiled, returning the loving embrace, closing her eyes and feeling the love.

"Sorry I'm late - my driver had never heard of Zone Two," she said stepping into the garden. Her beauty beat the temperature of the sun. Maud nearly vomited - Simone Delvin was actually in the same garden as her. Simone was an idol of Maud's; Maud decided to play it cool, but would corner her later for a selfie. Troy leaned in to Alex, "She's no Marilyn," with a wink to ease his fiancée at the beauty of Simone. Alex smiled, feeling the knot of excitement twisting her stomach. She hoped the baby was a contortionist. Stepping from behind a glamorous Simone was Leon.

"Don't even think about cashing that 'celebrity crush card' in," Troy quickly whispered, jealously jumping on each word making

Alex laugh. She turned, planting a massive kiss on her baby daddy; Troy embraced her rubbing her small bump - his family. "Hi everyone" Leon dressed like a young James Dean with shades and a white shirt, adding to the furnace in the garden looking cool and defined. He raised a shy wave. His sexiness shimmered in the sun, rubbing its randy rays all over the hunk. "I'm definitely climbing that!" Aoife screeched like a sexually frustrated town crier. She searched between Troy and Leon - Aoife was in male ecstasy, mental spit roast in her deluded mind had her gasping for air.

"You would sit on a bomb just to get a bang! Now sit down and behave," Granny C scolded her daughter, who winked a predator purple eye at Leon. Simone and Leon passed around pleasantries and took their plastic seats.

"That fucking cat best behave, or it will get this." Simone produced a Taser from her Chanel bag, ignoring the fact that they were illegal in Britain. The jet lag kept her in America in her head, "Right, now we're all here I would like to raise a toast," Joe-Ryan spoke.

"To Saffron, dead and buried," Simone shouted with glee.

"To Chad Rise - ruined and banned from keeping animals, for like, ever," Troy chipped in. shockingly video ended Chad's luxury life, instead of winning roles for films, he was hiding out in his cell in state prison, where beastiality got him beat up on a regular basics, he was down to his last three reminding veneers. The name had no effect on Mindy whatsoever, and her strong smile reassured Joe-Ryan and Alex of this. Even finding out that Chad Rise had led a previous life and that life was as 'Him', Edward, her cheating bastard of an ex, had no effect on her. She had been shocked, but she had overcome it with family support, four bottles of wine and six weeks with a therapist. Revenge is something that people always think should hurt or destroy another being - sinister, and deadly sometimes - yet Mindy gained the ultimately revenge by moving on from the hurt of her past and finally found a happy present, and hopefully a future. Looking at Joe-Ryan her heart leapt; she had got revenge on her past by simply becoming happy and in love.

"My weight loss," Maud muttered as a pork pie wrestled with her hungry tongue.

"My pregnancy" Alex curled a loving hand around Troy, who landed a kiss to her head and stroked her tiny bump.

"To me, for finding my marbles" Poppy laughed and Mindy rolled her eyes while the rest laughed. Joe-Ryan was starting to lose confidence in his announcement.

"To Cher" Sabrina sang, out of tune.

"Who the fuck is Cher?" Simone pulled a face.

"Let the poor eejit speak! I'm fucking gasping for a drink," holding her champagne flute up like a priest does with wine to be blessed. Joe-Ryan cleared his throat, brought back to centre stage with Granny's C comment, and took a huge breath to inflate his waning confidence.

"Thank you. I raise a toast to Mindy." The pause was due to nerves; to his small audience of family and friends they had mistaken the big build up to the confession as to why they were congregated in the garden like slugs as dramatic effect.

"Fucking hurry up, gasping here," Aoife howled, but what she was really gasping for was anyone's guess. She gave Leon and Troy a wink each with an individual eye at the same time - the poor sods were in a game of Russian roulette, but no gun, worse, Aoife.

Joe-Ryan took a deep breath. All of his life he had dreamt of this moment; the next step in his life story, a chapter that if he wrote an autobiography would come in a Bible-fat trilogy, a true classic romantic novel of two hearts. Finally, he had found love - a true love to last forever. He turned to the object of his deep love, and paused for dramatic effect before he spoke those life changing words, *here goes* he told his old self, *thanks for the ride* he got of the ride.

"Mindy said yes to becoming my wife." The familiar faces on all of the loved guests dropped to the crazy paving floor, *so glad I jet washed the pavement* strangely ran in his confused mind. Silence muted the garden and the heat from the sun became a furnace as if it was too embarrassed by the mute, stale reaction. The chorus of joyful screams they thought they would receive had failed to get off the bus at the end of the street.

Mindy and Joe-Ryan stood staring at their parents and friends, mirror imaging said look at each other. This was not the reaction they had expected; even Granny C was quiet. Even the passing birds didn't make a peep, and not even traffic from the road filtered into the silence.

Did they not agree with their commitment?

Maybe after three months since meeting they thought it was a tad quick for an engagement. Did they disagree with their decision?

Maybe it was the idea that they were only together because they had both shared that tragic night, and were both suffering from post-traumatic stress? Teatime magazines forever filled their pages with such articles. Poppy twisted her lips as if she was thinking about what to say. She made Mindy feel like her heart was about to bungee jump off her bottom lip.

On the other hand, was the silence more from the fact that everyone thought Mindy was a closet lesbian? Maud seemed to Morse-Code her suspicions to a stunned Eric with the fast flickering of her heavy eyelashes.

Maybe Joe-Ryan was after a visa, the blank look that Simone bore questioned - she had asked if Ireland was in the Congo. Silence overtook the birdsong piercing Mindy and Joe-Ryan's ears, invading thunderously. They forgot the joy of sound.

Suddenly, a horrific explosion of noise chased E.T into the house for safety in a flash. *'Congratulations!'* deafened Mindy in a chorus of different tones and pitch like a group singing of happy birthday; any pitch any tone welcome. She couldn't tell who was hugging her she felt that many arms around her, as if she was in a dark room at a swinger's party. She was sure she heard a dozen gunshots mistaking the sound of the champagne popping and cheers all around, and a few tears of happiness from Aoife who insisted and forced Leon to comfort her. The round of applause beat the time that Mindy had picked up her Oscar for best make-up in a film.

Half an hour settled. There were overflowing congratulations, and every question possible about the wedding was settled, Aiofe 'will you wear red? Granny C asked 'you up the duff? 'Defiantly have to get my dress took in few times' Maud promised swallowing a sausage roll. Conversation amongst the guests to return to normal, the girls went inside to fetch more champagne and boys place more meat on the BBQ. Mindy jokily refused Simone and Alex as bridesmaids for fear of them outshining her, and told Maud the same just to make her feel better as they entered indoors.

Joe-Ryan approached his new mother-in-law as she sat staring out into the trees that were guarding like soldiers, her wine spritzer still full, her heart occupied by memories. "You ok, Poppy?" Poppy turned on the call of her name. By now they were all used to the enlarged eyes of her goggles, but he could see tears. "What's up?" His strong arms were comforting on her shoulders, and she leaned in for emotional support.

"I'm just so happy."

"Come here, mother-in-law" hugging his soon to be mother-in-law. She smelled of vanilla ice cream, and her frail frame was strong despite its weak appearance of late due to Aoife's trial of healthy foods to combat the illness.

"God help you with me for a mother-in-law!" Poppy joked. "It's only fair - Mindy's got Aoife as hers." Joe-Ryan put his hands across his eyes mocking his faux shame of his crazy mother, they both turned, seeing Aoife sitting on Troy's lap ignoring Granny C's pleas with her daughter to stop showing her up.

Poppy's smile, happily content lay in a hammock between her enlarged goggle eyes. "Thank you for making her happy. It makes a mother's heart glow when their baby is happy." She planted a soft kiss on Joe-Ryan's stubble shadowed cheek, blessing their marriage. "Can I ask you something, Poppy?" The coast was clear, so his question was safe from interruption or attack.

"Course you can, dear."

"Did the Viennetta melt?" It had bugged him all afternoon, taking over every spare moment he had to think.

Poppy smiled. "No sweetheart, it didn't melt. Viennetta was the lazy-arse camel I was riding at the time." Her smile reached her kind eyes, plucking joyful tears like a ripe apple from a tree, slapping her knee laughing, belly rumbling laugh, so sweet, birds in the trees joined in as the chorus line.

Joe-Ryan laughed hard. "Come here you crazy bat," hugging his mother-in-law to be into a giant loved filled embrace.

"I'll call in Donatella, she owes me a favour," Simone declared to Mindy, twirling a strand of her silky golden hair around her finger blind to her million-pound rock that was on that finger. She made it sound as if the Italian fashion power player was her personal dressmaker losing sleep every night until Simone called, popping fluffy popcorn into her luscious mouth; Simone chewed with elegance of gazelle.

"She'll be honoured to make all of the dresses." Simone staked her couture claim as a bridesmaid, and was egging Alex on to claim 'chief'. *As if Ms. Versace has got nothing better to do than make a wedding dress for a fatty* - her old self-doubt tried one last time to keep a fat foot in the door of self-loathing. *Screw you!* she thought, slamming the door hard on self-doubt and trapping its toes. She decided on engaging in self-humour instead. Mindy would certainly diet for the wedding; Donatella would be repulsed at having to make a dress in a size that was double figures. Luckily for Ms Versace, Mindy's wedding dress was already stored in the airy loft. She wasn't a Bridezilla, or a wedding dress hoarder, or handy with a sewing machine herself. No, her late Grandma's lace dress that she had bought in Italy on a surprise engagement slept in a polystyrene plastic bag ready to wake from its vacuum coma.

"Thanks, Sisi, but that's a long way off yet." Simone rolled her sapphire eyes and flicked back her golden hair with perfect annoyance as another popcorn kernel entered her mouth. "Fine," admiring the gold glitter nail varnish that had been painted on in St Tropez that morning.

Mindy had been worried since the proposal the weekend before if unpredictable time was on her side. Poppy had been blessed with a clear run of good days. It was only a matter of time before the good times stopped and the bad took over - that was life's balance, and you can't have the good without the bad. In addition, Granny C was not getting any younger, nor was Alex getting any skinnier; the delicious baby bump glowed on her best friend. Maybe she could have a surprise wedding, or a shotgun wedding in Scotland while hiking. Either way, Mindy knew that one day she would marry Joe-Ryan. Just the mention of his name simply made her look out to him as he engaged in conversation with her mother holding a sausage on a fork in the air, who was on the floor mimicking a camel arching her back. *Crazy old bird*, she laughed.

"More drink?" Simone filled both flutes up without waiting for a reply, the fizzing bubbles dissolving any further wedding talk. The rampant baby-making had been put on hold; even the mile-high club was not safe from Simone and Leon's frantic shagging. The reason that the baby-making was on hold was that Leon was directing a cult documentary on soup kitchens of the world, and Simone was on location filming the film version of the explosive memoirs of the late Saffron's house cleaner, Helena's international bestseller *What the Scrubber Saw* written about the deceased broad. Simone won the lead role of young Saffron, while new British hunk Jude Waters played opposite her while his flamboyant husband Lucas worked new interiors on the extension to her New York apartment, finally able to buy Saffron's apartment.

"Where's your ring, anyway?" Simone adored diamonds; the bigger the better, and if it was a blood diamond then she was in heaven.

"It's in the cat basket," Mindy said. Simone pushed her reply into a pout, declining to entertain what she thought was a lie. "Just remembered, I found this on my way in on your doormat." Simone fished in her ceramic Tom Ford clutch and pulled out an anorexic postcard she had almost forgotten to pass on. Simone at first thought it was a perfume sample, Simone never seen mail, she had Gloria for that.

"Fuck knows who it's from." She was not at all sorry for invading her privacy, reading the postcard as she passed it over.

"Who on earth sends postcards nowadays, anyway?" Maud asked, popping a dozen nuts into her mouth with the force of suicidal person taking a overdose, following Simone - her idol - and Alex back into the garden, chatting about babies until they became distant noise leaving only Mindy and E.T in the living room. A bunch of Pride colour-sprayed tulips drew attention on the glass table; Mindy dropped a gentle touch of her fingertips to a purple bud. Studying the front of the postcard with a picture of a donkey in a beautiful field full of sunflowers and a bright, big sun, the words *'loving life'* were emblazoned across in clouds. She took a seat on the sofa and E.T joined her lap, his ginger fur warm from the hot sun's kiss, grey starting to flood his muzzle gave him a distinguished look in his twilight years.

She turned over to read it, but a blade of sunlight through the bay window made it difficult. Was it interfering to stop Mindy from reading? Did it want to stop Mindy, or protect her, even? She stood and walked over towards the fireplace by the mirror framed in a rustic gold frame that Joe-Ryan had made. It became the equivalent of sunglasses, and gave her some vision back.

Thank you so much for everything; revenge is a bitch, darling. Enjoy the ring! All my love always - M x

She smiled. Heading towards the cat bed and slipping her hand under the tartan cat bed, she pulled out her ring. The bright blue stone gleamed as if the stone was happy it was finally allowed out, showing off its beauty to the whole world. Mindy slipped the ring onto her finger; it fitted like a glove. She nearly pulled her neck out hearing a horse neigh - was it Ballet Foot's approval? Was he now at rest? But she looked in the garden to see Aoife riding the back of Troy, and she chuckled.

The sun leaked into the open kitchen wrapping her up in its glorious glow giving E.T's ginger fur a shine. She could identify the culprit in sense of smell alone lifting the postcard to her petite nose. The scent of the freshest peaches ever to grow and ripen signed the card with adoring love; it fluttered delicate butterflies all through her body - Mabel. Mindy came to the conclusion over three bottles of wine with Alex one Friday night, Mabel's revenge simply was about the cursed ring no longer being in the cruel procession of Saffron. Saffron losing power she held over Mabel for decades gone in the ring being took. Mabel was not a woman to rack and ruin another woman not matter what that women may have done. All her glamorous life she helped women, fighter for their rights, put them up in hardship despite she suffered negativity thorough the abuse and lies her sister put on her life like a crown made of thrones, pain became part of her. For Mabel not to crack to repent revenge on Saffron, even with the ring, power turned hands was not Mabel's style. No one would blame Mabel if she dragged Saffron through the mud by her dyed perm all over New York City; yanking the evil bitch kicking and screaming to a public execution to be hanged not by a rope but by being outcaste to the social wasteland called the Z-list. Receive a global apology but no, Mabel knew she was dealt that cold hand for a reason and the reason was Mabel could handle it with a smile and fur coat and a filthy joke. Revenge for Mabel was that Saffron lost the ring which lead to the bitter old board's death, due to her own greed and obsession with power, undoubtedly and unknown to Saffron; led Saffron to kill herself, that for Mabel was enough.

An unexpected knock on the front door stopped Mindy from sniffing the postcard again like a bloodhound. "Wonder who that is?" she asked E.T, who looked up with his brown eyes. Would he need to get his claws out?

She opened the door to see none other than the acting legend Henry Dooley on her doorstep looking very savvy. *Why would he be knocking at my door*, she questioned the baseball bat lying in the umbrella stand her hand in reaching distance in case she needed it. Was he the new neighbour? Maybe he was researching a role as a bailiff for new film. Or maybe he was a friend of Simone's, coming to say hello while she was in London? Mindy tried to act cool and calm, but inside she wanted to get his autograph and was thinking of whipping a boob out for the film legend to sign.

"Can I help you?" She smiled her best 'it's not every day that a national treasure knocks at your door' smile. Thankfully, her fringe was now at a length associated with a typical fringe, her make-up was beautiful on her glowing face kissed a shade darker by the summer sun, and a shimmering aqua blue summer dress came alive like a fish in water on her body toned from romantic walks and passionate nights with Joe-Ryan, igniting her skin to that of a Raphaelite.

"Yes. I'm awfully sorry for intruding on your day, bright day if I say so." His voice was posh, slightly trembling, not like the harsh common cockney his many film characters spoke with. "But I'm looking for a-" he gave a slight cough, and carried on his question, "Mindy Moore?"

Finishing his sentence he prayed that it was this beautiful woman, wiping his forehead with a checked handkerchief. She was a vision of elegance standing there in her blue dress with a bit of cleavage on show - but in a classy way - and her red hair moved. It reminded him of the elegant winding colourful Chinese dragon he witnessed at a festival for New Year when filming in China in the eighties; she looked like her mother did back then.

"Who's asking?" Mindy was a little defensive. She declined to give her identity away too quickly and spoke with a tone you expect when knocking on a redneck's trailer home, just in case the dead witch had one last trick up her sleeve, horror film style. She eyed the baseball bat again that Aoife had bought them as a housewarming gift, lurking in the umbrella stand itching to be used like a dormant dildo lying in the ghetto of the bottom draw of old dying knickers and agoraphobia gym gear. She noticed his famous eyes were a kind shade of grey - gently reassuring, and his posture professional and tall more importantly friendly, no need for the bat.

"Well, this is slightly awkward, so please forgive me," taking a crisply folded letter out from the pocket of his very posh jacket. He opened it up; it shook gently in his hands, either due to nerves or maybe he could have been a secret alcoholic. Mindy wasn't one to judge, after all she been though Maud told her 'surprised you're not fucking sitting on a park bench in just ya underwear. Pissed as a fart smoking crack' she meant it well, proud Mindy didn't restore to this. He took a deep breath and gave a nervous cough, pulling at the smart cuffs of his jacket, she noticed HD gold buttons, the jacket which was a little too thick to be wearing on such a pleasant afternoon, woven with expensive and Saville Row tailoring. Being a prestigious actor he had delivered some famous lines, but this next line was life-changing - for the better, he hoped. "I'm asking for a Miss Mindy Moore as well, this sounds a little bizarre, but you see, well" he paused, smile grew across his aged handsome face.

Life as always was the best director he ever worked with and gave him one of his favourite lines. "I believe she's my daughter - and I am her dad."

Printed in Great Britain
by Amazon